NAGUIB MAHFOUZ

Respected Sir
Wedding Song
The Search

———

Naguib Mahfouz was born in 1911 in Cairo. He began writing at the age of seventeen, and his first novel was published in 1939. Since then he has written over thirty novels and more than a hundred short stories. In 1988, Mr. Mahfouz was awarded the Nobel Prize in Literature. He lives in the Cairo suburb of Agouza with his wife and two daughters.

THE FOLLOWING TITLES BY NAGUIB MAHFOUZ ARE
ALSO PUBLISHED BY ANCHOR BOOKS:

The Beggar
The Thief and the Dogs
Autumn Quail
The Beginning and the End
The Time and the Place and Other Stories
Midaq Alley
The Journey of Ibn Fattouma
Miramar
Adrift on the Nile
The Harafish
Arabian Nights and Days
Children of the Alley
Echoes of an Autobiography
The Day the Leader Was Killed
Akhenaten, Dweller in Truth

THE CAIRO TRILOGY:

Palace Walk
Palace of Desire
Sugar Street

Respected Sir

Wedding Song

The Search

Respected Sir
Wedding Song
The Search

——

NAGUIB MAHFOUZ

ANCHOR BOOKS
A DIVISION OF RANDOM HOUSE, INC.
NEW YORK

Respected Sir was originally published in Arabic in 1975 as *Hadrat al-Muhtaram*.
Copyright © 1975 by Naguib Mahfouz. The English translation was first published in Great Britain by Quartet Books Limited, a member of the Namara
Group, London in 1986 and subsequently in the United States by Anchor Books,
a division of Random House, Inc., New York, in 1990. *Respected Sir* was translated by Rasheed El-Enany.

Wedding Song was originally published in Arabic in 1981 as *Afrah al-Qubbah*.
Copyright © 1981 by Naguib Mahfouz. The English translation was first published by The American University in Cairo Press, Cairo, Egypt in 1984 and subsequently in the United States by Anchor Books, a division of Random House, Inc.,
New York, in 1989. *Wedding Song* was translated by Olive E. Kenny; edited and
revised by Mursi Saad El Din and John Rodenbeck.

The Search was originally published in Arabic in 1964 as *al-Tariq*. Copyright ©
1964 by Naguib Mahfouz. The English translation was first published by The
American University in Cairo Press, Cairo, Egypt in 1987 and subsequently in the
United States by Anchor Books, a division of Random House, Inc., New York, in
1991. *The Search* was translated by Mohamed Islam and edited by Magdi Wahba.

Library of Congress Cataloging-in-Publication Data

Mahfuz, Najib, 1911–
[Novels. English. Selections]
Respected sir ; Wedding song ; The search / Naguib Mahfouz.
p. cm.
ISBN 0-385-49836-5 (pbk.)
1. Mahfâò, Najâb, 1911——Translations into English. I. Title: Respected sir ;
Wedding song ; The search. II. Title: Wedding song. III. Title: Search. IV. Title.
PJ6846.A46 R4713 2001
892.7'36—dc21   2001022743

Book design by Oksana Kushnir

www.anchorbooks.com

Printed in the United States of America
10 9 8 7 6 5 4 3 2 1

CONTENTS

Respected Sir

Translator's Acknowledgment

I am deeply grateful to my colleague Mr. G. Balfour-Paul CMG, for his meticulous and painstaking revision of my translation, a task which he undertook with the patience and thoroughness of a scholar coupled with a poet's sensitivity for words.

One

The door opened to reveal an infinitely spacious room: a whole world of meanings and motivations, not just a limited space buried in a mass of detail. Those who entered it, he believed, were swallowed up, melted down. And as his consciousness caught fire, he was lost in a magical sense of wonder. At first, his concentration wandered. He forgot what his soul yearned to see—the floor, the walls, the ceiling: even the god sitting behind the magnificent desk. An electric shock went through him, setting off in his innermost heart an insane love for the gloriousness of life on the pinnacle of power. At this point the clarion call of power urged him to kneel down and offer himself in sacrifice. But he followed, like the rest, the less extreme path of pious submissiveness, of subservience, of security. Many childlike tears he would have to shed before he could impose his will. Yielding to an irresistible temptation, he cast a furtive glance at the divinity hunched behind the desk and lowered his eyes with all the humility he possessed.

Hamza al-Suwayfi, the Director of Administration, led in the procession.

"These are the new employees, Your Excellency," he said, addressing the Director General.

The Director General's eyes surveyed their faces, including his. He felt he was becoming part of the history of government and that he stood in the divine presence. He thought he heard a strange whispering sound. Perhaps he alone heard it. Perhaps it was the voice of Destiny itself. When His Excellency had completed his examination of their faces, he opened his mouth. He spoke in a quiet and gentle voice, revealing little or nothing of his inner self.

"Have they all got the Secondary Education Diploma?" he inquired.

"Two of them have the Intermediate Diploma of Commerce," Hamza al-Suwayfi replied.

"The world is progressing," said the Director General in an encouraging tone. "Everything is changing. And now here is the Diploma, replacing the Certificate of Primary Education."

This was reassuring, but they all sought to conceal their delight under still greater submissiveness.

"Live up to what's expected of you," His Excellency went on, "through hard work and honesty."

He looked over a list of their names and suddenly asked, "Which of you is Othman Bayyumi?"

Othman's heart pounded within him. That His Excellency had uttered his very own name shook him to the core. Without raising his eyes he took a step forward and mumbled, "Me, Your Excellency."

"You got an excellent grade in your Diploma. Why didn't you go on to finish your education?"

In his confusion he remained silent. The fact was he did not know what to say, even though he knew the answer.

The Director of Administration answered for him, apologetically, "Perhaps it was his circumstances, Your Excellency."

Again he heard that strange whispering, the voice of Destiny. And for the first time he felt a sensation of blue skies and of a strange but pleasant fragrance pervading the room. The reference to his "circumstances" was no worry to him, now that he had been sanctified by His Excellency's kindly and appreciative notice. He thought to himself that he could take on a whole army and vanquish it all alone. Indeed his spirit soared upward, higher and higher, till his head disappeared into the clouds in a surge of wild intoxication. But His Excellency tapped the edge of the desk and said, by way of ending the interview, "Thank you. Good morning."

Othman went out of the room, silently reciting the Throne verse from the Qur'an.

Two

I am on fire, Oh God.

Flames were devouring his soul from top to bottom as it soared upward into a world of dreams. In a single moment of revelation he perceived the world as a surge of dazzling light which he pressed to his bosom and held on to like one demented. He had always dreamed and desired and yearned, but this time he was really ablaze, and in the light of this sacred fire he glimpsed the meaning of life.

But down on earth it was decided that he should join the Archives Section. It did not matter how he started; life itself evolved from a single cell or perhaps from something even less. He descended to his new abode in the basement of the ministry, his wings still fluttering. He was greeted by gloom and the musty smell of old paper. Outside, through a barred window, he saw that the ground was on the same level as his head. Inside, the huge room spread out in front of him. Rows of filing cabinets stood on either side, and another long row divided the room down the middle. Staff desks were placed in gaps between cabinets. He walked behind one of the employees toward a desk at the front placed crosswise in a recess like a prayer niche. At the desk was seated the Head of the Archives Section. Othman had not yet recovered from the upsurge of divine inspiration. Even his descent into the basement could not wake him up. He walked behind the clerk, perplexed, distracted, and excited.

"Man's aspirations are infinite," he said to himself.

The clerk introduced him to the Head of Section: "Mr. Othman Bayyumi, the new clerk," he said, and then introduced the Section Head to him: "Our chief, Mr. Sa'fan Basyuni."

He recognized something familiar in the man's features, as if he were a native of his own alley. He liked the protruding bones of his face, its dark and taut skin and the white, disheveled hair of his head. He liked even more the kind and friendly look in his eyes which strove in vain to reflect an air of authority. The man smiled, revealing his ugliest feature: black teeth with wide gaps in between them.

"Welcome to the Archives Section! Sit down!" he said, and started to shuffle through the documents of his appointment.

"Welcome! Welcome! Life," he went on to say, "can be summed up in two words: hello and goodbye." Yet it was infinite, Othman thought. There blew around him a strange mysterious wind, full of all kinds of probabilities.

It was infinite, he thought again, and because of that it demanded infinite willpower.

The Head of Section pointed to a vacant, neutral-colored desk whose leather top was worn-out and spotted with faded stains of ink.

"Your desk," he said. "Examine the chair carefully. The tiniest nail can rip a new suit."

"My suit is very old anyway," replied Othman.

"And remember," the man carried on with his warning, "to recite a prayer before opening a filing cabinet. On the eve of last Bairam festival a snake, at least three feet long, came out of one of the cabinets." He choked with laughter and continued, "But it wasn't a poisonous one."

"How can one tell whether it is poisonous or not?" asked Othman anxiously.

"You ask the section messenger. He comes from Abu Rawwash, the city of snakes."

Othman took the warning for a joke and let it pass. He chided himself for failing to study meticulously His Excellency the Director General's room and print on his mind's eye a full picture of the man's face and his person, for not trying to unravel the secret of the magic with which he dominated everyone and had them at his beck and call. This was the power to be worshipped. It was the ultimate beauty too. It was one of the secrets of the universe. On earth there existed divine secrets without number for those who had eyes to see and minds to think. The time between hello and goodbye was short. But it was infinite as well. Woe betide anyone who ignored this truth. There were people who never moved, like Mr. Sa'fan Basyuni. Well-meaning, but miserable, paying tribute to a wisdom of which he had learned nothing. But not so those whose hearts had been touched by the sacred fire. There was a happy path which began at the eighth grade in the government service and ended at the splendid position of His Excellency the Director General. This was the highest ideal available to the common people, beyond which they could not aspire. This was the highest heaven where both divine mercy and human pride became manifest. The eighth grade. The seventh. The sixth. The fifth. The fourth. The third. The second. The first. Director General. The miracle could be brought about in thirty-two years. Or perhaps rather more. Those who fell by the wayside were innumerable. Still the celestial order did not necessarily apply to mankind, least of all to government employees. Time nestled in his arms like a gentle child, but one could not prophesy one's future. He was on fire: that was all. And it seemed to him that this fire blazing in his breast was the same as that which lit the stars in their courses. We were creatures of mystery whose secrets were hidden to all but their Creator.

"You will first learn to handle the incoming mail," said Mr. Basyuni. "It is easier." He then added, laughing, "An archivist should take off his jacket while working. Or at least have elbow patches sewn on his sleeves to protect them against dust and paper clips." All that was easy. What was really difficult was how to deal with time.

Three

In his one-room flat he could subject himself to scrutiny. There, the meaning of his life took shape before him. He lived with his senses always on the alert and with heightened awareness, constantly seeking to provide himself with every possible weapon. From his small window he could see the place where he was born: al-Husayni Alley, an extension of his body and soul. A long back street with a sharp bend, famous for its parking area for carts and its watering trough for donkeys. The house where he had been born and brought up had been demolished. In its place there was now a little plot for pushcarts. Few of the natives of the alley ever left it for good except for the grave. They went to work in various quarters: al-Mabyada, al-Darrasa, al-Sikka al-Jadida, or even beyond, but they came back at the end of the day. One of the characteristics of the alley was that it knew no murmurs or whispers. Voices here were very loud, sometimes crude, sometimes full of wisdom. Among them was one very close to him, a strong, coarse voice which age had not weakened, the voice of Omm Husni, the landlady. Dreams of eternity were wearisome indeed. But what had he been yesterday, and what was he today? He would do well not to recoil from the impossible. He would do well not to surrender himself to the current without a definite plan. An exact plan. He often dreamed that he was urinating, but always woke up at the right moment. What did that mean? Omm Husni had been a workmate of his mother's. A lifetime friend and confidante. Both were married to cart drivers and both had slaved away with the patience and persistence of ants for a few piastres with which to help their husbands and keep their homes together. They had worked as peddlers, hairdressers, marriage brokers, and so on. His mother was still working when she died. As for Omm Husni, she went on slaving away with great zeal. She had more luck and earned more than his mother and thus was able to save up enough money to build her three-story house: a timber store on the ground floor and two flats above. She lived in one and Othman in the other. As for her son Husni, the days of war and hardship had led him to distant lands where he settled down, and all he had left behind was his name.

Did he not have the right to dream? Dream he did, thanks to the holy flame burning in his breast. Thanks to his small room too. He got used to his dreams just as he got used to the bed, the settee, the chest, the mat, and, for that matter, the sound of his own voice, sometimes shrill, sometimes melodious, which echoed against the dark, solid walls.

What had he been yesterday? His father had wanted to make of him a cart driver like himself, but the sheikh of the local Qur'an school said to him, "Put your trust in God, Mr. Bayyumi, and enroll the boy at the primary school."

His father did not seem to comprehend.

"Has he not learned enough Qur'an for him to perform the prayers?" he asked.

"The boy is clever and intelligent. One day he could make a civil servant," replied the sheikh.

Mr. Bayyumi guffawed incredulously.

"Try the charity schools. He might be accepted free," the sheikh said.

Mr. Bayyumi had hesitated for a while, but eventually the miracle took place. At school Othman achieved astonishing success until he finally obtained the Primary Certificate. He drew ahead of his barefooted playmates from the alley and was acutely aware of the first holy spark from his throbbing heart. He was certain that God had blessed his footsteps and that the gates of infinity lay open before him. He joined a secondary school, also free, and achieved greater success than anyone in al-Husayni Alley could believe. But when he was still in the second form, his father contracted a terminal illness. He felt miserable at what he had "done" to his son.

"I am leaving you behind a helpless schoolboy," he said to him. "Who will drive the cart? Who will provide for the family?"

His father died a sad man. But his mother worked twice as hard, hoping that God would make a great man of her son. Was not God all-powerful? If it had not been for the unexpected death of his mother, Othman would have completed his higher education. His anguish was great, all the more so because of his heightened awareness of his ambition and the sacred aspirations throbbing within him. Sacred too was the memory of his parents. And on every religious occasion he would visit their grave, a paupers' grave which lay in an open piece of land amid a host of the forgotten. Now he was alone. A branch cut off a tree. His elder brother, who had been a policeman, had been killed in a demonstration. His sister had died of typhoid in the fever hospital. Another brother had died in prison. The memory of his family was painful to him, and how he mourned for his parents! He linked these happenings with an exalted drama which he contemplated with respect and awe. For fortunes were determined in the alley through conflicting wills and unknown forces and then consecrated in eternity. By this token his belief in himself was boundless, though in the end he depended on Almighty God. And for the same reason he would never miss a prayer, least of all the Friday service at al-Husayn Mosque. Like the people of his alley, he made no distinction between religion and life. Religion was for life and life for religion, and a glittering jewel like the position of Director General was only a sacred station on the divine and infinite path. Living among his colleagues with his senses alert and shining, he picked up the sort of ideas and maxims that seemed important to him. He then devoted himself to laying out a precise plan for the future, which he translated into a working schedule to be studied every morning before going out to work:

Program for Work and Living
1. fulfillment of duties with care and honesty;
2. study of the Financial Bill as if it were a holy book;
3. studying for a university degree as an external student;
4. a special study of English and French, as well as Arabic;
5. acquisition of general knowledge, particularly of the kind beneficial to a civil servant;
6. demonstration, by every proper means, of piety and rectitude as well as diligence in work;
7. efforts to gain the confidence and friendship of seniors;

8. seizing useful opportunities without the sacrifice of self-respect. For instance: helping out someone in a position of influence, making useful friendships or a happy marriage conducive to progress.

He often looked at a small mirror which was nailed to the wall between the window and the clothes stand to examine his appearance and reassure himself on this point. Certainly his appearance would not be an obstacle. He was well built like the people of his alley. He had a dark, longish face with a high, clear forehead and well-trimmed hair. On the whole, his physique would qualify him to fill any position, no matter how important.

He drew courage and strength from the depths of his soul and thought to himself: Not a bad start—and the road is endless.

Four

The tryst on the edge of the wasteland was also sacred. He hastened to it with ardent heart and with the gaiety of one who has cast aside the heavy weight of life's burden. There on the skirt of the desert stood the ancient, abandoned fountain at the foot of whose steps they would sit side by side in the infinite bosom of the afternoon. Before them the desert stretched as far as the foot of the mountain and silence would sing in its unknown tongue. Her dark brown color resembled that of the tense evening, a hue inherited from an Egyptian mother and a Nubian father who died when she was six. Their old companionship in the alley reached back into the remote past until it vanished into the very spring of life. When he looked into her big, wide eyes or saw her small, firm body brimming with vitality, he felt himself in the presence of an ideal which excited his whole being and awakened in his instincts a kind of humble yearning. She was his childhood friend in the alley and on the roof. Although hardly sixteen, she was considered a good housewife. In fact, she had been her mother's only helper after all her seven sisters had married.

Sayyida smiled. Her face was always smiling, her eyes radiant and her limbs constantly moving with a sort of restless grace. Tresses of her thick, curly hair danced in the dry breeze coming down from the mountain. The silence was sweet. Breaking out of it she said, "My mother is pleased that you have joined the civil service . . ."

"And you?" he asked teasingly.

Her smile grew bigger, but she did not reply. He put his arm around her and their lips met, hers full, his sharply defined. No mention of love had been made between them, but whenever they were alone together they expressed it through kisses and embraces. She satisfied in him that aspect of his soul which craved the simple pleasures of life. He also loved her with his mind because he appreciated her virtues and her sincerity and had an instinctive feeling that she could make him happy.

"You are now a government employee . . ." Her voice disclosed her admiration and he kissed her again. "No one in our alley has ever achieved that," she added.

All his friends worked in various manual trades. They watched him go by, whenever he passed, with admiration, and sometimes with envy. This would have pleased him had he not been acutely and bitterly aware of the long and difficult path ahead of him.

"You are the only white-collar worker!"

"Outside our alley that's worth nothing," he said quietly.

"Outside doesn't matter. Our alley's just a place for carts!"

He kissed her for the third time and said, "Never speak of carts without respect . . ."

"Well said! You are so noble . . ."

Her father had been arrested in the same brawl as his own brother. He went to jail, where he died of his injuries. However, these happenings were considered among the glories which made the good name of the alley. But Sayyida obviously had only one thing on her mind and it was no use ignoring it. There she was, asking the question: "And what next?"

He was aware of her yearning for a word that would set her heart at ease and make her happy. He knew too that on no account would his happiness be less than hers; it might even be greater. He loved that girl as she loved him and could not do without her. But he was afraid. He had to think a thousand times. He needed to refer to the bitter Work Program. He still had to ponder a long while on the life that lay before him, welcoming him and challenging him at the same time.

"What do you mean, Sayyida?"

"Nothing!" she answered lightly, but with an undertone of insistence.

"We shouldn't forget we are young . . ."

"Me?" She said this with mild protest, hinting sweetly at the womanhood that cried aloud within her. "Grow your mustache. That's what you need."

He took her jest seriously and thought the idea could be of real help to him in his struggle. For who could imagine a senior official without a mustache?

"I will carry on with my education, Sayyida," he said quietly.

"Do you need more education still?"

"A university degree."

"What for?"

"A useful asset for promotion."

"Will it take you long?"

"Four years, at least."

With concealed anguish, he noticed an expression of coldness in her eyes, perhaps also of shame, with something of anger in it too.

"And what do you need promotion for?"

He laughed and kissed her hair but did not dare go beyond that. The scent of her hair reminded him of childhood games and a punch in the back when they were caught playing bride and groom. The darkness of night loomed over the hilltop and a sound of singing came from a distant gramophone.

"It seems promotion is more important than I imagined . . ."

He took her hand in his and murmured, "I will love you forever . . ."

What he said was the truth, a truth accompanied by a sense of dejection and grief; and he hated himself. He said to himself that life was a grand and awesome experience, but tiresome.

Five

He stood at his parents' grave, lost among other countless graves, and recited the opening verse of the Qur'an. Then he said, "God have mercy upon you . . ."

Next he whispered to them in a spirit of gratitude, "Othman is now a respectable government employee taking his first steps on a difficult path, but he is resolved to follow it to the end." He bowed slightly and added with humility, "All the good things I have I owe to the Lord and to you . . ."

A blind boy was reciting some of the shorter chapters of the Qur'an. He gave him a half-piastre. Yet, insignificant as the amount was, he still had that feeling of resentment which always possessed him when he gave someone money. When the boy was gone, he addressed his parents again: "Before God I vow to move you to a new grave when He has made my wishes come true . . ."

He had no idea how much of their dead bodies would remain with the passage of time, but he reckoned that there would be something remaining at any rate. To his surprise his thoughts reverted to Sayyida, and her smiling image took shape before his eyes. It seemed to him that she was on the verge of passing some pointed remark, outspoken and sarcastic. His heart contracted with pain and he murmured, "Guide me, Oh God, onto the straight path, for all I do is done at Your inspiration."

He lived once again his father's last days. There was no escape from this. Sickness and old age had crippled him till his only recreation was to sit on a sheepskin in front of the house, hardly able to see or hear. He would contemplate his helplessness, crying aloud in his grief, "Oh Lord, have mercy . . ."

In his day, he had been counted among the strong men of the alley. Throughout his long life he had relied on the muscles of his arms and legs, toiling without a break and enduring to the end a harsh and poverty-stricken existence. His strength, which had nothing to nourish it, had been wasted; and in his misery he would break into a cackle of laughter, without meaning or reason. One evening he was found dead where he customarily sat on the sheepskin. So no one ever knew how death had come to him or how he had met it. As for his mother, her death was even more shocking. She had been doing the washing when suddenly she had bent over and begun to scream in terrible pain. An ambulance had come and carried her to Qasr al-'Ayni Hospital, where she died during an operation for appendicitis.

His family was singularly victimized by death. Something inside told him that, for this reason, perhaps he himself would live long, and a wave of sorrow swept over him. Every manner of death was reasonable compared with his brother the policeman's: a man big as an ox killed by the brickbats of the demonstrators. What a death! He had not known who they were nor had they known who he was. Othman regarded what had happened with the eyes of a spellbound spectator. It made absolutely no sense to him. True, he learned a lot from the perusal of history; he knew about history from the most ancient times up to the eve of the Great War. He knew about revolutions, but he had never lived them or reacted to them. He had seen and heard about things, but always kept aloof and wondering. No common sympathy had ever gripped his heart to draw him to the battleground; and he was always bewildered at the way groups of eminent statesmen and their supporters fought each other. He had been hounded all his life by poverty and hunger, and this had left him no time to extend the range of his thought to the outside world. The alley shut him in, its preoccupations unknown to everyone else, savage, violent, unending. Today, he was conscious of one goal only, a goal at once sacred and profane, which had nothing to do, as far as he could see, with the strange events that took place in the name of politics. He told himself that man's true life was his inner life, which governed his every heartbeat and which called for toil, dedication, and enterprise. It was something holy, something religious, and through it he could achieve self-fulfillment in the service of the sacred apparatus known as the Government or the State. Through it the glory of man was accomplished on earth, and through man God's will was accomplished on high. People applauded other, indeed quite contrary, things; but these people were foolish and fraudulent. So he never forgave himself for not having secured a full view of the Director General's room and of his singular personality which set the entire administration in motion from behind a screen—in precise order and perfect sequence, recalling to the ignorant the stars in their courses and the wisdom of heaven. He sighed deeply. He recited the *Fatiha* once more and said by way of farewell, "Pray for me, Father!" He moved around the grave, whose two headstones had fallen and whose corner had cracked, and said, "Pray for me, Mother!"

Six

How wonderful is the turning year. He lived through its seasons, working without pause. Winter in the alley was pretty severe but it spurred a man to work; spring with its sandy khamsin wind was a curse, summer an inferno, and autumn a mysterious, meditative smile. He kept on working with an iron will and a burning passion. His law books were ranged under the bed and on the windowsill. He spent little of the night in sleep. He embraced ideas and wrestled with the inscrutable. Success alone was not enough to satisfy him. Friday was usually set aside for acquiring general knowledge worthy of directors and those in their service. He paid special attention to poetry and learned plenty of it by heart. He even tried composing it but failed. He told himself that poetry had always been the best means of currying favor with superiors and of shining at official parties. It was a heavy loss not to be able to write poetry. Still, learning it was at any rate the best way to perfect one's prose. The art of public speaking was no less important for success than poetry, and eloquence was essential, so his heart told him. Even more so were foreign languages. All these branches of knowledge were useful, and there comes a time when their value goes up in the stock exchange of officialdom. For a civil servant did not live by financial regulations alone. Indeed, he must equip himself with a measure of everything useful, for who knew what might happen? He would tell himself that his life was an unbroken stream flowing in the direction of light and learning, loaded with its cargo of all sorts of novelties and fed by tributaries from the fields of thought: a stream carried forward by the intensity of faith, nobility, and human pride to reach in the end its estuary at the divine threshold.

As for peace of mind, that he attained on the steps of the ancient fountain, in the embrace of fervid love, in the arms of the pretty, loving girl, and her burning, virgin bosom. He allowed himself no commitment in word or deed. Yet he was as fond of her as of life itself. If only life could be satisfied with love and simple happiness, he thought. So anxious was Sayyida that she cast off her natural reserve. She no longer shrank from expressing her true emotions, or revealing the ardor of her yearning for him. On one occasion she said to him in a tone of reverence, "I cannot live without you."

But her words were tepid compared with the generosity of her full lips. On another occasion she said, "You are everything to me: the past and the future . . ."

Her brown eyes glowed with fidelity, with apprehension, and with real yearning. And in the melting moment of a passionate embrace she sighed, "We lack something . . ."

"Our perfect love lacks nothing," was his dull and selfish answer.

She shrugged her shoulders in protest, while seeking not

to embarrass him. She thought it better to be patient with him and to preserve.

He found that he suffered from a fearful repression that could eventually place him at the mercy of the unknown. Thus he yielded to the temptation of a colleague who invited him to visit the official prostitutes' quarter. As one of the breed of al-Husayni Alley, he did not lack the necessary courage. He walked ahead into a lane lit by two gas lamps standing wide apart and covered in so thick a layer of dust that the lane was sunk in that semi-darkness which arouses desire; and he looked excitedly from place to place until his eyes settled on a prey. Those visits were usually followed by a wholehearted plea for forgiveness and a prolonged resort to prayer and worship, the sort of thing he habitually did each time he faced up to his deeply hidden intentions toward Sayyida. Thus in addition to the hardship of continuous work, he suffered even harsher hardship from the pangs of conscience. His long exhausting nights would terminate in severe mental fatigue, almost to the point of fainting. And sometimes tears would come to his eyes almost without his realizing it.

Sa'fan Basyuni, the Head of Archives, watched his work with both admiration and misgiving. He appreciated his perseverance, discretion, and good manners. But from the start he was uneasy about his Secondary Education Diploma, which set him apart in the Archives Section, and also about his ambition for further education that would raise Othman even higher above his own solitary Certificate of Primary Education. Othman became aware of this quite quickly but he counted on the man's good nature and redoubled his efforts to ingratiate himself with him and comply with his every direction until Sa'fan fully trusted him and opened his heart to him with rare candor. Thus in his spare time he would draw closer to Othman and speak his mind openly. Even in politics he disclosed his views and inclinations to him. So zealous was the man that Othman shrank from ignoring his interests or declaring his own cold neutrality toward them.

"The truth is," he would say with wary ambiguity, "we are of the same turn of mind . . ."

Such words pleased the man in a way that Othman could not comprehend. The man's involvement in such things amazed him. And more amazing was the involvement of his wretched colleagues. What was it that they found attractive in them? Had they not more basic worries to occupy their minds? But he told himself with no little scorn that they were people without a fixed aim in life, that their religious faith was only superficial and that they never thought enough of the meaning of life or of what God had created them for. Thus their thoughts and their lives were wasted in empty amusement and sophistry and their true potentialities were dissipated without achievement. Illusions deceived them and they stood idle as time went by.

Seven

One day, after receiving the incoming mail from him, Sa'fan Basyuni said, "Come and spend an evening at my place. You'll enjoy it." Despite some surprise and misgiving he did not think of declining. The man went on: "Our neighbors are having a wedding party. We'll have an ox head for supper together and sit on the balcony to listen to the singing . . ."

He lived in a flat on the third floor of a block in al-Bahr Close in the Bab al-Shariya quarter. Othman found that he was the only person invited and felt gratified by the honor that his chief bestowed on him alone. They had together a delicious supper which consisted of ox tongue, brain, cheek, and eye, along with sausage, bready beef soup, and fried onions in addition to radishes and pickles, as well as melon for dessert. It was a superb and bountiful meal and he ate his fill. They sat on a balcony overlooking the court-yard of the house where the wedding took place. The courtyard was brightly lit by numerous pressure lamps. Inside were rows of chairs and sofas packed with guests.

The gangways thronged with boys and younger children while scores of others pressed around the outside fence. Lights shone inside the house as well and women were seen coming and going. The whole place reverberated with voices of every pitch and kind; bursts of laughter and coughing as well as cries of joy resounded in the air. Othman was stirred by the wedding's air of happiness and its heartwarming scents of sexuality and love. When the band struck up, he found it more moving than he expected or was accustomed to, for he did not like music particularly, though it was all right when it came his way. Indeed, music was not all that bad sometimes. It was something good and comforting. Marriage was a splendid relationship, a joy and a religious duty. A deep splendid sadness came over him.

"Perhaps you need some fun. That's what I keep telling myself . . ." So spoke Sa'fan, looking in his direction, his face partly lit by the wedding lights, partly hidden in shadow. "Your days are slipping by in work and study, but life demands much more of us than that," he added.

He pretended to listen attentively but inside he felt contempt. He despised homilies which encouraged indolence and considered them a blasphemy against God. At the same time his thoughts returned to Sayyida in her long agony, to the duties he must fulfill and the facts he must bear in mind and reconsider. He felt a meaningless smile on his face. Sa'fan started talking again. "You are a man of high ambition, but peace of mind is a precious possession too . . ."

"You are very wise, Mr. Basyuni . . ." he said, his contempt rising.

At the doorway of the balcony a shadow appeared. It was a girl carrying a tray from which rose the aroma of mint tea. Lights from the wedding below were reflected on her face, revealing some of her features in spite of the darkness of the room behind her. She had a pale round face, evidently attractive but its charms were veiled in mystery. He felt apprehensive. As he bent slightly forward to pick up his cup, he saw from close up the smooth tender skin of her arm and felt as if the scent of mint emanated from it. She was hardly there for a minute before disappearing into the darkness, the smile that had nearly escaped her timorously concealed. Silence reigned like a feeling of guilt, the atmosphere charged with a sense of conspiracy. His apprehension heightened.

"My daughter . . ." said Sa'fan. Othman nodded respectfully.

"She'd completed her primary education before she stopped going to school." He nodded again, this time in admiration. The voices of the group accompanying the singer were wafted up to them. Sa'fan went on: "Home is the real school for a girl." He did not comment. He did not know what to say. At the same time he was annoyed at his own silence.

"What's your view on the subject?"

"I agree with you completely."

Yet he recollected his mother's life of bitter struggle. He felt he was being pushed into a trap. The soloist began to sing in a soft, gentle voice. Sa'fan murmured, "How beautiful!"

"Indeed."

"Life is beautiful too."

"Absolutely."

"But it demands wisdom from us if we're to enjoy its sweetness."

"Isn't wisdom difficult to attain?"

"No. It's a gift from God."

God did not create us for a life of ease or the taking of shortcuts. The man was laying siege to him, but he was not going to give in. Yet how could he keep his freedom and gain his chief's favor at the same time? He no longer listened to the music. But Sa'fan went on listening, keeping time with his hands and feet and occasionally casting an inquiring look at him. He concluded that, by way of self-defense, he had better repay his invitation with one even more generous—a conclusion that caused him no slight pain. For he would never spend a single piastre except to meet a pressing need, and on the very day he received his first salary he opened a deposit account with the post office. It never occurred to him to change the place where he lived or the food he ate. He believed that thrift was an important element in his long struggle as well as a religious duty. It was also a safeguard against fear in a fearful world. Yet what must be must be. He would repay the treat with a more generous one. Moreover, it would be in a restaurant, not in his room, jam-packed with books as it was and poor in everything else. As a result, he would be spending a positively enormous amount of money. A curse on all stupid people! The sounds of music turned into a meaningless din and the gates of hell flew open. Yet the old man swayed his head to the tunes, oblivious of the offense he was committing. The world was inflicting on Othman another of its mockeries.

Eight

Before the end of the month, he had treated the man to dinner at al-Kashif restaurant. They had delectable fish and dessert. The old man was so happy he looked as if he expected an angel of mercy and joy to descend from heaven.

"What about spending the rest of the evening at al-Fishawi's café?" he suggested, apparently not satisfied with the dinner alone.

Othman's heart throbbed painfully, but he took his arm and said, "What a wonderful idea!"

As they sat in the café he remembered a Bairam festival in the past when his new galabiya was torn in a brawl in al-Husayni Alley. His father later gave him a beating and he had to wear the galabiya for a whole year, patched up by his mother. The old man's joviality irritated him. It was obvious he expected to hear good news. He sat there with a glow of expectation in his drab eyes and an air of general satisfaction.

"Are you happy with your colleagues in the Archives?" he said.

"Yes. I believe I am."

"They are a poor lot, but good-natured enough."

"Yes. Yes, indeed."

"As for you, you are an excellent young man. Will you become a barrister when you've got your degree?"

"No. But I hope to better my position."

"A good idea. I admire your high ambition."

Othman abandoned his hesitancy, determined to escape even if it meant stifling the man's hopes.

"My cares are greater than you imagine," he said.

The man looked at him apprehensively and said, "Heaven protect us! What's the matter?"

"It's not ambition I care about as you think. My concerns are of a humbler kind."

"Really?"

"If circumstances weren't so difficult, I would desire nothing more simple or natural than marriage."

The old man failed to disguise the disappointment which choked him. "What sort of circumstances, if I may ask?" he said.

"Huge responsibilities." Othman sighed wistfully. "People like me, brought up in poverty, cannot escape its grip . . ." With bowed head he added in a voice of melancholy, "How I wish . . ."

He fell silent as if overcome by emotion. The old man leaned back out of the lamplight till he was in shadow. Othman could not retract what he had said but he must preserve the man's friendship as best he could. Out of the shadow the man's voice came to him: "And when will you be able to stand on your own feet?"

"I have small children and widows to look after," he said in a tone of despair. "I'm just an ox tied blindfold to a waterwheel."

Everything went dead. Even the banging of backgammon pieces was no longer audible. He murmured again, "How I wish . . ."

The old man did not utter a word. He wanted to pay the bill but Othman would not let him. He paid out of his own pocket, feeling utterly miserable. All enjoyment had gone from the party and no pretense could revive it. They left the café and walked up to Bab al-Shariya Square, where the man took his leave and went off toward his home.

Othman was left in a wretched state of nervous tension. A surge of lunatic rashness swept over him, driving him to desperate extravagance of a suicidal nature.

Without wavering he made his way to the prostitutes' quarter, where he could bury his tensions and sorrows and his pangs of conscience.

"Even the sins of man must be hallowed," he said to himself in his misery.

Nine

Omm Husni stopped him as he was going downstairs. She would not do that without a good reason. He looked at her face furrowed with wrinkles, her hair dyed with henna, and her body still strong in spite of her old age. It made him think of his mother, and he shook her hand smiling.

"I've got news," she said.

"I hope it's good news."

Narrowing her single eye (the other one she had lost in a fight in the alley), she said, "There's nothing good in it."

He looked at her intently.

"A suitor. There's now a suitor standing in your way."

"Eh?"

"Somebody has proposed to Sayyida."

A sense of grief and bafflement overwhelmed him as if the news was something he could not have expected. He was lost for words.

"A tailor."

He knew this was something inevitable. He would not try to prevent it nor could he hope to. It was like death. He did not utter a word. She dragged him by the hand to her room and seated him on the settee next to herself.

"Don't you care?"

He felt a sharp pain in the depth of his soul. It was as if the world was fading away. He said angrily, "Don't ask meaningless questions!"

"Calm down!"

"I'd better go."

"But you won't be able to meet her."

The world faded more and more.

She went on: "You should have realized that by yourself."

"How do you mean?"

"Her mother is keeping a strict eye on her movements. A real man is better than an illusion . . ."

"A real man is better than an illusion," he mumbled in a stupor.

"You love her, don't you?"

"I love her," he said disconsolately.

"A well-worn story in our alley."

"Yet it is true."

"Great! And why haven't you popped the question?"

"I can't," he said poignantly.

"Listen, the girl has begged me to tell you!"

He sighed in total despair.

"Go at once and propose to her or let me do it for you," the woman said.

He murmured something incomprehensible as if he were speaking an unknown language. The woman was baffled. He continued his soliloquy: "And God will not forgive me."

"God forbid! Do you think her unworthy of a civil servant like yourself?"

"Don't put words in my mouth, Omm Husni!"

"Speak your mind to me! I'm like a mother to you . . ."

"I can't get married . . ."

"Let her wait for you as long as you wish."

"It would be a long wait . . ."

"Give her your word. That would be enough."

"No. I'm not selfish. For the sake of her happiness I must say no."

Before she had time to reply he had left the room. He walked slowly through the narrow lanes. His tribulation was profound and he bitterly accepted that he would not see her again. Yet, despite his anguish, he experienced a kind of relief, desolate and mysterious. If he was relieved, he felt equally certain that he was damned. He loved her, and no one else would fill the void she would leave in his heart. The love he had known would not be easily erased. It would teach him to hate himself and his ambition, but he was determined to cling to it with all the power of loathing and despair. Mad he was, but his was a hallowed madness that slammed the door on happiness with disdain and pride and drove him irresistibly along the path of glory, rough and strewn with thorns. Happiness might lure him into thoughts of suicide, but misery would spur him to pursue life and worship it. But oh, Sayyida, what a loss she was!

Ten

He made progress in every direction, but his torment hardly abated. He was now firmly established at work, and Sa'fan Basyuni, in spite of the failure of his own plans for him, testified to his assiduity, proficiency, and good behavior. He would say of him, "He is the first to arrive and the last to leave, and at prayer time he leads the worshippers in the ministry's prayer hall."

He would often do his own work as well as that of those who fell behind with theirs, and people spoke of his helpfulness no less than of his ability. The tremendous determination with which he advanced in his study promised brilliant success. Obsessively he frequented the National Library, where he read avidly in various fields of knowledge in addition to his difficult study of law. He also became a familiar figure at the Friday prayers at al-Husayn Mosque. He thus became known in the area for his piety and rectitude. Nevertheless his torment was unabated. Sayyida continued to dominate his thoughts.

"She is the one precious thing in my life," he would tell himself.

On the days when they had once had their assignations he would go and sit on the steps of the ancient drinking fountain and suffer the pangs of memory. He would indulge in them until they took form and substance in his mind. In moments of extreme passion he expected to hear her light footsteps and see her approaching, her face aglow with longing and timidity. He yearned for their long talks, their passionate embraces, and each precious spot he had washed with his kisses. But she did not come, nor would she. She had cut him off. Perhaps she had forgotten him, and if his image crossed her mind, would curse him as he well deserved. One afternoon as he was passing under her window, he thought for a moment that he glimpsed her head behind a pitcher placed on the sill to be cooled by the air. But she was not there. Or perhaps she had hurriedly drawn back in disgust. Man was sanctified by suffering, he told himself. Work and worship were inseparable, he told himself again.

One Friday morning he bumped into her in al-Khiya-miyya, in her mother's company. Their eyes met for an instant before she turned them away indifferently. She did not look behind her. He had a revelation of one meaning of death. Like the voluntary exodus of his ancestor from Eden. Like his own lofty struggle with agony.

In his emotional wretchedness he continued to pay cautious visits to the prostitutes' quarter. Time strengthened his relationship with a girl of the same age as he who called herself Qadriyya. Her dark brown complexion, like Sayyida's though darker, attracted him. She was plump but not excessively so. Once their paths had met, quite a long time since, he had never looked elsewhere. Her room reminded him of his. Nevertheless, it was more primitive with its bare floor, its raised bed, its mirror, its solitary chair used both for sitting and for hanging clothes, its washbowl and jug. Because of this he was not able to take off his suit on wintry nights. Years had passed without a word exchanged between them except for greetings on arrival and departure. Deeply devout though he was, she taught him to drink the necessary little amount. A glass of the hellish Salsala wine at half a piastre was sufficient to blot out his mind and infuse madness into his blood. So much so that one time he said to her in a moment of ridiculous ecstasy, "You are the mistress of the universe."

He would contemplate the bare room, smell the incense, notice the insects, imagine the hidden germs, and ask himself: was this accursed corner burning with the flames of hell not part of the kingdom of God? On one occasion there was a thunderstorm and he was incarcerated in the naked room; the lane was deserted, there was no sound and darkness reigned. Qadriyya squatted on the bed while he sat on the bamboo chair. The room was lit by a solitary candle. As time seemed endless, he took a notebook from his pocket in which he had written down some notes from his lectures. He started to read out loud, as was his habit.

"Qur'an?" Qadriyya asked.

He shook his head, smiling.

"Dates with girlfriends?"

"Lectures."

"So you're a student? Then why do you wear a mustache?"

"I'm a government employee. I go to evening classes."

He craved for Sayyida with an aching heart. But an idea occurred to him which brought him comfort: that the pouring rain was washing the lane and wiping its face clean.

One day he went back to the alley to find the ground in

front of Sayyida's house strewn with sand, while flags flut-
tered on either side. His heart gave a final beat. On the
stairs to his flat he came upon Omm Husni—perhaps she
had meant to wait for him? He greeted her as he passed
and went on. Her voice called after him, "May God give
you what you want and make you happy!"

He could not concentrate on his lecture notes. His small
room was invaded by voices, women's cries of joy, children's cheers, and the wedding music. Yes. There was Sayyida entering the kingdom of another man. A period of his
youth was over and buried.

*He went out with a new determination. He told himself
that life was something greater than all its aspirations, that
the wisdom of Omar al-Khayyam was more beautiful than
al-Ma'arri's* and that a man's heart was his only guide. He
stormed into the wedding and the people said he was crazy.
He pointed at Sayyida and said to her, "The decision lies
with you." She responded to his appeal in spite of the crying and the wailing, because in the critical moments which
precede execution the truth is laid bare and death is van-
quished. Away they went, running together up three back
streets through Bab al-Nasr to the City of the Dead, both
staggering with happiness.*

The noise, the cries of joy, and the singing continued till
dawn broke. He kept looking at his notes without compre-

---

*Omar al-Khayyam was a twelfth-century Persian poet whose famous *Ruba-
'iyyat* or quatrains were translated in 1859 by Edward FitzGerald. His verse
mocks the transience of human grandeur and calls for the enjoyment of the
pleasures of the fleeting moment. Al-Ma'arri was a renowned eleventh-century
Arab poet who led a life of celibate solitude and renunciation and whose austerity was reflected in his poetry. *Translator's note*

hending a thing. He was overcome by loneliness, slumped in an empty world without sound or hope. His anguish bore down upon him on the wearisome path. He reminded himself of the battling of nations and the battling of germs and the battling of health and strength, and he shouted, "Glory be to God on high!"

Eleven

His Excellency the Director General

Sir,

I have the honor to advise Your Excellency that as an external student I have, this year, obtained the degree of Bachelor of Laws, seeking to acquire more knowledge and to perfect the tools necessary for a government employee. All along, Your Excellency's genius has been my inspiration under the protection of His Majesty the King, God save him.

Please take note and authorize the enclosed certificate to be kept in my record of service.

I am, sir, with the highest respect,
Your obedient servant
Othman Bayyumi
Archives Clerk
(Incoming Mail)

He had achieved a brilliant record among external candidates. His note addressed to His Excellency would take its splendid course and proclaim to the world his superiority. It would first go to his immediate senior, Sa'fan Basyuni, to authorize its submission to His Honor the Director of Administration, Hamza al-Suwayfi. That meant it would first be recorded in the Archives' register of outgoing mail and then recorded again in the department's register of incoming mail. This done, it would be taken to Hamza al-Suwayfi to approve its submission to His Excellency the Director General. Thereupon it would be recorded in the department's register of outgoing mail and then in the register of incoming mail in the Director General's office. Then His Excellency the Director General would read it. He would take it in with his eyes, absorb it in his mind, and maybe it would move him. Then he would sign it and pass it to the Personnel Office for disposal. Whereupon it would be recorded in the register of outgoing mail at the office of the Director General and then in the register of incoming mail in the Personnel Office. Thus action would be taken and a copy would be sent to Archives, where the letter was first issued, for retention in his service record. In this way the astronomical orbit would be completed and those who did not know would know.

He was drunk with happiness for a day. But days went by. What then? Would everything be swallowed up in silence? Nothing happened. The sacred fire burned in his heart. The shrine of al-Husayn bore witness to his prolonged prayers. The path stretched ahead without a single flicker of light. He had finished his studies but his quest for culture never ceased. It satisfied his yearning for knowledge, refining his spiritual qualifications for the position he was one day, by the grace of God, going to fill. It also fortified him in his long and bitter struggle in the jungle of officialdom where everyone in power claimed sacrificial offerings from him. He did not possess the magic of wealth, nor did he enjoy the privileges which belong to a great family. No political power was behind him. Nor was he prepared to play the part of a clown, a servant, or a pimp. He was one of the wretched people who had to arm themselves with every weapon available, seize every chance, rely on God and seek His eternal wisdom which ordained that man should fall on earth in order to rise again, through sweat and blood, to heaven.

With the passage of time in its eternal course a post in grade seven became vacant in the Archives Section when its occupant was transferred to another ministry. Sa'fan Basyuni said to him, "I've recommended you for the vacant post. Nobody in Archives deserves it more than you do."

He shook his hand gratefully and felt he wanted to kiss him.

The old man spoke again: "You've spent seven years in grade eight during which you became a Bachelor of Laws and showed beyond doubt unmatched efficiency." The man laughed, revealing his black teeth with gaps in between, and went on: "It will be yours for sure. People with connections wouldn't be interested in a post at an office inhabited by snakes and insects."

Waiting was long and days went by. Seven years I have spent in one grade, he told himself; at this rate I will need sixty-four years to achieve my ambition. He had not seen the Director General, who had kindled the sacred flame in his heart, since the day he had stood in audience before him among the new appointees. It was his great joy to stand in a corner of the square and watch his procession as he left the ministry with the pomp and circumstance of royalty. That was the goal, the meaning and glory of life.

Work intensified in the department during the preparation of the budget. The Director of Administration needed additional officers from his subordinate sections and Othman was seconded from the Archives. This pleased him and he thought his chance had come. He braced himself for the task with great eagerness. He worked with the auditors and also with the deputy directors. Moreover, he attended meetings with the Director of Administration himself. It was like a volcanic eruption—as if he had just been waiting for the chance ever since his heart had taken fire with sacred ambition. He did not hesitate to place himself at the disposal of his seniors from early morning until midnight. In conditions so critical and delicate the administration was oblivious to everything save true competence. The budget was a serious business connected with the Director General, the Under Secretary of State, the Minister, the Cabinet, the Parliament, and the press. In those busy strenuous days nepotism stood no chance; rather, natural selection prevailed, the competent came to the forefront, and personal ability was recognized, though not, perhaps, rewarded. Othman attracted attention and won full confidence. His extraordinary capacity for work was evident and so was his knowledge of laws and regulations. As if he had not achieved enough success, he volunteered in secret to draft the budget statement which was normally written by the Director of Administration himself. On one occasion he had a chance to see the Director on his own on some business. When he had shown him his papers, he said with great deference, "Director, allow me to present to you some notes I took during work. They may be of some use in the editing of the budget statement."

Hamza al-Suwayfi did not seem to take him seriously. "You are an excellent young man as everyone says . . ." he said kindly.

"I do not deserve the compliment, sir."

"By the way, congratulations! Your promotion to grade seven has been approved today."

This was Othman's moment of triumph. "It's thanks to you and your help," he said gratefully.

"Congratulations!" the Director said, smiling. "But as for the budget statement, that's a different matter."

"Forgive me, sir," said Othman apologetically. "I wouldn't dare to handle the budget statement itself. It's just that I made some notes during work. They're the notes of a hard worker who has studied law and finance and only wished to be of some service to you when you set about composing the real statement."

The man took the notes and started to read them while Othman watched attentively. He found the work absorbing. That was obvious. At last he said with an air of superficial calm, "Your style is good."

"Thank you, sir."

"It seems you are an excellent reader."

"I believe so, sir."

"What do you read?"

"Literature, biographies of great men, English and French."

"Can you do translation?"

"I spend my spare time perusing dictionaries."

Hamza al-Suwayfi laughed and said, "Splendid! Good luck to you!"

He gave him permission to leave and kept the notes. Othman walked out of the room drunk with happiness, convinced that earning the confidence of the Director as he had just done was more valuable than the grade seven itself.

When the draft budget was printed several months later

Othman anxiously read the preamble—and there was the passage he had written with his own hand, apart from a slight alteration of absolutely no consequence. He was thrilled, full to the brim with faith in himself and his future. He was wise enough, though, not to divulge the secret to anybody.

It was not long before a decision was made to transfer him from Archives to the Budget Department. That night he stood behind the window in his room and gazed down the alley sunk in darkness. He lifted his eyes to the sky and the wakeful stars. They looked motionless. But there was nothing static in the universe. He thought God had created the beautiful stars to entice us to look upward. The tragedy was that one day they would look down from their height and find no trace of us. There was no meaning to our life on earth save by sweat and blood.

Twelve

"I'm sorry at your leaving the Archives Section and happy for your sake, in equal degrees," said Sa'fan Basyuni.

In the emotional atmosphere Othman's heart melted with momentary sincerity. Tears came to his eyes as he murmured, "I will never forget you, Mr. Basyuni, and I'll never forget the time I spent in Archives."

"Yet I'm happy because you are."

Othman sighed and said, "Happiness is very short-lived, Mr. Basyuni."

Sa'fan did not understand his remark but Othman lived it. He carried time on his back moment by moment and suffered patience drop by drop. He soon forgot that he was promoted to grade seven or that he worked in the Budget Department. He worked at the ministry like a man possessed, and in his tiny room he delved into more knowledge. Occasionally he would tell himself apprehensively that life flitted by, youth flitted by, and that the river of time flowed on and would not rest . . .

He was still at the beginning of the path. His frugality

increased with time and his attachment to his primitive house grew stronger. Money was a safeguard, he felt; and, if need be, it could be a dowry for the bride of his dreams. The bride of his dreams who would open closed doors and entice the treasure of the future out of its hiding place. Officials had a whole lore of wise sayings and proverbs on the subject. The right bride would be either the reward of glory achieved early or the key to glory that otherwise could hardly be achieved at all. The path seemed long and difficult and he needed succor. Rumor had it that His Excellency the Director General reached his unique position when he was fairly young thanks to politics and family connections and that as a result he married a girl of ineffable beauty from a highly respected family.

It was also rumored that the First Deputy Director of the department was promoted because of his wife, or more correctly his wife's family.

Othman had equipped himself with every possible weapon. Nobody could blame him, then, if he sought the support of a wellborn bride; otherwise how was he to stand against the ruthless current of time? So he started to do translations for newspapers and magazines to earn more money and build up his savings. In this too he was by no means unsuccessful, but he did not spend a single piastre more to alleviate the harshness of his life. Of all the fun in the world he knew only one thing: his weekly visit to Qadriyya in the lane and that hellish glass of wine at half a piastre.

Once she said to him, "You never change this suit. You wear it summer and winter. I've known it for years just as I've known you."

He frowned and said nothing.

"Don't be cross! I like a good laugh."

"Have you counted the money I have given to you over the past years?" he said to her naively.

"I once had a crush on a man," she retorted sardonically, "and he stole two hundred pounds from me. Do you know what two hundred pounds means?"

At the thought of such a disaster he prayed to God for protection from the countless afflictions of life.

"And what did you do?" he asked her.

"Nothing. God keeps us in good health. That's what matters."

He told himself there was no doubt that she was mad and that was why she was a whore. But she was the only recreation in his rigorous life and she gave him comfort of sorts. Sometimes he yearned for real love and its charms which gave life a different savor. He would remember Sayyida and the steps of the forlorn fountain and the desert, but in the end he would surrender to the harsh jests of life, resting content with himself, despite the torment in his soul, for having chosen the arduous path attended by the blessing of God and His lofty glory.

One night Qadriyya said to him, "Why don't the two of us go on a picnic on Friday morning?"

He was astonished and said, "I steal my way to you in the dark like a thief . . ."

"What are you afraid of?"

What could he say? She understood nothing. "It wouldn't be right if anyone saw me . . ." he replied in a tone of apology.

"Are you committing a crime?"

"The people . . ."

"You are the bull who carries the earth on its horns . . ." she said satirically.

He was a godly and righteous man with a good reputation to take proper care of.

"You could keep me all to yourself for a whole night," she said seductively. "We could make an arrangement . . ."

"And the cost?" he said warily.

"Fifty piastres."

He contemplated the idea with concern. It would bring him, despite the terrible price, real consolation. And he needed consolation.

"A good idea," he said. "Let it be once a month."

"Would once a month be enough for you?"

"I might come more often, but in the normal way."

He admitted he could not live without her. She was his age, but she appeared insensible to time and the effect it was rapidly making on her. She lived without love and without glory as if, in a kind of fury, she had made a pact with the devil. And how it galled him when she once confessed to him that she had taken part in a demonstration.

"A demonstration!" he shouted angrily.

"What's the matter? Yes. A demonstration . . . Even this back street felt patriotic once . . ."

He told himself that insanity was more widespread than he had reckoned. Political interests exasperated and amazed him. Yet he was determined not to pay attention to them. He believed that man had only one path along which he had to trek without flinching and all alone, taking no part in politics and demonstrations, that only a solitary man could be aware of God and what He wished him to do in this life, and that man's glory was fulfilled in his muddled but conscious effort to distinguish good and evil and in resisting death until the last moment.

Thirteen

One day Othman came across an advertisement of some interest. It had been put out by his ministry to fill a vacancy for a translator with a knowledge of both English and French at a salary of thirty-five pounds per month. A date was announced for a competition. He entered the competition without hesitation and without giving it much thought. It so happened that he won it, and this increased his self-confidence and the pride he took in his own talents. He was called to see Hamza al-Suwayfi in his office (the new appointment was under his direct supervision).

"I congratulate you on your success. It shows how versatile you are," he said.

Othman thanked him with his usual politeness.

"But that's a post with a fixed salary," the man said. "If you take it, you will be excluded from the ordinary promotion scale. Have you thought about that?"

He had not in fact realized this and soon his enthusiasm for the job's relatively high salary subsided.

"Actually I do not wish to withdraw from the ordinary scale . . ." he said.

"That means we should appoint the runner-up."

Othman thought of a good idea and said, "Wouldn't it be possible to have me promoted to grade six, add the translation work to my responsibilities, and thus save a considerable sum in the budget?"

The Director of Administration thought for a long while and then said, "The question must be raised with the Personnel Office and the Legal Department."

"Very well, sir."

Hamza laughed and said, "You are ambitious as well as wise. I hope your suggestion will be accepted."

His promotion to grade six was settled at a monthly salary of twenty-five pounds. And though he had to sacrifice ten pounds a month, still he earned a promotion that otherwise he would not have reached for years, quite apart from the special importance attached to him because of his dual job. As usual, he enjoyed a brief spell of happiness. His acquaintance with happiness was ephemeral, like chance encounters on the road. He went back to measuring the long path and groaning at its infinite length. What use was grade six when he was nearing the end of his youth and about to enter a new phase of his life?

Sa'fan Basyuni embraced him and said, "You are making marvelous leaps ahead, my son . . ."

"But days are swifter than a fleeting thought," he said wistfully.

"They are indeed. Heaven protect you from their evil . . ."

Othman gazed at his wrinkled face and said, "Tell me about the ambitions you had when you were young, would you?"

"Me? God be praised! The position of Head of Archives was greater than anything I dreamed of."

"Didn't you aspire to become Director General?"

The old man broke into a fit of laughter until tears came to his eyes. "Common people like us cannot aim at anything beyond being the head of a section," he said.

He was wrong. What he said was true of reaching the position of Minister or Under Secretary of State, but to become a Director General was not impossible for ordinary people. It was their ultimate aspiration, particularly for those special cases who prepared themselves for that exalted glory. But days went by incessantly and stealthily. And the position of Director General would be of no avail if it were not held long enough for it to be enjoyed, for life to be appreciated under it, and for the most sublime of services to be rendered in its name to the sacred apparatus called the government.

When was he going to fulfill the requirements of his faith? Before achieving his life's ambition or after? He must have a family and father children or else he would be damned. Either the bride that exalts a man to glory or the glory that attracts a dazzling bride. Under the intensity of his anguish, he sometimes craved for tranquillity and leisure as he brooded over the hard struggle which gave life its sole meaning and sacred agony.

One day he learned that the Director of Administration, Hamza al-Suwayfi, was complaining that his son was falling behind at school over foreign languages. He offered to help him.

Hamza was undecided and said, "I'd better find him a private tutor. I don't want you to waste your time with him."

"Your Honor," replied Othman in words chosen with his usual care, "you have used words I cannot allow."

So he paid frequent visits to the Director's house and took singular trouble with the boy, with the result that he passed his examination. The Director tried to reward him but he recoiled as though from fire and said, "I shall not permit Your Honor that either . . ." And he stood his ground until the man succumbed. Then he added in a grateful tone, "I owe so much to you for your kindness and encouragement . . ."

However, he felt in the depths of his heart a pain of similar dimensions to the sum he had magnanimously declined to take. But that was not the only frustration he suffered in frequenting the Director's house. For he had dreamed of coming upon a "suitable" bride there, and who could know? He also dreamed that his services might intercede for him with Hamza al-Suwayfi and enable him to overlook the humbleness of his birth and admit him into a new class that would help him make progress. But the dream did not come true and on his visits the only people he met were males. Sa'fan Basyuni would not have cared about his birth: the origins of the two of them were much the same. But what benefit could he expect from marrying his daughter? Nothing but children and cares and poverty. Not even love. For he only loved Sayyida and his heart had been dead since he abandoned her. But those who aspired to glory on the path to God did not concern themselves with happiness.

Days went by as they always would: the scorching days of summer, the dreamy days of autumn, the cruel days of winter, and the scented days of spring. And he himself would always maintain his patient determination and his soaring ambition, along with the bitterness in his heart and the grinding of his desires.

Fourteen

Omm Husni came to see him as was her wont. She presented him with a jar of pickled lemons and sat down on the settee eyeing him carefully and making him curious. She slapped her knee suddenly and said, "By the holy Husayn, your loneliness makes me sad . . ."

He smiled impassively.

"Are you not aware you're growing old?" she said.

"Of course I am, Omm Husni."

"And that nothing is more treacherous than the passing years?"

"You're right."

"Where are your children to keep you company?"

"In the realm of the unknown." He kept quiet for a short while, then said, laughing, "The matchmaker's instinct is stirring in you, Omm Husni . . ."

She laughed and said, "Listen, I've got something special . . ."

In spite of his restraint, the conversation with its engaging air of mystery attracted him.

"You've always got something special."

"A pretty, middle-aged widow," she said hopefully. "A sensible woman. The daughter of the late sheikh of the quarter."

"Eh?"

"She's got one daughter. Fourteen years old."

"They're two women then, not one . . ."

"The girl will live with her uncle. You can be assured of that."

"Great!"

"She is a house owner."

"Really?"

"In Birjwan. It's got a garden with a mulberry tree." She stared at him with her poor eyes to assess the impression her words made. She imagined he was pleased and added, "You'll see her for yourself."

Omm Husni pointed her out to him in al-Sikka al-Jadida. She had a coat on, but he could tell from the slow and swaying way she walked that she had learned it from wearing the long native wrap. She was short and plump with a round face and black hair. She aroused a primitive desire in him. Like Qadriyya. Maybe she was cleaner, he thought, but her troubles were immeasurably greater. He felt sorry for Omm Husni, who knew so little about him despite their long familiarity. How could she grasp what it meant to be an auditor and translator in the Budget Department? Humankind began from clay and was then expected to take up its place among the stars; and that was its tragedy.

"What do you think?" said Omm Husni.

"She's a fine woman," he replied, smiling. "You're still an expert."

"Shall I get on with it?"

"No," he answered calmly.

"Didn't you say she was a fine woman?"

"But she isn't a fit wife for me."

The old woman proved to be more obstinate than he thought, for one afternoon she came to him and said, "What a happy coincidence: Madame Saniyya's come to see me."

His primitive desire was aroused and he yielded to a transient weakness. Omm Husni repeated with fresh emphasis, "She's come to visit me . . ."

"Maybe she will come to visit me too," he said mischievously.

"You could come down if you wished . . ." she said as she was going.

He did go down, without hesitation. As silence prevailed, Omm Husni was able to go on chattering nonstop. Othman remembered that he had never talked to anyone seriously except to Sayyida.

"This is an honor . . ." he was obliged to say.

"Thank you," she mumbled.

"It's cold today."

"Yes."

Omm Husni said to her, "Have you finished redecorating your house?"

She nodded.

Omm Husni also tried to bring him around to talking about his official position but he wouldn't. He was inflamed with desire, but it was desire without hope. Finally Saniyya made as if to go and he got up at once, said goodbye, and left. But instead of going upstairs to his flat he went downstairs and waited below with a daring plan in his mind. He heard her footsteps as she came down the stairs. She was surprised to see him. He feigned surprise as well and said, "Nice meeting you . . ."

He made way for her and whispered as she went past him, "Would you care for a cup of tea upstairs?"

"No, thank you," she said hurriedly.

"Please, I've got something to say . . ."

"No," she said, protesting.

She went away as fast as she could. He had rushed things, he thought, his limbs trembling with desire. How on earth could he have imagined that she would accept! But what was to be done with sexual desire, impatience, and human frailty? He climbed the stairs, ashamed and infuriated. He would remain an adolescent, he told himself, until he settled down in a respectable family.

Fifteen

The state of his purse improved constantly. He received a pay increase and his income from freelance translation was growing. And because he spent only what was absolutely necessary, his balance with the Post Office Savings Bank was steadily going up. His fervor for work never slackened and his relationship with the Director of Administration became close, almost as if they were friends.

One day Hamza said to him, "His Excellency the Director General has expressed his admiration for your style in translation."

A wave of joy overwhelmed him. He became certain he wouldn't be able to sleep a single hour of the night. Naturally, His Excellency did not remember him personally, but he still knew of him, if only as an abstract name. The Director of Administration went on: "His Excellency the Director General is a great translator. He's translated many important books himself, and he certainly knows what he's talking about when he praises your work."

He mumbled gratefully and said, "I only got His Excellency's appreciation through you."

"I've been invited to give a lecture at the Civil Servants Society," the Director said, smiling in a very friendly way. "I've jotted down the basic points. How about writing it up with your excellent style?"

"It would be a great pleasure, Director," he said in a tone of enthusiasm.

He wished he could be given a similar task every day. For his work in the department, extensive and well appreciated as it was by everybody, was not going to be enough on its own. So the least he should do was to render services to his seniors, and make them feel his importance and outstanding merits. And that might mollify his dismay at the smallness of his achievements when compared with his ambitions. It was something to comfort him as he proceeded on his long path. In the night he was seized with sudden dejection and cried aloud:

"What madness! How could I imagine that one day I would achieve what I desire!"

He counted the grades he needed to pass through before ascending to the pinnacle of glory: grade five, grade four, grade three, grade two, grade one. He counted them and he counted the years they would claim of his life. It made him giddy and a sense of profound sorrow overwhelmed him. Some great event, he said to himself, must take place; his life could not be wasted away in vain. As he had an appointment with Sa'fan Basyuni at the café, he put on his clothes and went out. He found Omm Husni waiting for him on the landing in front of her flat.

"I've got some visitors," she said. "You should come in and say hello. It's Sayyida and her mother . . ."

He walked in and greeted them. He was a little fright-ened at first, but he soon realized that everything was dead and buried. Not a single look of aversion or reproach, but one of unaffected disinterest without a glimmer of recollec-tion. It confirmed for him that the past had fallen into the infinite abyss of death. What added to his profound aware-ness of the passage of time was the hearty reception the mother gave him. He saw death devouring a loved image which he believed to be eternal; and all it amounted to was a mere memory that hardly seemed to have once been real, any more than Adam in the Garden of Eden. There was Sayyida, growing fat and stupid. She reminded him of Qadriyya and his agitation grew. The top of her wrap had slipped from her head and rested on her shoulder, leaving both her head and neck free. Her embroided kerchief was drawn back to disclose a shiny forehead and parted hair. As for the luster he used to gaze at in her eyes, it had gone out. The meeting passed in a lifeless atmosphere tinged with an ironic sense of estrangement. And he tried in vain to trace on those thick lips any sign that his own lips had kissed them. He stayed only as long as courtesy demanded, and when he left, his heart was beating in supplication to the mysterious unknown which wreaked havoc with a smile at once soft and cruel. He was going to meet his old chief, who was going to be pensioned off in a few days, and spend a friendly evening with him. The old man had become skin and bone and lost the last hair on his head, not because of senility, but because of a stomach disease. However he was still as kindhearted and resigned as he had always been. It was obvious that he faced the end of his service in a depressed and melancholy state of mind. Oth-man tried to cheer him up.

"I wish you a long and happy rest," he said.

"I can't think what life will be like away from Archives," said the old man with a meaningless burst of laughter. "And I haven't got a hobby to keep me busy. That's what really upsets me," he added with a sigh.

"But you're so popular. Everybody loves you."

"True, and I haven't got any family obligations left. But still I'm frightened."

They sipped at their tea while Othman cast furtive glances at him with a feeling of compassion, till the man went on: "I still remember the day I was appointed in the civil service as vividly as yesterday. It is an unforgettable occasion, like one's wedding night. I still remember its every detail. How could a lifetime flit by so swiftly?"

"Yes," murmured Othman with a pang in his heart, "like so many other things . . ."

The man smiled at him as though announcing a change of mood and said, "What about your own family responsibilities?"

He remembered his false claims and replied, "The burden is still heavy."

"You were just a big lad when I first took you on," he said, looking at him with affection. "And now you've become a full-grown man, and soon . . . But anyway, just make sure time does not cheat you. Be very careful."

"Fine! And what good does that do?"

"At least, you mustn't let life pass you by."

"You're speaking of marriage?"

"Of everything. You've always seemed on the lookout to me. But what for? And till when?"

"But life's like that . . ."

The man waved his hand in protest and said, "We all speak confidently about life as if we knew the truth about it."

"What else could we do?"

"Without the existence of God life would be a losing game with no meaning to it."

"It's lucky for us that He exists, and that He knows what He's doing better than we do."

"Thank God for that!" said the old man with feeling.

They fell silent and then talked again, and again they fell silent and again they talked, until it was time to part. Othman felt he was never going to see him again. There was nothing between them but an old comradeship and a sense of duty on his part. Yet he felt for him, momentarily, no little compassion. As they shook hands the old man said, "I trust you won't forget me."

"God forbid!" he answered warmly.

"Forgetfulness is death," said Sa'fan in a pleading tone.

"God give you a long life!"

Othman had no intention of seeing him again, nor had he come to say goodbye to him in response to any genuine feeling, but only for fear of being charged with ingratitude. For this reason he was oppressed by his conscience and his fear of God, and he walked away hardly conscious of his surroundings. In spite of himself, his thoughts were focused on grade five, which was due to be vacant in a few days.

His standing with the Director of Administration was now so good no obstacle of any consequence stood in his way.

So he was promoted to grade five that same month and made Head of Archives.

Sixteen

Patience, however vacuous, may have its reward. Othman's new leap forward was a real one and its great advantage lay in the fact that the Head of Archives presented important mail in person to His Excellency the Director General to receive his instructions confidentially and see that they were carried out. God was pleased with him at long last and the celestial gates were now opened to him, leading to the sublime administrative presence. Here was a royal opportunity that required him to exploit all his experience, culture, suavity, and sincerity. Here was the room, vast as a public square, from which he dreamed he would one day rule. It was a dream that had to come true, no matter what offerings must be made at its altar: a dream to which nobody had access save the meritorious who purchased it in exchange for the cheap and ephemeral pleasures of life.

He studied the enormous room meticulously: the smooth white ceiling, the crystal chandelier, the neatly decorated walls, the tiled fireplace, the blue carpet whose dimensions exceeded anything he had ever imagined possible, the conference table with its green felt cover, and the desk facing him with its strong, curved legs and glass top on which stood an array of silver objects: paper holders, inkpots, pens, a clock, a blotter, an ashtray as well as a wooden cigarette box from Khan al-Khalili.

Now he had ample opportunity to cast furtive looks at the lucky Director as he sat on his large chair: sharp dark eyes and a well-shaven face, a dark red tarboosh, a fragrant scent, a black mustache of medium length and width, an aura of vitality all around him, his girth moderate, though his height could not be ascertained with accuracy. Above all an air of solemn and unbending reticence, which made the earning of his friendship an aspiration difficult to achieve.

There he stood in audience before him, conscious of his breathing and within the aura of his fragrant scent, almost hearing his pulsebeat and reading his thoughts. He stood there seeking to learn his wishes and eager to obey his commands before they were uttered. In the light of his smile he read the future; and his dearest dream was always that he would one day sit in his place.

With pious deference he bowed and said, "Good morning, Your Excellency."

The man looked up and mumbled some sort of reply to his greeting.

"Othman Bayyumi, Head of Archives," he announced by way of introducing himself. In the way the Director lifted his normally level eyebrows Othman read the equivalent of a smile, though no smile showed on his lips.

"The new one, sir," he added.

"And the translator. Isn't that so?"

"Yes, Your Excellency," he answered, his heart beating.

"Your style is good," he said in a low voice.

"Your encouragement is a great honor, sir."

"Any important mail?"

He began opening the envelopes dexterously, showing the Director their contents and scrupulously taking down his instructions. He bowed again and left the room drunk with happiness. On his way back to Archives he thought how Hamza al-Suwayfi was now passing out of his life into the shadows, until the darkness should swallow him as it had swallowed Sa'fan Basyuni, and how from that moment his future was in the hands of (next to Almighty God) His Excellency.

"Beware of slow progress, Othman," he told himself. "One or two leaps forward will be essential."

"When Sa'fan Basyuni was pensioned off he had spent the last half of his service in the same grade," he told himself again.

He knew only too well that the department had two Deputy Directors, which meant that a leap forward could only materialize through Hamza al-Suwayfi: through either his promotion, his retirement, or . . . his death. The thought made him feel ashamed, as his thoughts often did, and he prayed to God for forgiveness.

"Why did God create us in such a corrupt image?" he wondered.

He was anything but pleased with that aspect of his own nature, but he accepted it as it was. He believed that on either side of his sacred path the waves of good and evil clashed together, and that nothing could affect its sanctity except weakness, frailty, self-satisfaction, and indulgence in easy delights and daydreams. He prayed: "Forgive me, Oh almighty God! For my only sin is the love of glory You have instilled in me."

"How can you convince His Excellency of your usefulness? That's the question," he said to himself with determination.

How and when would he have the opportunity to render services without immorality or shame: not as a debtor but as a creditor, in the same way as he treated Hamza al-Suwayfi, and within the limits of dignity and pride, yet according to the dictates of official decorum and its usual obsequious language? "My struggle is noble," he thought to himself. "As for my feelings and thoughts, these belong to God alone."

He believed that God made man for power and glory. Life was power. Survival was power. Perseverance was power. And God's heaven could only be attained through power and struggle.

His chance came when His Excellency Bahjat Noor, the Director General, was awarded the Order of the Nile. He composed a congratulatory column and published it in a newspaper he usually supplied with his translations. He hailed the man's firmness, propriety, good character, administrative talent, and idealism, and declared him a model Egyptian director, a species once thought incapable of replacing the English one.

When he entered the grand room with the mail, His Excellency smiled at him for the first time and said, "Thank you, Mr. Bayyumi."

"Thanks are only due to God, Your Excellency," he said as he bowed.

"Your style is really enviable."

He admitted that it was not only vile wine that made man drunk. But drunkenness did not last and was often followed by a hangover. And he thought the chariot of time was going ever faster. He only remembered that in the distant past, time did not exist: al-Husayni Alley was simply space. Grade five was nothing great for a middle-aged man, a man who constantly lifted up his eyes toward the polestar, who confined himself to his tiny room packed with books, whose best food was ox cheek and kebab on feast days, and whose only pleasures in life were vile wine and the Negress Qadriyya in the bare room.

He needed real human warmth. A bride and a family. He could no longer bear to be consumed in the fire of life on his own.

How he needed a companion in this universe crammed with millions of universes.

Seventeen

He invited Omm Husni to visit him. He made her a cup of coffee on his little stove. She must have felt he was preparing to say something in a mixture of agitation and pleasant anticipation. She said expectantly, "My heart tells me you've called me in for a serious purpose. God be my witness, last night I dreamed . . ."

"Forget about dreams Omm Husni," he broke in. "I want a wife."

Her face beamed with joy and she shouted, "Hurrah! What a happy day!"

"A suitable wife."

"You can pick and choose."

"I've got certain conditions, Omm Husni. Try to understand me!"

"I've got virgin girls, divorcées, and widows both rich and poor."

"Take your mind off our alley and the whole area," he said in a voice of decision.

"What do you mean, my son?" she asked, puzzled.

"I want a wife from a good family."

"What about the daughter of Mr. Hassuna, the owner of the bakery?"

"Forget about our area! A good family, I said!" he interrupted her impatiently.

"You mean . . ."

"Distinguished people . . . senior officials . . . people in power . . ."

The woman was dumbfounded, as if he were talking about the inhabitants of a different planet.

"It seems you're no good in this field."

"You've got strange ideas, my son," she said desperately.

"So?"

"I'm no good, as you said, but I know Omm Zaynab, a matchmaker who lives in al-Hilmiyya."

"Try her, and if she succeeds, I will reward you as if you had done everything."

"You're mean, Mr. Bayyumi," she said laughingly.

"That's unjustly said, woman. I give you my word."

"I'll do my best."

"I don't care if she has been married before. Let her be a widow . . . a divorcée . . . a spinster. Good looks don't matter as long as she is acceptable; and she doesn't have to be young or wealthy either."

The woman shook her head in bewilderment as he went on: "As for my origins, you can say that my father was a merchant, for example. Do they look into these things to check up?"

"Yes, they do. God bless your parents' souls!"

"Anyway, my person may intercede for me. Just let's try!"

Days went by tiresomely as he waited. And every time he went to Omm Husni, she told him to be patient. His imagination brooded on the reasons for the delay and his spirits were plunged in gloom. He began to frequent the shrine of al-Husayn.

During that period it happened that the Director of Administration, Hamza al-Suwayfi, was confined to bed for some time with high blood pressure. The general situation was critical because the administration was about to start drawing up the new budget. Othman visited the man on his bed of sickness and sat by him for long hours. He showed such sorrow and sympathy that the man sang his praises and prayed that God might protect him against the days of evil. As he sat there, Othman remembered how he had not visited Sa'fan Basyuni and had heard nothing about him as if he had been dead. He said to Hamza al-Suwayfi, "You must rest completely and stay in bed until you're fully recovered. Have no worries about work. My colleagues and I are at your service."

The man thanked him and mumbled anxiously, "The budget draft!"

"It will be done," he answered him confidently. "They're all your pupils and their work under your direction has taught them how to go about it."

At the ministry, there was gossip about the sick man and his illness. It was said that high blood pressure was a grave indication and an incurable disease. It was also said that Mr. al-Suwayfi might have to retire or at least give up his chief responsibilities. Othman listened to these surmises with interest and his heart pounded with secret delight. He deplored and resented this feeling, as usual; but it also roused his dreams and ambitions. Suddenly the Director General set up a special committee, of which he made him president, for the preparation of the draft budget. The

implications of his choice were clear to all. True, nobody
questioned his competence, or the propriety of the decision
from that point of view. But, it was said, would it not have
been more appropriate if the Deputy Director of Administration had presided over the committee to satisfy formali-
ties? Nevertheless, he dedicated all his strength to drawing
up the draft so that it might emerge perfect and without a
single flaw. He demonstrated his skill in the assignment
and coordination of duties as well as in gathering the data
required from other departments of the ministry. He personally undertook to do the final balance and write up the
preamble to the budget. The work required direct contact
with His Excellency the Director General in the form of
daily meetings which lasted for an hour and sometimes
two, until familiarity replaced formality between them.
One day the meeting went on for four hours and the man
ordered coffee for him and offered him a cigarette, which
he refused politely, as he was not a smoker. Days which
filled his heart to the brim with happiness, pride, and hope
went by. The man was pleased with his work and he felt
that God was pleased with him and that fortune smiled on
him. He drew up a model preamble to the draft, which the
Director particularly liked, and he felt that he was standing
on the very pinnacle of glory.

Hamza al-Suwayfi regained his health and returned to
work on the last day of the committee's work. Othman
showed his delight by embracing him and wishing him
long life.

"We were lost without you. The Lord be thanked for
your recovery!" he said to him.

"What about the draft?" the man inquired.

"It's been done and the preamble has been written and

both are now with His Excellency for consideration. You will see them tomorrow or the day after. But how are you?"

"I'm all right, thank God. They cupped me and prescribed a strict diet. It's all in God's hands."

"Don't worry. The whole thing is only a passing cloud."

During the course of his long service he got used to his own split personality and the moral conflicts it had to go through. He also got used to disappointments, both those which can be expected and those which cannot—like this one, for example. A feeling of lassitude, almost of despair, oppressed his innermost soul. Thus when a grade four position in the Legal Department became vacant, his anxiety prompted him to speak out. He had never done so before: in the past his habit had been to let his deeds and services speak for him. Thanks to the general atmosphere which his work with His Excellency the Director General created he was able to say to him, "If Your Excellency would be so kind, you might agree to my using my knowledge of the law in the Legal Department."

"No! The Legal Department is a monopoly of people with certain privileges and will be better left alone," the man answered decisively.

Alas, it was the same story as the wife for whom he had been waiting for so long. He was annoyed, but he answered deferentially, "As you wish, Your Excellency!"

He was walking toward the door when he was stopped by the man's voice: "I've proposed in the new budget that the Head of Archives post be raised to grade four."

He turned, took one long step, and bowed until his head nearly touched the edge of the desk.

Eighteen

This was assuredly a gratifying leap forward. If fortune continued to smile on him, he might achieve his ambition in twelve or fifteen years and still have a few years ahead of him in which to exercise high administrative responsibilities like His Excellency. But, as for Omm Zaynab's mission, it was certain she had failed. That could no longer be doubted. A Head of Archives (he thought) was simply not acceptable. A Director of Administration might be accepted, but a Director General would never be rejected, not even if he was a senile dotard.

The reasons for marrying were countless. Marriage was a consolation to the lonely heart and the agonies of solitude. Marriage would also satisfy that religious aspect of his soul which regarded his celibacy as a sin. The tensions in his life were alleviated by the role Qadriyya played in it, but she did not provide him with those feelings of lovingkindness, tenderness, and human understanding which marriage offered, not to mention that she intensified his sense of guilt. The only comfort he had was his work, knowledge, and the exercise of thrift. And whenever he was tired of frugality, he told himself, "That's how the Orthodox Caliphs lived!"

One day, as he was working in the Archives, he was taken aback to find Sa'fan Basyuni standing in front of him, decrepit and emaciated like a ghost bidding life farewell. He stood up to welcome the man, ashamed of how grossly he had been neglecting him. He sat Basyuni down, saying with affected geniality, "How nice to see you again!"

The old man pulled himself together with great effort and mumbled, "How I missed you, man!"

"To hell with work!" cried Othman in a burst of repentance. "To hell with home and everyone there! I'm so sorry, dear friend."

"I'm ill, Othman," the man said plaintively.

"Don't worry! You'll be all right . . . Shall I order a coffee for you?"

"Nothing at all. Everything is forbidden."

"God give you back your health and strength."

He was extremely vexed and embarrassed and could see no way in which this unfortunate meeting could be brought to an end. Sa'fan was quiet for a short while and then murmured in tones of humiliation, "I'm in bad need of three pounds." He choked as he spoke and then went on: "For treatment, you see."

Othman trembled. He saw danger about to engulf him, no mercy shown; and he cried out passionately, like a man being chased, "How horrible! I would never have . . . I would never have imagined myself turning down a request from you. Particularly this request. I'd sooner steal than say no to you . . ."

The man swallowed hard and said despondently, "Not even one pound?"

"Don't you believe me, dearest of men? Oh, God! If only I could tell you! If only I . . ."

The man despaired completely and was lost in unknown thoughts. He got to his feet with difficulty, saying, "I believe you. God help you! God help us all!"

Othman's eyes brimmed with tears as he shook hands with him—genuine, unaffected tears, condensed out of the vapors rising from the tortuous conflict raging deep down inside him. He nearly went after him, but let him go and walked back to his desk muttering to himself, "Oh, God!"

"We should have been hewn out of stone or iron to be able to stand up to life," he said to himself.

"The path is very long," he also said. "My only consolation is that I hold life, the gift of God, as sacred and do not make light of it."

During the same week he heard the news of Sa'fan Basyuni's death. It was not unexpected, but he was deeply shocked. From the sheer intensity of his pain, he screamed inwardly, "Stop suffering! You've got more than your share of pain."

And he said, "People envy me, but am I happy?"

And he asked, "What's happiness?"

"Our real happiness," he told himself, "is that God exists," and he then added with determination, "Either we live or we die!"

Nineteen

Time cuts like a sword. If you don't kill it, it kills you. He had become an authority on getting the better of time, but had he really escaped its sharp edge? The previous day a new young employee had spoken to him privately, asking his advice on a personal matter.

"I really feel embarrassed about this, sir," the young man had begun, "but I come to you as a father or an elder brother!"

The words sounded so strange he thought the man was being sarcastic. As a father! True, he could have had a son of his age. And why not? Yet he never failed to attend to techniques of mastering time.

One day Omm Husni said to him, "This time it's a headmistress."

He shook with unconcealed pleasure. But although a headmistress could perhaps make a suitable wife, yet what he really desired was someone to lift him to a higher plane. So what was to be done?

Unable to resist his curiosity, he asked the old woman, "Old?"

"In the prime of womanhood. Thirty-five years at most."

"A widow or divorced?"

"A virgin, as God made her. Headmistresses were not allowed to marry in the old days, as you know."

He did not think he would be any the worse for seeing her, and see her he did, in al-Sayyida. He liked her appearance and she had a good figure. (His instincts had been aroused by Saniyya before.) So he saw her and learned that she too had seen him.

Later on Omm Husni said to him, "She won't cost you a penny."

He realized the woman had approved of him. For here she was, offering to furnish a house and provide the wedding requirements. All he would have to attend to were minor matters.

The old woman went on: "Only the ring and a wedding present and some sundries. So, can I congratulate you?"

"Let's be patient a little!"

"Her only condition is the promise of a hundred and fifty pounds in case of divorce."

Everything was fine and in perfect harmony with his cautious nature. Had he wished only to satisfy his religious faith by getting married, nothing would have been more suitable. But what about his worldly ambitions? He sank in a whirlpool of thoughts, perhaps because of his feeling that he was growing old. Because of the secret revelations which enveloped him from the world of the unknown. Because of the irony and cruelty and treachery of appearances. Because of the roses he never smelled and the songs echoing beyond the range of his hearing. Because of life's harshness and deprivations. In spite of all this he said to himself, "What's all this brooding and hesitation for? Rubbish! All is rubbish! I will not do something crazy after all that waiting."

He wished he could establish a relationship with her: an unholy relationship! But he was only likely to be rejected, even more flatly than he had been by Saniyya. Even if she agreed, it would not be an occasion for happiness, as one might think, for that would require him to rent and furnish a flat somewhere else. His heart was full of apprehensions and in the end he simply said to Omm Husni, "No."

"You can't be serious!" the old woman shouted.

"I said no."

"You're a riddle, my boy."

He laughed mirthlessly.

"What do you want? Do you not like the female sex?"

He laughed again.

"God forgive you!"

"I'm sad, my son," she said.

"In sadness," he said to himself, "man is hallowed and made ready for divine joy."

Twenty

Onsiyya Ramadan arrived at a time when Othman had fallen victim to feelings of melancholy and depression which he had not experienced with such force before. He told himself that he was lost in an arid and blazing desert, that he had gained nothing of value, that ambition needed time, and life was short and the past despicable. For all his intimate personal emotions, he was despicable. His true emblem was a charity grave and the prison. The one martyr in his family had died on the side of oppression and injustice. He was friendless. Relations between him and the companions of his boyhood had ceased altogether. At work he had colleagues who respected and envied him but he had no friends. The only man with whom he could sit and talk was a servant at al-Husayn Mosque, and the only touch of romance in his arid life was a bare room and a whore who was half Negro. "What's the meaning of this life?"

True, he had dedicated himself to the glorious path of God, but he was wading in sin and suffering pollution hour

by hour. And it seemed he did not resist death with sufficient fortitude. "It looks like a losing game!"

As he burned in the furnace of his mental hell, a soft
breeze with a new fragrance was wafted into Archives. It
was new not only to Archives but to the whole administration, and new in the full sense of the word. It was the first
girl to join the administration and, specifically, the Archives
Section. A handsome dark-skinned girl of delicate features
and simple dress. Her appearance as she stood in front of
his desk to introduce herself left him at once confused and
astonished and moved. As he asked her to sit down, he
glimpsed the clerks' heads beginning to protrude from
between the lines of filing cabinets. They were amazed and
unable to believe what they saw.

"Welcome!"

"Thank you! My name is Onsiyya Ramadan."

"Pleased to make your acquaintance! You seem to be
very young?"

"No, I'm eighteen!"

"Wonderful . . . wonderful! And what qualifications do
you have?"

"The General Certificate of Education in science."

"Splendid! Why didn't you carry on with your studies?"
He regretted that question, remembering the first day of his
service at the office of His Excellency the Director General.

The girl answered shyly, "Certain circumstances com-
pelled me to stop."

He cursed circumstances and sought relief in the fact
that the two of them shared the same dreadful predicament.

"You reminded me of myself. But let me tell you this: I
got my degree while working. Closed doors will open
before those who try hard," he said affably.

Her eyes clouded over with a wistful look and she said, "But we live in a harsh and unfair society."

He found that the "revolutionary" ideas which he had no knowledge of and deliberately sought to ignore were threatening again to assault him. He said with determination, "It's better to rely on oneself than to attack society. God addresses His commandments to us as individuals and brings us to account also as individuals. And to cleave a path through rocky ground is better than begging charity from society. It seems you're interested in politics and what they call sociological thinking?"

"I believe in it."

"This means you don't believe in yourself. As for me, I only believe in my own willpower and the unknown wisdom of God!"

She smiled and did not utter a word. He smiled too and said, "I will give you the incoming mail to look after. It's the best job for a new employee."

"Thank you, sir."

"I will expect you to prove yourself always worthy of my confidence."

"I hope I'll never give you reason to be disappointed."

"If you meet with any annoyance from your colleagues, do not hesitate to tell me!"

"I hope I won't need to."

He handed her over to one of the clerks to initiate her in her job.

"Incoming mail," he said tersely.

He felt that Archives had made a gratifying leap toward the luminous life and that from now on it would not lack something to move the heart and excite the senses. The clouds of melancholy memories lifted a little, and instead his thoughts turned back to Sayyida, to Saniyya, to Asila the headmistress, and to Qadriyya, and he told himself that the world of women was endlessly variable and sweet and painful. He asked himself in puzzlement, "Which is the means and which the end: the woman or the position?"

And he also said to himself, "Many men live without position, but who lives without a woman?"

At his age a man thinks twice. He gets tired of the company of books and grumbles about work. He finds deprivation and austerity difficult to bear and is conscious of the past pursuing him without mercy. At his age a man's awareness of his isolation and estrangement grows more intense. So does the anxiety of waiting for uncertain glory. The previous day Hamza al-Suwayfi had said to him, laughing, "Look! There's a gray hair on your head, master of financial statutes!"

He started as if he was caught red-handed.

"Your eyes may have deceived you, sir."

"Let the mirror be the judge between us. Have a good look at home."

"It's come too early," he muttered in defeat.

"Or too late!" the Director of Administration said, laughing. "I knew gray hair when I was ten years younger than you."

He gave another long laugh and then went on: "Yesterday you were the subject of a conversation I had with some colleagues. We wondered how you lived. They said no one ever met you on the street or saw you at a café or a party, and they wondered where you spent your time. 'What does he live for without a family?' they said. And 'He's not interested in any of the things that interest most people; what does he really care for in this life?'"

Othman smiled weakly and said, "I'm sorry to have been a source of trouble to you."

"You're an able and honorable man, but you're mysterious. What is it you care about in this world?"

His heart raced as the questioning closed in upon him, and he said, "There's no mystery, Mr. Suwayfi. I'm a man whose interest is in carrying out his duty and who finds his heart's content in worshipping God."

"Well said! I hope I haven't upset you. To be at peace with oneself is what really matters."

But where was this kind of peace? Where?

Here was gray hair advancing on him. Life's splendors, like its trivialities, drew to an end. How much time was left for him?

Twenty-One

One day while Othman was doing some routine work with Hamza al-Suwayfi, the latter remarked in the course of a conversation, "Happiness is man's goal in life."

"If that were so," Othman replied with concealed contempt, "God wouldn't have banished our first ancestor from Paradise."

"So what do you think the purpose of life *is*?"

"The sacred path," he answered proudly.

"And what's the sacred path?"

"It's the path of glory. Or the realization of the divine on earth."

"Do you really aspire to dominate the world?" Hamza asked in surprise.

"Not exactly that. But there's an element of divinity in every situation."

The man gave him a strange look which made him regret his words. "He thinks I'm mad," he said to himself.

A rumor spread around that His Excellency Bahjat Noor was going to be transferred to another ministry. When he heard this, his heart nearly jumped out of his breast. He had done the impossible to gain the great man's confidence. How long would it take him to gain that of his unknown successor? But the rumor proved false. One day Bahjat Noor handed him a huge bundle of papers as he said, "This is a translation of a book on Khedive Isma'il. It took me half a year to do it!"

Othman looked at the papers with interest.

"I'd like you to look over the style," the man continued. "Your style really has no equal."

He received the commission with total happiness and addressed himself to it zealously, energetically, and with meticulous care. Within one month he had returned the manuscript to His Excellency in perfect style, thus rendering the sort of service he had always yearned for. His Excellency was now his debtor, and at every meeting he was now greeted with a smile that even the most favored were not honored with.

Despite all this, his soul was still scourged by apprehension. He saw time running past him until it disappeared into the horizon, leaving him behind, all alone in the wilderness clasping his sacred ambition. His anxiety drove him to visit a woman who read fortunes from coffee cups, half Egyptian, half European, in al-Tawfiqiyya. She stared into the cup while he watched her, half excited and half ashamed. He told himself he should not have given in to superstition.

"Your health is below par," she said to him. His physical health was good beyond question. But his mental health was not. Perhaps she was right after all . . .

"You will get plenty of money but only by dint of much trouble," the woman went on.

He was not after money, albeit he held on tight to every piastre he earned. Perhaps she meant salary increases that would come with promotions ordained in the world of the unknown.

"An enemy of yours will go on a journey from which he will not return."

Enemies were legion. They hid behind charming smiles and sugarcoated speeches. In his way there was a Deputy Director in the third grade, another in the second, and a Director of Administration in the first. They were all friends and enemies at the same time, as life with its pure intentions and its cruel demands dictated.

"I see two marriages in your life."

He had not even succeeded in finding one, but such was the punishment of those whose misgivings led them into superstition. On his way home he remembered Onsiyya Ramadan. She was growing healthier in appearance and better-looking: a good job was quick to show itself on the faces of the poor. He was a kind chief to her. A tender and decent human relationship, as yet difficult to name, bound them together. At any rate, he no longer was able to imagine Archives without the fragrance of her presence there.

When he had returned to his room, Omm Husni came up to him and said with an air of concern which made him smile, "Madame Asila is at my place. She . . ."

"The headmistress?"

"Yes. She wants to ask your help with some of her affairs."

He realized at once that she had come to snare him with her charms. His natural expectancy drove him toward adventure. He shook hands with Asila for the first time. She was wearing a blue dress which did justice to her breasts and forearms and emphasized the attractions of her figure. There she was, offering herself to him, no matter what true or false stories she had to tell. She excited him as Saniyya and Qadriyya had done. They were of the same type: voluptuous and exciting but not fit for marriage.

Omm Husni said, "I'll go and make you coffee."

Always the same tactics! An old woman whose sole concern was to see people lawfully wedded. Here they were, sitting on the same sofa with nothing between them but a cushion. He tilted his head to straighten his mustache, meanwhile casting a glance at her well-rounded leg firmly planted in a masculine-style low-heeled shoe.

"I'm honored, madame!"

"The honor is mine."

She clasped her hands in her lap and said with a firmness which displayed her ability to face up to the situation, "May I ask you a question?"

"Madame?"

"I own a piece of land which has been expropriated by the government. I'm sure you understand these matters?"

"Of course."

"The road they're going to build covers most of it but leaves bits which cannot be put to any use."

"I believe this is taken into consideration when the valuation is made."

"But the procedures are complicated, as you know."

"You may depend on me."

By the same measure as he sensed the strength of her personality he despaired of seducing her. She was prepared to marry him and in fact she came for nothing else. But for her to acquiesce to an illicit relationship with him looked impossible. Omm Husni came back and they started to drink coffee in total silence. Perhaps she was the most suitable wife on several counts, but she was not the one he wanted. Out of the blue came the image of Onsiyya Ramadan placing itself between them and effacing the woman completely. Since the days at the ancient fountain, his heart had not moved as it did for that young girl. His strained nerves relaxed and his mind was set at ease as he received from his imagination a fresh breeze reawakening his noblest feelings. When the woman had gone, he found Omm Husni looking at him anxiously for reassurance on the success of her purpose in life, on which she spared no effort and which had become part of her faith. The old woman had come to worship marriage and children and the festivities associated with them, and she praised God for the miracle of love which He had created. When his silence continued, she said hopefully, "Maybe you've changed your mind?"

"Why should I?"

"Didn't you see how beautiful she is?"

He remained silent, adamant in his rejection of the hand she stretched out to him in kindness.

In a voice of disappointment Omm Husni began: "As the proverb says . . ."

He left the room before he could hear the proverb. What a pity! Unless a valuable marriage came to his rescue, his pains were likely to be wasted and his hopes destroyed in midcourse. His life had become the object of endless questions and criticisms. People wondered why he didn't marry and have children and make friends. They also wondered how he could live entirely in his private world and ignore the national events taking place around him which excited people even to the point of giving up their lives. And what were the causes which preoccupied them and possessed their hearts, hovering above the noise of their conversations and hindering their work? They talked endlessly about children, diseases, food, the system of government, class conflict, political parties; they repeated proverbs and clever sayings and they cracked jokes. They did not live a true life: they ran away from their sacred duty. They recoiled from taking part in the fearful race against time and glory and death, and in the fulfillment of God's word, which was withheld from the unworthy.

Twenty-Two

Onsiyya Ramadan came to submit her monthly report on the incoming mail. It was the morning of an autumn day and the cool weather breathed into the recesses of the spirit a feeling of sweet wistfulness. His eyes turned now to the paper he was examining, now to her fingers spread out on the edge of the desk. He thought he saw something move in one of her hands. Something which moved and came nearer, delicately inching its way as if bearing a secret message. It was a small package, which she neatly slipped under the blotter after making sure he had seen it.

"What's this?" he asked in a low voice which instinctively responded to the air of caution evident in her gesture from the start. He lifted the blotter a little to reveal a silver-colored case half the size of an open palm.

"What's this?" he asked again.

"A small present," she whispered, blushing.

"A present?" he asked, though he did remember.

"It's your birthday!"

A surge of ecstatic joy overwhelmed him. Today was indeed his birthday or, to be precise, coincided with the date of his birth. But it was just another day. He might remember it a few days before it came or a few days after it had passed or even on the actual day, but this never made any difference except perhaps in that it served to intensify his apprehension of the future. He never celebrated the occasion. That tradition was unknown to him and to the alley he had been brought up in. But here was Onsiyya announcing new traditions. New too was her innocent maneuver to show affection and her marvelous power of opening up the gates of mercy.

"As a matter of fact, I never bother to remember it."

"That's strange!"

"But you shouldn't have taken the trouble!"

"It's only a very simple thing."

"I really don't know how to thank you."

"There's nothing to thank me for."

"What a lovely person you are! But how did you know the date of my birth?" he asked, then laughed and went on: "Ah, I forgot that . . . You've dug out my service file and now you know my age!"

"It's the age of reason and maturity."

He put out his hand and shook hers. He pressed her hand, smooth as silk, and all this time sweet thoughts poured over him. He would buy her an even better present on *her* birthday, which he would learn from her service file too. In spite of his radiant happiness he wished she could have chosen a way to express her feelings which had nothing to do with money; for the spending of money hurt him and upset the balance of his life. But he did not dwell on this for long. He was slipping into an abyss, flying toward the unknown, his heart filled with delight and longing. When he pressed her hand, she accepted it with a conscious smile, which gave him encouragement as well as pleasure.

And after this, what? Was this in harmony with his one and only path? He was confronting something greater than a delicate and transient moment perfumed with enchantments. He was confronting the unknown: Destiny itself. He was knocking on a door behind which time was stopped in its tracks or even made to go backward. "Come back," a call resounded, "or thou perishest!" But no ear listened, no heart responded.

On the following day she stood in front of him transmitting looks full of submissiveness and sweetness. His head was on fire, his throat scorched. His fingers were drawn toward hers and touched them where they rested on the files spread out between them. He looked warily around, while he mumbled some meaningless instructions. He bent forward and kissed her lips, then sat back again in his chair, shivering, burning, intoxicated with life and the fear of the unknown.

Twenty-Three

They met early one Friday afternoon. Their assignation grew out of an irresistible urge to surrender, coupled with a hope that he would be able to escape in the end. He felt it a fall from grace but it was seeped in happiness. He had no knowledge of places where lovers met. She suggested al-Azbakiyya Garden. He objected on the grounds that it was unprotected and open to view from all directions. But the Zoo was sufficiently far away and deserted, lying outside the built-up area and safe from the eyes of busybodies. To reach it the tram had to pass through open fields and wastelands. They walked side by side enjoying a "real" life in the few hours before closing time. He had not been to the Zoo since visiting it on a school outing. He had no idea what was customary when taking a girl out: what may be said and what may not, what may be done and what may not. They walked together happily and quietly; yet there was that uneasy feeling nagging at him and telling him that the meeting was something irregular and wrong, that he should not have given way to the impulse. To ward off his feelings of confusion and frustration he expressed his admiration of the trees, the bridges, the grotto, the streams, the ponds, and the different kinds of animals. But he remained convinced that he had not yet said a single word to the point and that he was trying to escape when it was already too late. She walked beside him, her eyes melting with a dreamy and triumphant look, her head raised and her breast thrown proudly forward. Her air suggested to him a tide race of demands within. And in her breathing he felt that she took in the most beautiful mysteries of life. Their eyes met, and in her glowing look he read the purest innocence, sweet cunning too, and the rush of secret desires.

"Even now that I've got a job I can't easily get out of the house," she protested.

"Don't let it make you cross, my dear," he answered in a ludicrously paternal tone.

"But it's unnatural and humiliating."

"An inaccurate translation of the parental sentiments."

"I don't think you really believe that."

"Really?"

She laughed with complete assurance and added: "If my mother had known I was coming to see you, I don't think she would've minded."

"But she didn't know?" he said anxiously.

She laughed again and was silent for a moment until his mouth went completely dry. Then she said, "Our meeting remains a secret as agreed."

"Of course, dear."

"To tell you the truth, I'm not happy about this."

It was obvious she wanted everything out in the open, and what that meant was also obvious. Was he then at her mercy already? Would circumstances compel him to accept things that were not in his plan? Would the powers of destruction besiege him and shatter for good his solitary, sacred, unattainable dream? Through his fearful thoughts he challenged the unknown and threatened it with murder. But then he felt ashamed of his thoughts as he noticed the gazelle-like figure prancing merrily along beside him, her arm in his, while the clouds moving through the sky above the gardens seemed to give a benison to her joy. He soon calmed down and buried his misgivings. He made peace with his importunate ambitions so that he might melt away into the glow of enchantment and swallow down the taste of hellfire burning inside him. He felt his elbow touch her supple body and receive from its youthful and untrodden territories vibrations of magic. He looked carefully around with a stealthy and guilty look, then kissed her cheek and her neck. Their lips met. He said in a voice which he did not recognize, "You're adorable, Onsiyya."

She smiled coyly and happily.

"I wish," he murmured passionately, "I wish I could . . ." and then he fell silent, breathing audibly.

"Yes?" she said.

"It's as if I'd known you since eternity."

She smiled contentedly, though her eyes asked for more.

"How beautiful the place is!" he said. "Everything is so unspeakably beautiful."

"You love nature!"

Her remark struck him as strange and ironic, seeing that the reality of his life was so different.

"It's you who have made everything beautiful."

"Don't exaggerate! Would you mind if I told you something?"

"Not at all!"

"You don't seem to be interested in anything."

"Really? And do you believe that?"

"I don't know. But I feel you're a man of riddles just as I feel you're a good man."

"All this is nonsense! There's only one universally acknowledged truth: that you're charming."

"And so?"

"What's between us must remain forever, whatever happens in the future."

"In the future?"

"Didn't you learn something unpleasant from my service file?"

"Nothing at all."

"You're the most beautiful thing in my life."

"And you too," she said in a quiet voice of surrender.

He kissed her cheek again as he passionately squeezed her hand.

"I'm torn between what I want and what I am able to do."

"Is there something that you wish for and cannot do?"

"Life is full of unattainable wishes."

"Tell me about what concerns *me*!"

She was right. His mouth was still moist from kissing her and his elbow still touched her soft sweet body as they paced in front of the elephant which saluted them by lifting its trunk.

"Let our relationship remain a secret!"

"Why?"

"So that nobody may think badly of us."

"And why should anybody do so?"

"People would."

"There's nothing bad between us."

"But that's what people are like, my dear."

She laughed lightheartedly and asked, "Did you ask me to go out with you, sir, in order to preach to me?"

"I asked you because I wanted us to get to know each

other and because I wanted to make sure my heart was right."

"And what did you find out?"

"I have become certain that the heart is the best guide!"

All the way back he was wondering why he had not revealed his love to her in direct terms. Why did he not ask her hand? Even supposing she would turn his life upside down and make him face a new direction at the altar of life, was she not more capable of making him happy than the polestar?

Twenty-Four

Asila Hijazi, the headmistress, came again on the pretext of asking whether his good offices had succeeded—or so Omm Husni told him when she invited him to come down to her flat. He was staggering under the weight of his usual cares in addition to the new love which intensified the conflict inside his mind to the point of madness. Thus he welcomed the visit of Asila Hijazi in the hope of escaping from himself. Even if that meant committing a folly that would cost him nothing. He needed a way out and Qadriyya was not available every day. He shook hands with the headmistress and sat down, saying, "Your problem is moving toward a solution."

Soon her physical charms, emphasized by her flower-spotted dress, began to chant their infernal song. She looked at him affably and asked, "Will I have to wait long?"

Omm Husni thought she would go and make the coffee and he was seized with an insane determination to settle the matter there and then and strike an unexpected blow regardless of consequences.

"No, you won't have to wait for long."

"I'm really grateful."

"In fact, everything depends on the strength of your nerves."

"It seems I will have to wait for some time?"

"Allow me to express my admiration!" He said this in a completely different tone as if to introduce an entirely new subject. She blushed and lowered her eyes.

"I really admire you," he went on, "as a man admires a woman. You understand what I mean."

She did not utter a word, but she looked happy as though she were about to be admitted to Paradise.

"But we must be careful. I must tell you something else which I know you might not like."

She gave him an inquiring glance.

"The idea of marriage is out of the question!" He watched her as she turned into ashes, then added boldly and ruthlessly, "I've got a thousand and one reasons, and life, you know, is full of secrets."

"What makes you tell me that?" she asked weakly.

"It's not as though we were two adolescents," he answered politely, but persisting in his cruelty. "Let's talk like adults and look for happiness with sincerity and courage."

"I don't see what you mean."

"Well, I admire you, but I am a bachelor forever."

"Why do you tell me that?"

"I thought you might have a solution for my incurable case."

"You insult me inhumanly," she said with great indignation.

"Forgive me! I speak out of a deep sense of agony."

She frowned and kept quiet.

"A little courage could give us considerable happiness."

"How do you mean?"

"Isn't my meaning clear enough?"

"I don't think I understand you."

"We need a safe place to meet at," he said, with a presumption he never thought he could muster.

"Mr. Bayyumi!" she shouted.

"It'll be a real consolation for two people in need of love and intimacy," he went on heedlessly.

She stood up in a fury, saying, "Either you go or I go."

"I'm going, but think about it calmly and objectively. And don't forget I'm a poor man!"

Twenty-Five

It was no longer a question of a single silver hair difficult to spot. Every now and again a new one would peep out with a chilling white look which threatened a change in the rhythm of life. And what was life? A passing game that a man played with reluctance until he found himself face-to-face with his ultimate fate. Then he would survey his life in its entirety, weigh his deeds and assess their fruits, suffer however resentfully the breath of the unknown, brace himself for further struggle, and then accept defeat. But at least let that defeat be hallowed in the event. There was no promotion to look forward to in the near future. His savings increased, his nervous tension grew more acute, his efforts redoubled. His relationship with Onsiyya was growing more and more intimate, slowly but surely. As for Qadriyya, she truly deserved to be described as a lifetime companion. At the end of his prayers he would say to God, "What's life, Oh God, without You?"

But apparently others did not have his staying power.

For his telephone rang one day and the caller was none other than Asila Hijazi, the headmistress.

"I wanted to thank you for your successful mediation."

"Don't mention it, madame."

"And how are you?"

"I'm fine, thank you."

"I'm glad to hear it."

"Thank you."

"I'm really grateful for your help."

"You're very kind."

A few seconds of silence and then: "But I have a bone to pick with you."

"God forbid!"

"Last time when I left you I was angry, don't you remember?"

"I'm sorry, but there was nothing to make you angry."

"You think so?"

"Yes."

"But you didn't try to get in touch with me."

"I'm sorry, but I don't know your phone number."

"But I managed to get yours!"

"I'm sorry again."

"I hoped you'd try to make the situation easier with a kind word."

"I'm more than willing."

"Really?"

"Positive."

"How?"

"Let's agree on that!"

"Are you still poor?" she asked, muffling a laugh.

"There's no helping that."

"We're lucky I've got enough money."

"May God give you more!"

"Should I be more explicit?"

"I'm more than willing!"

"Lovely! Let us each do our part then!"

This was no surrender, it was a breakdown. He could imagine what lay behind it. She was in her middle years, approaching her decline, lonely and trembling at the advance of age. No youth, no real beauty. Certainly there had been a conflict in her mind which he had not perceived, but he was now witnessing its distressing consequences. What was he to do? He was frightened of Onsiyya and had no real desire for Asila. In his moments of despair he often wished that his heart could die and his lust could be quelled, so that he could go forward carefree on his arduous journey. And to himself he said sorrowfully, "I can't blame people who think I'm mad."

Twenty-Six

How would he find the time to look for a flat and furnish it? He let days go by without doing anything. He forgot the matter altogether until one day he found Asila standing in front of his desk. He received her with a smile, though silently cursing her.

"Excuse my boldness . . ." she said.

He smiled without comment.

"I couldn't get any sense out of you on the telephone."

"I'm much too busy these days," he said with a solemnity to match the official surroundings.

"What have you done?"

"Nothing."

"Nothing at all?"

"Work doesn't give me a free minute. Believe me!"

"I expected to find you more eager." She spoke with a boldness which sounded like desperation; like one whose patience was ebbing as his fears increased.

"I am eager enough, but I have no time."

"There's a flat in Rawd al-Faraj . . ." She held out a

folded piece of paper as she went on: "Here's the address. Go and have a look at it yourself. And if you like it, go ahead and have it furnished." Then temptingly and beseechingly: "I hope you'll like it. Who knows, it may bring us happiness."

He felt the crackle of approaching fire. When the woman had gone, he thought of the long nights that would be added to *The Thousand and One Nights* rather than of the nights he was accustomed to spend studying, translating, and performing services for His Excellency: nights of sacrifice on the path of glory. That path which he had chosen from the first day as an emblem to which his infinite yearnings could legitimately aspire. His desire for the woman subsided as a result of her thoughtless impetuosity and the way she had freely offered herself. Actually she was not bad as a substitute for Qadriyya. But in her he felt the crackle of approaching fire, eager to swallow him up together with those sacred hopes linked to the mystery of God's word. He would not let himself be destroyed by any power on earth save death itself—which was another of God's mysteries, like His inspiring glory. And while he had not been accepted by that unknown wife after whom he had striven for so long, it would be wrong to give up the struggle and surrender to pathetic widows and spinsters.

One night he heard a knock on his door. He was dumbfounded to see Asila sneak in, stumbling over her shame and humiliation.

"I was determined to come and told myself that if somebody saw me I would make for Omm Husni's flat as if it had been her I had come to visit." She spoke in tones of embarrassment as she sat down panting on the settee.

"Well done!" he said, trying to comfort her.

"Do you mind my coming?"

Life had begun to stir in his depths.

"Of course not. I'm more pleased than you imagine."

"Omm Husni will soon be going to bed," she went on. "Do you mind if she suspects what's happened?"

"Not at all!"

They exchanged a long look. Beneath its darkly flowing current she seemed without a trace of pride, merely a woman in love with her defenses down.

"What've you done?" she asked in tender expectation.

He recovered completely from his surprise. He did not want to talk about anything at all; all he was aware of was carnal desire embodied in a woman prepared to give herself to him. He took her soft hand. It felt cold; the contraction of her heart had stopped her blood from circulating. He squeezed it repeatedly, as if passing a secret message. She wasn't expecting this—or so she pretended—and tried to take her hand away. But he did not let her.

"What've you done?"

"We'll discuss that later."

"But you haven't tried to get in touch with me." He bent toward her and kissed her cheek as he whispered in her ear, "Later . . . later . . ."

"But this is what I've come for."

"You'll get what you're after . . . but later . . ."

She opened her mouth to speak but he stopped her with a long and heavy kiss, saying sharply, "Later."

Nature played one of her infinite tunes with joyful bravura, which seemed like a miracle. But soon the tune died away, receding into oblivion and leaving behind a suspicious silence and a feeling of languor full of sadness. He lay on his side on the bed while she stayed where she was on the settee, exposing her slip and the drops of sweat on her forehead and neck to the unshaded light of the electric bulb. He looked at nothing and wished for nothing, as if he had accomplished what was required of him on earth. When his eyes turned in her direction, they denied her completely, as though she had been some strange object sprung from the womb of night, and not that enchanting person who had set him on fire: a dumb thing with no history and no future. He said to himself that the game of desire and revulsion was no more than an exercise in death and resurrection, an advance perception of the inevitable tragedy, matching in its grandeur such fleeting revelations of the unknown, in its infinite variety, as are granted. The position of Director General was one such revelation, but it could only emerge in response to a soaring effort of the will, not to its capitulation, however attractive. Thank God he was barricaded behind sensible impassivity, lethal though it was. Here was this woman, eager beyond question to return to her important subject but hesitant and ashamed. She must have hoped that he would make the first move; but despairing of this, she cast him a wistful beseeching glance and mumbled, "So?"

The unfamiliarity of her voice astounded him with its intrusion on his sacred solitude. He felt a steady repulsion toward her which nearly turned into hatred. What she was seeking to do was to pull down the edifice which he had been constructing stone by stone

"What do you think?" she asked.

"Nothing!"

The roughness of temper characteristic of the back streets, and latent in him, was discernible in his voice.

"But surely you must've done something!"

"Nothing at all."

"Haven't you even had a look at the flat?"

"No."

Her face darkened with chagrin.

"Forgive me for saying this, but . . . should I put the money in your hands?"

"No!"

"Frankly, I don't understand you."

"I've spoken clearly."

"What do you mean? Don't torture me! Please."

"I don't intend to do anything."

"I thought you had agreed and promised," she said in a trembling voice.

"I don't intend to do anything."

"If you have no time now . . ."

"I have no time now, nor will I in the future."

Asila breathed heavily and said with a break in her voice, "I thought you felt differently."

"There's no good in me," he confessed. "That is the fact of the matter."

She shied away as if she had been stabbed. She put on her dress in a hurry, but she collapsed again onto the settee, overcome by fatigue. She rested her head in the palm of her hand and closed her eyes; he thought she would faint. His heart beat violently, rousing him from his impassive cruelty. If the unthinkable happened, he might well face a scandal with profound repercussions. The path was rough and arduous enough in spite of his good reputation. What would happen if he suddenly found himself involved in a scandal of the kind the newspapers like to gloat over? He nearly changed his whole attitude and risked a new lie, but at the last moment she moved. She got up with some difficulty, made her way, subdued and crestfallen, to the door and disappeared from his view. He sighed deeply with relief, then stood up and walked to the window. He looked out at the alley, nearly covered in darkness, until he saw her pass, swiftly and ghostlike, out the front door. She went on through the alley toward the end leading to al-Jamaliyya and soon vanished completely into the dark.

Nobody, he told himself, knew the unknown, and for that reason it was impossible to pass comprehensive judgment on any of our actions. Yet for man to define a goal for himself provided him with a guide in the darkness and a justification in the clash of fortunes and events. It was also an example of the design Nature seemed to adopt in her infinite progression.

Twenty-Seven

He loved Onsiyya Ramadan. He had to confess that before his own conscience and before God. Since the time of the ancient drinking fountain his heart had not sung so sweet a song. And for this reason he should be more afraid of her than of any other woman on earth. What made it even worse was that she too loved him; yet a wife who could not push you forward would only pull you back. He might perhaps have married her without hesitation if there had been only one step between him and the Director General's position. But things being what they were, what would he gain from marriage save the daily troubles and cares which consumed a man's energy in ways it had not been created for?

One day Mr. Husayn Jamil brought him the mail as usual. When he had put his signature to it with his instructions, the man did not leave as he normally did. He was a young Archives employee who had worked under Othman for five successive years and who was known for his perseverance and good manners.

"Is something the matter, Husayn?"

The young man was quite clearly confused. There was something he wanted to say. What could it be?

"What's wrong? Is it something to do with your work?"

The youth came closer as though to make sure his voice was not heard by others.

"I'm afraid something is the matter, sir," he said.

"What is it, my son?"

"I'm awfully sorry, but I must speak up."

"Well, I'm listening."

He was quiet for a moment while he pulled himself together.

"It's something to do with Miss Onsiyya Ramadan."

Later on Othman told himself that he probably had not heard the name uttered or that he had heard it without comprehending what it meant.

"Huh?" he said, stupefied.

"Onsiyya Ramadan!"

"Your colleague? What about her?"

"The truth is," came the almost inaudible answer, "I'm in love with her."

Othman frowned and his heart missed a beat.

"And what has that to do with me?" he asked angrily.

"I wanted to propose to her."

"Fine! But what have I got to do with it?"

The youth looked down and mumbled, "But Your Excellency . . ."

Othman's limbs were trembling. The questioning stare he gave the young man was tantamount to surrender.

"Yes?"

"Your Excellency knows everything."

"How do you mean, please?"

"The truth is, if it hadn't been for you, I would have proposed to her."

Othman was certain it was all up with him. Nothing was any longer of value. Not even life itself.

"If it hadn't been for me?"

"I've seen everything . . . here and outside," came the despondent reply.

With the strength of despair, Othman prepared to defend himself to the end. He was not so much sorry for his lost love as he was afraid for his official position.

"Young man, you have a nasty mind. What is it you've seen, you wretch? But of course, this is just what lovers do! I've always treated her as if she were my own daughter: a totally innocent relationship. I'm very much afraid you have damaged her good name without knowing what you were doing."

"I know when and how to bury my sorrows and protect the reputation of someone I love." There was a certain nobility in the young man's innocent and grave rejoinder.

"Good . . . good . . ." sighed Othman. A wave of sorrow swept over him. "You've behaved like a man." The force of the initial shock and the relief brought by his unexpected escape were so jarring that he felt sick. "A man like you deserves to be happy with the person he loves."

His tormentor left him and he remained alone with his sorrow, a sorrow as solid and as gigantic as fate itself. It brought back to him old memories of long, sad nights. He thought to himself that if life was measured by its share of happiness, it was certain that his own had been a sheer waste. Why did the pursuit of glory demand such suffering?

Twenty-Eight

He asked Onsiyya to meet him in the desert by the Pyramids on a Friday morning. This time he planned the assignation with more caution than was his custom, stealthily giving her a piece of paper on which he had scribbled the arrangements and the route each of them should separately take. It was one of those wintry mornings, dry and cold, though both of them felt the sun's rays warm and invigorating. He watched her all the time with genuine anguish, though he was conscious that the role he was playing was cruel and debasing. From the first, the girl seemed unusually anxious.

"I had such a strange feeling when I read your note," she said. "My heart just shriveled up inside me."

Woman, he thought to himself, possessed an instinct which guided her in the knowledge of her most intimate affairs without recourse to the intellect; and if humanity as a whole had this sort of instinctive access to the unknown, it would not have remained unknown.

"The truth is," he said with increasing sadness, "we've got to think about this thing."

"Which thing do you mean?"

"Our close and sacred relationship."

"What's wrong with it?"

"You must have wondered at my silence. We've talked about everything except the most essential, and naturally you may never have realized that all the time I've been suffering the torments of hell."

She touched his arm concernedly.

"I must admit you're making my heart shrink even more!"

"And I must admit that I'm a selfish man."

"No. You are not selfish at all," she protested.

"Yes. Selfish in the full meaning of the word. And because of my selfishness I've led you on and given you false hopes. I shall never forgive myself."

"You've been so kind and good to me."

"Don't try to acquit me. You must have often wondered, 'When is that man going to speak? What does he want of me? How long shall we go on meeting and parting without really getting any further? Is he toying with me?'"

"I've never thought ill of you."

"In fact I have asked myself these questions many times, but the illusion of happiness has always got the better of me, and I wasn't able to face up to reality before things got out of hand. How often have I been determined to tell you the truth, but then weakened and given in!"

"What truth?" she asked in a tone of frustration.

"Er . . . Why I haven't proposed to you . . ."

Her eyelids quivered when she heard the beloved word. She stared at him in alarm and then turned away, raising her eyes to the unknown as though in silent prayer to ward off disaster.

"Surely you must have asked yourself this question? Otherwise what's the meaning of life?"

She fixed her gaze on the ground as though, expecting only the worst, she no longer wanted to know more.

"I'm ill," he went on.

"No!" she exclaimed in genuine fear.

"I'm not fit for marriage."

She stared at him, stunned.

"Don't let my appearance deceive you . . . My illness is not fatal, but it makes it impossible for me to marry."

He looked down in distress. The sharp sigh he heard transfixed his heart. He was on the point of casting off the shackles of his ambition, throwing himself down and kissing her feet and begging her to accept him as husband. But another force held him back and paralyzed him.

"I've spared no effort. I've been to more than one doctor. I never lost hope, or else I would have told you a long time ago. But it's no use. I should put an end to my selfishness, otherwise I will have destroyed your future forever."

"But how could I live without you?"

"You're still young. The wounds of youth are quick to heal."

"I can't believe it. It must be a nightmare."

"It wouldn't be wise for us to carry on together any longer."

"I can't believe it."

"Sudden disasters are always hard to believe, but life sometimes seems a series of sudden disasters. What matters is that you should find your way before it's too late."

"What do you want to do?" Her voice broke with anguish.

"We should stop traveling up a dead end."

"I can't."

"It's got to be done. It would be sheer madness to continue."

He avoided her eyes. He had carried out his plan successfully to the end. But success was harsh, and he now found himself alone in a wilderness of desolation, alone with his anguish and shame, without faith, without solace. Madness was the only way out, he told himself. Madness alone had room for both belief and disbelief, glory and shame, love and deceit, truthfulness and lies. For how could sanity stand the absurdity of life? How could he look up at the stars when he was sunk up to the neck in slime? Through the long night he wept and wept.

Twenty-Nine

It seemed that a gleam of light sought to pierce the dark clouds. He learned that Onsiyya Ramadan had become engaged to Husayn Jamil. He delighted in this happy development which made him feel secure at last, and he said to himself, "Now I can mourn for my lost love with my mind at rest and no apprehensions to bother me. I can drink out of the well of anguish until it runs dry and I gain my freedom. And in this I'm an expert."

Throughout his life he had met no woman more fitted than her to make him happy. Not even Sayyida. She was beautiful, intelligent, and pure and she had truly loved him. He now had come to believe that he was never going to find anyone like her again, no matter how lucky he was; and that, after all, was a just punishment.

The tide of time brought about another event. Hamza al-Suwayfi, the Head of Administration, was absent from work one day and it was learned that his blood pressure had risen to an even more critical level than that of his first attack. Othman went to visit him. This time he found him prostrate and completely resigned, the shadow of the other world looming in his clouded eyes. His appearance moved Othman greatly and he saw in it the final scene which awaits all men, whatever their position.

"You'll be all right, my dear fellow," he said. The sick man smiled, feeling grateful in his utter helplessness for any kind word.

"Thank you. You are a good man, just as you're a capable and efficient one."

"This is only a passing cloud. You'll soon be back running the administration."

The man's face contracted as he tried to hold back a tear.

"I won't be going back."

"Oh, come on!"

"It is the truth, Mr. Bayyumi."

"You always exaggerate."

"It's what the doctor says. He told me frankly that if I did exactly what I was told I could survive this attack, but that I had to retire from my work at once."

Othman's feelings were mixed, but for the moment compassion was dominant.

"Put your trust in God's mercy," he said. "His miracles are endless."

"Work isn't important to me anymore. I've married off my daughters and my youngest son is now in his final year at the School of Agriculture. I've fulfilled my calling and all I need now is peace of mind."

"May God grant your wish!"

Despite his exhaustion, the sick man went on with an air of pride: "God be praised, I've done my duty toward my job and toward my family. I've never been in need and I've always had many good friends. What more could one hope for?"

"A man of your fine character deserves all that and much more."

"We pass away one after another. Do you remember the late Sa'fan Basyuni? Men go, but their good deeds remain forever."

"True, true!"

The sick man stared at him for a long while and then said, "May God guide you to where your happiness lies."

Othman was much moved at the time and for a long while after. The moral of the situation pierced his heart as if he was returning from the burial of a close friend. But he roused himself in the nick of time and said to himself, "The sorrows of this world exist to sharpen our determination, not to dull it."

His thoughts were riveted on the position which would soon be declared vacant. He was by general agreement an able, honest, and upright man. In fact, nobody doubted that he was even more efficient than the two Deputy Directors of Administration. But one of them was in grade two and the other in grade three. If justice was done and efficiency alone was the yardstick, he would become Director of Administration; but how could he jump straight from grade four to grade one?

Hamza al-Suwayfi was pensioned off at his own request and consequently a flurry of promotions took place throughout the administration from grade one down to grade eight. So Isma'il Fayiq became Director while Othman Bayyumi moved up the scale to grade three and became Deputy Director. Thus an attack of high blood pressure had given a nudge to the wheel of fortune, bringing good luck to some and ill luck to others.

Othman was happy with his promotion for a day or two but his happiness soon wore thin. Hamza al-Suwayfi had been an able official, but now that he had gone, nobody was better qualified to replace him than Othman; and it was really grotesque that a man like Isma'il Fayiq should become Director of Administration.

Othman went to His Excellency the Director General's office to thank him. He had no doubt that of all the employees he was the one the Director General liked and valued most, relying on him in the official work of the administration as well as in his own private activities. They shook hands and Othman expressed his gratitude with his usual eloquence.

His Excellency said, "You didn't know the full story. I had on my desk a pile of recommendations from the Minister, the Under Secretary, and many members of Parliament . . ." The great man stared at him for a while before going on.

"I told them, 'You can have anything you want, except that *one* promotion must go to someone whose only recommendation is his ability and character."

Words of gratitude poured from Othman's lips; the frustration he felt in his heart he did not mention. The Director General continued: "We both know that Isma'il Fayiq is weak and ignorant."

"Yes, of course, Your Excellency," he replied, annoyed at the mention of the man.

"This means that actual responsibility will be yours alone to shoulder even though you are only Second Deputy."

"I shall always be at your service."

"What could I have done?" Bahjat Noor went on apologetically. "He is a relative of the Under Secretary, as you know."

"It's not your fault, Your Excellency."

"Anyway, congratulations again. And rest assured you are going to get your full rights one day."

He left the room satisfied in some degree, but his irritation soon got the upper hand and the joys of promotion were forgotten. He cursed everybody without exception and said to himself in terror that life went faster than any kind of promotion.

Before he left the Archives Section, his staff came to congratulate him on his promotion and say goodbye to him. When it was Onsiyya's turn to shake hands with him, he noticed, in a welter of confused emotions, the swelling of her belly with its promise of happiness. Already a wife and expectant mother! No doubt her husband, Husayn, would be particularly glad about his transfer to the administration.

He took his seat as Second Deputy Director, but he felt superior to all those around him. He stood first in the Director General's confidence, being an authority on administrative matters, regulations, and the budget, not to mention his mastery of law and economics, his general knowledge, and his erudition in languages. But he asked himself, "What's the use of all these advantages when life flies by or a sudden illness descends?"

He knew that both the First Deputy and the Director of Administration were younger than he. Consequently their positions were unlikely to become vacant unless an unpredictable miracle, a sudden death or a road accident, occurred.

"Forgive me, Oh God, for my wicked thoughts!" he prayed. Each of them (he kept thinking) enjoyed good health, a carefree nature, as well as a closed mind. And nothing, nothing save the lofty position he longed for could make up for the tremendous sacrifices he had made at the expense of his life's happiness and peace of mind. Perhaps he had never felt at any time in the past as he did now the need for the sort of wife who would help him up the ladder before he reached retirement age or fell sick or died. So he asked Omm Husni to speak again to Omm Zaynab, the marriage broker, about him, now that God had raised him to grade three as Deputy Director.

He was extra careful nowadays when he visited Qadriyya in the prostitutes' quarter, and he decided to disguise himself as a member of the lower classes so that nobody would recognize him. So one night he went to her wearing a loose galabiya, a cloak, and a scarf. She did not recognize him until she heard his voice.

"Been sacked from the government?" she asked, almost beside herself with laughter.

She had been slowly going downhill, growing all the time more fleshy and more debauched. Yet the relationship between them had grown stronger and developed into real human intimacy. It had passed through all the natural phases of desire, boredom, and then indispensable habit. Thus she and the bare room and the horrible wine had together become something integral and familiar, which simultaneously gave him comfort and sorrow as well as something to think about. It also impelled him to face up to life, harsh and primitive as it was. He took no notice of the woman's indifference or of her despicable behavior. In fact, these very elements made it possible for him to enjoy, even while he was with her, his sacred solitude.

"Strange," he would say to himself, "that in all my years I haven't made love to an ordinary woman except once!" He remembered Asila, but he also remembered that what he had done with her was a criminal act and not an act of love.

And he would also say to himself, "There is a humane and wholesome way of making love."

Then he would sigh and say, "But there is glory, too."

Then he would sigh more deeply and say, "There is God as well and He is the origin of everything."

Then he would sigh more deeply still and add, "And we remember Him when times are good and also when they are bad!"

Thirty

Despite her resistance to the passage of time, age had left its imprint on Omm Husni. Her eyesight was almost gone and she limped so badly that she could only walk by supporting herself with an old broom handle. Meanwhile Othman had so completely despaired of Omm Zaynab, the marriage broker, that he told himself indignantly that those who chattered about class conflict had good reason to!

Omm Husni was no longer fit for her noble profession. Her senility was such that once she suggested a woman for him forgetting that she had died years before.

One afternoon, after Friday prayers at the mosque, he was sitting in the Egyptian Club coffeehouse when he saw Asila passing, accompanied by another woman. He recognized her at once, though the extent to which she had changed was dreadful. She was as flaccid as a punctured ball, and in her face the springs of femininity had dried up, leaving behind an ambiguous shadow that was neither feminine nor masculine. She walked clumsily, a model of misery and degeneration. Something told him that death was hunting her down and that it also was drawing closer to his own time and place; that his time which had once seemed hallowed in eternity was no longer secure behind the screen of sweet illusions and that the proud and everlasting truth was now revealing itself to him in all its awesome cruelty. Did Asila still remember him? She could not have forgotten him. He had penetrated into her very depths with the full weight of his deceit and egoism, leaving her thereafter to hate him and curse him.

As for the companions of his boyhood, they were petty by profession and all they did was father children and fill the air with meaningless laughter. And gone were the innocent passions and the unruly imagination of childhood, buried under thick layers of dust like al-Husayni Alley, which had changed its skin. Many old houses had been demolished and small blocks had taken their place. A small mosque now occupied what used to be the donkey park and a lot of people had left the quarter and gone to al-Madhbah. Everything was changing: electricity and water had been introduced into houses, radios blared night and day, and women were abandoning their traditional wrap. Even good and evil had changed and new values arisen.

All this took place while he was still in grade three and growing old. Was this the reward for his extraordinary effort and dedication? Did they not recognize him as the epitome of expertise based on both theory and practice? That if his official memoranda, his budget analyses, and his original pronouncements on matters of administration and on the purchase and storage of goods were collected in book form, they would constitute an encyclopedia of government affairs? For such a shining light to be hidden away in the position of a Second Deputy Director of Administration was like hanging a 500-watt electric bulb on the wall of a toilet in a tiny village mosque.

He also told himself that "government official" was still a vague concept inadequately understood. In the history of Egypt, an official occupation was a sacred occupation like religion, and the Egyptian official was the oldest in the history of civilization. The ideal citizen of other nations might be a warrior, a politician, a merchant, a craftsman, or a sailor, but in Egypt it was a government official. And the earliest moral instructions recorded in history were the exhortations of a retiring official to his son, a rising one. Even the Pharaohs themselves, he thought, were but officials appointed by the gods of heaven to rule the Nile Valley by means of religious rituals and administrative, economic, and organizational regulations. Ours was a valley of good-natured peasants who bowed their heads in humility to the good earth but whose heads were raised with pride if they joined the government apparatus. Then would they look upward to the ascending ladder of grades which reached right to the doorstep of the gods in heaven. To be an official was to serve the people: the competent man's right, the conscientious man's duty, the pride of the human soul— and the prayer of God, the creator of competence, conscience, and pride.

One day he went for an inspection tour of the Archives Section. There he saw Onsiyya, whose womanhood had now reached the stage of maturity. She had also moved up the official scale to become a supervisor, occupying the post which was made empty by her husband's transfer to the Ministry of Education.

"A long time!" he could not prevent himself from saying as he shook her hand.

She smiled in unaffected shyness.

"Are you happy?" he asked.

"I'm all right."

"The ability to forget is one of fortune's blessings," he said, yielding to an irresistible impulse.

"Nothing is forgotten and nothing remains," she said with friendly simplicity.

He thought about her words for a long time, and as he left Archives, he repeated to himself, "I loved you so much, Onsiyya, in the old days."

He returned to his office to find on his desk a circular from the Public Relations Section. He could tell from its appearance that it was the kind which announced the death of an employee or the relative of one. The circular read: "Mr. Isma'il Fayiq, the Head of Administration, died this morning. The funeral will take place . . ."

He read it a second time. He read the name over and over again. Impossible. Only yesterday he had been working in full health. Othman had had his morning coffee with him in his office. Indeed the man had said, giving voice to his familiar worries, "The country is awash with contradictory opinions," at which Othman had smiled without comment.

"Everyone," Isma'il had gone on, "believes he's been sent by Providence." Then he had shaken his head and said, "In what frame of mind can one begin to prepare the final accounts?"

"In one like mine," replied Othman in an undertone of sarcasm.

The man had given a loud laugh. He had never questioned the efficiency of his deputy or the fact that he was the backbone of the administration. How *could* the man have died, in heaven's name?

Othman went to the First Deputy, who had been an intimate friend of the Director.

"Do you know anything about this tragedy?"

"He had just started on his breakfast," the First Deputy replied in a stunned voice, "when he suddenly felt tired. He got up and went to lie on the couch. When his wife came up to him to see what was wrong, she found him already dead!"

One felt relatively secure, thought Othman, because one believed that death was logical, that it operated on the basis of premise and conclusion. But death often came upon us without warning, like an earthquake. Isma'il Fayiq had enjoyed perfect health until the last moment, and what happened to him could happen to anyone. Wasn't that so? Health then was no guarantee, nor was experience, nor knowledge. Fear shook him to the depths. "The best definition of life is that it's nothing . . ." Othman said to himself.

But was death something so unfamiliar? Certainly not, but seeing was not like hearing, and his fright would surely persist for a day or two. For in moments like this, profit and loss and joy and sorrow canceled each other out, and things lost their meaning.

"What's the value of a lifetime of dedicated work?" he would ask himself.

His misgivings stayed with him during the funeral. Even the chitchat of the employees did not deflect his thoughts from their wistful course. But he felt grateful to be alive. "What is true heroism? It is to go on working with undiminished zeal in spite of all that."

His preoccupation with the post of Director of Administration soon drove all other thoughts from his head. The First Deputy had been nominated for a job in the judiciary system. This left the way clear for himself. He would be promoted to grade two and appointed Head of Administration. After a year's work in the post he would be eligible for substantive appointment in the post. Hope was now something he could really and truly grasp.

But he was totally dismayed by the decision to appoint someone from the Ministry of Transport as the new Director of Administration.

Thirty-one

No . . . No . . . No . . .

This possibility had never crossed his mind. He hated His Excellency Bahjat Noor and cursed him a thousand times. Bahjat Noor should have stood up for him. Damn them all! Did they think he could work for the benefit of others all his life? And who was this new Director? Who was this Abdullah Wajdi? How could he introduce himself to him as one of his staff? The shame of it! Shame would pursue him down the corridors of the ministry, and many were they who would gloat over his plight!

Bahjat Noor called him to his office.

"I'm very sorry, Mr. Bayyumi."

"I've come to despair of doing my best in life," he answered, not seeking to conceal his indignation.

"No, no. He is a relative of the Minister."

"I have learned to envy lazy officials."

"I repeat, I'm sorry, and I can tell you His Excellency the Under Secretary is sorry too." The Director General was silent for a moment and then went on: "Don't despair! It's

been agreed to promote you to First Deputy this month as
soon as the present one has left."

No use. Promotions did not matter except as a means to
his most cherished hope, the hope to which he had dedicated his life. The new Director was a young man of only
forty, which meant that, if things went their natural course,
he would be pensioned off as a Deputy Director or at best,
and then only by a miracle, as Director of Administration.
The dream of his life was shattered and the past was dead
and buried, leaving behind it only the blackness of illusion.
Perhaps he would have been better off driving a cart like
his father. For the first time in his life despair overcame him
and he felt the end of his life much closer than the achievement of his precious hope.

A new idea possessed him with a force he had not experienced before: marriage. He should not procrastinate any
longer; procrastination would serve no purpose. It was
enough that the best time of life for love and marriage was
gone. How he yearned for a wife, for genuine affection, for
an honest partnership, a warm house, children, a human
relationship, a loving heart, a kind touch, conversation, a
refuge from torment, a shield against death, a savior from
loss, a prayer niche worthy of true faith, a resting place
secure from foolish dreams, a truce with frugality and deprivation and loneliness.

"Woman is life, and in her presence Truth is crowned by
Death itself with all Death's solemnity."

He would not resort to Omm Zaynab, nor was there
now anything to be gained from Omm Husni, crippled as
she was. But there was a new girl in the administration called
Ihsan Ibrahim to whom he had unhesitatingly expressed
his affection. For now he did not want to delay his marriage for a single day if he could help it, and each extra

night he slept alone made him all the more frightened. It was as though the desire for marriage had constantly smoldered inside him until it finally erupted like a volcano.

But Ihsan did not take his affectionate hints in the right way. She probably thought it inappropriate for a man of his age to court her. But what could he do, since he was no longer capable of the kind of love he had experienced in the days of Sayyida and Onsiyya, or the wild passion he knew in the days of Saniyya and Asila.

One day Ihsan happened to be in his office on some business or other. He seized the chance and said to her, "Do you mind, Miss Ibrahim, if I ask you a question which may sound a bit curious?"

"Of course not, sir."

"Are you engaged?" he inquired after some hesitation. She blushed and for the first time glanced at him with the eye of a female rather than an employee working under him.

"Yes, sir."

He was disappointed.

"Forgive me, but I hadn't noticed a ring on your finger."

"I mean, I'm almost engaged."

After a moment's reflection he said, "May I ask you something . . . something that must remain a secret between us?"

"Sir?"

"Could you help me find a wife?"

She was confused for a while and then said, choosing her words, "All my friends and relatives are about my age. They wouldn't suit you, I'm afraid."

A polite way of saying, "You wouldn't suit them," he thought.

"Is it impossible for a man of my age to get married?" he asked, his desperation nearly driving him beyond the limits of propriety.

"Why not? There's a suitable wife for every sort of age."
"Thank you, and please forgive me for bothering you!"
"I hope I may be of some service to you."

When she left, he was burning with anger. She should have accepted him for herself, he thought, or for one of her friends or relatives. He had become unwanted scrap then, like the rubbishy surplus from the ministry's Supply Section, which he put up for sale every year after the annual stocktaking. Evidently his lot in the marriage stakes was to be no better than that. Not even if he achieved his most cherished hope and the dream of his life, by occupying the office of His Excellency the Director General. The whip of time continued to lash his back, and he could run no longer. And with each day that passed he became more and more obsessed with the idea of marriage till it bulked as large as his obsession with promotion. Ihsan brought him back no answer. Madly he began to make advances to women in the streets and on buses but he had no experience in that sort of thing and had to give it up. "What a waste my life has been," he would often sigh to himself.

Indignantly he asked himself what it was which so stood in the way of his getting married even after he had relinquished his early cumbersome conditions. Age was no doubt a negative factor, but it was not everything. People probably inquired about him and knew all there was to know about his origins. That was the other shameful fact. The truth was, he was a man past his prime and also of lowly background. God knew what else they said about him; for an outstanding personality like himself would naturally arouse envy in the hearts of others. He had long felt that he was without a true friend in this world; that he stood aloof, high above human frailty.

Night took him as usual to Qadriyya and the bare room.

"How nice," he would say to himself with bitterness, "to have a Deputy Director's job and a whore who is half Negress as my lot in life!"

"This is the first time you have drunk a second glass of wine!" she said laughingly. "It must be the end of the world!"

The end of the world it was, for he felt a strange giddiness in the head.

"Qadriyya, you must know I'm a man of faith," he said apropos of nothing in particular.

"Thank goodness!" she said as she tied a red kerchief around her coarse hair.

"And if I didn't believe that the world is sanctified by being the creation of God," he went on, "I would be content to live like an animal."

She gazed at him stupidly and said, "They've decided to abolish us, damn them!"

"And God in His greatness . . ." he continued, disregarding what she said.

"They've decided to abolish us," she interrupted.

"I beg your pardon?"

"Haven't you heard the news about the abolition of prostitution?"

No, he hadn't. All he read in the papers were obituaries and affairs of state.

"Really?" he asked with alarm.

"They've actually told us so."

"Unbelievable!"

"They've promised to help us find work. Work indeed! God damn them in this world and the next! Have they reformed everything till they've only got us left to worry about?"

"Maybe it's only a rumor. This country is full of rumors, you know."

"I'm telling you, we've been officially informed."

"And when is this going to take effect?" he asked in real consternation.

"Before the end of the year."

They were quiet, and for some time the noise of revelers in the lane could be heard in the room. He had imagined many disasters but this one never crossed his mind.

"There'll be brothels everywhere," he observed wistfully.

"And VD will spread."

"Thousands of innocent girls will be corrupted."

"Those wretched idiots! Just for the want of something to do!"

"What are you going to do?" he asked her with a sigh.

"Whatever happens, I am not going to work as a washerwoman in a hospital."

"Could I have your home address?"

"We'll be watched."

"Haven't you thought about the future?" he asked, his despair becoming unbearable.

"I will get married," was her confident reply. "There's nothing else for me to do."

Her words fell on him like a blow. He poured himself a third glass.

"Anybody in particular?"

"It won't be difficult to find somebody."

"But how?"

"I've got five hundred pounds," she replied boastfully. "I could furnish a flat for a hundred and fifty and keep the rest as something to fall back on. That being so, wouldn't lots of men be keen to marry me?"

"I'm sure you're right."

"If you find a suitable husband for me, let me know," she added, laughing.

At midnight, as he stealthily found his way under the arches, he bumped into a drunken man being sick. He was nauseated beyond endurance. A sense of his loneliness, of despair, and of the emptiness of life overtook him: he felt an urge to do away with himself. He changed his direction without thinking and staggered his way back to the lane. He saw Qadriyya coming down the stairs on her way home. He stopped her with his hand and said, "Qadriyya, I've found a suitable husband for you." He did not see her face in the dark but was able to guess the impact of his words.

"Let's get married at once!"

Thirty-Two

The marriage took place on the following day. His decision did not stun the woman as he had expected. She just looked at him closely for a while to make sure that he was serious, then she nodded her head with approval. He told himself that she probably considered him the real beneficiary in the deal because of her five hundred pounds.

"Let's go to the Registrar's Office at once!" he said with a sense of urgency.

"Sober up first and wait till morning," she said, laughing happily.

He spent the night in her little flat in al-Shamashirji Close and in the morning he said to her, "Let's furnish a new flat and then get married."

"No, we get married first and then furnish a flat," she retorted in tones of determination and finality.

The Marriage Registrar was called to the house. The contract required two witnesses and she could only find two pimps who used to procure men for her. He watched in a stupor during the simple ceremony. What was happening? A feeling of anxiety, almost of terror, took hold of him and tore him apart and he prayed that the unknown might intervene to rescue him from his nightmare. This feeling then gave way to one of resignation, almost of recklessness.

When he stated his name and occupation to the Registrar, both the woman and the pimps were amazed. He told himself they would declare him crazy, as others had done. Certainly he himself might as well admit, from now on, that he was out of his mind. A woman who was half Negress, gross as a fat cow, and laden with half a century of lechery and dissolute living. So the crazy longing he had sought to satisfy had come true: he had become a husband and Qadriyya, the companion of his youth, had become his wife. What had he done to himself?

"I must begin a new life . . ." he said.

Because he had come to like the Rawd al-Faraj quarter since he used to visit Hamza al-Suwayfi, he rented a flat there consisting of three rooms and a lounge and they set about furnishing it together. He forced her to wear the veil, ostensibly in the name of modesty, but his real motive was to guard against her being recognized by one of her old customers. They bought furniture for a bedroom, a dining room, a living room, and a study. They also bought new clothes for both of them, a radio, and a few other things. They contributed a hundred pounds each toward the cost, for with the same spirit of recklessness he had changed his policy and spent money freely wherever the need arose with a sense of desperate resignation which blacked out the pain he usually felt in such circumstances. A strong desire possessed him to enjoy the pleasures of life of which he had always deprived himself.

He said goodbye to Omm Husni in a touching scene.

The old woman was taken aback at his decision to move. She wept and said to him, "Don't run away from the place you were born! It's not good."

But run away from it he did, and without regret. In any case he couldn't conceivably bring Qadriyya to live in al-Husayni Alley. He generally thought of the place as a symbol of decay, of privation, of a wasted life, and of sad memories. He sought to drown his visible as well as his secret sorrows in what pleasures were available. And he determined to remind himself, or rather convince himself, that Qadriyya was the only woman he had really loved. Or else how could he have kept up his relationship with her for a lifetime? As for her, she spared no effort in playing her part as a housewife in her new and "fashionable" surroundings which represented a fantastic leap from the old lane. He prayed to God that none of her old customers would ever set eyes on her and advised her not to mix with the neighbors.

"Why not?"

"I don't like their manners."

But what he really feared was that she might have a disagreement with one of her neighbors and that this would put an end to her reserve and cause the volcano of obscenities latent in her to erupt. Otherwise, he could not deny that she was making a real effort to make him happy and to adapt to her new situation, and as time went by he grew more confident about his new life and accepted it for what it was. He enjoyed the company and the comfort, the discipline and the cleanliness that it afforded him. And now he was able to perform his prayers with a clean conscience. He even felt that having saved a soul that had gone astray (perhaps two souls rather than just one), he was closer to God than ever before.

Thus he bought a plot in al-Khafir Cemetery, after consulting people who knew about such things, and made preparations for the building of a suitable tomb. He frequently went to inspect the progress of the work in the company of an architect from the Engineering Section in the ministry. The architect asked him once, "Hasn't the family got an old tomb?"

"A very old one indeed," he answered, unshaken by the question. "It's become pretty crowded with so many generations of the family. There was nothing for it but to have this one built."

"There's no comparing old tombs with new ones," commented the architect. "A new tomb is a beautiful, modern structure."

"Personally I wouldn't bother to own a house in this world; a rented flat will do. But a tomb is a must, or else one's dignity is lost."

"In India they cremate the dead," the architect said, laughing.

"How awful!" Othman said with disgust.

The architect laughed again and went on: "If you want my opinion, a dead man loses dignity less by being burned than by being buried. Do you ever think about the process of decomposition that a corpse undergoes in the grave?"

"No," Othman replied with annoyance. "Nor do I want to know about it." He thought for a while and then said to the architect, "Shouldn't we provide a lavatory?"

"It will be used by strangers and made filthy."

"But surely we could plant some kind of a tree or ivy, couldn't we?"

"That won't be a problem. It could be watered from outside."

When the work had been completed, he went to examine the tomb and pay the balance. He looked over it admiringly. The door was open, and through it he could see the stairs leading down to the burial place, brightly lit by the sun. He bent forward a little to look at the floor of the tomb. It was smooth and fresh and spotlessly clean, bathed in light. He felt it was his eternal home, all ready for him; and his bones were not going to be lost in a heap of others like his parents'. Out of the depths of his soul came a soft strange voice whispering to him like a lover to lie down on the clean, bright ground, have a taste of the comforts of which he had had no share in life, and enjoy the peace which he had never experienced in the tumult of his raging emotions. For a moment he wished to obey that mysterious call and be through with the world, both its cares and its hopes.

He remained in the grip of these enigmatic thoughts until he left the cemetery and made his way back to town. And how he wished to transfer the remains of his parents to the new tomb so that he would feel more at home in it! But that, he had learned a long time ago, was not feasible, for the paupers' burial ground was so crammed with corpses, it was impossible to tell them apart.

"There's no doubt that my life today is better than it was before," he thought, desperately trying to convince himself that he had done the right thing.

This of course did not mean that he had abandoned the path of God's eternal world, even though his zeal had noticeably waned.

Thirty-Three

Let the days go by!

Whatever happened, he had become a family man and the owner of a tomb; he had come to know new kinds of food, other than sheep's head, rice, lentils, and beans, and he had also discovered something to be done with money other than mummifying it in the Post Office Savings Bank.

But were days not heavy and monotonous in their passage? Had he lost hope irretrievably?

Out of the stream of days there rose, quite unexpectedly, a high and powerful tide which changed fortunes and created the world anew. One morning the whole ministry learned of the decision to appoint Bahjat Noor, the Director General, as Under Secretary of State. Thus the position of Director General became vacant for the first time in a very long period. For two weeks many hearts were beating in continuous and uneasy expectation until it was decided to promote Abdullah Wajdi, the Director of Administration, to Director General; so he became a full-fledged "Excellency." Another heart which had been tranquil for a long time began to beat with excitement.

"I'm the only eligible person," Othman said to himself. "I'm first in line for promotion and nobody has got my ability or experience. What are they going to do?"

A few weeks elapsed without anything happening. Othman spared no effort in pleading his cause with both the new Director General and the Under Secretary of State.

In a conversation, he heard someone express the opinion that the position of Director of Administration was a sensitive one. He asked him what he meant.

"It is not only experience and qualifications that count when such appointments are made. Social status matters too," said the man.

"That's only true in the case of an Under Secretary of State or a Minister," Othman retorted with indignation. "As for Director of Administration or even Director General, these are jobs open to the common people. This has been the case since British officials stopped taking them."

His anguish did not last for long, for the decision to promote him to Director of Administration was made the same month. Later he used to remember that day with a kind of passionate excitement, and he would say to himself, "The miracle took place in a twinkling!" And he would also say, "In terms of seniority there is no one now between me and the Director General."

But how did the miracle take place? He had already come to believe that he was going to be pensioned off before anybody ahead of him in the official line had moved. But a Cabinet change took place in which the Under Secretary of State was made Minister, and as a result there was that happy and unexpected shuffle lower down.

Bahjat Noor, now Under Secretary of State, said to him, "I've promoted you in the face of many objections."

Othman thanked him warmly. "But why the objections?" he inquired sadly.

"You've been too long in government service not to be able to guess the answer to your question."

However, he now set about his work with the same old vigor as in the past. He pledged before God to make history during his directorship of the administration and to create an unmatchable record full of expert and ingenious administrative practices that would last forever. He was going to demonstrate to everybody that a government post was something sacred, a duty to humanity and a form of worship in the full sense of the word.

From the first day he determined to give Abdullah Wajdi the fullest cooperation. For cooperating with the Director General was a sacred ritual of government service, and he had never been unfaithful to the duties of his office. Moreover, he was determined to use his own experience to cover up the Director General's incompetence, and even to offer him what private help he needed just as he did with the Under Secretary of State. Perhaps one day he might reap what he had sown.

"It's true that Abdullah Wajdi is still a young man," he would tell himself, "but the age of miracles has returned." But in point of fact he did not pin his hopes on miracles alone. He watched Abdullah Wajdi's corpulence with interest and listened with secret happiness to gossip about his overindulgence in food and drink.

"There is no end to the diseases that people like him are exposed to," he would think to himself.

And it was only fair, wasn't it? For in spite of his limitations, he himself was a believer, a man of God, a follower of al-Husayn, the Prophet's grandson; and God would never abandon him. On the Day of Judgment what better could a man plead than the noble ambitions he had entertained, the achievements with which he had been blessed, the steady progress he had made, and the record of the services he had done for the state and the people? The state was God's temple on earth, and our standing in both this world and the next was determined by the extent to which we exerted ourselves for its sake.

Meanwhile, the peace and quiet of his matrimonial life did not last long. However much he deceived himself and hoped for the best, the difficulties were predictable. He reproached his wife, "Qadriyya, you drink too much."

She looked at him with astonishment.

"Yes, I know, and I've always done so."

"It's never too late to overcome our bad habits," he said hopefully.

"Not worth the effort."

"But it is," he went on in the same vein, "and my hope is to see you praying and fasting. We need God's blessing."

"I believe in God," she retorted angrily. "And I know He is merciful and forgiving."

"You are a respectable woman, and a respectable woman wouldn't get drunk every night."

"How often then does a respectable woman get drunk?"

"She shouldn't at all."

She gave a hoarse laugh, and then quickly her look darkened and she said wistfully, "It's hopeless!"

"How do you mean?"

"We can't hope to have a child. It's too late."

He was conscious of sharing her sorrow but said, "We can still live happily."

She made a halfhearted attempt to keep off the drink but

went on much as before. Indeed, Othman's renewed absorption in his work and her brooding about the dreadful emptiness of life without companionship may have made her an even worse addict than she already was. One evening Othman was appalled to see her taking opium.

"No!" he screamed.

"Let things be!" she said sharply.

"Since when have you been . . ." he inquired anxiously.

"Since Noah and his Flood."

"But . . ."

"Oh, lay off! It's stronger than death."

"But death and opium are one and the same."

"I don't care," came the reckless answer.

He was overcome with horror. What had he done with himself? He had gone after illusory happiness and now he had to pay the price. It was useless to think of divorce, for that would lead him into a fierce dispute which could finally destroy him.

"How do you get it?" he asked her.

She did not reply.

"So you're going to those old contacts that were always suspect. Don't you know how dangerous that can be?"

"Don't exaggerate!"

"Qadriyya, think about it, please! If you do not change your lifestyle, it will be the end of us."

To protect his reputation and his future he managed, by a great effort of will and after what nearly amounted to a fight, to get her to a rehabilitation center in Hilwan, where she stayed for a few months until her addiction was cured.

He imagined she had come back a new woman. But now food became the only consolation in her life and she ate gluttonously. She kept putting on more and more weight until her body became so grotesquely fat as to invite not just ridicule but pity. He never ceased to worry about her. All day long his attention was divided between her and his work. And he would say sadly to himself, "I have even lost the one thing that made those nights of animal behavior enjoyable, for all that's left of her now is a miserable wreck: no manners, no faith, no sense, and no taste."

He recalled the arguments which some of his politically minded colleagues advanced to justify cases like his wife's by blaming them on social injustice and class inequality. But he also recalled his own "case." Did he not grow up, like Qadriyya, poor, helpless, and deprived in every sort of way? Yes, but he discovered at the right time the divine secret in his feeble heart, just as he discovered the eternal wisdom of God and thus found the path of glory along which he walked and suffered in a manner worthy of Man, the creature of Almighty God. For this reason he hardly pitied her and again he asked, "What have I done with myself?"

What indeed was the meaning of married life without real love, a spiritual bond, the promise of posterity, or even mere human companionship? Then he addressed this warning to himself: "Take it easy! Don't let your sorrows get the better of you. You are not as strong as you used to be. There's been a new change, soft as a breeze, but cunning as a fox: it has to do with age, with the passage of time . . ."

He thought for a little while and then added: "It is Time we must thank for every achievement, and Time we must blame for every loss . . . *And nought abideth save the face of the Almighty One.*"

Thirty-Four

As usual he forgot his new promotion completely. Joy disappeared and a cloud of worries built up. The duties of his Director's job soon became a familiar routine: something that he had to transcend, and quickly, for not much of life was left. Otherwise his service would come to an end while he still stood like a beggar at the door of the Blue Room. Ambition was ruthless and marriage no longer a comfort.

"God, I'm trying to guide her. In Your mercy, grant me the strength!"

But his effort was of no avail. Indeed, he had brought to her a degree of misery she could never have imagined. In the past she had been miserable, but hardly realized it; and in drink and opium she found a welcome refuge. But today she faced the void with hideous awareness, her eyes wide open and full of terror. There was nothing to console her: no love and no children.

"As a prostitute," he would say to himself, "she was a consolation to me and a pleasure, but in this comfortable home she is hell itself."

"If we each went our own way," he would also tell himself, "with a miracle I might still attain happiness. Where's my old solitude? Where?"

One evening he went back home to be greeted by bloodshot eyes and a stupefied grin.

"Have you been drinking again?" he said with horror. She nodded with an air of resignation. "Yes, thank God!"

"And soon you'll be taking opium again too," he sighed.

"It's already happened," came the sarcastic reply.

"What do we do then?" he asked sharply.

"Everything is fine," she said calmly. "Last night I dreamed of my mother."

"I shall absolutely despair of you."

"That's all I want you to do."

He watched her as she gradually dissolved into her own world of illusions, keeping out of his way. He felt somewhat relieved, for in this way he was able to regain his solitude. And he decided, with an uneasy conscience, that this time he would let her go to pieces without opposition on his part. Addressing himself to God, he said, "Forgive me my thoughts, Oh God! They are part of life and therefore cruel like it."

While he was on fire with these thoughts, Radiya Abd al-Khaliq was appointed his secretary. The Head of the Personnel Office had asked him to choose a suitable secretary for himself.

"It's your right to choose your own secretary," he said. "You may even appoint a relative of yours, somebody you trust." Did the man really know nothing about his origins? Throughout his long service he had known the ingenuity of employees in digging up the most hidden secrets. It was certain that his "donkey cart" origins were no secret to anybody anymore.

"I leave the choice to you."

"You really are a model of propriety, sir," the Personnel Head flattered him.

On the following morning a young woman introduced herself to him.

"Radiya Abd al-Khaliq, Your Excellency's new secretary if you will be so kind as to approve the appointment."

"How do you do," he said, feeling gratified. "Which section do you come from?"

"Personnel."

"Fine, and what are your qualifications?"

"A B.A. in history."

He nearly asked her about her age, but he checked himself. He put her at about twenty-five. She had a remarkably good figure and her coal-dark hair flowed on either side of her long, brown face, enveloping it like a halo. Her eyes were small, clear, intelligent, and attractively bright. She had protruding incisors, sometimes considered a defect, but in her case they made her face even more attractive. Her prettiness excited him and he privately cursed the Personnel Head for his happy choice. "In this inferno of mine how I need a place of refuge!" he thought.

From the first look he took to her, perhaps driven by a secret desire for protection. And as days went by his affection for her grew even stronger, particularly when he knew that she was an orphan who lived with a spinster aunt. His inner dreams and desires were no secret to himself, but he was in no frame of mind to consider, even to consider, committing a folly.

"It's enough that I can see her face every morning," he said to himself.

The refinement of her manners, coupled with her gentle nature and the mellow look in her eyes, captivated him. All this he explained as the proper behavior of a secretary toward her boss, especially when the boss was as old as her father. But why was he thinking of her more than he should? His whole being was suffused through and through with the scent of her. He told himself that there were moments in life when those who took life seriously and those who made a joke of it were equal.

"Lord, have mercy!" he prayed.

He watched her work with interest and one day he asked her, "Do you find work in my office demanding?"

"Not at all. I love work," came the warm answer.

"So do I. Indeed, I've always done so since the day I first took up a job. And I can assure you, hard work is never wasted effort."

"But they say . . ."

"I know what they say," he interrupted her, "and I don't deny it. Favoritism . . . nepotism . . . party politics . . . preference for members of the ruling party . . . and even worse things. But efficiency is also a factor that cannot be ignored. Even incompetent people in high positions find themselves in need of someone with real talent to cover up their own inadequacy." He smiled, secretly overcome by her charm, and went on: "I have forced my way up relying on Almighty God and my work alone."

"So I've heard everywhere."

Had she? And what else had she heard? The thing that stopped Omm Zaynab, the marriage broker, from ever coming back? But that didn't matter any longer.

"I ought to tell you that I'm very pleased with your work," he said to her.

"It's all due to your kind encouragement," she said with a delighted smile.

Such purity of atmosphere was unmatchable. A purity

pregnant with promise, distilling into the heart of holy joy. From such a starting point as this the lover sets out on the road that leads to happy marriage and true friendship. In this way, a man in his perplexity may stumble on situations rich with the prospect of happiness in unpropitious circumstances. The place, for instance, may be right but the time wrong: or vice versa. All this confirmed that happiness exists, but that tracks leading to it may not always be smooth. And from the interplay of time and place came either good fortune or absurdity. But you shouldn't forget mistakes either. Mistakes? Sayyida, Asila, and Onsiyya.

As days went by he would tell his heart to beware. As usual, he started to fear Radiya as much as he liked her. And as usual too, he surrendered himself to the current and waited for life's course to be determined by an unknown destiny.

Thirty-Five

As the days passed by, compounded of work in the office and wretchedness at home, secret longings took fire in his heart. It appeared that the universe had come to a standstill and that Abdullah Wajdi had become as immovable in the position of Director General as the Great Pyramid.

"There isn't a flicker of hope!" he thought.

How would the miracle happen this time? There he was with only a few black hairs remaining on his head: his eyesight was now poor and he had to wear glasses, his digestive system had lost its usual rigor so that he had to use drugs for the first time in his life, and his back had grown humped from years of bending over a desk and taking no exercise.

"I'm still strong, thank God!" he would say to himself. And he would spend a long time looking at himself in the mirror, which was not his habit, and thinking, "I still look all right!"

At that time he had written a comprehensive book on employment regulations which caused a sensation in official circles. Despite his advancing age he continued to slave away both at his office work and on his translations—partly because he enjoyed it and partly as an escape from the burden of his marital life on the one hand and his emotional excitement, reckless and frivolous as he thought it, on the other.

"There's no denying that the hour I spend with her looking at the mail every morning is my share of happiness!"

The exchange of greetings and smiles. Comments on work. Disguised flirtation. Discreet compliments on her hairstyle, her shoes, or her blouse. On one occasion he was admiring her hairstyle when she said, "I'm thinking of having it cut short."

"No, no!" he protested.

She smiled at the warmth of his protest over something quite unconnected with administrative statutes.

"But . . ."

"Leave it as it is!" he interrupted.

"But the fashion . . ."

"I know nothing about the fashion, but I like it the way it is."

She blushed. He studied her carefully but found no trace of displeasure in her face. He decided to put to use the lessons he had learned during the happier moments of his past. So one morning he presented her with a handsome little case. Radiya was taken aback.

"What's that?" she asked.

"A small thing for a great occasion!"

"But . . . but how did you know?"

"Many happy returns."

"In point of fact it really *is* my birthday."

"Of course it is."

"But . . . you're so kind . . . I don't deserve . . ."

"Say no more! With you, silence is more expressive!"

"I'm really grateful."

"And I'm really happy!"

He sighed, gathered his strength, and then surrendered completely to his emotions. Without further thought he burst out, passionately and in dead earnest, "What can I do? I'm in love!"

She looked down, accepting his confession and happily surrendering to whatever it should bring.

"It is the last thing I ought to speak about," he went on, "but what can I do?"

Her brown face flushed darker, but she stayed where she was sitting submissively as if waiting for more.

"I'm not a young man, as you see." He was quiet for a long while and then went on: "And I'm married." What was it he wanted? Perhaps what he didn't want was to face the possibility of failure or in the end death, all alone; without the warmth of love and without children.

"But what can I do?" he said again. "I'm in love."

Silence reigned again. Nothing mattered any longer and he asked her almost jokingly, "What do you say to that?"

She smiled and mumbled something indistinct.

"Maybe you think I'm selfish?"

"No, I don't," she whispered.

"Or senile?"

She laughed softly and answered, "Don't do yourself an injustice!"

"What you say is very kind but what shall we do?" For the third time there was silence.

"I really do want to know what you think," he said again.

"It's a delicate situation and rather bewildering," she said gravely. "And I don't like to be inhuman or cruel."

"Are you hinting at my wife?"

"That's something you surely must consider."

"Leave that to me, it's my responsibility."

"Very well."

"But I want to know what you think apart from that."

She was now in much better control of her emotions and said, "Haven't I already made that clear in what I've been saying?"

"I'm so happy, Radiya, to hear that . . . It shows that my love for you has your blessing."

"Yes, it does," she said without hesitation. He was drunk with rapture.

"I don't mind what happens now!" he said with royal abandon, and then added in a voice that pleaded for sympathy: "I must tell you that I have never known happiness."

"Can that really be so?"

"I've had a difficult life and a miserable marriage!"

"You never gave me that impression."

"How so?"

"You have always seemed such a wise person to me, and it's my belief that wise people are happy people."

"What an idea!"

"I'm sorry."

"But your love makes me happy."

He believed he had won the greatest prize of his life and that next to the power of almighty God, the power of love was the greatest.

Later on he went with her to her place in al-Sayyida Zaynab. She introduced him to her old spinster aunt. From the beginning it was obvious to him that the woman was not in favor of the marriage and she made her feelings only too clear. The matter was discussed from all aspects.

"Divorce your wife first!" she said.

But he rejected the idea, explaining apologetically that his wife "was ill."

"You are an old man and an untrustworthy one," she blurted out sharply.

Radiya rushed to his defense.

"Don't be cross with my aunt!" she said.

"What do you propose to do?" asked the aunt after a while.

"I want our marriage to remain secret for a short period until the time is suitable to make it public."

"Well, that's a fine story, I must say!" cried the aunt. "And what do you think of that?" she asked, turning to Radiya.

"It's something we have agreed on. I'm not very happy about it, but I haven't turned it down."

"Do as you please!" she shouted at her. "But the whole thing seems to me wicked and sinful."

"Aunt!" screamed the girl.

"Are you trying to take advantage of us because we're poor and have got no one to protect us?" said the aunt angrily, turning on Othman.

"I've known poverty and loneliness more than anyone," retorted Othman, feeling exasperated for the first time.

"Then let each of you go your own way," answered the aunt imploringly.

"We've already made up our minds to stay together," came Radiya's adamant reply.

"What can I do? God's will be done!"

One month later the marriage took place in the aunt's house. They bought furniture to suit their new life. Othman said to himself that life was a series of dreams and nightmares and that his last dream was the happiest of all.

He would stay in Radiya's flat until about midnight and then go back to Rawd al-Faraj, where Qadriyya, lost in her own world, never asked him where he had been or what he had been doing. Wisely he decided to postpone having children until he had made the marriage public, so that his new wife would not find herself in an embarrassing situation at the office.

In his overwhelming happiness he forgot how old he was and how totally bogged down were his hopes for the Director General's position; and he forgot Qadriyya. He told himself that life had only been created as a stage for the performance of the wonders of Providence.

Thirty-Six

For the first time in his life he was seen striding about in handsome clothes: a gray suit made of English wool and English shoes too. As for his shirts and ties, Radiya had chosen them herself. For the first time too he used eau de cologne and shaved every day, and if he had not been too shy he would have dyed his hair. And again for the first time he took vitamins, and he looked after his health and cleanliness more than he had ever done in the past. He said to Radiya, "With you, my darling, I will begin a new life, new in the full sense of the word." He kissed her and went on: "We shall have children . . ." He paused for a long while and then continued: "Nobody knows when his time will be up, but I come from a long-lived family. May God give us long life!"

Radiya kissed him and said, "My heart tells me we'll have a happy future."

"The heart of a believer is his guide! I've got enough faith to make up for a multitude of sins and I've served the state with enough devotion to atone for many transgressions; and when things have settled down, I will go on the pilgrimage to be reborn, soul and body."

As for Qadriyya, she was steadily going downhill, and this relieved him altogether of responsibility for her. He was not without sympathy for her but he remained afraid of telling her about his second marriage.

He did not forget that he was approaching the end of his service with no real hope of attaining his life's most treasured dream. But as the days went rapidly past, something unexpected took place. Abdullah Wajdi was appointed Under Secretary of State for Foreign Affairs, so all of a sudden Othman saw the Director General's post vacant in front of him. He closed his eyes and tried to master the beating of his heart. With the vacant post occupying the foreground, everything else in his life—his bride, his joys, his hopes—was consigned to oblivion. His suppressed ambition exploded and once again he worshipped in the sacred temple of advancement.

Radiya said to him, "Everybody is talking about you as the only candidate."

"God grant our hopes come true," he said piously, and went on in an air of genteel thanksgiving: "Isn't life amazing? In just one moment it wipes away sorrows that the oceans themselves could not wash off. A kind mother, that's what life is, though sometimes she treats us cruelly."

Othman went without delay to the Foreign Office to congratulate Abdullah Wajdi. The latter welcomed him. "Let me confess to you, Mr. Bayyumi, that I was doubly gratified," he said courteously. "Once at my own appointment as Under Secretary, and once because I knew for sure you would replace me at the ministry."

Othman left the Foreign Office intoxicated with happiness. He wondered whether they would first appoint him Acting Director General and then give him substantive promotion or let him stay where he was until he was promoted. Every day of waiting was a torment. Suffer indeed he did, despite his knowledge that the Minister had a good opinion of him and that he was the special protégé of the Under Secretary of State. When his patience had been exhausted he went to see Bahjat Noor, the Under Secretary of State. The man gave him a warm welcome as he said, "It's as though I read your thoughts."

Othman smiled in confusion and was lost for words.

"But you do not read my thoughts," the man went on.

"I owe to you everything good in my life," Othman answered pensively.

"A little patience is all I ask of you," the Under Secretary of State said, smiling. "I trust I will have good news to tell you in the end."

Othman left the man's office feeling grateful but wondering why he had asked him to be patient. He told himself that the omens were good but even so he did not feel completely secure. Patiently he suffered. After one week the Under Secretary of State called him to his office. Othman thought he read a cool look in the man's eyes and his heart pounded.

Bahjat Noor said, "You're probably wondering why your promotion has been delayed."

"Indeed I am, Your Excellency."

"Well, you know my opinion of you and I may tell you that the Minister's opinion is the same as mine."

"I'm most gratified."

The Under Secretary of State was silent. They looked at each other for a long while.

"What do you deduce from this?" the great man asked.

"That there must be objections from above?" Othman answered, feeling very low.

"Frankly there's a bit of a battle going on."

"And the outcome, Your Excellency?"

"I don't think the Minister will give in."

"How much hope do you think there is?" he asked, feeling his mouth go dry.

"Oh, plenty! Just put your trust in God like the devout believer you are."

His trust in God was boundless, but the devil had long been active in the department. Othman was constantly having to cross a bridge of nails.

"There's little chance left," he sighed.

"Don't be sad!" said Radiya. "Promotion is not the only thing in life to look forward to."

But sad he was, and his sadness settled deep in his heart. He aged, as it were, by a whole generation and all life's dreams turned to ashes. Radiya suggested that they spend a day the following weekend in al-Qanatir Gardens. He welcomed the idea and let her lead him away to wander with her in the huge park. She was the only happy thing in his whole life.

"People have always forgotten their worries in nature's arms," she said, laughing.

She squatted on the grass and gave herself up, soul and body, to the water, the green lawns, and the cloud-dotted sky. He watched her with admiration and warmly endorsed what she said about the beauties of nature. But when he looked around all he saw was scenery that had never meant anything to him in the past, nor did it now. The fact was, he was always absorbed in an inner world, a world of restricted thoughts and fancies conjured up by instinct, a world in which God and God's earthly glory, and the conflict between good and evil, predominated. These things apart, he saw nothing of life.

"Surely you love nature!"

"I love you."

"Look at these happy couples all around us!"

"Yes, there are so many of them!"

She rested her palm on his hand as she said, "Let's forget our worries, it's so refreshing here."

"Yes, let's!"

"But you're so sad."

He sighed without speaking.

"Look," she said, "you are a senior official in grade one. Others would be happy with much less than that." He nearly told her that true faith was the contrary of trivial happiness.

"I'm not like other officials, and to prevent me from occupying the position I deserve is despicable behavior and a blatant breach of the moral system the state operates on."

"Don't you think you set too high a value on government positions?"

"A government position is a brick in the edifice of the state, and the state is an exhalation of the spirit of God, incarnate on earth."

She gazed at him with amazement and he realized that she did not comprehend the nature of his faith and all it comprised.

"That's a new idea to me," she said. "But I've often heard that the spirit of the people comes from the spirit of God."

He smiled scornfully. "Don't speak to me about political conflicts!"

"But that's the real life."

"What absolute rubbish!"

"But the whole world . . ."

"The real world," he interrupted her, "is in the depths of the heart." His heart ached at the thought that she might think he was mad, as some idiots did, and he said to her, seeing a way out, "Let's not argue!"

She gave way and smiled sweetly.

"It's time," he went on, seeking refuge in a new hope, "to make our marriage public."

She blushed. "Is our way clear now?"

"We must face life with courage to be worthy of happiness."

"How beautiful to hear you say that!"

"I'm going to tell my wife." His face brightened with a smile. "A sacred power calls on me to start life afresh and father children I can be proud of."

Thirty-Seven

He declared his good intentions again in the presence of Radiya's aunt.

"For the first time you appear to be a sensible man," said the old woman.

Both Othman and Radiya laughed.

"Our life is worth nothing without you, Aunt," he said. The old woman showed her approval with a smile.

"We've spent a good day in al-Qanatir Gardens and it's time for me to go," he said.

"Will you tell your wife tonight?" asked the aunt.

"The sooner, the better!" he answered as he got up. He took one step forward and then stopped, his expression visibly changing.

"What's the matter?" Radiya asked.

He pointed at his chest without uttering a word.

"Do you feel tired? Sit down!"

"A severe pain here!" he mumbled, indicating his chest again.

She rushed forward to help him but he fell back into his chair and fainted.

When he came to he found himself lying in bed, his clothes still on except for his tie and shoes. He saw in the room a new person, who, despite his weakness, he realized was a doctor. Radiya's face was sad and drained of color and even her aunt's face wore an expression of dejection.

"How do you feel?" asked the doctor as he looked into his eyes.

"What's happened?" answered Othman.

"Nothing very serious."

"But . . ."

"But you will need quite a long rest."

"I feel perfectly all right," said Othman, greatly disturbed. "I think I can get up."

"If that's the case, I must tell you that your condition is critical," the doctor said firmly. "In medical terms it is not serious, but any failure to do what I tell you can make it so. You need complete rest for at least a month."

"A month!" exclaimed Othman.

"You must take the treatment regularly, and rigidly follow the prescribed diet. This is no matter for argument. I will look in again tomorrow." He put his instruments back in his bag and added: "Make sure you remember every word I've said!"

The doctor went out, Othman's eyes pursuing him with a look of anger and despair. Radiya came nearer until she was standing next to the bed. She stared at him and smiled encouragingly.

"A little patience and everything will be all right." The look on his face reflected his anxiety. Tenderly she touched his forehead with the tips of her fingers.

"Don't worry! You'll be fine."

"But there are so many things . . ."

"I will take care of the situation at the ministry."

"How?"

"The truth must be known. There's nothing wrong with that."

"What a situation!"

"Your wife must know too."

"That's even harder."

"We must face reality at any cost."

"You just rest!" Radiya's aunt interrupted.

Radiya was right. He mustn't give up. The will to live in him rejected despair and surrender, come what might! In the end the whole thing was something of a joke.

He shut his eyes, and let events outside weave their way as if they had nothing to do with him, though he was in fact their very center. His colleagues in the office soon came to see him, and as he was not allowed to receive visitors, he was flooded with dozens of get-well cards. He read the prayers and good wishes they contained and remembered Sa'fan Basyuni and Hamza al-Suwayfi. His thoughts reverted to memories which made him feel uneasy. He wondered how Hamza al-Suwayfi was and whether he was still alive. Then he reflected that new employees who did not know him, and who probably would not have a chance to, were joining the department now. And overhead, above all this, clouds raced in the sky and vanished beyond the horizon. Only now did he understand the meaning of the movement of the sun.

He closed his eyes for a while and then opened them to find Qadriyya sitting near the bed gazing at him. In her eyes he saw a stupefied look, soft, dark, and indifferent, like the moon when veiled with a transparent cloud. He realized she no longer lived in this world and was not to be feared. However, she seemed to have been told to be nice to him, for she asked him calmly, "How do you feel?"

He smiled in confusion and gratefully murmured, "Fine, thank you."

"They told me that moving you to your 'original' home might be dangerous," she said, as though reproaching the unknown. "I would have liked to look after you."

"Thank you, Qadriyya. You've always been so good to me."

"You must rest until God helps you out of your illness." She shook her head with an air of wisdom that was not typical of her and went on: "I don't blame you. I understand everything. You want a son, and you're right. God grant you your wish!"

"You are so good and kind, Qadriyya."

She relapsed into silence and was then transported into a world of her own suffused with the perfumes of Paradise. He felt deeply relieved because the secret was out, and the critical and potentially explosive moment had passed. On the other hand, he fully realized the meaning of his illness. What hope was there now for promotion? And . . . and what hope was there of having children?

"I didn't have the slightest warning," he said to Radiya.

"The doctor wasn't surprised."

"This has certainly taught me what it means to be taken unawares."

"It's only a passing cloud."

"I'm very sorry for you, I really am."

"Me? All I care about is your health and well-being."

He looked at her with affection. "One can never tell what's going to happen to one in this world."

She bowed her head in silence till he feared she was seeking to hide a tear.

"I'm grateful to you," he said. "You are a spark of light in this world of ours, which has no logic and no real existence."

"Look on the bright side of life, for your sake and mine!"

He sighed. "Has Qadriyya gone in peace?"

"Yes."

"I thought I heard her voice rend the air. What was the matter?"

"Nothing at all. She's an unlucky woman."

"Yes. One makes mistakes as often as one breathes."

"You must rest completely."

He looked at her tenderly. "Will we be able to realize one of our hopes?"

"Yes, with God's help."

He stared at her sadly. "In a moment of despair I put the thought of promotion behind me and all my hopes centered on a single dream—a child."

"We shall have one."

"Thank you, darling."

"You just take it easy and everything will be fine."

"But how could a hope of immortal kind be lost? It would mean that the annihilation of the world is possible and may, quite simply, happen . . ."

"Wouldn't it be better to keep philosophy for another time?"

"Very well."

"Is there anything you want before you sleep?"

"Just to know the secret of existence," he answered with a smile.

Thirty-Eight

At last he was able to receive his visitors. Everybody came to see him: his colleagues, the staff working under him, and even porters and messengers. Gatherings took place in the bedroom, lasted a long time, and seemed to promise full recovery. Conversations went on about health and illness, miraculous recoveries, and the mercy of God. They also discussed the skill of doctors, the news of the ministry and the department, the cards sent by the Minister and the Under Secretary of State.

"Why didn't the Under Secretary come himself?"

"He's been up to his neck in work. Still, he has no excuse."

"Well, and what does that matter?"

Soon conversations turned to public affairs: the latest radio concert, prices, the generation gap, etc.

Othman took some part in the conversation, but mostly he just listened, and suddenly he found them discussing politics. Once again talk about the conflict raging in society and the slogans that go with it resounded in his ears: freedom, democracy, the people, the working masses, revolutionary ideologies, and confident predictions about the upheavals of tomorrow.

He told himself that every individual staggered under the weight of his own ambitions: was that not enough? But they believed that each man's hopes were dependent on his dreams of revolution. Well! What revolution could guarantee *him* recovery, a child, and the fulfillment of God's word in the sacred state? But he kept his thoughts secret. They were a paltry flock, grazing in the pastures of misery. They hung their hopes on dreams because their faith was weak and they did not know that solitude was an act of worship.

A feeling of warmth generated by the assurance of imminent recovery made him want to try his strength. Being on his own in the room was a good opportunity, so he moved slowly to the edge of the bed and lowered his legs carefully until his feet touched the floor.

"My trust is in God," he mumbled.

He stood up and leaned against the bed until he gained confidence in himself, then he moved his feet tentatively like a child taking its first steps on its own. His legs barely supported him, so weak was he, and so long had he been on his back. He walked till he reached the door. He opened it and continued to walk in the direction of the living room. He wanted to give Radiya and her aunt a pleasant surprise. As he approached the room, he heard voices: an argument between Radiya and her aunt.

"Who? Who?" Radiya was asking sharply.

Uncharacteristically the aunt answered in soft tones, "You've brought it all on yourself. I warned you long ago."

"What's the use now?"

"See what your greed and miscalculation have brought you!"

"Go ahead and shout so he will hear you!"

Then they fell silent.

He returned to his bed stunned. What were they arguing about? What was it she had brought on herself? What greed? What miscalculation? He closed his eyes and bit his lip.

"Oh God! What does that mean? Could it be true?" Why shouldn't it? He himself had always wanted to play that game, but had been unlucky. So strong was his feeling of frustration he was completely carried away with it.

"What a fool I have been!"

He had a setback, suffering a further attack. For days life and death fought over him. He appeared determined to cling to life despite everything and despite telling himself it would be a long and losing battle.

"God's will be done!" he said.

People said he had passed the critical stage, but it was known from the beginning that he would have to stay in bed indefinitely. He revealed his secret to nobody. When Radiya came in he kept his eyes closed. He bore her no grudge nor was he angry with her.

"I have no right to hate her more than I hate myself," he would tell himself.

"If one day I can have a child by her, I will not hesitate, so the game of life will have its bright side as well as its dark," he thought. And in the end he sighed. "What a fool I was! What a bad end I have come to!" He was not angry but he no longer had any confidence in space.

One evening Radiya entered the room, her face flushed.

"The Under Secretary of State has come to visit you," she said.

Bahjat Noor came in with his usual dignified bearing. He shook his hand and sat down as he said, "You look marvelous!"

Othman was touched. "This is a great honor, Your Excellency."

"You deserve to be honored. Good services cannot be forgotten."

Tears came to his eyes.

"Your absence has created a vacuum that nobody else can fill," said the Under Secretary.

"You're so kind . . . That's why you say these things . . ."

"Soon you'll be all right and you'll come back to us. I have brought you good news." The man smiled while Othman gazed at him with incomprehension.

"A decision has been made today to promote you to the position of Director General." Othman continued to gaze at him blankly.

"Right and justice have won in the end."

"I owe everything to your kindness," murmured Othman.

"His Excellency the Minister has asked me to convey to you his best wishes for a speedy recovery."

"I'm most grateful to His Excellency."

The man went away, leaving him in seventh heaven, as though he had been a messenger of mercy sent by the unknown. Othman received the congratulations of Radiya and her aunt with his eyes shut. And again he felt he no longer had any confidence in space.

"How happy I am!" he heard her say.

He savored his success tranquilly. He was now "His Excellency," the occupant of the Blue Room, the authority on legal rulings and administrative directives, the inspiration behind perceptive instructions for wise administration and the efficient manipulation of people's interests, one of God's faithful empowered to do good and prevent evil.

"My cup shall be full, Oh Lord," he addressed himself to God, "the day I am enabled by Your gracious mercy to get up and exercise power and exalt Your word on earth."

But the doctor said to him, "What matters to me is your health, not your job." Indeed, the doctor was unbendingly obdurate, and if his prognosis proved correct, that promotion would never take effect.

"Health alone is not enough to make a true believer happy," Othman said to him.

"I've never heard *that* before."

"If I use up my sick-leave entitlement, I'll be pensioned off."

"Well, there's nothing we can do about that."

Othman was depressed and he thought to himself, "Perhaps they only promoted me as an act of charity, knowing all the time I would not be able to take up the job."

He called Radiya and said to her, "I don't want to trouble you any more."

She was puzzled. "How do you mean?"

"Nursing a sick man is a horrible business."

Radiya protested again but he was determined. He discussed the idea with his doctor, who agreed and arranged for him to be moved to a private room in the hospital. Visitors apart, he had reverted to his old solitude.

Days went by in their endless progression. He was almost cut off from the outside world. Qadriyya too stopped visiting him, her condition having gotten worse. He resigned himself to his fate and he no longer bothered about the past, the present, or the future. He tolerated the hours Radiya spent by his side with extreme irritation but kept his sorrows to himself, believing them at the same time to be merited. His staunch faith in the sanctity of his convictions, in the harshness and holiness of life, the struggle and the agony, and the faraway and exalted hope, all remained unshaken. And he said to himself that occasional failure to achieve one's aspirations did not undermine one's belief in them. Not even illness or death itself could do so; for all that was noble and meaningful in life came from one's determination to pursue them.

Empty words of encouragement were hateful to him, and he resigned himself to the fact that taking up his new position was a dream. He was also resigned to the fact that fathering children was another dream. Yet, who knew?

What hurt him most was that everything went on without any attention being paid to him: appointments, promotions, and pensionings, love, marriage, and even divorce, political conflicts and their feverish slogans, the succession of day and night . . .

Down there, he could hear the cries of hawkers announcing the approach of winter.

Maybe it was as well that the new tomb out there in the sunlight had given him such pleasure.

Translated from the Arabic by
Dr. Rasheed El-Enany.

Wedding Song

———

Contents

The English title *Wedding Song* is an attempt to preserve some of the multiple ironies in the Arabic title *Afrah al-Qubbah*. Literally, *Afrah al-Qubbah* might be interpreted as meaning something like "wedding festivities at the saint's tomb." This is a Cairene tale, however, and in this instance *al-qubbah* refers to a palace that was one of the official residences of the former khedives of Egypt. Naguib Mahfouz explained to me that the weddings of the khedivial family were marked by processions with singing and dancing, and that songs sung on these occasions, popularly repeated, came to be known as *afrah al-qubbah*. Hence *Wedding Song*.

O.E.K.

Tariq Ramadan the Actor

September. The beginning of autumn. The month of preparations and rehearsals. In the stillness of the manager's
office, where the closed windows and drawn curtains allow
no other noise to intrude but the soft hum of the air condi-
tioner, the voice of Salim al-Agrudy, our director, erupts,
scattering words and ideas, sweeping through the scaffold-
ing of our silent attentiveness. Before each speech his
glance alerts the actor or actress who will be playing the
part and then the voice goes on, sometimes soft, sometimes
gruff, taking its cue from whether the part is a man's or a
woman's. Images of stark reality rush forth, overwhelming
us with their brutal directness, their daunting challenge.

At the head of an oblong table with a green baize top,
Sirhan al-Hilaly, our producer, sits in command, following
the reading with his hawklike features fixed in a poker
face, staring at us while we crane in al-Agrudy's direction,
his full lips clamped around a Deenwa cigar. The intensity
of his concentration makes any interruption or comment

impossible; the silence with which he ignores our excitement is so arctic that it compels us to repress it.

Doesn't the man understand the significance of what he's reading to us?

The scenes that unroll before my imagination are tinged with bloodshed and brutality. I'd like to start talking with someone to break the tension, but the thick cloud of smoke in the room deepens my sense of alienation; and I am sodden with some kind of fear. To hold back panic, I pin my eyes to the impressive desk in the rear of the room or a picture on the wall—Doria as Cleopatra committing suicide with the viper, Ismail as Antony orating over the body of Caesar—but my mind shows me the gallows. I feel devils inside me carousing.

Salim al-Agrudy utters the words "Final curtain," and all heads turn toward Sirhan al-Hilaly in bewilderment, as he says, "I'd like to know what you think of it."

Doria, our star, smiles and says, "Now I know why the author didn't come to the reading."

"Author?" I venture, convinced that somehow the world has come to an end. "He's nothing but a criminal. We ought to hand him over to the public prosecutor."

"Watch yourself, Tariq!" al-Hilaly barks at me. "Put everything out of your mind except the fact that you're an actor." I start to object, but he cuts me off irritably—"Not a word!"—and turns back to Salim, who murmurs, "It's an alarming play."

"What do you mean?"

"I'm wondering what kind of impact it'll have on the public."

"I have approved it and I feel confident."

"But the shock is almost too much."

Ismail, the male star of the troupe, mutters, "My role is disgusting."

"No one is crueler than an idealist," says al-Hilaly. "Who's responsible for all the carnage in this world? Idealists. Your role is tragic in the highest dimension."

"The murder of the baby," Salim al-Agrudy interjects. "It will destroy any sympathy the audience might have had for him."

"Let's not bother with details now. The baby can be left out. Not only has Abbas Younis persuaded me at last to accept a play of his, but I also have a feeling that it will be one of the biggest hits in the history of our theater."

Fuad Shalaby, the critic, says, "I share your opinion," and adds, "But we must cut out the baby."

"This is no play!" I exclaim. "It's a confession. It's the truth. We ourselves are actually the characters in it."

"So what?" al-Hilaly retorts, dismissing my objection. "Do you suppose that escaped me? I recognized you, of course, just as I recognized myself. But how is the audience going to know anything?"

"One way or another, the news will leak out."

"Let it! The one who'll suffer most is the author. For us, it can only mean success. Isn't that right, Fuad?"

"I'm sure that's true."

"It must be presented," al-Hilaly says, smiling for the first time, "with the utmost subtlety and propriety."

"Of course. That goes without saying."

"The public," Salim al-Agrudy mutters. "How will it go down with them?"

"That's my responsibility," replies al-Hilaly.

"Fine. We'll begin at once."

The meeting is over, but I stay behind to be alone with

al-Hilaly. On the strength of the fact that we're old friends and comrades as well as former neighbors, I take the liberty of urging him to put the matter before the public prosecutor.

"Here's an opportunity for you," he says, ignoring my agitation, "to portray on the stage what you have actually experienced in real life."

"Abbas Younis is a criminal, not an author!"

"And it's an opportunity that could make you an important actor. You've played supporting roles for so long."

"These are *confessions*, Sirhan. How can we let the criminal get away with it?"

"It's an exciting play. It's bound to attract audiences and that's all that matters to me, Tariq."

Anger and bitterness well up inside me; past sorrows, with all their attendant regrets and failures, spread over my consciousness like a cloud. Then a thought comes to me: now I'll have a chance to get back at my old enemy. *"How do you know all this?"* *"Pardon me, but we're going to be married."*

"What are you going to do?" says Sirhan al-Hilaly.

"My primary concern is to see that the criminal gets what he deserves."

"Better make it your primary concern to learn your part."

I give in. "I won't let this chance slip by me."

At the sight of the coffin, a sense of defeat overwhelms me, and to everyone's astonishment, as if it were the first coffin I've ever seen, I burst into tears. It is neither grief nor contrition I suffer, but temporary insanity. The contemptuous expressions of the other mourners waver like water snakes in my tear-filled eyes, and I avoid looking at them, afraid my sobbing will turn to hysterical laughter.

What melancholy engulfs me as I plunge into the

crowd—the men, women, and children, the dust and the din—at Bab al-Shariya!* I haven't gone near it for years, this district of piety and depravity, where everything under the clear autumn sky seems draped in contempt and depression. My memories of this place—bringing Tahiya here for the first time, her arm gaily tucked in mine—disgust and pain me, as much as the way I live now, mixing with scum, crouching under Umm Hany's wings. Damn the past and the present. Damn the theater. Damn its bit parts. Damn my hopes of success in a lead role—at my age, over fifty, in a play by my enemy, who is a criminal! I walk down the narrow serpentine length of the gravel merchants' market, past its ancient brooding gates and its two apartment buildings, stark and new, to the place where the old house, a dark and bloody past locked up inside it, still lurks.

Some changes have been made, though: the ground-floor reception room has been converted into a shop where watermelon seeds are roasted and sold, and Karam Younis sits in it ready for business, with his wife, Halima, beside him. Prison has transformed them completely. Their faces incarnate resentment and at the very time their son's star is on the rise they seem to have sunk into total despair.

The man catches sight of me, the woman looks in my direction, and their gazes are neither affectionate nor even cordial. I raise my hand in greeting to Karam, but he ignores it. "Tariq Ramadan!" he rasps. "What brings you here?" Hardly expecting a better reception, I pay no attention to his brusqueness. She jumps to her feet, then immediately sits down again on her straw-bottomed chair. "The first visit we've had since our return to the face of the

---

*A quarter in the northwest section of the old Fatimid quarter of Cairo.

earth!" she says coldly. Her features still clutch at some memory of beauty and he seems to have his wits about him in spite of what he's been through—this pair who have engendered the criminal author.

Feeling that I should say something to soften the situation, I remark that the world is full of trouble and that I am merely one of the lost.

"You're like a nightmare," says Karam.

"I'm no worse than anyone else." Since neither invites me to sit down in the shop, I have to stand there like a customer, which makes me more determined to stick to the purpose of my visit.

"Well?" Karam barks at me.

"I have bad news."

"Bad news doesn't mean a thing to us," says Halima.

"Even if it's about Mr. Abbas Younis?"

Her eyes become apprehensive. "You'll always be his enemy," she spits at me, "right to the end!"

"He's a devoted son. When I refused to return to my old job at the theater, he set us up in this little shop."

"And his play's been accepted," Halima adds proudly.

"It was read to us yesterday."

"I am sure it's a marvelous piece of work."

"It's horrible. Do you know anything about it?"

"Nothing."

"He couldn't tell you."

"Why?"

"Why?! Because his play takes place in this house of yours! It tells exactly what went on inside. He exposes a crime. And it throws new light on everything that's happened!"

Karam is suddenly concerned. "What do you mean?" he asks.

"You'll see yourselves in it, just as the rest of us do. He shows everything. Everything! Don't you want to hear about it?"

"Even prison?"

"Even prison—and Tahiya's death. It shows who betrayed you to the police, and it shows that Tahiya didn't just die. She was murdered."

"What kind of nonsense is this?"

"It's Abbas, or the one who represents him in the play, who kills her."

"What do you mean?" Halima screeches in sudden fury. "You hate Abbas!"

"I'm one of his victims, and so are you."

"Isn't it just a play?" says Karam.

"It leaves no doubt about who squealed on you or who the murderer is."

"Nonsense!"

"Abbas can explain everything," Halima says.

"Go see the play for yourselves."

"You crazy fool! You've been blinded by hate!"

"Not by hate. By the crime."

"You're nothing but a criminal yourself. And it's only a play."

"It's the truth."

"You're a spiteful lunatic! My son may be stupid, but he's neither an informer nor a murderer."

"He's an informer and a murderer, and not at all stupid."

"That's what you want to believe."

"Tahiya's murderer must be brought to justice!"

"The same old spite. How did you treat Tahiya when she was with you? Did you treat her right?"

"I loved her, that's enough."

"Yes, the love of a layabout."

"I'm a better man than your husband or your son!" I shout.

"Just what do you want?" Karam growls, his voice harsh with loathing.

"A piastre's worth of melon seeds!"

"Go to hell!"

As I wade back through a swarm of children and women, my thoughts are fixed on the play. I am certain that Abbas has not revealed the plot of his play to his parents, which in itself is a proof of his guilt. But why should he divulge such a dark secret when nobody dreamt of suspecting it? Yearning for success at any price? Will he be rewarded with fame, I wonder, rather than the gallows? *"Tariq! What can I say? It's fate. And luck!"* At the corner where the road meets Sharia al-Gaysh, I turn to the left in the direction of al-Ataba, walking toward the apartment building down a street that over the years has become shadowy, pockmarked, and constricted.

Tahiya, you got what was coming to you. If the man who killed you is the one you left me for, that's justice. Soon it'll be so crowded that people will start eating each other. If it weren't for Umm Hany, I'd be a derelict. The height of your glory, Abbas, will be the hangman's noose. And what about me? The only distinction I have is virility. My failure is otherwise indelible. Is there any meaning in the life of a third-rate actor?

Lust was my teacher in the good old days and it was lust that educated me in the sweet talk of a perfect man-about-town. Our affair was born backstage: I got Tahiya's first kiss while the others were onstage plotting the death of Rasputin.

"Tahiya, you deserve to be a star, not a second-rate actor like me."

"Do you really think so? You're exaggerating, Mr. Tariq."

"Not at all. It's the voice of experience."

"Or the eye of approval?"

"Even love doesn't color my judgment."

"Love!"

We'd been walking after midnight along Sharia Galal, oblivious to the biting cold, intoxicated by the warmth of our dreams. "Of course," I answered. "Shall we take this taxi?"

"It's time for me to go home."

"Alone?"

"There's no one else in my little flat."

"Where do you live?"

"Sharia al-Gaysh."

"We're almost neighbors. I have a room at Bab al-Shariya, in Karam Younis's house."

"The prompter?"

"Yes. Are you going to ask me up to your flat, or shall I invite you to my place?"

"What about Karam and Halima?" I laughed, and she smiled. "There's no one else in the house?"

"They've only got one kid. He's a student." She was pretty. She had a flat. And her salary was the same as mine.

Why has Sirhan al-Hilaly sent for me in the middle of rehearsals? Leaning across the conference table in the warm sunlight, he speaks before I have a chance to say anything: "You've asked to be excused from rehearsals twice, Tariq?" I say nothing, and he goes on: "Don't mix friendship with work. Isn't it enough that you have driven Abbas into hiding?"

"Perhaps the reason he fled is that he's been exposed."

"Are you still clinging to those strange ideas of yours?"

"He's a criminal. No doubt about it."

"It's a play. And you're an actor, not a public prosecutor."

"But he's a criminal. And you know it as well as I do!"

"Your judgment is blinded by hate."

"I don't bear any grudge."

"Haven't you recovered yet from unrequited love?"

"Our rehearsing is going to bring success to a criminal!"

"It will be our success—and your chance after years of obscurity to be seen in the limelight."

"Please, Sirhan, life . . ."

"Don't talk to me about life. Don't start philosophizing! I hear that stuff onstage every night and I'm sick of it. You've neglected your health. Sex, drugs, and the wrong kind of food. In that play about the female martyr you took the role of the Imam* when you were drunk, without the slightest twinge of conscience."

"You're the only one who knew it."

"There was more than one member of the faithful out front who could smell your breath. Are you going to force me to . . ."

"Don't treat the friendship of a lifetime as if it were nothing," I break in, alarmed.

"And you recited a verse from the Qur'an incorrectly. That's unpardonable."

"Nothing happened."

"I beg you, please. Forget this obsession of yours, this prying and spying, and concentrate on learning your part. It's the chance of a lifetime." As I leave the room he adds,

*Prayer leader in Muslim prayers.

"And you'd do well to treat Umm Hany better. If she leaves you, you'll really be in a bad way."

She's the same age as I am, damnit, and doesn't have the sense to feel grateful. She watched Tahiya die, and couldn't see that she'd been murdered, leaving me to play the role of the forsaken lover night after night, to cry again and again—in front of her coffin, because she died without remorse, without even thinking about me, without knowing herself that she'd been murdered, killed by that idealist who commits suicide in the play, and should be hanged in real life.

This crime is creating an author and an actor in one stroke.

"Isn't Tahiya coming?"

"No."

"I didn't see her at the theater."

"She's not going to the theater."

"What do you mean, Abbas?"

"Mr. Tariq—excuse me—Tahiya isn't coming here and she's not going to the theater."

"How do you know all this?"

"Pardon me, but we're going to be married."

"What?!"

"We've decided to get married."

"You son of a bitch. Are you crazy? What are you saying?"

"Be reasonable. We wanted to be nice to you, to treat you with respect. Allow me . . ."

I slapped his face and all of a sudden he became a tiger, snarling with hatred. He punched me—a powerful young man despite his clouded left eye—and my head swam.

Karam Younis and Halima came up yelling, "What happened?"

"It's ludicrous!" I shouted. "A joke! Mama's boy is going to marry Tahiya!"

"Is that so?" said Karam in the dim voice of an addict still on a high, remote and uninvolved.

"Tahiya!" Halima exploded at her son. "What kind of lunacy is this? She's ten years older than you?"

Abbas said nothing.

"Kids' games!" I shouted. "I'll find a way to stop this!"

"Don't make matters worse!" Halima screamed.

"I'll bring destruction on this house and everyone in it!" I shouted.

"Take your clothes," she told me coolly, "and get out."

"You can stay here and rot!" I shouted, storming out of the house.

I was shattered, though. My self-esteem went down like a stallion biting the dust. And it was just at this point, when my spirits were at rock bottom, that my heart leapt aflame with love. I'd thought my feelings were smothered in routine. I'd taken it for granted that Tahiya belonged to me, like a comfortable old shoe. I'd harangued her, demeaned her, and beaten her, but she couldn't live without me, I thought, and she'd sacrifice her life rather than leave me. Now I knew that if she walked out on me—so cunningly and so cruelly—she was taking my trust in life, my confidence, and my sense of mastery with her. What replaced them was madness—in the shape of love, which broke out of the dark corner of its lair, shook off the lethargy of long hibernation, and went to seek the food it had been missing.

When she appeared at the judas, summoned by my ringing, Tahiya's eyes showed confusion, as if she might be faltering. But they didn't flinch, there was no sign of cringing from challenge at this crisis in her life. And in what seemed

a new personality, courageous, freed from continual submission, looking forward to a new life, I sensed that she
was slipping across some kind of border into a region of
potential violence.

"Open the door, Tahiya," I pleaded.

"You know everything now."

"Are you going to leave me outside, like a stranger?"

"Tariq, what can I say? Perhaps it's for the good of both
of us. It's our fate."

"This is some crazy joke."

"I should have told you myself."

"But I don't believe it. Open up!"

"No. I'm treating you honorably."

"You're nothing but a whore!"

"Fine, then. Leave me in peace."

"I'll never do that."

"We're getting married right away."

"A student. Mad. Half blind."

"I'll try my luck."

"Open the door, you fool."

"No. It's all over between us."

"It can't be."

"That's life."

"You'll never know love except with me."

"We couldn't go on living like that."

"You're not old enough to have given up hope. Why are
you acting in this stupid fashion?"

"Please, let's be friends, I beg you."

"You acted in a fit of despair. It was a mistake."

"No."

"People like you—I know what odd phases they go
through."

"May God forgive you."

"You lunatic! When did you change?"

"I haven't committed any sin against you."

"You've lived a lie for quite some time."

"Don't keep on insisting. It's no use."

"You're the biggest whore around."

She clicked the judas shut.

For a while I actually stayed on at Karam Younis's house—Abbas Younis had left, taking over his father's job as prompter, which the old man no longer needed, being content with the earnings the house made for him—and the atmosphere to begin with was somewhat strained. Sirhan al-Hilaly took me aside. "Don't spoil our soirees," he whispered. "Be sensible. You can get Umm Hany back with a wink, you know. She earns twice as much as Tahiya." Al-Hilaly is crazy about women and he'd had Tahiya once or twice, but he knows nothing about love and can't see any connection between suffering and sex, which he ordains or disdains as if it were a matter of administrative routine. When he wants it, it's simply served up immediately. I had no doubt about his good intentions toward me: he'd given me many chances, all of which came to nothing only because of my own limitations—and now in Abbas's play he believes I'll finally be a success—so that when he told me he'd already given hints to Umm Hany about my returning to her, I went back to the company's seamstress. I did it more for the sake of escaping loneliness and shoring up the sad state of my finances than to get over any bitter emotional experience. The fact was that I expected Tahiya's marriage to fail: she'd always had attachments—she needed the money—but I was sure she'd never love anyone except me, in spite of my poverty. On the face of it she belied my expectations, keeping up her marriage until her death. The play, however, unveils her secret: she is shown confessing on her sickbed that she's sold herself to a foreigner, whereupon her husband decides to kill her by replacing her medicine with plain aspirin. So my doubts were justified without my knowing it. This man, whose idealism had been a thorn in our flesh, killed her—this man who, if it is left to me, will never escape punishment.

What have I hoped to gain? I'm face-to-face with Abbas in the flat that was once Tahiya's, having gone there the day after the reading, after seeing his parents in their shop. So he's now a playwright—a playwright at last, after dozens of rejections—this scribbling phony who plunders reality without shame. He's astonished to see me.

Don't be surprised, I want to tell him. What's past is past, but its aftermath, thanks to you, is going to be felt far and wide, all over again.

Al-Hilaly made peace between us one day and we've shaken hands, but we haven't buried our feelings. Here in his study—the flat consists of two rooms with a little foyer—we look at each other sullenly until I say, "No doubt you're wondering why I came."

"I trust it's good news."

"I came to congratulate you on the play."

"Thanks," he replies lukewarmly.

"Rehearsals begin tomorrow."

"Your producer is full of enthusiasm."

"Not like our director."

"What's he say?"

"The hero is a disgusting creature and the public won't like him."

He shrugs, frowning.

"Why weren't you at the reading?" I ask him.

"That's my business."

"Didn't you stop to think? What takes place in the play could create suspicion about you."

"I don't care if it does."

"They will think, quite understandably, that you're a murderer, and a traitor to your parents."

"That's ridiculous. And anyway, why should I care!"

Losing control, I blurt out, "You're a self-confessed murderer!"

"And you're nothing but a shit," he mutters, looking at me with scorn.

"Will you be able to defend yourself?"

"I haven't been accused. I don't need to defend myself."

"You'll be accused—sooner than you think."

"You're an idiot."

I get up. "She may well have deserved to be killed," I say. "But you deserve to hang."

The next day, at the first rehearsal, I'm welcomed by one of al-Hilaly's tantrums. When our producer gets angry he's a hurricane! "You! You! You're behaving like a ten-year-old!" he shouts. "An imbecile! If you weren't so stupid you could have developed into a fine actor. But you insist on turning yourself into a public prosecutor. Why did you go see Abbas Younis?" Has that bastard been complaining about me? I choose to say nothing until this storm blows over a little. "You'll never get a grip on your role," he yells, "until you concentrate on it, instead of on him."

"Today's the first day," I mumble. "It's just as important that the criminal gets what he deserves."

"There's not one of us," he bellows sarcastically, "who hasn't got some misdeed hanging around his neck for which he deserves to go to jail."

"But we haven't gone so far as to commit murder!"

"Who knows? Tahiya—if it's true that she was killed—had more than one man possibly involved in her murder. And you are chief among them."

"He doesn't deserve your defense."

"I don't consider him accused. Have you got one bit of evidence against him?"

"The play."

"No play is devoid of some charge or other. The office of the public prosecutor demands quite a different kind of evidence."

"In the play he commits suicide."

"Which means that in real life he does not commit suicide. And it's our good fortune that he'll be around to write some more."

"He never created one line, and he'll never write one. You know perfectly well what kind of plays he offered you before."

"Tariq Ramadan, don't be so tiresome! Pay attention to your work and take advantage of this opportunity, because it isn't going to come your way again."

I become absorbed in my role. Rehearsing that murderer's play, I relive my life with Tahiya, from its beginning backstage and the old house in the gravel market where we made love in my room, to the denunciation of Karam and Halima, and finally to my crying at her funeral.

"You're acting like you never acted before," Salim al-Agrudy remarks, "but you must stick to the text."

"I'm repeating what was actually said."

He laughs. "Forget about real life and live in the play!"

"You're lucky to have the right to change it."

"Just the necessary cuts. I dropped the scene about the baby."

"I have an idea!" Al-Agrudy looks annoyed, but I go on anyway: "As the heroine is dying, she asks to see her former lover."

"What lover? Every actor in this theater was her lover at one time or another."

"I mean the lover whose part I'm playing. He goes to see her, and she apologizes to him for her infidelity and dies in his arms."

"That would mean introducing major changes in their personalities and in the relationship—the bond of affection—between the husband and the wife."

"But . . ."

"You're inventing a new play. The heroine here forgets her former lover altogether."

"Impossible. And unnatural, too."

"I told you to live in the play and forget about life. Or go ahead and write a new play. There's quite a lot of sloppy, offbeat writing on the market these days."

"But you cut out the baby!"

"That's different. It has no connection with the basic plot, and the killing of an innocent baby is enough to deprive the hero of any sympathy."

"But he kills his wretched wife."

"Listen, hundreds of men in the audience wish, in their hearts, that they could kill their wives, too!"

Isn't that Karam Younis? That's him, for sure, leaving al-Hilaly's office. Only two weeks to go before the play opens. At the doorway of the cafeteria I stand chatting with Doria, the star of our company, the two of us with coffee cups in hand. As Karam approaches, dressed in his old suit, the neck of his black sweater pulled right up to his jawline, I call out, "Glad to see you here."

Casting a look at me, he growls, "Get out of my sight," nods at Doria, and goes on his way.

Doria breaks off what she was saying about the high cost of living to remark, "He must have come to ask about Abbas's mysterious disappearance."

"Abbas is hiding because he's a criminal."

"He didn't kill anyone," she assures me with a smile, "and he hasn't committed suicide."

"He may not have committed suicide. But he's certainly going to hang."

"Victory* should have led us to a more prosperous life," Doria goes on, returning to the subject at hand.

"Only the corrupt have it easy. The whole country's become one huge brothel. Why did the police bother to choose Karam Younis's house for a raid? He was only doing what everyone else does."

"We're living in times when sex has become a national pursuit," Doria says, laughing.

"I'm a man so sunk in corruption that I've been disowned by an old respectable family. So why am I still bogged down in failure?"

"The eternal failure! Poor man. No field of operation left to exploit but Umm Hany!"

On opening night, the tenth of October, the air outside is mild, but inside it feels as though it's going to be steamy. Karam and Halima, al-Hilaly, and Fuad Shalaby are among the audience. Though I'm the only one acting out on the stage what he experienced in reality—Ismail has the part of Abbas—the life of the old house is lived again in all

*Refers to October 1973.

its shamelessness with new and more brutal crimes added. Scandals follow one after another—the producer takes the risk of actually sneaking into Halima's bedroom—and are crowned with betrayal and murder. And during all this, for the first time in my career, my acting is greeted with applause. Is Tahiya watching us from her grave?

Pouring us out success like wine, the crowd either listens in deathly silence or bursts into wild applause. The author, of course, criminal and cowardly, is absent. But how are Karam and Halima taking it? Before the final curtain they're going to have a few more wrinkles in their faces.

After the show, when we have our usual celebration in the cafeteria, people, for once, seem aware of my presence. I am altogether a different person. From a nobody, Tahiya has made me more than a man. The broad grin on Umm Hany's face spreads until her mouth is as wide as a bull-dog's. Behind every great man there's a woman.

"Didn't I tell you?" says Sirhan al-Hilaly.

"A great actor has been born," adds Fuad Shalaby.

Ismail's simper shows his jealousy: it's I who've played the complex role of a lover, a madman, and a heel. I fill my stomach with shawerma and cognac; and the cognac reacts with the wine of success to the point where, seeing Halima in a suit she's rented from Umm Hany, I even drink a toast to the absent author.

Around three o'clock in the morning I leave the theater, arm in arm with Umm Hany and Fuad Shalaby. "Come on," says Fuad. "Let's take a stroll around Cairo at the only time it has a chance to be respectable."

"But we're a long way from home," protests Umm Hany.

"I have my car. I need to get some information."

"You're going to write about me?"

"Of course."

I crow with laughter.

Answering his questions as we walk, I tell him about my past: "I was born in Manshiyyat al-Bakri. There were two villas side by side—the Ramadan family and the al-Hilaly family. My father, Ramadan, was a major general in the cavalry, one of the pashas of the old order; al-Hilaly's was a landowner. I was the eldest in our family, and Sirhan was an only child. One of my brothers is a consul, another is a judge of the High Court, and the third is an engineer. My story in a nutshell is that we were expelled—Sirhan and I— from school. Not that we'd learned much, except about whorehouses, taverns, and drugs. My father left me noth- ing. Sirhan inherited seventy feddans,* though, and to sat- isfy his craze for bossing and for girls, he founded a theatrical troupe. I was one of his actors. My brothers cut off relations with me completely. A low salary. Debts all over the place. If it hadn't been for women . . ."

Umm Hany sighs, "Ah."

Fuad asks, "You were active politically, of course?"

I laugh again. "I have no affiliation with any entity but life. You know what Karam Younis is like. He and I are twins in spirit. People say in his case that being brought up by a mother who was a prostitute has made him what he is. Well, I grew up in a respectable family. So how do you explain our similarity? Environment can't change natural gifts. We despise respectability, both of us. The difference between us and other people, in fact, is that we're honest and they're hypocritical."

*A feddan is roughly equivalent to an acre.

"Are you going to write this drivel?" asks Umm Hany, turning to Fuad.

"Fuad belongs to the same breed himself!"

"You're a real bastard," she bubbles gleefully. "Don't you believe there are any decent people at all?"

"Sure. Mr. Abbas Younis, for example, the author of *Afrah al-Qubbah*. He's such an idealist, you know. That's why he throws his parents into jail and kills his wife and baby son!"

"What are you going to write?" Umm Hany asks Fuad.

"I'm not a lunatic like him," he says, guiding us to his Fiat.

We drive to the Citadel quarter. At the corner where our alley meets the main road, we get out of Fuad's car, unable to take it any farther because of overflowing sewers. The stench accompanying us as we stumble over the crumbling pavement drives the drink from our heads.

Can the success I have now be sustained? Will I ever be able to escape from this slum, from this woman in her fifties who weighs a hundred kilos?

Tahiya and I had left the old house in the gravel market and were on our way to the theater, braving together the cold blast brought by the evening darkness, she with her black coat tightly wrapped around her voluptuous curves, I with the thought that her body was made for bed, not the theater, and that we were both in the wrong profession.

"I caught the boy during tea break sneaking hungry looks at you," I said.

"Abbas? He's only a kid."

"He's going to make an expert pimp someday."

"He has nice manners. And he's not to blame for what goes on in his house."

"He's Karam and Halima's son. And in these times what can you expect?"

I realize now that I hadn't understood at all what was going on in her mind.

"I never pictured you as the grieving lover," Sirhan al-Hilaly said with a chuckle.

"Did you ever imagine that one day we'd cross the Canal and win?"

"She's as poor as you are."

"Tell her—please . . ."

"You imbecile! She'd already decided to leave the stage. What's turned the trick is the fascination of marriage."

"Go to the devil! I'm almost out of my mind."

"You're angry, that's all."

"Believe me."

"The clever operator can't take a defeat!"

"It's not like that."

"That's all it is. Go back to Umm Hany right away, because you're not going to find anyone else to support you."

I hesitated before answering, "Sometimes I almost believe there is a God."

Sirhan guffawed. "Tariq son of Ramadan, even madness has its limits!"

Afrah al-Qubbah proves to be a real hit, with success confirmed night after night. Sirhan al-Hilaly has at last found the play that will enrich his theater, and the daily wage he agrees to pay me revives both body and soul.

Fuad Shalaby asks me, "Are you pleased with what I wrote about you?"

I press his hand gratefully. "After more than a quarter of a century I finally have my picture in your magazine."

"You'll never look back from now on. But did you know that Abbas has come out of hiding?"

"Really?"

"He paid a call on al-Hilaly yesterday at home. Do you know why?"

"Why?"

"He demanded a share of the profits."

I laugh so loudly that Amm Ahmad Burgal, behind the bar, almost jumps out of his skin. "Halima's son! What did al-Hilaly say to that?"

"He gave him a hundred pounds."

"Hell! He doesn't deserve it!"

"Abbas has no job and he's working on a new play."

"Bloodsucker! He'll never write anything new that's worthwhile."

"The future's in God's hands, not yours."

"Where was he hiding?"

"He didn't tell anyone."

"Fuad, my friend, aren't you convinced he's guilty?"

"Why would he kill Tahiya?"

"Because she confessed her infidelity."

He shrugs his shoulders and says nothing.

When I saw her coffin being hauled through the entrance of the apartment building, a terrifying sensation of emptiness slammed the pit of my stomach and spread until I felt my whole self turning to nothing. Then came an attack of weeping, catching me unawares. It was only my sobs that disturbed the other mourners. Even Abbas was dry-eyed.

I left in Sirhan al-Hilaly's car. "When I heard you crying," he said, "when I saw what you looked like, I almost burst out laughing, God help me."

"It surprised me, too."

"I can't remember ever having seen you cry before."

I smiled. "Every racehorse has a tumble."

Death brings back memories of love and defeat.

The news arrives at the artists' coffeehouse where I always stop before leaving for the theater, and I rush to Sirhan al-Hilaly's room to ask if it's true.

"Yes," he says guardedly. "Abbas was staying in a pension in Helwan. He hadn't been seen for a long time. A suicide note was found in his room."

"Has his body been found?"

"No, they haven't found any trace of him."

"Did he give any reason for committing suicide?"

"No."

"Do you really believe he's killed himself?"

"Why should he have gone into hiding at exactly the time when success invites him to display himself along with his work?" There is a depressing silence. Then I hear him ask, "Why would he commit suicide?"

"For the same reason the hero of the play does."

"You're determined to accuse him."

"I challenge you to find any other reason."

Among artists and theater people the news spreads like wildfire. The usual measures, in such circumstances, are taken, but the search for Abbas uncovers nothing, at which I feel a deep sense of relief.

The success of this play, I say to myself, will be limitless.

Karam Younis

Autumn, "harbinger of winter cold." How will we be able to stand it? A lifetime peddling peanuts, melon seeds, and popcorn. And of this woman I've been sentenced to, like another imprisonment. In this country nearly everyone deserves to be locked up. Why single us out for jail? A law not founded on respect for its own workings is insane.

What are all these young boys going to do? What will happen to them? Wait till you see these old houses blown sky-high! A history reduced to rubble is pretty sad.

The woman never stops dreaming.

But what's this? Who is this? Some ghost from the past? "Bring me a poisoned dagger." What is it you want, you plague, you swamp of insects?

I turn to Halima and bark at her, "Look!" She jumps and we both speculate as to whether he's coming to congratulate us or to gloat, while he stands there grinning, with his little eyes, thick nose, and heavy jaws, like a pig. Be tough with him, the way you were the other times.

"Tariq Ramadan! What brings you here?"

"Our first visit from a loyal friend," Halima sneers, "since we returned to the face of the earth!" She's agitated, unnerved.

"I couldn't help it. I've been in a whirl, too."

"You're like a nightmare," I say, turning my back on him to busy myself with a customer.

"I have bad news," he says.

"Bad news doesn't mean a thing to us," says Halima.

"Even if it's about Mr. Abbas Younis?"

"He's a devoted son," I snap back. "When I refused to return to my old job at the theater, he set us up in this little shop."

"And his play's been accepted," the woman adds.

But it's precisely about Abbas's play that Tariq's come here. Has jealousy driven him crazy? He'd rather die than see Abbas succeed. So let his jealousy kill him. He's the source of all our trouble. No one can understand you better than I, Tariq: we both crawled out of the same dung heap.

"The setting is this house," Tariq persists. "It's about you, and it reveals other crimes no one ever imagined."

Is that possible? Abbas never said a word about the subject to anyone. But then he's such a perfect little moralist. "What do you mean?" I ask.

"Everything. Everything! Don't you want to know about it?"

What's he getting at? Why should Abbas compromise himself? "Even prison?" I ask.

"And that he's the one who denounced you to the police and that he killed Tahiya."

"That's nonsense!"

"What do you mean?" the woman shouts. "You hate Abbas!"

But he's said enough already to disturb me deeply. "Isn't it just a play?" I say feebly.

"Abbas can explain everything," Halima says.

"Go see the play for yourselves!"

"You've been blinded by hate!"

"Not by hate. By the crime!"

"You're the only criminal! You're crazy with spite!"

"My son may be stupid, but he is neither an informer nor a murderer," I retort, hiding my anxiety.

"Tahiya's murderer must be brought to justice!" he yells.

He and the woman begin a terrific row, but my own thoughts wander, until I finally get rid of him with a curse.

It is then that I find myself drowning in a sea of suspicion. Would Tariq have taken the trouble to come out this way to tell tales about Abbas that were groundless? The man is vicious, but he's not stupid. When my doubts finally get the better of me, I glance at the woman, only to find her staring back at me.

We live together in this old house like two strangers. If it weren't that Abbas would suffer, I'd divorce her. Abbas. The only thing that gives savor to this bitter life. He's the only hope I have left.

"He's lying," the woman mutters.

I feel much more concern than she does, almost to the point of being sympathetic with Tariq. "Why should he lie?"

"He still hates Abbas."

"But there's the play, too," I venture.

"We don't know anything about it. Go and see Abbas."

"Yes, I'll certainly go and have a talk with him."

"But you aren't making any move!" Stupidity and stubbornness can make Halima quite intimidating.

"There's no great rush."

"He has to know what's going on behind his back."

"And if he confesses?"

"What do you mean?"

"What if he admits that his play really does say what that swindler claims it does?"

"You'll get an explanation for everything."

"I wonder!"

"A real murderer doesn't expose himself."

"I don't know."

"Go see him, that's the main thing!"

"Of course I'll go."

"Do you want me to go?"

"You haven't got anything fit to wear," I point out, reminding her how they'd seized all our money and how that son of a bitch of a detective beat me. "But that's all in the past. It's finished. We've got to concentrate on what happens to us now."

"That cheap swindler. He's lying."

"Abbas just couldn't accept our way of life, could he? So virtuous! You'd think he was a bastard, not my son! But he's always been loyal to us. And why would he kill Tahiya?"

"You're asking me?"

"I'm thinking aloud."

"You believe what the wretch said!"

"And you believe him, too."

"We've got to hear what Abbas has to say."

"As a matter of fact, I don't believe him."

"You're raving."

"Damn you!"

"I was damned the day I got tied to you."

"The same applies to me."

"I used to be pretty."

"Did anyone else want you but me?"

"Everyone always wanted me! Just my bad luck, that's all."

"Your father was a postman, but mine was employed on the Shamashirgi family estate."

"Which means that he was a servant."

"I come from a family."

"What about your mother?"

"Just like you."

"You're a windbag. You don't want to go, do you?"

"I'll go when it suits me."

Collecting my wits, I decide that, come what may, nothing worse can happen to us. To think that when this woman and I came together for the first time it was with feverish passion, beautiful dreams! What's happened to us? I'll have to make this trip. Some afternoon. That'll be the best time.

I don't know anything about the place where my son is supposed to be living. After his marriage we lost contact and we've had nothing to do with each other since. He despised us and rejected our way of life, and I despised and disowned him. When he moved to Tahiya's apartment I was glad not to see his scornful looks anymore. But now I'm running to him. It's the only hope left. When we came out of prison he treated us with understanding, as a dutiful son should. How can he be the one who threw us into it?

I go up to the porter at Tahiya's address a few days later to inquire about Abbas, only to be told that he left a couple of hours earlier, carrying a suitcase.

"Is he traveling somewhere?"

"He told me he'd be away for some time."

"Didn't he leave an address?"

"No."

This unexpected obstacle upsets me. Why didn't he tell us? Have Tariq's accusations reached him? I decide to look up Sirhan al-Hilaly at the theater in Sharia Imad al-Din. I ask to see him and he lets me in immediately, standing up to welcome me, full of sympathy over my safe homecoming: "If it weren't for my circumstances, I'd have come to see you and offer congratulations."

"Sirhan Bey," I say coolly, "that excuse is unacceptable."

He laughs. Nothing fazes him. "You're right."

"Our association has been a long one. A lifetime. My lifetime as prompter of your company. And you had the use of my house. Until I was arrested."

"I haven't treated you right," he mumbles. "How about a cup of coffee?"

"No coffee, no tea. I've come to see you about Abbas, my son."

"You mean the controversial playwright? His work is going to be an unprecedented success. And you, Karam, above all people, should understand how I feel."

"Good. But I didn't find him at home. The doorman told me he'd left carrying a suitcase."

"And why are you so upset about that? He's started on a new play. Who knows? Perhaps he's found a quiet place . . ."

"I've heard things about the plot of the play and I'm afraid it's got something to do with his leaving."

"Don't get the wrong idea, Karam."

"Tariq is malicious, and he . . ."

"Don't talk to me about Tariq," he interrupts. "I know him better than you. There's no need whatever to worry about your son."

"I'm afraid he may have . . ." I leave the sentence unfinished.

"The play is a fantasy. And even if it were true . . ."

"Tell me what you really think."

"I don't bother my head, not for one minute, about anything but the play itself. Any crime the hero commits onstage is good for the play. That's all that concerns me."

"But doesn't he betray his parents and kill his wife?"

"And a very good thing, too."

"What do you mean?"

"The elements of tragedy!"

"Don't you believe that's what actually happened?"

"It's got nothing to do with me." He shrugs.

"I want to know the truth."

"The truth is, we have a great play. And I am, as you know, the owner of a theater, not a public prosecutor."

"And I am in agony."

Al-Hilaly laughs. "What are you talking about? You never loved him!"

"The present isn't the past. You should understand that better than anyone else."

"A play is just a play. Nothing more. Otherwise the law would have the right to put ninety percent of our authors in the prisoner's dock."

"You don't want to offer me any comfort."

"I wish I could. Karam, don't get worked up over absurd conjectures. No one could share them with you anyway except your most intimate friends. As for the public, they won't look beyond the play itself. By the way, why did you turn down your old job as prompter?"

"Thanks for asking. Abbas suggested that, and he told me you'd agreed. But I have no wish to go back to the past."

Al-Hilaly laughs again. "I can see that. You're your own boss now. And perhaps you make more money from the shop. That's all right, my friend. But don't get upset over

Abbas. He's trying to establish himself. He'll surface at the proper time."

Our meeting is over and I take my leave, weighed down by contempt for all mankind and thinking: *No one cares about me, and I care for no one.* I don't even love Abbas, though my hopes are pinned on him. A treacherous murderer. Why should I blame him, though? I'm just like him. His outer paint has been peeled off, and he's shown the true colors he's inherited from his father—the naked self everyone pretends to honor these days, revealed without hypocrisy. What is goodness but mumbo jumbo, empty words said over and over in the theater and the mosque? There are pickup joints and rooms by the hour all along the Pyramids Road. How could he get me thrown into prison?

Who's this? At the door of the cafeteria I run into Tariq Ramadan, who holds out a slimy hand. I refuse it and tell him to get out of my sight.

I didn't do anything wrong. Drugs were chic, weren't they? And I was a man with no inhibitions. I followed my instincts, that's all. Other men were no different from me. What happened later was bad luck. Halima would say to me, "Do you expect my salary by itself to be enough to support your family?"

"You want a quarrel? I'm ready."

"Opium ruins everything."

"So what?"

"What about your son? Such a wonderful boy deserves to be looked after."

It wasn't my fault. My mother taught me what's right, instilled the fundamental principles. Halima wanted to play at being respectable, to forget the way she used to live. But I won't tolerate hypocrisy in my household.

"If you have trouble finding a suitable place some-times," I said to al-Hilaly, "you can use my house." He gave me a searching look. "In the heart of Bab al-Shariya," I assured him, "even the jinn wouldn't suspect it!"

I was right. The old house took on new life: it was cleaned up from top to bottom and the largest room was transformed into a salon for the hell-raisers. Those aristo-crats. Those playboys—al-Agrudy, Shalaby, Ismail, Tariq—and Tahiya the playgirl. I respected them. They did as they liked without hypocrisy. There was a storeroom for snacks, drinks, and drugs, and Halima really took to the trade. A total hypocrite. I despise hypocrisy. Her true nature came right to the fore: the expert mistress of a new establish-ment, pretty, sharp-witted, as open-minded as I was and even more so, quite adept at running a brothel. The sky rained down gold.

What made the boy look at us in disgust? *Whose son are you anyway? Who's your father? Who's your mother? Who's your grandmother? You're a bastard, you are—off-spring of a theatrical marriage!* An idiot, taken in by hypocrisy.

"The boy's sorrow is killing him," Halima sighed.

"Let him die of grief, the way every idiot should."

"He refuses to accept the situation."

"I don't like that word *accept*."

"He deserves some sympathy."

"He deserves to be throttled."

As he grew to hate me, my love for him was likewise uprooted. "Understand your life! Live in the real world! It's only the chosen few who have as good a life. Look at the neighbors! Don't you hear about what's going on around you? Don't you understand? Who are you anyway?" His eyes gave off a queer look, as if he lived outside the walls of time. What did he want?

Listen, I'll give you some advice: Your grandfather built this house. I don't know anything about him. Your grandmother—a young widow no different from your mother—made it a lovers' nest. Your father grew up in the bosom of reality. I'd really like to tell you everything. Should I be scared of you? If your grandmother hadn't died suddenly she would have married the master sergeant and lost the house. After she died he wanted to lord it over me. I beat him up and he tried to get me drafted into the old regular army, but the house stayed mine. It was Umm Hany—my mother's cousin and al-Hilaly's pimp—who got me the job as prompter. I'd like to lay these facts before you someday so you'll know what you came from, so you can trace your origins back to their roots without any sham reluctance. Be like your father, and love will unite us the way it used to when you were small. Don't be misled by your mother's hypocrisy. Someday you'll find out everything. Should I be afraid of you, son?

Back at the shop I have to face Halima's dreary questioning. What had Abbas told me? she wants to know.

"I didn't see him. He left the flat with a suitcase, and no one knows where he went."

She beats her thighs with her fists. "No one knows! Why didn't he let us know?"

"He doesn't think about us."

"He's the one who helped us start this shop."

"He wants to forget us now. As far as he's concerned, we belong to a past that's best forgotten."

"You don't understand my son. You should've gone to

see al-Hilaly!" Exasperation makes me speechless, and she goes on: "You're not careful!"

"I'd like to bash your head in."

"Have you gone back on opium?"

"Only government ministers can afford it these days!" I retort. "Al-Hilaly doesn't know where he is either."

"You visited him?"

"He has no idea where he is," I repeat.

"My God! Did he move out of his flat?"

"No."

"He'll come back. Maybe there's a woman involved."

"That's what a woman like you would think."

"You don't care about him at all!" she screams. "You don't care about anyone but yourself!"

"I have been condemned to leave one prison for another."

"I'm the one who's living in a prison cell!"

The woman begins to sob, and that makes me even more exasperated. How could I ever have loved her? I wonder.

The red cafeteria. Walls and ceiling painted deep red, tablecloths and a thick carpet of the same color. I sat down at the barman's counter on a high leather stool, next to a young woman I hadn't noticed at first. Amm Ahmad Burgal, the barman, brought me the usual fava beans and a sandwich with a cup of tea and inevitably I glanced sideways, to be instantly dazzled by a young creature of extraordinary beauty. It struck me that she must be an employee of the theater, like myself, since the public wouldn't show up at the theater until well after eight o'clock. I heard Amm Ahmad ask her, "Any news about a flat, Miss Halima?"

"Searching for gold is easier," she replied, in a voice that oozed honey.

"Are you looking for a flat?" I butted in, bewitched.

She nodded, took a sip of tea, and Amm Ahmad introduced us. "Mr. Karam Younis, the company's prompter. Miss Halima al-Kabsh, the new cashier."

"Getting married?" I said with my usual brashness.

Amm Ahmad answered for her. "She's living with an aunt in a cramped little apartment and dreams of having a small place of her own. But there are the problems of rent and key money."

"I have a house," I piped up at once.

She turned to me, interested for the first time. "Really?"

"A large house. It's old, but it has two floors."

"Is each floor an apartment?"

"No. It isn't divided into flats."

Amm Ahmad asked me if she could have a floor to herself.

"Of course she could." She asked if that wouldn't inconvenience the family. "I live there alone," I replied, at which she raised her eyebrows and turned away, prompting me to explain, in defense of my good intentions: "You and your family would find yourselves quite safe there."

She made no comment, but Amm Ahmad asked me, "What's the rent?"

"No one's ever taken it before. I'm not at all greedy."

"Shall I bring you a tenant?" he inquired solicitously.

"Oh no, I don't want that. It's the family house and it has its memories. I just wanted to help out the young lady, since we both work here in the theater."

Amm Ahmad laughed. "Give us a chance to think about it."

The young woman went out, leaving me charged with pangs of desire.

There she is now, sitting bent over in her chair with her

arm folded, disgust and anger in her eyes, her forehead knitted in a scowl like a curse. Wouldn't it be better to live alone than share a life of wrangling? Where is the old enchantment—the sparkle, the foaming intoxication? Where in this world has its mummified corpse been interred?

Whenever I saw her in the red cafeteria I'd say to myself, "This girl grabs me like hunger." I'd imagine her and her high spirits in the old house, the way it would be rejuvenated, warmed. I fantasized about her curing me of deep-seated ills.

Amm Ahmad Burgal kept encouraging me in private. "Halima is a relative of mine," he said one day, "on my mother's side. She's educated and she's clever. I'm the one who got her her job here with al-Hilaly Bey."

"She's a wonderful girl," I responded, encouraging him to go on.

"Her aunt's a good woman. She herself is a very virtuous girl."

"There's no question about that."

His smile was so promising that it ignited my feelings, which were already pretty volatile; and I let myself surrender to the enticements of my own imagination, allowed myself to be lulled into daydreams, overpowering visions of sweet sensation, unbearably sustained. One day I finally said to him, "Amm Ahmad, I sincerely want . . ."

The rest of my unfinished sentence he understood. "Good for you!" he mumbled, full of glee.

"I have no income except my salary, but I own the house, and that's not something to be sneered at these days."

"Having a roof over your head is more important than keeping up appearances." And a little later that same week he was able to meet me with the words "Congratulations, Karam!"

During the days that followed, I floated on the tenderness of a tranquil engagement, wrapped in a veil whose silk translucence was woven from gossamer dreams and only the most dulcet of realities. The leather shaving kit she gave me made me so pleased that I felt like a child. Sirhan al-Hilaly raised my salary by two pounds and congratulated me on entering a new life. The theater people gave a party for us in the cafeteria and saw us off with flowers and sweets.

What's on the woman's mind? Her veined hand toys absentmindedly with a heap of popcorn. She hasn't a cheerful thought in her head. We're condemned to venting our mutual irritation on each other alone. We live in a prison cell. Only the light streaming down on the rubbish strewn along this ancient street makes it look a little different, as gusts of wind pick up the lighter bits, blowing them here and there to be kicked about by the feet of countless boys. What's on the woman's mind?

On our wedding night, with a cock crowing on a neighboring rooftop, she made the revelation that dragged us both to the edge of a bottomless pit, down which everything seemed to plunge but history itself. My first bewilderment turned to a numbness so deep that except for hearing the sound of her choking sobs, I almost thought I'd died. The sobs said everything. "I'll never forgive myself," she whimpered. *Really?* "I should have . . ." *What for? There's no need to say any more.* "But I loved you," she murmured a second time.

I'd found out her secret. But she hadn't yet found out mine. How could she know that her man had likewise come to her with something of a past? Or even understand how wild I'd been? I'd had a nasty surprise, but her deception didn't bother me, and even my surprise, once the numbness wore off, seemed silly. "The past doesn't matter to me," I declared heroically.

She bent her head, in what looked like grateful humility. "I hate the past," she said. "I'm becoming a new person."

"That's good," I said magisterially. Any desire to learn more I put aside. I was neither angry nor glad. I loved her. I entered into my new life with all my heart.

Hours go by, and we don't exchange a word. We're like two peanuts in a shell. Every customer complains about the rise in prices, the overflowing sewers, the exhausting queues at the government food stores, and we exchange condolences. Sometimes they look at the woman and ask, "What makes you so silent, Umm Abbas?"

What have I got left to look forward to? She, at least, expects Abbas to return.

I began my married life with genuine ardor. Halima announced the news of her approaching motherhood, and I was annoyed at first, but it was only a passing feeling. When Abbas was a child I loved him passionately.

Then things began to change. It was Tariq Ramadan who came up to me one day and said, "Hamlet's a tough role. Why don't you dissolve this in a cup of tea?" That was the beginning of a mad course. The man who cared about nothing was taken in. As time passed, the springs of life dried up and finally all joy was throttled in the grip of a crisis.

"Is this what you want? To blow you earnings on poison and leave me to face life on my own?" Halima's voice was now as disgusting to me as the stench of backed-up sewers.

We'd become like two bare trees. Hunger was knocking at the old house's door.

I was relieved to be able to say to her one day, "The end is in sight."

"What are you talking about?"

"We'll fix up the east room upstairs as a place for entertainment."

"What?"

"They'll come every night. We won't have to worry about being poor anymore."

She gave me a look that boded ill, so I said, "Al-Hilaly, al-Agrudy, Shalaby, Ismail. You know. But we have to organize something that will keep them coming."

"That's a dangerous game."

"But it's a very shrewd one. The profits will be incredible."

"Isn't it enough for us that Tariq and Tahiya are staying here? We're sinking to the lowest depths."

"We are rising to new heights. You and your son can both shut up."

"My son's an angel. He's the one I'm worried about."

"Just let him try defying his father, damn him. You're ruining him with your silly ideas."

She gave in, but with resentment. She'd forgotten her wedding night. It's strange: people always yearn to be free of government regulations, but they're delighted to load shackles on themselves.

Here she is returning from her mission. Except for her services in the house, I'd have wished she'd never come back. There's disappointment in her face and I don't ask her any questions, ignoring her until finally she sighs, "His apartment is still locked up." I'm glad to have a customer.

It's an excuse to avoid her. When he's gone, she hisses at me, "Do something."

My mind isn't with her: it's busy pondering how the government could throw us into prison for doing what it practices itself quite openly. Don't they operate gambling houses? Don't they promote brothels for their guests? I'm full of admiration for them. It isn't operations like that that drive me to rebel. It's the hypocritical injustice.

"Go and see al-Hilaly again," the woman says in a louder voice.

"Go yourself!" I say sarcastically. "You know him better than I do."

"God have mercy on your mother!" she says, stung to fury.

"At least she wasn't a hypocrite like you."

Then she sighs, "You don't love your son. You never loved him."

"I don't like hypocrites. But then, again, I don't deny he helped us."

She turns her back on me, muttering, "Where are you, Abbas?"

Where's Sirhan al-Hilaly? He'd gone out and hadn't come back. He was hardly likely to have gone to sleep in the bathroom. Meanwhile the gambling was still going on, and I was raking my percentage of the winnings after every round. Wasn't it time for Halima to serve drinks? Where was she? "Where's our producer?" I asked.

Everyone was busy with his cards and no one answered me. Was Tariq giving me a funny look? Halima should bring the drinks. "Halima!"

No answer. I couldn't leave my place or I'd be robbed. "Halima!" I shouted at the top of my voice. A little while later she appeared.

"Where were you?"

"I fell asleep."

"Make some drinks. And take my place until I come back."

I left the card room. Downstairs I found Abbas. "What woke you up at this hour?" I asked him.

"I couldn't sleep."

"Have you seen Sirhan al-Hilaly?"

"He left the house."

"When?"

"A while ago. I don't know exactly when."

"Did your mother see him?"

"I don't know."

Why had he left? Why was the boy looking at me so quietly, with such despair in his eyes? I smelled something fishy. I may be many things, but I'm not a sucker. When there was nothing left in the house but cigarette butts and empty glasses, I gave the woman a long accusing look and then confronted her: "What went on behind my back?" Staring back disdainfully, she ignored my question altogether. "Did Abbas see?" She still didn't answer, and her silence irritated me all the more. "He's the one," I said, "who gave you the job. Everything has its price, that's what concerns me." She stamped her feet with fury. "As for you, though," I went on, "you aren't worth being jealous over."

"You're the lowest kind of vermin," she snarled, marching off to her room.

I guffawed. "Except for one little worm!"

She's returned from another outing. I hope you suffer more and go even crazier. Standing facing me in the shop, she says, "Fuad Shalaby is quite sure."

"Did you see him?"

"In the actors' coffeehouse."

"How does he know?"

"He said it's just an author's whim and that he'll show up at the right time with a new play in hand."

"A few words of comfort to a poor, infantile mad-woman."

She dragged her chair into the farthest corner of the shop and sat there talking to herself. "If God had only willed it! He could have given me better luck. But He threw me into the arms of a junkie."

"That's what happens to a man when he marries a whore."

"God have mercy on your mother! When Abbas comes back I'm going to live with him."

"I hope he returns, then, for my sake."

"Who'd ever imagine you're his father?"

"Any boy who's killed his wife and thrown his own parents in jail is my son and I'm proud of him!"

"He's an angel. And he's the product of my upbringing."

I wish she'd talk herself into a straitjacket.

The karate chop that detective gave me on the neck. The punch that made my nose bleed. The raid was like an earthquake. It flattened everything, even Sirhan al-Hilaly: he was so frightened he just stood there blinking. And the savings we'd sold our souls for—confiscated. My God, it was awful!

What the devil was going on out in the hall?

I left my room to find Tariq and Abbas fighting, and Halima screaming.

"What's this nonsense?" I roared.

"It's ludicrous!" Tariq shouted. "Mama's boy is going to marry Tahiya!"

Everything seemed ludicrous, alien, incompatible with the euphoria beginning to rise from the drug I'd just taken.

"What kind of lunacy is this?" Halima shouted. "She's ten years older than you!"

Tariq spat out threats so vehemently that saliva was sprayed in every direction.

"Don't make matters worse," Halima pleaded.

"I'll bring destruction on this house," Tariq shouted, "and everyone in it!" Whatever excitement I could have felt had receded. All I could muster was scorn and indifference, but before I could express anything, Halima told Tariq to take his clothes and get out.

"Behind my back!" he yelled. "In this filthy house!"

"It's your presence that makes it filthy," came my rejoinder, in so calm a tone that it sounded very strange in this stormy atmosphere. He didn't bother to look at me.

Then Halima asked Abbas, "Is it true, what he says?"

"We've reached an understanding," said Mama's boy.

"Why weren't you considerate enough to consult us?" I said with lofty indifference and, getting no response, went on: "Will her salary be sufficient for running a home?"

"I'm going to take your place as the company's prompter."

"From author to prompter?"

"There's no inconsistency between the two."

"My son's gone mad!" cried Halima convulsively. Then she told Tariq, "Don't you act like a crazy fool, too."

He began making threats again, whereupon she yelled, "Get out of our house!"

"I'll stay here until Doomsday!" came his parting shot. Exit Tariq, leaving the scene to the Noble Family. I looked maliciously from one to the other, enjoying myself.

"I don't even know her except as this or that person's mistress," Halima said to Abbas, imploring him to reconsider.

I roared with laughter. "Your mother's an expert. Listen and take note!"

She went on pleading with him. "Your father, as you well recognize, has become a good-for-nothing. You're our only hope."

"We'll begin a new life," said Abbas.

I laughed. "Why have you deceived us all this time with your high-flown morality?"

Abbas strode out, and she broke into sobs. In the depths of my heart I would welcome his final departure, exulting over the collapse of the alliance between him and his mother against me. His had always been a dissenting voice, and I was fed up with him. Let him leave, and the house would become calm and harmonious. I'd even been afraid of him at times. He personified the meaning of words I hold in contempt, the nature of acts I abhor.

Halima was bewailing her fate. "Alone! Alone!"

"Alone! Don't pretend to be what you are not. In what way are we different? The same source, the same life, the same final goal!"

She stared at me with eyes that spoke loathing and contempt, then went to her room, with my loud, disdainful laugh following her all the way.

I look at her back over the mounds of peanuts, melon seeds, popcorn, and dried chickpeas heaped up in their bins along the counter. What kind of existence is this, so totally joyless, in this atmosphere laden with smoke and aversion? The boy's return and his success should have been enough to give her new life.

For once, I was really feeling quite cheerful, while Halima was hiding her gloom.

Sirhan al-Hilaly had been asking, "Where are Tariq and Tahiya?"

"A severe shortage of players," said Salim al-Agrudy.

I laughed. "Exciting news, Sirhan Bey: my crackpot son has married Tahiya."

The whole table burst out laughing. "It appears," said Ismail, "that your son is a real artist."

"The kid," exclaimed al-Hilaly.

"The marriage of the season!" added Shalaby.

"You'll now find Tariq," said Ismail, "wandering in the desert, like Magnun Layla."*

The table burst out laughing again.

"But Halima isn't joining in our happiness," observed Sirhan.

"Halima is at a funeral," she said, and went on mixing drinks.

"Who knows? Perhaps he's found the happiness that evades the rest of us."

"In spite of everything!" I laughed out loud.

"These days only mules are lucky enough to be happy," Halima said bitterly.

"Will he go on trying to write plays?" said Sirhan.

"Of course," Halima replied.

"Great. Tahiya will be able to supply him with lots of useful experience."

After that I became absorbed in collecting the money. It

---

*Refers to the theme of a love lyric by Gameel (d. 701), a poet from Medina. Magnun was the self-immolating lover and Layla his ever-inaccessible inamorata.

was the first night I'd done business with no one to spy on me and I thoroughly enjoyed it.

The woman is out searching for her son. Alone in the shop, I wonder what kind of end he's assigned her in the play. I forgot to ask about that. Has he lowered the curtain over the time we spent in prison? Over this shop? Customers come one after another. These people don't realize how much I despise and detest them. Hypocrites! They carry on exactly the same way we did, then offer up prayers at the proper times. I'm better than they are. I'm liberated. I belong to the good old days, before religion and moral behavior became all the rage. I'm besieged in this shop, though, by an army of hypocrites, every man and woman. The state, too. That's why it neglects the sewers, leaves us to line up in queues, and deluges us with bombast. And my son gives me a splitting headache with his silent reprimands, then commits betrayal and murder. If only I could get hold of a little opium. It would make everything bearable. Why were we so beguiled at the time of our engagement? Why did it whisper to us so insinuatingly of a sweetness that didn't exist?

"I am indebted to Amm Ahmad Burgal for a joy that is almost more than a man can bear."

"Don't exaggerate."

"Halima, who can be happier than a man whose heart has not beaten in vain?" Her radiant smile was like a flower in full bloom.

Where does she hide this sweetness now?

Ah, if only it were possible to go back in time as it is to go back in space. Somewhere in my primeval being is a soft spot that makes me want to cry over these ruins. Somewhere a Karam who no longer exists is weeping over the Halima of the past.

The woman has returned. She comes in and sits down without even a nod at me. I ignore her completely, and she doesn't speak, but her eyes look serene. What has she found out? She's no doubt withholding good news from me, the sow: if it were bad news she'd have poured it over my head the minute she came in. Has Abbas returned? I refuse to ask. Several minutes pass before she says, "We're invited to see the play!" She hands me a printed notice.

My eyes come to rest on the name of the author: Abbas Younis. I'm carried away with pride. "Shall we go?"

"What a question!"

"We may get a shock when we see ourselves."

"What matters is that we see Abbas's play," she says. "My heart tells me that the playwright is bound to appear."

"Who knows?"

"My heart knows."

We do our best to look presentable: I wear a suit that isn't too bad, and Halima has rented a *tailleur* from Umm Hany. At the theater they receive us graciously.

"But I don't see the playwright," Halima says.

"He didn't come," says Sirhan al-Hilaly, "but I've told you enough." So she's met him and managed to get considerable news from him.

Since we're early, we go to see Amm Ahmad Burgal, who gives us each—on the house—a sandwich and a cup of tea. "It's like old times," he remarks, but we neither smile nor comment. At curtain time we take our seats in the front row. The theater is packed.

"It's a success," observes Halima.

"You can't judge until a week's gone by." Despite the

ironic detachment I feel—how can I take a play seriously when life itself does not mean anything to me?—my nerves are on edge.

Ah, the curtain is rising—to reveal our house. Our house, no other. Was it al-Agrudy or Abbas who wanted it this way? The father, the mother, and the son. A brothel and a gambling den, that's what it is. There's more than crime and betrayal there. The stage mother is an uncontrollable whore, her relations with the director, the producer, the critic, and Tariq Ramadan follow one after another: and I look swiftly at Halima, whose breath is coming in rough gasps. It's sheer hell. Now you can wallow in your son's opinion of you. What he thinks of his father and mother is painfully clear. Who would have imagined that his serene head could hold all this devastation? I'm glad he sees his mother this way, glad he's come out with what he really thinks of her. This piece of drama is his way of wreaking vengeance on me, punishing me for what I am.

But in this moment of scandal I experience a sense of triumph over both the mother and the son, over my two mortal enemies. He doesn't understand me. He presents me as someone fallen, a man who has resorted to corruption in reaction to the challenge of reality. I'm not like that, you fool. I never had any stature to lose. I grew up untamed and free, watching the hypocrites, learning from them. That's what you cannot understand. What's the secret of your success? You flatter them, you pander to their sense of superiority. I spit on you and your evasions!

Thunder of wild applause.

We're invited—as is customary—to the party in the cafeteria, in celebration of a successful play. "Shall we join them or leave?" I whisper.

"Why shouldn't we join the party?" *It's no use pretend-*

ing to be above it all, Halima. You don't have the same wings I have. "He didn't need to commit suicide," she murmurs.

"What kind of an end did you expect for a murderer?" I ask, hoping to nettle her.

"He got a lot of sympathy."

Sirhan al-Hilaly declares loudly, "My intuition says that it won't be a flop," and they begin drinking toasts.

"It's brutal, of course," says Salim al-Agrudy, "but it's impressive."

"It reminds the audience of their everyday hardships," says Fuad Shalaby. "But it's terribly pessimistic."

"Pessimistic?" scoffs al-Hilaly.

"He needn't have committed suicide. The audience's hopes and aspirations were all pinned on him."

"Don't look at it as a suicide," answers al-Hilaly.

"It's just a way out for the new generation."

"God protect all bastards!" roars al-Hilaly. And turning to Tariq Ramadan, he raises his glass and says, "To the revelation of a great actor, discovered in his fifties!"

"A discovery more significant," Fuad Shalaby exclaims, "than finding an oil well!"

Al-Hilaly turns to us for a response, but I anticipate him and raise my glass. "A toast to the absent playwright."

A surge of acclaim turns into a riot of drinking at the theater's expense. I revel in scandals recalled about every man and woman present. Why were we the only ones imprisoned? Friends, libertines—drink a toast to me! I am your true symbol!

When we return to the old house, it is dawn and we have no wish to sleep. I light the charcoal in the heater in the hall, where the tiles are covered by an old Assiut rug, and Halima and I sit down, as if, in spite of our mutual aversion, we want to be together for a while. Which of us will start the conversation? How very difficult it is for us to talk to each other. We are always on guard.

"Did you like the play?" I ask.

"Very much. Very much."

"And the subject?"

"What a silly question from someone who's spent a lifetime in the theater!"

"Why do we always deceive ourselves? There's no doubt about what he intended."

"I won't accept this silly way of thinking!"

"It was even more true than the real facts."

"There's no connection between the way I appear in that play and the real facts." I can't help chuckling at that, which annoys her. "It's just a fantasy."

"All of them just as we know them in real life?"

"An author is free to do as he likes, to keep some characters as they are in real life and change others, as he wishes. There were completely new elements in the plot."

"Why did he portray you as he did?"

"That's his business."

"I thought he loved and respected you!"

"There's no doubt about that."

"You give yourself away with that bitchy look of yours!"

"I know I'm right."

"Even Tariq!" I say with contempt. "I never imagined you'd sink to such depths."

"Spare me your filthy thoughts."

"If it hadn't been for your fun and games on the side we'd have made a lot more money."

"What about you? The fact is that he shows you much better than you really are, which proves that he really was using his imagination." I laugh so loudly that she says, "Quiet! People returning from dawn prayer will hear you."

"So what? That strange boy of yours. He threw us into prison."

"How can you expect anyone to lead a decent life? You don't follow any rules but your own."

"But he claimed to be so perfect. That's what gave me a pain in the neck!"

"He's a wonderful boy. A well-known playwright. My son." Outwardly, at least, she's pleased with things.

"What I admire is his brutality!"

"When he comes back I'm going to leave this damn house and live with him."

"This house? Where every room bears witness to our past glory?"

She leaves me, and I sit there alone holding my hands over the heater. I'd like to know more about my father. Was he one of these hypocrites? He died young, my mother sank very low, and I grew up her way, under the devil's horns. But you, Abbas, are a dark horse.

How bored I am! I'm like a jinni shut up in a long-necked bottle. No room to maneuver.

I follow the play's success with fascination, expecting the playwright to surface, even to come up with a new play, hoping that his success will change the course of my tedious life.

I make frequent visits to the theater to nose around for news; and one morning as I enter Amm Ahmad Burgal rushes up to me and takes me into the empty cafeteria. His downcast face alarms me. I sense that behind it lies bad news.

"Karam! I was just about to come see you."

"Why! What's wrong?"

"Abbas."

"What about him? Say it, Amm Ahmad."

"He disappeared from the pension in Helwan, the place where he was staying, and he's left a strange message behind."

"What message? Don't you want to tell me?"

"A note, saying he was going to commit suicide."

My heart sinks, pounding, like anyone else's. We look at each other silently. "Have they found . . . ?"

"No," he says. "A search is being made, though."

"Ah. Probably . . . who knows? But he wouldn't have written the note, would he, if he hadn't . . . ?" My mouth says the words, my thoughts are astray.

"May the Lord help you." He sounds like someone who believes the matter is ended.

"I must go to Helwan!"

"Sirhan Bey al-Hilaly has already gone."

A futile, painful trip. There is nothing but the suicide note. Abbas has vanished, disappeared once and disappeared again. Finding his body will be the only proof of his suicide. Would he have written the note if he hadn't really made up his mind to commit suicide?

"If he really wanted to commit suicide," al-Hilaly muses, "why didn't he do it in his room?"

"So you doubt the seriousness of his intentions?"

"Yes, I do."

I do not return to the old house until evening. Halima isn't there and I realize that she's gone to the theater to find out why I'm so late. I close up the empty shop and sit in the hall waiting for her. An oppressive hour goes by before she comes in, her eyes ablaze with madness. We gaze at each other for a second, then she cries, "No! Even if he wanted to kill himself he wouldn't do it! He couldn't! He couldn't kill himself! It's not possible!"

Sinking into a sofa, she bursts into wild tears, slapping her cheeks with both hands.

Halima al-Kabsh

From the bowels of prison, born again to the face of the earth! Abbas's face appears before me, and I take him in my arms. Weighed down by shame and humiliation, I bury my face in his chest. "How badly we've treated you," I whisper. "I wish we'd died. Then you'd be rid of us."

"It's only your words that hurt me," he answers gently. I can't help weeping. "We should be thankful now," he says. "Let's think about the future."

"You're all alone, son. God has seen fit to take away your wife and child," I say, shaking with sobs, "and we weren't there to comfort you."

"What's past is past."

With his father he scarcely exchanges a word. We are all together in the hall of the old house the way we used to be, sometimes, in the old days.

"I beg you not to bring up the past," he says. Then, pausing for a moment, he goes on: "I've been thinking things over. Does Father want to go back to his old job in the theater?"

"No. Never, damn them!"

"I can turn the reception room into a shop. We'll sell some of the furniture and set up a snack shop. It's an easy business and fairly profitable. What do you two think of that?"

"Just as you see it, son," I say with gratitude. "And I pray to God that I may hear good news about you soon."

"I hope so. I think I'm about to come up with a winner."

I invoke God's blessing on him over and over, until he says, looking at us from one to the other, "What matters most is that you cooperate with each other and that I don't hear things that hurt me."

"I have often dreamed of living with you," I say with a sigh.

"If God means me to be successful, everything will change."

"Why don't you go ahead and take her with you!" Karam says, growling.

"You must cooperate with each other. I'll do all I can to give you a decent life, but you must learn to get along together."

What cooperation? The poor boy doesn't understand anything; he's too naive to comprehend the secrets of the heart even when they're displayed right under his nose. How can he understand what his father did when he's never seen anything but the man's melancholy exterior? My son can make sacrifices and be as generous as his devoted heart wants to, but doesn't he realize that he's shutting up two adversaries together in a single prison cell? From one prison to another, from loathing to sheer hatred. There's no hope for me, son, unless you can succeed, unless you can rescue me.

I glance at him as he works, selling peanuts, melon seeds, popcorn, and chickpeas, throwing the piastres into a half-open drawer. He wallowed so long in a life of sin that he's probably dreaming now about going back to the habit that prison cured him of. If it weren't for Abbas, his stipulation that we divide the earnings between us, we'd have been ruined again by now. That permanent look of melancholy he has! Except when customers come in, the gloomy mask never falls from his face. He's aged so much he looks older than he really is, and that means I've aged too. *The years in prison. The night of the raid when detectives kept slapping my face . . . Ah, the bastards, not one of them came to see us! Al-Hilaly is as big a bastard as Tariq Ramadan. Detained at the police station just one night and then released. We bore the punishment alone. Our neighbors say the law is only hard on the poor, and they accuse us and gloat over our misfortune. They do business with us, though. My only hope is that you succeed, son.*

Time passes. We have nothing to say to each other. The fire of hatred is stronger than the heat of an oven. *When I clean this hateful old house, or when I cook, I feel so miserable. Why am I condemned to this wretched life? I used to be pretty, all piety and decorum. Fate. Fate. Who will explain the meaning of fate to me? But God is on the side of the patient, the long-suffering. My destiny is in your hands, Abbas. I'll never forget your visit that night, on the feast of the birthday of Sidi al-Sharany,* and your words, which relieved my torment and opened up the gates of heaven: "My play has been accepted at last!"*

I hadn't been so happy since he was a young boy. Even his father's face shone with joy. *What have you got to do*

---

*A holy man to whom a small local mosque was dedicated.

with it? I don't understand. You hate him just as you hate me. All right, he has grown up to be a dramatist, contrary to what you predicted. To you his idealism was stupidity, but good will always win out. His strength and energy will sweep away the dross of riffraff like you.

I don't like autumn, except that it brings us closer to opening night. *Where do they come from, these clouds that blot out the light? Isn't it enough that the clouds cover my heart?* I hear the man speaking to me:

"Look."

I see Tariq Ramadan coming toward the shop, looking as if he were someone bringing news of an accident in the street. *Has he come to congratulate us or to gloat over us?*

He stands there in front of us, his greeting lost in the empty air.

"Our loyal friend, paying us a visit for the very first time," I say.

I pay no attention to his excuses until I hear him intone, "I have bad news."

"Bad news doesn't mean a thing to us."

"Even if it's about Mr. Abbas Younis?"

My blood turns cold, but I remain as calm as I can. "His play's been accepted," I say proudly.

"It's nothing but a deplorable joke. What do you know about the play!" He goes on to summarize it, citing the most important episodes, and ends by saying, "That's it— everything!"

Hiding my anxiety with my head spinning, I reply, "What do you mean? You hate Abbas!"

"Go see the play for yourselves!"

"You've been blinded by hate."

"By the crime, you mean."

"The only criminal is you."

"Tahiya's murderer must be brought to justice!"

"You're a low-down crook yourself. Why don't you just get lost!"

"How can they say that prison teaches people manners?" he says, laughing sarcastically.

I grab a handful of chickpeas and throw them at him. He draws back jeering, then leaves.

What has Abbas written? What has he done? My son would never kill anyone or be disloyal; at least he wouldn't betray his mother. He's an angel.

The man and I look at each other. I must haul myself out of this unending loneliness. "Tariq is lying," I say.

"Why should he lie?"

"He still hates my son."

"But there's the play, too."

"Go and see Abbas!"

"I'll see him, sooner or later."

"But you aren't making any move."

"There's no great rush."

He exasperates me; like Tariq, he has no love for Abbas.

"He has to know what's going on behind his back!" I yell.

"And if he confesses?"

"You'll get an explanation for everything."

"I wonder!"

"A real murderer doesn't expose himself."

"I don't know."

"Go see him, that's the main thing!"

"Of course I'll go."

"Do you want me to go?"

"You haven't got anything fit to wear."

"Then it's up to you to go. That crook is lying."

"He detested the way we lived. He was so idealistic you'd think he wasn't my son at all, but someone else's bastard," the man says. Then he seems to change his mind. "But he didn't double-cross us. And why would he kill Tahiya?"

"You're asking me?"

"I'm thinking aloud."

"You believe what the wretch said!" I shout.

"You believe him, too."

I press my lips together to hold back the tears. "We've got to hear what Abbas has to say."

"As a matter of fact, I don't believe him."

"You're raving!"

"Damn you!"

"I was damned the day I got tied to you!"

"The same applies to me."

"I used to be pretty."

"Your father was a postman, but mine was employed on the Shamashirgi family estate."

"Which means that he was only a servant."

"I come from a family."

"What about your mother?"

"Just like you."

"You're a windbag. You don't want to go, do you?"

"I'll go when it suits me." Then, changing his tone, he says, "He's most likely to be at home in the afternoon."

Praying for patience, I surrender to his indolence, though doubt is killing me from my feet upward. *What is it they say about the best people? A rose among the ruins—in a community of thieves and their victims. The man has bought me material to make a dress so I could go out, but*

I've put off making it. I'll start cutting it out right away and then see about getting it made. The son of a whore insults me about my origins. But Abbas could never betray his mother. He may have scorned everything else, but not my love. Love is stronger than evil itself.

My happy childhood home in al-Tambakshiyya, where the sun always shone, even in the winter, even at night, the home of Halima, beautiful daughter of a beautiful mother and a father who always brought home nice things, things we liked. "Let her go on," my mother used to say to him. "Education will give her the opportunity of a lifetime. I wish I'd had the chance." That was before he died.

Our good cousin, Amm Ahmad Burgal, came visiting one day. "The girl's father is dead, and keeping her on at school has become a hardship."

Mother asked, "So what should we do, Amm Ahmad?"

"She has a certificate, and she's clever. She must find work. They'll be looking for a cashier at the theater."

"Would that kind of work suit you?" asked Mother.

I answered with apprehension, "I suppose practice will make up for what I lack in experience."

"El Shamashirgi is a friend of al-Hilaly Bey. Your father never worked for him, but he's the biggest man in the district and he's been our benefactor. If you mention his name when you have your interview, I'll take care of the rest."

And thus I was poised, the first time I set foot in the theater, to enter a different world. It was a marvelous place. It even had a special smell. Amm Ahmad shrank in stature: his work there was not very important. Summoned to meet the producer, I entered his magnificent inner sanctum in my old shoes and my simple white dress, and walked timidly, step by step, toward him. His tall frame, piercing eyes, and masterful expression made him almost awe-inspiring; and he scrutinized me at such length that I thought I'd nearly die. Finally, he gave me a sheet of paper to see how fast I could write the numbers.

"You'll need some practice before you can take over the job," he said in his domineering voice. "What's your name?"

"Halima al-Kabsh,"* I said shyly.

"Al-Kabsh!" The name made him smile. "What of it? You're a good deal more attractive than the actresses in our company. I'll want to examine you after you finish your training."

So I set to work in a burst of enthusiasm, inspired not by concern for my future, but by the wish to please that wonderful enchanter. I described him to my mother, and she said that was what the upper classes were like. If I could only win his approval, I thought, what a lucky break it would be for me.

When I stood before him, I was panting. "You're the jewel of the company, Halima. God is beautiful and He loves beauty." At what point did he begin to fondle me? Sunlight piercing the window shone full in my face; out in the street someone was playing a dance on a rustic flute. Gasping, I shoved his huge hand away, and said, "No, sir. I'm a respectable girl." His laugh made my ears ring.

In the silence that ensued in that vast locked room, my protests expired. A rush of hot breath, a cunning approach, and all my determined resolutions were confounded. It was a nightmare of the kind that draws tears but wins no sympathy. In the world outside that room other people came and went. My mother died before she found out.

In the afternoon he gets a move on at last. My taut

---

* Al-Kabsh—the ram.

nerves relax a little. I'm clutching at a straw, but what can I expect? I've got to get the dress ready, just so I can do something. My son will tell his secrets to me, but not to that despicable man. What have I got left now except Abbas?

The disappointments came with—no, even before—the opium. My expectations—all dead and buried now—had been so sweet. I remember one night when he drained the dregs from his glass, leered drunkenly, pointed to the room next to the reception room, and said, "My mother used to go into that room alone with the master sergeant."

The disclosure was so brutal it shocked me. Abbas was tucked up in his cradle, asleep. I couldn't believe my ears. "You're drunk, Karam."

He shook his head. "She used to warn me to stay in my own room."

"That wasn't right."

He interrupted me. "I don't like hypocrisy. You're a hypocrite, Halima."

"God forgive her. Do you still feel resentful toward her?"

"Why should I hold it against her?"

"I don't understand you."

"Your husband is unrivaled among men. He doesn't believe in any man-made lies." *What does he mean? He's not a bad husband, but he makes fun of everything. He ridicules my faith, the things I hold sacred, my principles. Doesn't that man respect anything at all? He's just exposed his mother shamelessly.* "And that's lucky for both of us," he went on, "because if it weren't so, I'd have divorced you on our wedding night."

I was pierced to the heart and tears welled up in my eyes. I'd just received the second cruel blow of my life.

"You can't help it, Halima. When are you going to become liberated?"

"You're wicked and cruel."

"Don't bother using words like that. They don't mean anything."

He told me how his mother had been madly in love with the policeman, how she'd neglected him, and how he'd grown up "liberated," thanks to her dissipations. "I owe everything to her," he said finally, with a drunken leer.

He was like some frightful object hung around my neck. I was living with a force that had no principles. On what basis, then, was I to deal with him? The letdown came before the opium. The opium found no spirit left to crush.

When I catch sight of him coming back, my heart leaps in spite of its aversion. He looks even older in the street than he does in the shop. He sits down without looking at me and I can't help asking, "What did he say to you?"

"He left the flat with a suitcase, and no one knows where he went," he says without emotion.

Ah! What instant trepidation, instant torment! Is there no end to calamity?

"Why didn't he let us know?"

"He doesn't think about us."

Pointing to the four corners of the shop, I say, "He treated us better than we deserve."

"He wants to forget us now."

"You should have gone to see al-Hilaly."

He answers me with a look full of scorn and disgust, and I, to provoke him, tell him he doesn't know how to act.

"I'd like to bash your head in!"

"Have you gone back on opium?"

"Only government ministers can afford it these days." He lowers his voice. "Al-Hilaly doesn't know where he is either."

"You visited him?" I ask anxiously.

"He has no idea where he is."

"My God! Did he move out of his flat?"

"No."

"Maybe there's a woman involved."

"That's what a woman like you would think."

"What can I say to someone like you? You don't care about him at all."

My misery is too much for me. I weep bitter tears.

Wearing my new dress, an old shawl around my shoulders, and without any hope, I go to Abbas's building, where my despair is confirmed when I question the doorman.

"You must know something about what happened?"

"Nothing at all."

I don't have the courage to go to the theater. My reluctant footsteps direct me homeward. I stop on the way and visit Sidi al-Sharany to seek his miraculous help, then come back to my prison cell to find the man joking and laughing with a customer, quite unconcerned. I sit down defeated, my spirits at lowest ebb, my endurance gone. "Do something," I manage to say to him. "Don't you have any plan in mind?"

"I'd like to kill you; someday I will kill you!"

"Go and see al-Hilaly again."

"Go yourself," he interrupts. "He gives special attention to his slave girls."

"The truth is, I'm your mother's victim! My torture comes from her grave. She's the one who made you such a brute!"

"Compared with you, she was a decent woman."

This theater—where I'd been raped and no one held out a helping hand—was the backdrop of my torment and my love. While its lofty dome echoed with admirable sentiments, phrased in the sweetest way, my blood spilled on its comfortable seats, the blood of my secret, strangling me. I was lost, lost. He wasn't even aware of my adoration. Nothing mattered to him. He probably even forgot my name.

"You're avoiding me! I can't take any more. I have to see you."

"Is there anything you need?"

"What? Have you forgotten? I've lost everything!"

"Don't exaggerate. I don't like it. What happened isn't worth troubling your head over." Tears welled up in my eyes. "No," he said, "no. Nothing that goes on in this theater should ever be taken to heart."

"But what about me? Don't you see what it means to me? Don't leave me!"

"The whole thing is much simpler than you imagine. No harm done. Cheer up—for the sake of your work and your future. Forget what happened. It's no use asking me to keep remembering it."

He was as hard as granite. My aversion for him was as strong as my love had been. *Abandoned, alone, in torment. Someday my aunt would guess the secret of my suffering. What could I expect from a world that knows no God?*

Late in the afternoon I go to the actors' coffeehouse, where I catch sight of Fuad Shalaby smoking a narghile and make a beeline for him. I may be the last person he's expecting to see, but he stands to welcome me and pulls up a seat for me.

"I should have come to visit you. Damn all the work!"

I ignore his words. "Nobody's visited us. Not that it makes any difference. I'm so upset over Abbas's disappearance that I had to come."

"There's no need to get upset." He smiles. "It's quite obvious he left to get away from spongers. It's a good thing he did. He's probably working on his next play."

254 / Naguib Mahfouz

"But he should have told me."

"Try to overlook his negligence. Don't worry. You're still as pretty as ever, Halima. How is Karam?"

"He's alive and active, pursuing his hobby of making mankind miserable."

He laughs, in a way that gets on my nerves, so much so that I get up and leave the coffeehouse.

This time I have the courage and the determination to go to the theater. I ask to see the producer and enter the room, the selfsame room—same leather couch, same man.

No, he's different: there's nothing left of the old self but the depravity, which seems to have aged him more than prison has us. *Which of us two is more to blame for my unhappiness?* He rises to greet me. "Welcome, welcome! I'm delighted to see you looking so well," he exclaims.

"Well?" I retort as I take a seat.

"As befits the mother of a successful playwright."

"At the moment, he's the cause of my suffering."

"That's suffering for no reason whatsoever. I have good news: He's contacted me by phone."

I interrupt, aflame with joy, "Where is he?"

"I don't know. That's his secret; let him keep it if he wants to. The important thing is that he's busy on a new play."

"Has he left his job?"

"Yes. It's a risk—but he's sure of himself, and I'm confident, too."

"He didn't bother to get in touch with me?"

"Well, he wants to avoid being interrogated about his play; that's what I think."

"Certain suspicions are being voiced, over and over. What do you think about it all?"

"A play is a work of art, and art is a fantasy, no matter how much it borrows from the truth."

"But what about people's assumptions?"

"The audience doesn't see anything in it. To think otherwise is idiocy, and if it weren't for Tariq's stupidity . . ."

"He's his enemy, damn him!" I interject.

"Now, I want you to cheer up!"

"I heard that Karam Younis is asking for your hand?"

"Yes, he is."

"The damage can be repaired."

"No, I refuse to go along with that kind of deception."

"You mean you're going to let him know the truth?"

"I think that's the best way."

"You're a remarkable girl! So many people are without principles these days. Are you going to tell him who it was?"

"That's not important."

"It would be better not to."

As I enter the cafeteria, Ahmad Burgal sees me and shouts, "Welcome!"

I sit in front of him, silent, while he begins to make a sandwich and tea for me. Just two people on this earth have brought about whatever happiness we have known: Ahmad Burgal and Umm Hany. Recollections come flooding in upon me: a cup of tea, a sandwich, a little flirtation, and the music of a flute heard in hell, like clear drops of rain falling on a pile of garbage.

Amm Ahmad says, "Abbas's success is a good omen. It'll make up for the past."

"But he's left without a word."

"Don't be upset. No one here is worried about it."

"And Tariq Ramadan?"

"He's half crazy."

*   *   *

I went through a terrible new ordeal. I'd been determined to confess—I was respectable and modest and I hated deception—but at the last moment I'd been silenced by fear. Karam seemed such a commendable young man, serious and loving. Would I lose him? Fear kept me silent until the door had closed on us. My weakness appalled me, I wept. The truth now stood between us, naked, taut, ready to serve any purpose. "I am a criminal," I whispered. "I just couldn't bring myself to tell you beforehand."

The grave look in his eyes baffled me. What I'd dreaded was taking place. "I was so afraid of losing you. You must believe me: I was raped."

I lowered my eyes, frightened by his agitation. I said things and he said things, but our words were lost in the intense heat of our agony. His voice was engraved on my consciousness: "The past doesn't matter to me." I cried all the more, but some unexpected ray of hope had appeared to me. I told him that he was gallant, that I would dedicate my life to making him happy. I dried my eyes. "How easy it is for the innocent to be lost," I whispered.

With a heavy heart, I return to the prison cell and sit down. I'll tell him about meeting Fuad Shalaby and nothing more. I won't offer him any relief. He doesn't love Abbas. He pretends to be quite disinterested in what I found out. If he only suffered as I do. The snacks we sell help other people while away the time, but our only distraction is exchanging abuses.

My letdown had continued step by step. A new vice was threatening the foundations of our home.

"Opium is a terrible thing. It will destroy you."

"I'm grateful for it, at any rate."

"You're running away from reality. And you're doing it faster and faster."

"Again, I say thanks to it."

"I'm doing my utmost. And there's Abbas to think about, your beloved son." He takes another sip of black tea. "My salary by itself isn't enough to keep the house going."

"You have the rent from Ramadan's room."

"And even that's not enough. Life is so expensive."

I understand you now. And I'm afraid of you. You aren't what I thought you were at the outset of our life together. You've lost everything, even the potency you used to boast about. We've moved into separate rooms. Between us there's neither love nor desire! You're the only thing left, Abbas. Pay no heed to what your father says. Don't believe him. He's sick. It's a good thing you're alone most of the time. God be with you—He is our sufficiency. Be an angel. Let your friends, your books, and the theater be your teachers. Be my son and the son of other good people. You're the only light in this old house steeped in darkness. Be unique in every way.

He steals a furtive glance at me now and again, hoping I might divulge what I know. Never. I'll challenge him to hate me more.

"Winter's coming. How can we stay in this open shop?" he says.

"When Abbas succeeds, our luck will change," I answer confidently.

"When Abbas succeeds!" he retorts, bitterness in every syllable.

"I'll go live with him," I say defiantly, "and he won't begrudge you an overcoat or a woolen cloak!"

*　　*　　*

The red cafeteria was always the same; it laughed at the shifts and changes in its patronage, hearing most of what was said, but believing no one. "Here's your sandwich. I'll get your tea ready," Amm Ahmad Burgal said.

A young man came and sat on the stool next to me. He ordered beans and a sandwich. He was one of the theater people, it appeared, but he wasn't one of the actors. A young man, attractive except for his large head and nose. Amm Ahmad asked me, "Any news about a flat, Miss Halima?"

In front of the stranger, I answered somewhat diffidently, "Searching for gold is easier."

"Are you looking for a flat?" the young man said abruptly.

I replied that I was, and Amm Ahmad introduced us.

"Getting married?" the young man went on to ask boldly.

Ah, the seduction's begun: Here in this theater it gets off the ground quickly and does not stop short of violence. The quarry is brought down to the accompaniment of a native flute.

"I own an old house that has two floors."

"Is each floor an apartment?"

"No. It isn't divided into flats."

Amm Ahmad asked him if I could have one floor to myself, and he said I could.

"Won't that inconvenience the family?" I asked.

"I live there alone," he declared.

When I turned away from him, indignant at his boldness, he went on cunningly: "You and your family would find yourselves quite safe there."

I thanked him and said no more. *He hadn't made a bad*

impression on me. What did he want? He knew nothing about my tragedy, my love, or my distrust of mankind.

I say that I'm going to Umm Hany's small flat in al-Imam, where Tariq Ramadan is staying. She receives me warmly, but I have to wait until Tariq gets up. He comes out of his room with his hair standing on end, looking like the devil.

"Welcome," he remarks, with unseemly sarcasm.

I ask him right off the bat, "I believe you went to see Abbas before he left?"

"Right."

"It's not far-fetched to suggest that you said things that made him leave."

"He felt trapped, so he skipped out."

His insolence brings tears of fury to my eyes.

"Don't you know the meaning of mercy?" screams Umm Hany. "What's all this talk that's been going around? I watched Tahiya dying; I saw Abbas crazy with grief!"

Her words astonish me, and I want to know if the talk that's being spread around fits with what she saw.

"There's nothing to it!"

"He wouldn't kill her before your very eyes, you idiot," says Tariq.

"To suggest Abbas is a murderer is lunacy."

"His confession is being played out on the stage night after night."

"Thanks to him you've become an actor that audiences applaud even more than Ismail," says Umm Hany.

"Thanks to his crime—the crime that made him run away."

"He's staying in a quiet place," I say stubbornly, "to finish his new play."

"His new play! Don't fool yourself, Umm Abbas!"

Ah—in those days he was reasonable and obliging in spite of everything.

"What do you think, Halima? Tariq Ramadan wants to rent a room from us."

I objected. "No. No. Let him stay where he is."

"He's had a row with Umm Hany and has to leave her place. He's wandering around with no place to go, and things get more expensive every day."

"It won't be very pleasant having a stranger in the house."

"He needs us. And we need the money."

"He's no better than a tramp."

"He'd hoped we'd be kindhearted, especially you. We've got enough empty rooms to house an army."

Grudgingly I gave my consent. I had no use for him at all—a no-good actor living off the sweat of women. But I never imagined he'd do what he did to us.

Umm Hany pays us a surprise visit in the shop the day after I visited her. She evidently wants to apologize for the rude way her man had treated me. Like Tariq, she's in her fifties, but she's still buxom, not bad-looking, and has money.

"They're all talking about the success of the play," she remarks. "It's the biggest hit the theater's ever had."

"But the playwright doesn't want to show himself," I say sadly.

"He'll show up when he finishes his new play." The woman is silent for a while, then says, "What's being said is really absurd. But then Tariq is crazy!"

"Wouldn't it have been better for him to kill his mother?" Karam says sarcastically.

I have always had a liking for Umm Hany, and the fact

that she is related to my husband hasn't lessened my affection for her.

The house in al-Tambakshiyya, crowded with people, smelling of rubber, as though it were a bus. My aunt cleared a corner to receive Amm Ahmad Burgal.

"Don't forget the provisions, because next to God it's them we depend on."

"I came for something more important than that!" he said, more serious than usual.

"Open the bag, you snake charmer."

"It's about Halima."

My aunt looked at him and then at me, while the blood mounted in my cheeks.

"What! A husband?"

"That just about sums it up."

She looked at him inquiringly, and he said, "Karam Younis."

"And who's Karam Younis?" asked my aunt.

"He's the company prompter."

"What does that mean?"

"He's a respectable employee of the theater."

"Do you think he's suitable, Amm Ahmad?"

"Yes, I do. But the important thing is what the bride thinks."

"The bride is a real beauty, as you know. But we are poor, Amm Ahmad."

It was my turn to speak. I'd been absolutely shattered by the bloody secret I was harboring; I didn't love the bridegroom, but I had no aversion toward him—a presentable young man. Perhaps he'd give me peace of mind, even happiness. Beleaguered by my aunt's stare, I mumbled, "I don't know anything about him worth mentioning."

"He has a job, he owns a house, and has a good reputation."

"By the goodness of God!" cried my aunt. Although she loved me, she'd be glad to be rid of me. As for me, I wanted to escape from that overcrowded house; and since Sirhan al-Hilaly was so rotten, there was no hope for me in that direction.

Life was unbearable, and hunger was knocking at the door.

"I've found the way to shut you up," he said, eyeing me disdainfully.

"Have you finally been cured of that hell of a drug?"

"Al-Hilaly has agreed to hold their soirees in our old house!" I didn't grasp his meaning, so he added, "We'll prepare a room for them to play cards in, and then we'll be on easy street."

"A gambling den?" I said, dismayed.

"You always describe things in the worst way. What would it be except a gathering of friends?" I protested, but he interrupted: "Don't you want a good life?"

"Yes, and a clean one, too!"

"If it's good, it will be clean. The only unclean thing is hypocrisy."

"And there's Abbas to think about," I murmured uneasily.

"I own this house, not Abbas. Your son is crazy. But surely you care whether he has enough to eat and clothes to wear!" he shouted.

The sun is hidden so often this autumn that I am grounded in melancholy. This narrow street sees at least one funeral going to Sidi al-Sharany every day. Whenever the man is not occupied with customers he starts talking to himself. I daydream of the things Abbas will do for me, but he has nothing to dream about.

Why don't we keep track of the happy moments, so that afterward we will believe them? Is he the same man? Was he really sincere? Is he the one who said, "I am indebted to Amm Ahmad Burgal for a joy that is almost more than a man can bear"?

I moved my head coquettishly. "Don't exaggerate!"

"Halima, who can be happier than a man whose heart has not beaten in vain?" He said it in a tone of voice that has vanished forever. Although I didn't love him, I loved his words, and their fervor warmed me.

On the appointed day waves of joy and fear roll over me. I go to the Indian bath, Umm Hany supplies me with a dress, a coat, and a pair of shoes, and I return from the hairdresser with a glorious halo, newly created from hair that had been neglected for a long time. The man looks at me disdainfully. "So you still have that weakness for playing the whore. Why don't you exploit it—in these illustriously dissolute days?"

I am determined at any cost not to ruffle the serenity of the evening. We go to the theater, where we are received with the respect we deserve. Sirhan al-Hilaly fixes me with an admiring stare.

"How is it that I don't see the playwright?" I say.

"He hasn't come, but I've told you enough about it."

My first hopes are shattered; and the internal radiance I'd been building up all day through a sense of renewed youth is extinguished. We go to see Amm Ahmad, who gives us tea and a sandwich as he always did. "It's like the old days," he remarks, laughing.

What are you talking about, Amm Ahmad? I wish it had never been. Even the one comforting result of it is absent. This place sets my nerves on edge and intensifies my sadness. At the proper time, though, we enter the theater and I am suddenly delighted to find it packed. "It's a success!"

I don't listen to his replies. The curtain is being raised on the old house. Events unfold one after another, and my agonies come to life before my eyes; now nothing is left of them except the memory of heaving sighs. Once more I find myself in hell. I condemn myself more than I ever have before. *That's when I should have left him,* I say to myself, *that's when I should have refused.* I am no longer the victim I thought I was.

But what is all this new damnation, this flood of crimes that nobody was aware of, this strange way I am being portrayed. Is it what he really thinks of me? What is this, son? You misunderstand your mother more than your father does and are even more unjust. Did I object to your marrying Tahiya out of jealousy and selfishness? What jealousy, what selfishness? No, no. This is hell itself. You almost make your father my victim. He was never the victim of anything except his mother. Do you see me as a prostitute, a madam? Do you think I'm the pimp who drove your wife to the tourist, greedy for his money? Is this a fantasy or is it hell? You are killing me, Abbas. You have made me the villain of your play. And the people are clapping—they're clapping!

The life has been knocked out of me. We're invited to the party in the cafeteria. "Shall we join them or leave?" the man asks. Feeling that he is trying to provoke and ridicule me, I challenge back: "Why shouldn't we join the party?"

But in spirit I cannot. I'm in a burning stupor; my head resounds with brawling voices as strange faces undulate before my eyes, shouting and laughing for no apparent reason. *My head is going to burst. The end of the world is approaching. Let the day of judgment come. I'll never obtain a fair judgment except before God. You murdered and betrayed and committed suicide! When will I see you? Will I ever see you again?*

We reach the old house at dawn. Throwing myself on the couch in the hall while he lights the heater, I hear him ask, "Did you like the play?"

"The audience liked it," I say lukewarmly.

"And the subject?"

"It's a powerful plot."

"Weren't we depicted as we really are?"

"Don't start thinking like that spiteful Tariq Ramadan."

"It's even more true than the real facts."

"There's no connection between the way I appear in that play and the real facts," I retort angrily. He lets off a repulsive laugh, while I suppress my anguish. "It's just a fantasy!" I say.

"All of them just as we know them in real life."

"It's largely imagination and very little actual fact."

"Then why did he portray you as he did?"

"That's his business."

"I thought that he loved and respected you."

"There's no doubt about that."

"You give yourself away with that bitchy look of yours."

"I know I'm right."

"Even Tariq! I never imagined you'd sink to such depths."

"Spare me your filthy thoughts!" I shout.

"That's the boy who threw us into prison."

"He wasn't describing himself, he was describing you!"

"How virtuous he made himself out to be!"

Fighting down my despair, I burst out, "When he comes back I'm going to leave this damn house and live with him!" and rush to my room. Behind the closed door my own tears strike me dumb. *How is it you don't understand your mother, Abbas?*

He came reeling, tumbling down the stairs, almost collapsing from fatigue and drunkenness. Then he spotted me. "Some eau de cologne!" he shouted. "I've had it!"

I went into my room to get the eau de cologne for him, and he followed me.

"Here you are."

"Thanks. I drank more than I should have."

"And you've had bad luck from the beginning of the evening."

After a while, he pulled himself together, looked up at me, then went to the door and bolted it. I prepared to resist.

"Halima, you're magnificent!" he said.

"Let's go back upstairs." He came close to me and I drew back scowling.

"Are you going to be faithful to that lout?"

"I'm a respectable woman and a mother."

I made a rush for the door and got it open. For a moment he hung back, then he stepped outside and left the house.

All of them tried to seduce me, but I refused them. A whore?! It's true that I was raped once, and that I slept with your father, though not for long, before I turned celibate. I am a nun, my son, not a whore. Was it your father who painted this false picture for you? Desolate woman that I am, with wretched luck—I have no other hope but

*you. How could you picture me like that? I'll tell you
everything! But when are you going to come back?*

At night those carousers would slink into our old house,
their shamelessness polluting the street that led to Sidi al-
Sharany. My heart sank as I read their debauched looks
and I worried about Abbas in his room. *But you are a
jewel, son. You must not be stifled in the mire of poverty.*
I'd put on a cheerful front as a welcome mat and take them
to the room on the upper floor that we'd furnished with
borrowed money. I was supposed to be the barmaid and
serve them food and drinks; little did I understand that we
were at the beginning of a slippery path downward.

"Don't be alarmed, dear. They're your father's friends.
All men do that."

"But, Mother, what have you got to do with it?"

"They're my colleagues from the theater and it wouldn't
be right for me to neglect them."

"A good, safe place," Sirhan al-Hilaly said, beaming as
he took his seat at the table, where Ismail was shuffling the
cards.

"Tahiya isn't allowed to sit next to Tariq," Fuad Shalaby said with a chuckle.

Karam stood behind the cash box at the edge of the table
and there was a laughing remark from Tariq: "A votive
offering box, Mr. Karam Younis?"

"No voice should be raised above the sound of battle!"*

Karam was dissolving some opium in black tea. What a
beginning that knew no end!

I have returned myself to my prison cell, just as I have

*This was a sentence used during the wars with Israel, and it has a special
connotation.

returned the clothes I wore to the theater to their owner. He sits here, his face morose and blank; sells peanuts and melon seeds and joins the customers in complaining about the times. Almost to myself, I murmur, "The play's a success, that's one consolation."

"One can't judge before a week has passed."

"What counts is the audience, their excitement, the effect it has on them."

"I wonder how much al-Hilaly paid him for it."

"The first work always brings in the lowest price. Abbas doesn't care about money." He bursts into that boisterous laugh of his, for which I curse him with all my heart.

In the vastness of his throne room, the evil deity gazed upon us smiling, "Welcome, Halima. I suppose your son is offering us a new play?"

"That's right."

"The last one was worthless," he said, addressing Abbas.

"I always profit from your comments," replied Abbas.

"I'd like to encourage you, at least for your mother's sake."

As the weeks roll by, it becomes apparent how successful the play is. Never has there been such a sellout at the theater. And the weeks turn into months. When will the playwright appear? He can think what he likes and let me suffer—but where is he? "I should think the people at the theater might have heard by this time from our absent one," I remark, loudly enough so that he has to hear.

"The last time I went there was ten days ago."

Tired of defending myself against his tongue, I make no demands of him. He has trotted off to the theater from time to time, whereas I haven't ventured to go since the opening night. On the next morning he goes again. A warm day, with the sun shining, and my heart flutters with consuming hope.

I could imagine miracles and strange happenings, but never that Abbas would marry Tahiya. Now Abbas was going to leave and Tariq Ramadan would be staying. Where was heavenly justice?

"Abbas, she's at least ten years older than you! She has a certain reputation and a history. Don't you understand what that means?"

He smiled. "Unfortunately you don't understand what love is," he said smugly. Bitterness welled in my soul, bringing back my buried sadness. "We're going to start a new life," he added.

"No one can escape his past."

"In spite of everything Tahiya is virtuous."

I wasn't being fair, I had forgotten about myself, but I wanted him to have a better lot in life. That's all there was to it.

Tahiya visited me, looking subdued, but determined. "Don't stand in the way of my happiness," she entreated me.

"You are stealing innocence."

"I'll be a devoted wife to him."

"You!"

The sharpness of my voice made her turn pale with anger. "Every woman in the theater began with Sirhan al-Hilaly!" she retorted.

My heart shrank. So they all knew or inferred what they didn't know. It was as if she were threatening me! I detested her. But he would remain my son, in spite of everything.

Surely, the man is later than usual? The last beams of sunlight are just leaving the walls along this narrow street.

What's keeping him? Has he at last discovered the hiding place and gone there straightway? Will they come home together? I can see his fine-featured face smiling as he apologizes. I will not believe that this torture can go on forever. The play may well have pointed out the sources of my weakness, but I've always kept my heart clean. Haven't I atoned, then, sufficiently for that weakness? Who could have imagined that this kind of life would become the lot of the beautiful, chaste Halima? My heart holds nothing now but tolerance and love. Oh God, I accept your judgment. I have such compassion in my heart that it even pities Karam in his misery. I'll even forgive his brutality to me. When he returns with my beloved absent one's arm tucked under his, I'll forgive him everything.

Elation floods my being, but the feeling diminishes with the passing of time. A customer remarks as he leaves with his package, "You're in another world, Umm Abbas."

From the mosque the call to evening prayer reaches my ears as darkness creeps over the short winter day. There must be a reason for his delay. He isn't worth all this anxious waiting. What's keeping him? The candle splutters in the winter wind; I stand up, not intending to sit down again. My mood has altered; he has deceived me unmercifully. My patience is worn out, and I'll have to go and look for him.

The first person I meet at the theater door is Fuad Shalaby, who approaches me with unaccustomed tenderness, holding out his hands to me.

"I hope it's false news," he says.

"What news?" I say as my last glimmer of hope disappears. The man doesn't seem to know what to say, so he remains silent. "Is it about Abbas?"

He nods his head, saying nothing more, and I lose consciousness.

When I come to, I find myself on the couch in the cafeteria and Amm Ahmad is taking care of me. Fuad Shalaby and Tariq Ramadan are also there. Amm Ahmad breaks the news to me in a funereal voice and ends by saying, "No one believes it."

Fuad Shalaby takes me home is his car. On the way he wonders aloud, "If he's committed suicide, where is his body?"

"Then why did he write the note?"

"That's his secret," he answers. "We'll find out in good time."

But I know his secret as I know my own heart and I know my luck; he has killed himself. Evil is playing flute music for Abbas.

Abbas Karam Younis

Loneliness and the old house were the two companions of my childhood. I knew it inside out: the big, arched portals, the door with its small hinged panes of red, blue, and brown stained glass, the reception-room window with its iron bars, the upstairs and downstairs rooms with their high ceilings and painted wooden rafters, their floors covered with Masarany tiles, the old, shabby couches, mattresses, mats, and carpets, the undaunted tribes of mice, cockroaches, and wall geckos, the roof, crisscrossed with clotheslines like streetcar and trolley-bus wires, overlooking other roofs that on summer evenings were crowded with women and children. I roamed around the house alone, my voice echoing from its corners as I repeated my lessons, recited a poem, did a part from some play, or sang. Looking down on the narrow street for what might have been hours at a time, following the flow of people, I'd yearn for a friend to play with. A boy would call to me, "Come on down!"

"The door is locked, and my father has the key!"

I got used to being alone night and day; I wasn't afraid of anything, not even evil spirits.

"The sons of Adam are the only devils there are," my father would say.

"Be an angel," my mother would hasten to add.

When I had nothing to do, I would amuse myself by chasing the mice, the geckos, or the cockroaches.

My mother told me once that when I was a baby she used to take me in a leather cot to the theater and set me on a bench in the ticket booth. "I often nursed you in the theater," she said. I don't remember those times, of course, but I do recall events from a stretch of time when I must have been four years old. I used to wander around the theater in front or backstage, where, among other things, I'd listen to the actors memorizing their parts. My ears were filled with lovely songs and speeches—and with wicked oaths and blasphemies giving me an education I'd never have acquired from my parents, who were always either sleeping or working. On the opening night of every new play I was there with my father, half the time bedazzled, the other half asleep. It was about that time that I was given my first picture book, called *Ibn al-Sultan and the Witch,* a present from Fuad Shalaby.

That was how I came to understand heroes and villains in plays. Neither of my parents had time to give me any guidance; my father took no interest in education in any case, while my mother was content to repeat her only piece of advice—"Be an angel"—explaining that to be an angel was to love good, not to harm other people, and to have a clean body and clean clothes. My real tutors were, first, the theater, then books, when their time came, and finally people who had no relation to my parents.

As soon as I started school I loved it: giving me so many companions, it rescued me from my loneliness. I had to be self-reliant, though, at every step. I'd wake up early in the morning, eat my cold breakfast of cheese and boiled eggs from a plate that had been covered with a napkin the night before, dress, and leave the house quietly so I wouldn't arouse my sleeping parents. I'd return in the afternoon to find them getting ready to leave for the theater. I'd stay alone doing my homework, then amuse myself with games or books, at first only looking at the pictures, then reading the printed words—I'll never forget the generosity of Amm Abdu, the secondhand bookseller, who crouched on the sidewalk beside Sidi al-Sharany Mosque—and finally, after a supper of cheese and halva, I'd go to bed.

So I never saw my parents except for a while before sunset, and even part of this brief period was lost as they got ready to go out. Perhaps because there was so little intimacy or attention given to me, I was all the more attached to them. I yearned for them. My mother's beauty, sweetness, and tenderness bewitched me and I was enthralled by a vision of that angelic nature she urged me to acquire. His gentle way of playing with me and his hearty laughter likewise made my father seem wonderful. He was full of jokes, full of fun, and the limited time we had together was never spoiled by instructions, threats, or warnings. There was only an occasional reminder. "Enjoy being alone," he used to say. "You're the king of the castle. What do you want more than that? The only son, independent of everyone. That's what your father was like, and you'll be even more wonderful."

"He's an angel," Mother would hasten to add. "Be an angel, dear."

"Did Grandfather and Grandmother leave you alone, too?" I asked him once.

"Your grandfather?" he replied. "He left me before I ever knew him. And your grandmother—she worked at home."

Mother glowered, and I sensed that these words carried a secret meaning. "Your grandfather died young and your grandmother joined him, so your father was left alone," she explained.

"In this same house?"

"Yes."

"If these walls could speak, they would tell you the most fantastic tales," Father said.

It was a lonely house, but a harmonious one. At that time Father and Mother were an agreeable couple, or so, as I saw them in the gathering twilight, they always appeared to me. They shared conversation, jokes, and a deep affection for me. My father had a tendency to express himself a little freely, but Mother would stop him with a warning look, which I noticed sometimes and wondered about. The moment of leave-taking was painful and I would await Thursday with dwindling patience, for that was the night I could go with them to see a play.

As my learning increased, enabling me to read more, I asked for more pocket money to buy books, until I had accumulated a library of secondhand children's books. "Aren't you satisfied with going to the theater every week?" Father asked.

But I wasn't satisfied. My dreams took me far away to new horizons. One day I went so far as to tell him that I wanted to write plays!

He guffawed. "Dream about being an actor! It's preferable and more profitable."

n idea, too."

to outline the story of *Faust,* which was the
...ung I had seen in the theater. I'd added nothing new
except that I made the hero a boy of my age.

"How did the boy triumph over the devil?" asked
Mother.

"You beat the devil by using the same tricks he does!"
answered Father.

"Keep your thoughts to yourself!" shouted Mother.
"Can't you see that you're talking to an angel?"

From an early age I was saturated with the love of art
and virtue. I used to make lengthy speeches about these
things to myself, in my solitariness, and I also learned about
them from my schoolmates, among whom I was pretty
conspicuous. Most of them were mean little devils, to be
sure: whenever the teacher got fed up with them he'd
shout, "You whorehouse brats!" There was a select little
group, however, who were known for their innocence and
good behavior, and I gravitated to them. We formed a
Morality Squad, to battle against obscene language, and
used to strike up the anthems of the New Egyptian Revolution, in which we believed implicitly. When a few of us
pledged ourselves to unprecedented bravery, military or
political, I pledged myself to the theater, seeing it as a plat-
form for heroism, too, and one that would suit me, with
my weak eyesight, which had obliged me to wear prescrip-
tion glasses while I was still at primary school. Whatever
differences there may have been among us, we all dreamed
of an ideal world in which we made ourselves its most
exemplary citizens. Even defeat failed to shake our basic
ideals. As long as the slogans did not change and the leader
remained the same, what did defeat mean?

Mother's face had grown haggard, though, and she muttered words I could not understand while Father would shrug his shoulders, as if things didn't matter, then burst out singing the national anthem in a raucous, mocking voice: "My country, my country, I have shed my blood for you."

The theater was shut down for some days, and for the first time I was able to enjoy having my parents at home all day long. Father even took me with him to the coffeehouse on Sharia al-Gaysh, a new experience. Defeat that time was not without pleasant side effects, but they were short-lived.

Mother was pouring tea. "Abbas," she said, "we are going to have a stranger living with us!" I stared at her in disbelief. "He's a friend of your father's. You know him, too. It's Tariq Ramadan."

"The actor?"

"Yes, he had to leave the place where he was living, and what with the housing shortage he hasn't been able to find a good place to go."

"He's a rotten actor. He doesn't look nice."

"People should help each other. And you're an angel, my dear."

"He'll come at dawn," said Father, "and sleep until the afternoon. So except for his room, the house will still be your own special domain."

I was never aware of his arrival, but he usually left with my parents or immediately after them. He was insolent-looking and rough-spoken. He took a sham interest in me to flatter my parents, but I had no respect for him. One day, having spotted my library from where he was sitting in the hall, he asked me, "Schoolbooks?"

"Literary books and plays," Mother answered proudly. "You're speaking to a playwright!"

"Damn the theater! I wish I were a junk peddler. Or a hawker of meat from animal heads."

At that I asked, "Why do you only play small parts?"

He coughed abruptly. "My fate! I'm stalked by such crippling luck that if it weren't for your father's decency I'd have to sleep in public toilets."

"Don't scare the professor with such talk, Tariq," cautioned Mother.

He laughed. "A playwright must learn about everything, the good and the bad. Especially the bad. The theater has its fountainhead in wickedness."

"But good always triumphs," I declared with naive fervor.

"That's the way it is—in the theater!" he answered.

Like the coming of night, a vague change crept over them. Their silence wasn't the same silence, their talk wasn't the same, Father wasn't the same, nor was Mother. Our household had not been by any means without its minor differences or petty bickerings, but in general our life together had flowed along quite congenially. What, then, was the dark mystery that had slipped in between them? Her radiance had vanished; and he, who had always been an extrovert, laughing boisterously, making fun of everything and treating everyone amiably, had now become withdrawn. My mother's attachment to me—though still full of the same old tenderness—was tinged with a kind of grief which she could not succeed in hiding, while Father neglected me completely. An anxious dread of something unpleasant and unknown penetrated my soul.

At teatime one day, before they left, I heard Tariq advising them "not to give in to the devil."

"There is no devil except you," Mother answered bitterly.

"I'm not an adolescent," protested Father.

In deference to my presence, I surmised, Mother said nothing more. After they left the house I was struck with a sense of sadness and loss.

It was painfully clear that something had happened. I asked Mother about it, but she evaded the question, pretending nothing was wrong. When she and Father were alone in the hall I would hear them arguing fiercely. I would cower behind the open door listening.

"There's still a chance to be cured."

"Keep out of my private affairs!"

"But what you're doing reflects on us. Don't you realize that?"

"I hate being preached at."

"Opium killed my aunt's husband."

"Which proves that it has its uses."

"Your whole personality has changed. You're unbearable!"

I was seized by fear. I knew what opium was. I had learned about it watching a play, *The Victims*, from which the scenes depicting those doomed addicts had haunted me. *Was Father to become one of them? Was my beloved father headed for ruin?*

Before Father and Tariq returned I found myself alone with Mother. I gazed at her sadly.

"What's the matter, Abbas?"

"I know all about it." My voice was trembling. "It's something dangerous. I haven't forgotten *The Victims*."

"How did you learn about it? No, son. It's not quite as you imagine."

Father arrived at this point, upset, revealing that he had heard me. "Mind your own business, boy!" he yelled.

"I'm afraid for you," I said.

He shouted, in a voice more terrifying than I'd ever heard before, "Shut up, or I'll bash your head in!"

In my eyes at that moment he was transformed into a beast. The happy dream I'd had for so long was shattered. I retreated to my room, there to conjure up the whole panorama of a play that began with Tariq's eviction from the house and ended with my father's rehabilitation—as a result of my efforts, naturally. I told myself that good would still triumph if he could only find someone to help him.

But conditions went from bad to worse. He became more withdrawn; the father I had known no longer existed, and in his new personality he cut himself off from us on every occasion except when his anger was aroused for whatever reason. Then he would rain down curses and insults on us. I began to be afraid of him and kept my distance. Mother was miserable and didn't know what to do. "My salary isn't enough for the household," she told him once.

"So go butt your head against a wall!" he said.

We were certainly no longer living as we used to, spending much less and eating very simply. Food and money didn't interest me, but how was I going to buy books? It is unfortunate that the life of the soul cannot do without money. The most terrible blow, however, was that I had lost my father. Where was the man he'd once been? The look in my eyes seemed to anger him. "You're a poor specimen, not fit for life," he'd tell me. Things between him and Mother deteriorated to the extent that they each went their own ways and had separate rooms. Our home was disintegrating and we were living as strangers under the same roof. My mother's fate was hard for me to bear. In my mind sprang a scene revolving around a fight between

Father and Tariq: Father kills Tariq and is arrested, and as he's leaving he turns to me and says, "If I had only listened to what you said," after which the old house regains its purity. Later, of course, I felt remorse for the cruelty of my imagination.

I asked Mother, "How do you manage to make ends meet all by yourself?"

"I sell little things. Pay attention to your work. You're the only hope we have left."

"My heart is with you."

"I realize that, son, but the time hasn't yet come for you to bear our burdens. You must study, to get a good job."

"My ambition is to become a playwright."

"A profession that won't guarantee you security."

"I scorn material possessions. You understand my nature."

"You may hate materialism, Abbas, but don't try to ignore it altogether."

"Good will triumph, Mother," I assured her fervently.

I was as addicted to my dreams as my father was to his opium. I imagined changing everything around me and shaping it anew: I swept the gravel market, sprinkled the streets, and dried up the ever-flowing sewers; I tore down old houses and replaced them with towering apartment blocks; I smartened up the policemen, improved the conduct of the students and teachers, condemned drugs and drink, and conjured food from the air.

One afternoon the two of them were sitting in the hall, Father plucking his mustache with a pair of tweezers, Tariq darning his socks.

"Don't be taken in by the destitution of the poor," Tariq was saying. "This country is full of rich people no one knows about."

"Al-Hilaly is mining gold," said Father.

"Don't talk to me about al-Hilaly and his gold. Talk about women—and the petrodollar glut!"

"This scheme appeals to me. But our hands are tied."

"Abu al-Ala* used to live on a diet of lentils," I piped up.

"Deliver these pearls of wisdom to your mother!" Father yelled at me.

I fell silent, telling myself that they were just a couple of savages.

There was Tahiya, standing right in front of me, so incredibly attractive with her captivating eyes that I looked at her in a daze, not believing what I was seeing.

During the period before exams I used to stay up late at night and sleep in the daytime. The door had opened while I was pacing up and down in the hall studying, and Tahiya had come in, with Tariq Ramadan close behind. Father and Mother had already gone to bed. I knew Tahiya. I'd often seen her onstage, doing bit parts, like Tariq, and I stared at her now in bewilderment.

"What's keeping you up at this late hour?" she said, smiling.

"He's a striver. He stays up at night in the pursuit of learning, and next week he is going to take the middle school exams."

"Good for you."

They went upstairs to Tariq's room. My head spun; my blood boiled. Was he bringing her to his room behind my parents' backs? Didn't she have a house they could go to? Was our house being brought down to the lowest depths? I

*Abu al-Ala al-Maarry (973–1057), born near Aleppo, was a blind poet-philosopher who is said to have been a skeptic, freethinker, and materialist.

couldn't concentrate. My head was aflame with all the unquenchable desires of puberty. Temptation had launched an attack, which, in my struggle for purity, I fought off by sheer willpower: my whole being raged furiously until at last sleep overcame me.

In the afternoon, when they were sitting in the hall, I approached my parents, and at the sight of me Father asked apprehensively, "What's the matter with you?"

"Something very strange! You'd never imagine!" I burst out heatedly. "Tariq brought Tahiya to his room last night!" His heavy eyes turned toward me, fixing on me. He said nothing, so I assumed he didn't believe me. "I saw it with my own eyes!"

"What exactly do you want?" he asked me coldly.

"I wanted to let you know, so you can set him straight and make him understand ours is a respectable home. You must tell him to leave."

"Pay attention to your studies, and leave matters belonging to the house to its owner," he replied sharply.

"She's engaged to him," Mother explained, in a voice that was muffled and abject.

"But they aren't married yet!"

"He wants to die of starvation," Father said to Mother sarcastically, pointing in my direction.

"We have made ourselves poor," I remonstrated in a burst of anger.

He seized his glass of tea to throw it at me, but Mother jumped between us and took me to my room. Her eyes were threatening tears. "There's no use hoping for anything from him," I said, trying to comfort her. "Just don't have anything more to do with him. I wish we could go away together, but where could we go? Where would we find a place to live? And where would our money come from!"

I couldn't find an answer. The truth stood before me in all its naked ugliness: Mother's moral reserves had collapsed in the face of the circumstances created by my father's addiction, for which he was obviously responsible, but from which he was helpless to escape. But even apart from his addiction, it struck me at times that he was totally without principles. I despised him and I rejected him. He'd made a brothel out of our old home. But I was weak, too. All I could do was cry.

I passed my examinations, but my success didn't make me as happy as it should have. I couldn't rid myself of my sense of shame; sorrow had settled deep within me. During the long vacation I took refuge in the library, and there I wrote a play. I begged Father to show it to Sirhan al-Hilaly, but he only replied, "We're not a children's theater."

Mother volunteered to submit it to him. Two weeks later she brought it back, saying, "Don't expect your first play to be accepted. What you must do is try again."

I was upset, but I didn't despair. How could I despair when my only hope was the theater? One day I happened to meet Fuad Shalaby in the reading room. We shook hands, I reminded him who I was, and his cordiality gave me the courage to ask, "How can I write an acceptable play?"

"How old are you?" he inquired. "What grade are you in now?"

"I'll be in secondary school next year."

"Can't you wait until you finish your education?"

"I feel as if I can write now."

"No, you don't understand life yet."

"I have a pretty good idea what it's all about."

He smiled at me. "What is life, in your view?" he asked.

"It's the struggle of the soul against materialism."

"And what role does death play in this struggle?" he asked with a broadening grin.

"It's the soul's final victory," I answered confidently.

"If things were only that simple." He patted my shoulder. "You need a lot more experience. Find out what interests people and what arouses them. I'd strongly advise you to plunge into life, taste it to the full, and wait for at least another ten years."

His words made me retreat even further within myself. He imagined that I'd been sheltered from temptation! Perhaps he was ignorant of what was going on in our house. And ignorant as well of the struggle in an adolescent soul, the unabating conflict of lust and loftiness, the battle in the mind between the erotics of Omar Khayyam and the epic romance of Magnun Layla, divided by the same contrast as between Tahiya, the wanton in the room upstairs, and the vision of her that haunted the imagination, or as between dirt strewn on the ground and banks of white clouds floating in the sky.

Strange things were going on in the room next to Tariq's. The old furniture had been sold, replaced by beautiful new things bought at a public auction. A table covered with green baize stood in the center on a large carpet that had been laid over the Masarany tiles, and against the middle wall was a buffet. These were mysterious preparations. When I asked Mother she said, "Your father is getting it ready to spend his evenings there with friends and colleagues, as all men do." I stared at her suspiciously, the very mention of Father filling me with misgiving. "They'll spend the rest of the night here after the theater closes," she added.

I got into the habit of crouching in my room in the dark so that I could see things.

The truth of what was going on in our house could only be seen at night. These friends used to arrive very late. I would watch them come dribbling in—first Father, then al-Hilaly, Ismail, Salim al-Agrudy, Fuad Shalaby, Tariq, and Tahiya—then I'd sneak up to the top floor in the darkness. They would be seated around the table and the cards would already have been dealt.

It was gambling, just as I had seen it in the theater. The dramas of the stage, with their heroes and victims, had moved into our house, with the difference that these people, who contested with each other on the stage, here stood solidly together all on the side of evil. They were all actors, even the critic, and nothing was sure except lies. If the Deluge came again and if good intentions are worth anything, only Mother and I would deserve a place in a lifeboat. These changes were not our doing. But even Mother went so far as to prepare the food and drink. "You shouldn't have to serve these riffraff," I protested.

"They are colleagues, and I am the mistress of the house," she said by way of excuse.

"What house? It's nothing but a whorehouse, a gambling den."

"I'd like to get away from it, if we could only leave together. But what can we do?"

"This is why I hate money," I said, exasperated.

"But we can't get along without it. That's the tragedy. In any case, you are my only hope."

What is goodness? What is it without action? I had no energy for anything but daydreams, imagination, the domain of the theater. The house was infested with obscenity, and youth was no excuse for accepting the situation, but my hands were tied. I had no other recourse. The lives my schoolmates lived I could share only in the fire of my imagination, where beautiful words became images, not deeds, a Danse Macabre that I could only applaud from the edge of the ballroom floor.

Then Fuad Shalaby began bringing Doria, so that they could whisper together in the third room under the framed Bismallah* that had been a gift from my grandfather. "Shalaby and Doria, too," I said to Mother. "We must leave."

"Not before you're able to," she replied, her eyes red.

"I'm suffocating."

"So am I, son, and more so."

"Is only opium responsible for all this?" She didn't answer. "Perhaps this opium itself is the result of something else. Perhaps it's not the real reason."

"Your father is mad," she sighed. "But it's my fault that I let him mislead me."

"I'd like to kill him."

She patted my arm. "Lose yourself in your studies," she whispered. "You are the only hope I have left."

The night that burned away my last illusion: through the doorway of my room I made out Sirhan al-Hilaly staggering downstairs in the dark, his hair disheveled, his eyes dull, driven by what looked like a kind of blind madness. I wondered why he'd fled so enraged from the battlefield of the card room. Mother came out of her room—I'd thought she was upstairs—to see what was happening, and met him below the last step. They whispered something I could not catch. She went into her room, and he slipped in after her. I jumped up, impetuously, but then stood stock-still, sensing that it was more important to me to learn the truth than to

*The first verse of the Fatha, Sura I, Qur'an.

try to stop her. *My mother, too?* It is possible that for a few minutes I even lost consciousness. This was the blow that would leave my world in scorched ruins, echoing with the jeers of demons. I darted into the hall, then into her room, drowned in darkness, where I switched on the light. It was empty. I turned the light off again, backed into the hall, switched on the light there, and stood in a quandary. At that point my father came leaping down the stairs to confront me.

"What woke you up at this hour?" he said brusquely.

"I couldn't sleep," I answered, not knowing what I was saying.

"Have you seen Sirhan al-Hilaly?"

"He left the house."

"When?"

"A while ago. I don't know exactly when."

I returned to my room and stood there, in the dark, my head burning with insane thoughts, oblivious to the passing of time until the sound of footsteps brought me to my senses. People were leaving. Then no one was left in the hall except Mother and Father. I put my ear to the keyhole to hear what they were saying. "What went on behind my back?" I heard him asking her. She didn't answer, so he asked her another question. "Did Abbas see?" Again no answer. "He's the one who gave you the job. It's common knowledge that al-Hilaly hasn't spared anyone, not even Umm Hany." I didn't hear a sound from her, and he went on: "Everything has its price, that's what concerns me. As for you, though, you aren't worth being jealous over."

At last she spoke. "You're the lowest kind of vermin."

"Except for one little worm."

This was the reality. This was my father and this was my mother. The flames consuming my world grew fiercer.

Sheathe your dagger, for even Caesar has been slain. Cyrano de Bergerac fought against ghosts.

I disowned both my parents, the pimp and the whore—whom I now remember having seen once whispering together with Fuad Shalaby, when I hadn't thought anything of it, and another time with Tariq Ramadan, when I hadn't had any doubts or suspicions. *All of them, all, without any exception. Why not? She is my foremost enemy: Father is insane, an addict, but Mother is the engineer of all the evil in the world.*

My mother's voice, calling my name, reached me in my room. How strange that my hatred of Father had taken a definite form, while my feelings toward her expressed themselves not in simple aversion, but in a confused tumult of resentment.

She hurried in and took me by the hand. "Leave your reading for a while—it's not often we have the chance to sit together and talk."

She took me into the hall, sat me down beside her, and served me tea. "I'm not pleased with you these days," I remarked.

"I understand what's grieving you," she said, "but don't make my suffering worse." I avoided looking at her. "The time of deliverance is drawing closer and we'll leave together."

What an impostor she is! "This house can only be purged by fire," I muttered.

"Isn't it enough that my heart worships you!" *Shall I dump the ashes of my burned-out heart? Shall I bury her?* But my fantasies had so destroyed every response within me that I could only stand bewildered before her gaze. "Are you writing another play?" she asked.

"Yes. It will remind you of the play called *The Drunken*

Woman," I said, referring to the one that dealt with the dark world of fallen women.

"Oh no," she said, "in your plays, son, you should let the light in your heart shine forth."

At that moment Father came out of his room, and Tariq and Tahiya came down. I got up to go back to my room, but Tahiya wouldn't let me pass. "Sit with us for a while, author," she said gaily.

It was probably the first time she had paid any attention to me, so I sat down. Tariq laughed. "He's going to be the author of a tragedy," he remarked.

"He's sick with the disease of virtue!" my father muttered.

Tahiya took a sip from her glass. "How beautiful," she murmured, "that anyone could be virtuous in these days."

"As you can see, his eyes are weak," said Father, "so he can't see what's going on around him."

"Leave him in his heaven," replied Tahiya. "I'm also a lover of virtue."

"Your virtue is the kind that puts everyone in a good humor," said Tariq, chuckling.

"He has his mother's good looks. He's strong like his father. He should be a Don Juan," said Tahiya, sipping her tea.

"Just look at his glasses!" scoffed Father. "His trouble is he can't see."

They went out, leaving me furious and full of rebellion. In my imagination I eagerly set about tearing down and rebuilding.

When Tahiya stood in my way, however, she had brushed against me and set a new dream in motion. She was no better than my mother. What made her seem so much less objectionable? Later, alone, I recalled her touch, and a new idea for a play sprang from the inferno inside me: it revolved around this old dwelling my grandfather had built by the sweat of his brow, and how it had become a whorehouse. This was the central conception. The only inkling I had that it might be a success was the trembling joy that permeated my being. *Would such a plot serve as the basis of an effective play? Could there be a play without love?*

A faint knock at my door. I answered it and found Tahiya dressed to go out. *What had brought her here before teatime?* With one remark—"Everyone's asleep except you"—she walked in and stood in the middle of the room. Her eyes took in everything. "A bed. A desk," she noted. "This is a home, not just a room. Have you got any sweets here?"

I apologized for having none.

Her ripe body spread an aura outward from the middle of my room, exuded allure. For the first time I noticed the translucence of her eyes, the color of honey.

"I guess I should leave, since you have nothing here except books." But instead of turning to go, she said, "You're probably wondering why I'm ready to leave so early. I'm going to my apartment in Sharia al-Gaysh. Do you know it? It's one streetcar stop from Bab al-Shariya. Building 117."

Her feminine fragrance had already intoxicated me. "Wait!" I exclaimed. "I'll get you some sweets."

"I'll find what I want in the street. You're very nice."

For an instant, because of her presence, I forgot the struggle that had raged in my conscience. "You're the one who is really nice," I answered.

She gazed at me with a look that inspired dreams, then moved languidly toward the door. In spite of myself, I murmured, "Don't leave. I mean, there's no hurry."

She gave me a winning smile, said, "Until we meet," and went away, leaving behind her, in that tranquil room, a storm of the most delightful excitement. *Why would she come without pretext, and why would she mention the number of her apartment so casually?* How my deprived, obstinate, and naive heart throbbed. For the first time it had discovered a real woman to take an interest in, rather than Layla, Lubna, Mayya,* Ophelia, or Desdemona.

Over the next few days every furtive glance we exchanged was imbued with a new meaning that confirmed our fascination with each other. Heedless of those present, we would converse warmly. I asked myself, with puzzled persistency, whether I was being transported upward or pushed down to the depths.

In spite of the Amsheer† wind howling outside, the shouting and the ruckus reached me from the upper floor. I leaped up the stairs to investigate and saw Tariq slapping Tahiya's face in the hall. Astonishment froze me in my tracks. She retreated into their room.

"Did we disturb you?" Tariq said coolly.

"Excuse me," I spluttered, suppressing my agitation.

"Don't be upset. This is part of our daily routine. Enjoy it."

"This time I'm not going to come back!" said her trembling voice, raised almost to a shout, from inside the room.

Tariq went in, closing the door behind him, and I went back down, a new sadness plunging me deeper into despair. *Why would a beautiful woman like Tahiya put up*

---

*Female characters in well-known Arab love lyrics.
†Coptic name of the windy month that follows Touba, the coldest month, corresponding to January. The rich weather lore associated with the Coptic calendar has kept it in use throughout Egypt by both Copts and Muslims.

with a life of abuse from a man like Tariq? Does love give light only so as to reveal tragedy?

For two days she stayed away, but on the third she came back, her face glowing. My heart contracted and my grief grew greater still. I despised her conduct, but my love for her now was so obvious that it could not be ignored. It had probably come into being, taken root, and continued growing for a long time without my being aware. That day as they were leaving she stopped to straighten her stockings and let fall a small piece of folded paper before catching up with the others. I opened out the paper, my heart trembling with joy, and read the address and the time.

There were only two rooms, with a small entrance hall, but her flat was attractive, clean, and redolent of sweet incense. A round orange vase on the table in the hall held a bouquet of roses. She received me wearing a dark blue dress. Pointing to the flowers, she said, "To celebrate the day of our meeting." Pent up desire drove me into her arms. We embraced for a long time, and if the choice had been mine, the encounter would have been finalized before we separated, while I was still tasting the delight of my first kiss. But she freed herself gently from my arms and led me into the blue sitting room, simple but tidy, where we sat down side by side on the large sofa. "It's daring of us," she breathed in a low voice, "but it is the right thing to do."

"The right thing!" I repeated emphatically.

"We can't possibly hide what's between us any longer."

"The right thing," I said, determined to do away with childishness. "I have loved you for a long time."

"Really! I've loved you, too. Can you believe that I am in love for the first time!" Incredulous, I said nothing.

"You've seen for yourself," she said earnestly, "and possibly heard more. It's been groping around, not love."

"A life unsuitable for someone like you," I said sadly.

"A beggar can't choose what's suitable and what isn't," she said.

"Everything has got to change."

"What do you mean?"

"We must begin a proper life."

"I've never met anyone like you before," she said with fervor. "They were all beasts."

"All of them?" I protested.

"I don't want to hide anything from you: Sirhan al-Hilaly, Salim al-Agrudy, and finally Tariq." I was speechless, my thoughts turning to my mother. "If you're the kind of person who can't forget the past," she went on, "there's still time to change your mind."

I took her hand in mine, possessed by a strong inner drive to meet the challenge. "The only thing that concerns me is true worth," I assured her.

"My heart always told me that you were bigger than any of my petty fears."

"I'm not a child."

"But you're still a student," she said, smiling.

"That's true; I still have a long stretch ahead of me."

"I have a little bit saved up," she said simply. "I can wait."

But I had been captivated not only by love but also by longing to escape from that sullied, joyless house. I therefore decided to take a step that would irrevocably open a new path.

"On the contrary," I said quietly, "we must get married right away."

She blushed, looking all the more beautiful, but seemed too shaken to speak.

"That's what we have to do," I repeated.

"I want to change my way of life!" she said, full of sudden excitement. "I want to get away from the theater, too. But are you sure your father will still support you?"

"He certainly won't do that." I smiled sadly. "And I'm certainly not going to accept his filthy money."

"How in the world are we going to get married then?"

"I'll be finished with secondary school quite soon and I won't be drafted, because of my eyesight. There's no reason why I shouldn't get a job. My talents depend on individual study, not on taking courses."

"Will your earnings be enough?"

"My father has asked to be relieved of his work in the theater. He can live easily on what he earns from gambling and other sources and he's been looking for someone to take his place as prompter. I'll apply for the job. At least I'll be in the theater, in the kind of world where I belong. And since you hold a lease on this flat, we won't have the problem of finding somewhere to live."

"Shall I go on working in the theater until our circumstances improve?"

"No!" I said sharply. "You must keep away from those men."

"I have a little put by, as I said, but it won't last until you can stand on your own feet."

"We'll just have to make do," I said fervently, "until we achieve our goal."

At that point we surrendered to passion and forgot everything for a while, not saying a word until she freed herself tenderly from my arms and whispered, "I have to get away from Tariq. I'm not going to see him again."

"He'll come here," I said. The very mention of his name upset me.

"I won't open the door to him."

"I'll tell him everything," I declared.

"Abbas," she said uneasily, "please don't let things get out of hand."

"I'm not afraid of facing him," I boasted.

I returned to Bab al-Shariya a new being. For the first time I had seen her through the eyes of a lover saying good-bye, and she appeared even lovelier and more worthy of sympathy. *I'll be moving soon,* I said to myself, *out of the audience to play a role on the stage of life, out of the putrid atmosphere of the old house to breathe a purer and newer air.*

I sat waiting in the empty hall until I saw Tariq coming downstairs. He greeted me and asked, "Hasn't Tahiya arrived?"

"No," I answered, jumping up to confront him.

"I didn't run across her at the theater."

"She's not going to the theater."

"What do you mean?"

"She's not coming here, and she's not going to the theater."

"Where did you discover all these secrets?"

"We're going to be married."

"What?!"

"We've agreed to get married."

"You son of a . . . ! Are you crazy? What did you say?"

"We decided to treat you honorably."

He took me by surprise, hitting me hard enough to make me angry. I punched him back and nearly floored him. All of a sudden, there were my parents, rushing blindly toward me.

"It's ludicrous!" Tariq yelled. "Mama's boy is going to marry Tahiya!"

"Tahiya!" Mother cried. "What kind of lunacy is this? She's ten years older than you!"

Tariq began to threaten us, so Mother told him to take his belongings and get out.

"I'll stay here until Doomsday," he shouted as he left.

For a while, no one spoke. Then Father muttered the words of an old song—"In love, you whom I mourned for"—tingeing them with scorn.

"Abbas," Mother said, "This is just a rash infatuation."

"No, it isn't! It's a new life."

"What about your dreams, your future?"

"I will attain them in the most praiseworthy way possible."

"What do you know about her?"

"She told me frankly about everything."

"A child of the theater," Father sneered, "who knows all the tricks. And you're a strange boy! Your knowledge of your mother should have made you forswear the female species."

At that my mother took me to my room. "She has a certain reputation and a history," said Mother. "Don't you understand what that means?"

I avoided looking at her, the old pain stabbing again. "Unfortunately you don't understand what love is," I retorted. "We're going to start a new life."

"No one can escape his past!"

Alas, she was unaware of what I knew about hers. "In spite of all that," I asserted, "Tahiya is virtuous."

I wish I could say the same about you, Mother.

No sooner had I completed secondary school than I went to see Sirhan al-Hilaly about taking over my father's job. Tahiya and I got married at once, and I bade farewell to the old house and its inhabitants without any ceremony, just as if I were going off to school or to the library. Father didn't utter a word of congratulation or wish us well.

"What made you put so much effort into your school-work," he said, "if all it amounts to is a prompter's job?"

Mother, however, hugged me and burst into tears. "May the Lord help you and protect you from evil people," she said. "Go in peace, and don't forget to visit us."

But I had no intention of ever coming back to hell. I was eager to lead a different life, to breathe pure air, and to forget the abyss I'd been mired in, the pain I'd suffered.

Tahiya was waiting for me and so was love. With her I found all the happiness that can arise from the union of two harmonious people. She was bewitching, whether talking or silent, serious or having fun, even cooking or cleaning. What my salary could not cover, she made up from her savings. The sense of peace I gained from her replaced all my earlier unrest, disorientation, grief, and suppressed anger. I would come home about three in the morning, wake up around ten, and after that there was ample time for both love and writing.

We pinned our hopes together on my expected success as a playwright. Until that success came, we were willing to live simply, even frugally, doubling our efforts, patience, and hopes because of the joy we shared. Tahiya proved her strength of will in a fitting way by not touching a drop of wine, thus breaking a long-standing habit. To save money, she even stopped smoking. She confessed that she would once have sunk to opium smoking if it hadn't made her sick and given her a permanent aversion. She was such a proficient housewife that one time I remarked, "Your house is always clean and tidy, your food is delicious, and you have good manners. You shouldn't have had to . . ."

"My father died and my mother married a bailiff," she said, interrupting my train of thought. "She neglected me, and he mistreated me, so I had to run away."

She didn't elaborate, and I didn't ask her to. I neverthe-less imagined what had happened to make her one of Sirhan al-Hilaly's actresses. And in spite of myself I recalled that my mother had worked in the same theater, likewise at his mercy. I was privately waging war, a campaign against all the kinds of enslavement to which people are exposed. *Would the theater be enough of a base for this war? Would my concept of the old house, which had sunk so low as to become a brothel, be a sufficiently strong ally?*

Tahiya's gentleness and sweetness never failed; even in my happy childhood, my parents' relationship had never been like that. She was an angel, the proof of which was her determination to cast aside the way of life that had tainted her sad past. And she truly loved me as was clear from her desire to have a child. I didn't want that to hap-pen, however, being afraid, with our limited income, that it would interfere with my life as an artist, which was dearer to me than anything else in the world, dearer even than love, though I hated to disappoint her, and my own ethics forbade me to give in to selfishness.

At exactly the time when the cost of living had soared beyond both our expectations and our means, and we found ourselves forced to think of different ways of surviv-ing, Tahiya's hope of being pregnant was fulfilled; and I was beset by a new anxiety, obliged now to take into account both the near and the distant future. Our state of affairs convinced me that there was no way out except to find another job, if that were possible.

I'd heard that American and European writers used typewriters instead of pens, so I'd learned to type. On my way to the theater I used to pass by a typing bureau called Faisal, and I applied there for a job. The owner immediately accepted me on his terms: I agreed to work from eight in the morning to two in the afternoon and to be paid by the piece.

Tahiya received the news with mixed feelings. "You're going to go to bed at three in the morning, wake up at seven, at the latest, instead of ten, work from eight until two, then come home at three to get another two hours' sleep, at most, between four and six. You won't get any rest. You won't have time for reading or writing."

"What can I do?"

"Your father has lots of money."

"I'm not going to accept one filthy millieme," I said indignantly.

I refused to go on arguing. She was certainly an exceptional woman, but she was quite practical when it came to matters of living, preferring in the depths of her heart to ask my father for help rather than see me bury myself in work that would impinge on my time, my creativity, and my strength.

I took two days off from work at Faisal in order to finish my play, which I offered to Sirhan al-Hilaly. He looked at me smiling. "You haven't given up?" he asked.

During the days of waiting for his reaction I lived with my beautiful dreams. Art had become not only the one way I had of satisfying my deepest longings but also my only route to actual living. I'd begun writing this particular play, however, before I'd had the idea about the house as a brothel; it hadn't yet jelled, but I'd finished it anyway, still happy with its idealistic moral philosophy.

Sirhan al-Hilaly returned it to me with one remark: "You still have a long way to go."

"What does it lack?" I asked, sighing.

"It's a story," he said crisply, "but it won't do as drama."
There was no encouragement for me to continue.

What unparalleled agony! Worse than what I'd gone
through in the old house. Failure in art is death itself—that's
the way we're made—and art, in my case, was not just art
but the surrogate for the action that an idealist like me is
unable to take. *What will I have done to combat the evil
around me? What will I do if I have not the strength to carry
on the struggle in the only field granted me, the theater?*

The days went by. I worked nonstop, like a machine,
making hurried love, cutting myself off from the life of the
spirit. No reading. No writing. Living—reduced to daily
encounters with universal blight, the filth and slime of
overflowing sewers, and a beastly transportation system—
lost all its joy. Examined during brief intervals of relax-
ation, with Tahiya close to me, my life seemed a calendar
of days dwindling away in sterile mockery. It was in such
an oppressive atmosphere that we exchanged endearments,
buoyed by cautious daydreams, the life that pulsated in her
womb playing on the strings of my hoped-for, dreamed-of
success—though sometimes the dreams burned with wild
anger, against shame and sin, with visions of fire destroying
the old house and the fornicators in it. I could never have
such visions, however, without feeling ashamed and self-
recriminatory afterward. It's quite true that my heart held
not one speck of love for my father, but I had a sort of
wavering compassion for my mother.

When I expressed this inner conflict, Tahiya said to me,
"A secret gambling den is a crime in the eyes of the law, but
the rise in prices is just as bad."

"Would you be willing to have that go on in your
house?" I asked.

"God forbid! But what I want to say is that there are people who, when they are in trouble, act like a drowning man and grab at anything to save themselves."

I told myself that I was acting like that drowning person, even though I had committed no crime according to the law: to earn our bread, I had filled all my time with worthless work, and life in consequence had become a dry reed. Wasn't that somehow criminal, too?

The days passed by, my agony increased, and some satanic power enabled me to give form to my innermost desire: sitting at the typewriter, I was suddenly overcome with a longing for freedom, for my lost humanity, and for my dissipated creativity. How could the prisoner break his chains? I pictured a world, a righteous world, with no sin, no bonds, no social obligations; a world throbbing with creativity, innovation, and thought, nothing else; a world of dedicated solitude, without father, mother, wife, or child; a world where a man could travel lightly, immersed in art alone.

Ah! What a dream. What kind of devil lurks in the heart that has consecrated itself to goodness? The image of my angel brought me remorse. *I should feel mortally ashamed before that woman, who exudes love and patience. May God protect my wife and forgive my parents.*

"What are you thinking about?" she asked. "You're not listening to what I'm saying."

I touched her hand tenderly. "I'm thinking about the new arrival and what we should have ready for him."

One day, about to sit down at Amm Ahmad's bar, I noticed a morose look on his face that portended bad news. "Are you all right, Amm Ahmad?" I asked.

"It seems you haven't heard yet."

"I just arrived. What's happened?"

"The police," he began. "Last night—I mean at dawn—they made a raid on the house."

"My father's?" He nodded. "And what happened?"

"The same as always happens in such cases: they let the gamblers go free and arrested your parents."

I was absolutely devastated. Filled with a suffocating anxiety, I forgot my former sentiments, forgot my enduring anger. My father and mother's dreadful fate stabbed me so deeply that I broke into sobs. Sirhan al-Hilaly summoned me at once. "I'll engage an expert lawyer as legal counsel for them," he told me. "The money has been confiscated. They came across quite a lot of drugs. There's some hope, though."

"I want to see them right away."

"No doubt you'll be able to, but I'm afraid I can't let you off work tonight. That's a matter of course in the theater. The show must go on, even when there's been a death. I mean, even the death of a loved one doesn't prevent a professional actor from playing his role. Even if it's a comic one."

I left his room feeling defeated, and the guilty memory of my frightful dreams intensified my suffering.

Taher was born just before the trial, into an atmosphere so heavy with dejections, so teeming with sorrows and humiliations that Tahiya hid even her joy in front of me. Before the baby was a month old his grandparents went to prison. He was sickly, which worried us both, but I fled, to drown my anxieties and sense of guilt in endless work. I was destined, however, to face another blow, so cruel that it would make me almost forget the sorrow I felt then.

When Taher was just over five months old, Tahiya's health broke down. We diagnosed the malady ourselves as influenza, but after a week had gone by with no signs of improvement, I fetched the local doctor. "She must have tests done," he said when we were alone. "I suspect typhoid." As a precautionary measure he prescribed some medicine and suggested moving her to a fever hospital.

Having made up my mind to look after her myself, I rejected the idea, though I had to quit my job at Faisal's typing bureau. To make up for the loss of income and to cope with added expenses, I sold the refrigerator. I became Tahiya's nurse and Taher's nursemaid, moving him into the other room and giving him his bottle while I tended her, applying myself to both tasks with devotion. Unlike the baby's, Tahiya's health improved.

Driven by love and a sense of grateful indebtedness to this woman who had always been so sweet and good to me, I did all I could for her. After three weeks of care she'd recovered enough strength to leave her bed and sit in a comfortable chair in the sunshine. She had lost most of her fresh beauty and all her vitality, but she asked incessantly about the baby. Her recovery gave me a little respite, despite Taher's continuing misery. He received no attention during my long hours at the theater, from eight in the evening until two in the morning, and I had hoped that Tahiya would soon be able to take over my duties. Suddenly, however, her condition deteriorated, so much so that I called the doctor again. "She shouldn't have got up," he said. "She's had a relapse. It often happens, with no serious results." I went back to my nursing feeling twice as depressed but with twice the determination. Umm Hany got to know about our predicament, and offered to stay with Tahiya during my absences.

Despite the assurance of the doctor's repeated visits, my heart contracted, and I had a sense of imminent sorrow. Was I going to have to go on living without Tahiya? Could

I bear to live without her? Torn between her and the weakening baby, I worried about how quickly the money was running out and wondered what else I could sell. I would gaze at her sallow, shrunken face, summoning up recollections of our beautiful relationship, as if I were bidding her farewell. The whole world seemed black to me. When the final warning came, I was outside the flat, returning from the theater, had just rung the bell, and heard Umm Hany's loud wailing. I closed my eyes in acceptance of my fate, and opened my heart to the blackest sorrow.

A week after Tahiya's death Taher joined her, as was to be expected. The doctor had predicted it. I hadn't had a proper chance to learn what fatherhood was like: his tortured existence had always been a source of pain to me.

I don't remember anything about those days except Tariq Ramadan's weeping. Having cried my heart out alone, I had been able to bear up fairly well in front of the people gathered for the funeral, when all of a sudden Tariq's outburst made everyone from the theater turn to look at him. I wondered what lay behind this show of emotion. Had he loved her, this animal, who had moved his canned imitation of love to Umm Hany's house? I couldn't help speculating on the meaning of his tears, not only in my capacity as a widower but also as a dramatist; for not even in my dazed grief had I forgotten my dormant aspirations.

This was loneliness: a silent house filled with memories and ghosts, a heart ravaged not only by sorrow but also by a sense of sin, for the icy reality that stared me in the face also whispered in my ear that my imaginings had been realized. I wanted to forget the imagination, even if it meant grieving more deeply.

Yet when grief is so intense, plunges so deeply that it finally hits bottom, it begins to radiate a strange intoxication, bringing a little solace with it. Could it be that Tariq Ramadan, when he affronted the mourners with an outburst of tears, deep down inside had been laughing? This, too, is loneliness: grief, accompanied by forbearance and challenge. Together they showed me a prospect that tempted me: lifelong bachelorhood, satisfied pride, and immersion in writing until death.

I had already begun drawing up plans for a play to be entitled *The Old House—The Brothel* when in a flash came a vision of Tahiya as she had been, strong and well, lusciously full of *joie de vivre*. A new idea sprang up: the setting would actually be the old house, its actual transformation into a brothel would still pertain, and the characters would be actual people themselves; but the plot would be what I'd imagined and not the actuality. Which— what I'd imagined or what had actually happened—was theatrically stronger? What I'd imagined, unquestionably. In reality the house had been raided by police and sickness had killed Tahiya and her son, but there was another murderer: my imagination, which had informed the police and had killed both Tahiya and the baby, and was thus the ultimate protagonist in a plot that fulfilled all the requirements of a drama—a plot through which I would confess, do penance, and write a real play for the first time. I would challenge Sirhan al-Hilaly to reject it, though he and a few others might think I was confessing to outward reality rather than to the substance of a dream. Inwardly, art is a means of expurgation, outwardly a means of battle, incumbent on men born and reared in sin and determined to rebel against it. Nothing else matters. The fever of creation had infected my whole being.

On my way to keep my appointment with Sirhan al-Hilaly, the month allotted to reading the play having now gone by, my heart had been beating wildly. A refusal this time would be beyond my endurance. It would finish me. The glee I saw hiding in his eyes made my heavy heart tremble, however, and I sat down where he indicated with increasing optimism, to hear his booming voice say, "At last you've created a real play," and to feel him staring at me interrogatively, as if to ask, "How did you do it?" At that moment all my cares momentarily evaporated and I could feel my face going red. "It's wonderful, terrifying, potentially a great success! Why did you call it *Afrah al-Qubbah*?"

"I don't know," I replied, bewildered.

"Artists' wiles are beyond me," he said with a resounding laugh. "I wonder if you're alluding to the joys—shall we say?—of moral struggle in the midst of spreading vermin? Or are you being ironic, the way we are when we call a black servant girl Sabah or Nur?"* I smiled in agreement. "I'll give you three hundred pounds," he said. "Generosity is, probably, my sole virtue. It's the largest sum ever paid for a first play." *If only you could have lived long enough to share my happiness.* "But don't you expect some embarrassing questions?" he asked, after a moment of reflection.

"It's a play. There's no need to look beyond it."

"Well answered. I'm not interested in anything but the play. It's bound to arouse a storm of suspicion, though, among people we know."

"I don't care if it does," I said calmly.

"Bravo! What else have you got?"

---

*Meaning *morning* and *light*.

"I hope to begin writing a new play soon."

"Good for you! It's the rainy season for you. I'm all anticipation. I'll spring it on the company as a surprise this coming fall."

My little flat made me subject to frequent fits of gloom and I wished I could find another place to live, but where? Changing the rooms around, selling the bed, buying a new one, I realized that Tahiya had penetrated much further into my life than I had ever imagined. My mourning was not the kind that began deep and became lighter. It had been comparatively bearable to begin with—probably because of the state of shock I'd been in—but then became so entrenched that I could only hope for forgetfulness through the passage of time. My apparent lack of reaction would look to many people like evidence that I had killed her. *But she knows the whole truth now.*

Shortly before the onset of autumn, my parents were released from jail. A sense of duty, which in my mind always overrides sentiment, led me to welcome them with sympathetic charity, but to see them so broken deepened my depression. I proposed to Sirhan al-Hilaly that they return to their former jobs in the theater; I would make work available for them, freeing myself from the job so as to spend all my time on my art. He agreed, but they absolutely refused, making it clear that they wanted to have nothing more to do with either the theater or its people, none of whom, with the exception of Amm Ahmad Burgal and Umm Hany, had even taken the trouble to visit them.

I was glad. Father now conformed to the picture I had drawn of him in the play. He was still strange, despite his forced withdrawal from opium; we had nothing in common, and I didn't understand him. But then I don't lay claim ever to have understood him with any certainty. It was the play that had willed me to present him as the victim of poverty and drugs. *I wonder what he'll say about his role. Will I be able to face him after its performance?*

As for Mother, she was still attached to me and still wanted to live with me, but I wanted to be unencumbered, to discover some new place to live on my own, even if it was only one room. If I didn't feel any love toward her, neither did I harbor any feelings of hate. *And she will be dismayed when she sees herself portrayed on the stage and realizes that I was aware of everything she had tried to hide from me.* After that, would I be able to look her in the eye? Never!

I would leave them to themselves, but in some security. The idea of the shop—Amm Ahmad Burgal had suggested it—was a good one. I hoped they would make a living, and sincerely repent.

I was face-to-face with Tariq Ramadan. We'd always exchanged the usual greetings in passing. This time, however, with typical insolence, he actually intruded into my solitude. Tariq is one of those few who have no notion at all of what it is to feel awkward or embarrassed over doing anything at other people's expense; I'd scolded Umm Hany several times for living with him.

"I came to congratulate you," he said, "on the play."

I didn't believe him. *You came, rather, to conduct a cruel inquiry.* I tried to be courteous, however, and thanked him.

"The hero is totally disgusting, an odious person," he said. "The audience won't have any sympathy for him." The remark was mainly his sly way of letting me know the director's opinion and I ignored this criticism completely: the hero wasn't like that, either in real life or in the play. I saw that Tariq was simply attacking me, nothing more or less, and I looked at him so contemptuously that he asked, "Didn't it occur to you that the events of the play would make people think the worst about you?"

"That doesn't matter to me."

"What a cold-blooded killer you are!" he blurted out, suddenly showing agitation.

"Now you're going back to the past," I said disdainfully. "As far as I'm concerned, the main thing was an attempt at love, whereas with you it was all nothing but an ordeal marked by your own spite."

"Are you going to be able to defend yourself?"

"I haven't been accused."

"You're going to find yourself in the office of the prosecuting attorney."

"You're a stupid ass."

He got up. "She deserved to be killed in any case," he said contemptuously. "But what you deserve," he added, "is hanging." Then he left.

This hateful visitation made me feel as if I were being caught up in a whirlpool; it convinced me that I had to hide myself somewhere, out of reach of these ignoramuses. *Did I really deserve to be hanged? Not in the least, not even if I were charged with my own hidden desires. My imaginings—symbols of escape from actual burdens, not of flight from love or my loved one—had arisen out of temporary agitation, not out of deep-seated feelings. Anyway, I could no longer go on living where this devil could get at me.*

An agent suggested a room in the pension La Côte d'Azur in Helwan.* This again was loneliness, but of a dif-

---

*A town about twenty-five kilometers south of Cairo. With its warm, dry climate and mineral springs, it was once a famous spa.

ferent kind: myself, my craft, and my imagination. Keeping mostly to my room, I set aside time during the night to get some exercise by walking. As I'd resigned from my job and had nothing to do but write, I told myself that I had to sit down and choose one of the dozens of ideas floating around in my head, then concentrate. When it came to it, however, it became quite clear to me that after all I didn't possess a single idea. What was wrong?

I wasn't living merely alone, but in a vacuum. My grief for Tahiya returned, penetrating, deep, and subjugating. Even the image of Taher took shape before my eyes, innocent, emaciated, struggling against some unknown entity. In my attempt to escape from my depression by writing, I would encounter only a void. I was burned out. And what had extinguished the flame had not only smothered my creativity but left nothing in its place except endless listlessness and aversion to life itself.

Meanwhile, much to my bafflement, I read a great deal about the success of the play, dozens of critiques lavishing praise on the author and predicting how much the theater would profit from his talent. This critical reception, coming on the heels of my tortured attempts at writing in this hell of barrenness, this hell of sorrow and want, with my resources dwindling every day, was sheer mockery. To the gloom enveloping me I said aloud: "You never expected this."

Far from enjoying the rainy season that Sirhan al-Hilaly had predicted, I could not even think. Any idea I conceived came to nothing, shriveling as the wells of contemplation dried up. It was death, a living death: I saw death, touched it, smelled it, and lived with it.

When the money was all gone, I went to see Sirhan al-Hilaly at home. He didn't begrudge me an extra hundred pounds over and above the contracted price.

I'd entered a race with death, but I was so dried up within me that mine had become a living body without a soul. The voice of annihilation stole into my ears, jeering, letting me know that I was finished—it had played with me as it wished, baring its fangs to pronounce a sentence of death.

When the money ran out again, I rushed off a second time to Sirhan al-Hilaly, who politely but firmly made it clear that he was ready to grant me another sum whenever I showed him a portion of a new play—and only then.

Returning to solitude, with destitution now added to grief and sterility, I contemplated seeking a haven—Bab al-Shariya—but something stopped me. At that point, willfully parentless, soon to be homeless, and no longer belonging to any quarter, I said to myself that nothing was left except the end I'd assigned to my own protagonist. And eventually I hit upon the appropriate exit line. I despised my burdens and afflictions. No mention of them. I would die keeping them to myself.

Shortly before the call to afternoon prayers, I went to the Japanese Garden* and sat down on a bench, oblivious of what was going on around me, aware only of my own thoughts in lurid collision with one another. *By what means? And when?*

I'd only slept an hour the night before. The wind blew, my head grew heavy, daylight was rapidly fading. Lassitude crept over me.

When I opened my eyes it was dusk, darkness falling with ponderous slowness; I must have slept for an hour or more. I got up from the bench—to find myself rising with

---

*A public garden at Helwan decorated with Japanese statues and laid out in Japanese style.

unexpected buoyancy, filled with energy. My head was free of fever, my heart from its weight—how marvelous!— gloom had dispersed, depression had vanished, and I was a completely different person. *When had he been born? How had he been born? And why?* What had happened in the space of an hour?

I hadn't slept through an hour, but an era, from which I'd awakened into a new one. Something had happened during my sleep, something so preciously significant that surely, had it not been for this joy at sudden recovery, this joy that had loosened at last my death grip on memory and cast into oblivion even the recollection of priceless things, I might have been able to call to mind at least an inkling of the onset of this miraculous change. I could only think that somehow I must have completed a long and successful journey. From where otherwise—and how—had the resurrection come? Incomprehensible, unbidden, perhaps undeserved—but so tangible, so real that it could be seen and felt, in the very midst of spiritual emptiness and physical destitution, despite all opposition, obstacles, losses, and sorrows—this joy was all I wanted to cling to, this ecstasy, as if to a talisman. *Let its strength remain unfathomably in its mystery! Lo, its life-giving force marches forward, bearing with it the fragrance of triumph!*

I set out at once for the station, which was no mean distance away, and with every step new vigor rushed in, as full of promise as great clouds laden with rain—potentiality, feeling, responsiveness, far above and beyond the fact that I was penniless and pursued and carried sadness with me. Only after I'd covered a considerable stretch did I suddenly remember the note and realize that it was too late to retrieve it. I told myself that it didn't matter, that nothing mattered now—let whatever might happen to that letter happen, whatever the outcome might be—except to keep on going. *This ecstasy at its peak may glow on a body stripped by penury, bared to its own aridity, but on a will that the challenge of joy has made free.*

Translated from the Arabic by Olive E. Kenny.
Edited and revised by Mursi Saad El Din
and John Rodenbeck.

The Search

———

One

Tears filled his eyes. In spite of his control over his emotions and the repugnance he felt at weeping before these men, he was quite overcome. With moist eyes he looked at the corpse as it was removed from the coffin and carried to the open grave, the dead body seemingly weightless in its white shroud. Oh, how you've wasted away, Mother.

The scene faded and he could see only darkness, and the dust stung his nostrils, and the unpleasant stench of the men around him filled the air.

The wailing of the women, mingled with the sting of the dust, utterly disgusted him, and he moved forward, leaning over the open grave, but a hand pulled him back and a voice said, "Remember your God."

He was repulsed by the touch and cursed the man inwardly. That man's a pig like the rest of them. But then the awe of the moment roused him with a pang of remorse and he said, "A quarter of a century of love, tenderness, care, all gone, swallowed up by the earth as though it had never existed."

A wailing heralded the entrance of a group of blind men who surrounded the grave and sat cross-legged. He felt eyes gazing intently upon him and others stealing an occasional glance. He knew what these looks meant and stretched his lean body in stubborn defiance. They must be wondering why he was so strange in his appearance and dress, as though he were not one of them. Why did his mother remove him from his environment, then abandon him?

They have not come here to pay their condolences, but rather to gloat over you.

The grave digger and his assistant appeared from below and proceeded vigorously to fill the grave with loose earth. The blind men were chanting on cue from their leader.

She will be truly lonely. What do these pigs have to say? Reverence, covering their faces like a summer cloud. He became impatient, craving the solitude of his house so he could meditate on his situation. Embarrassing questions will be put to his mother in the darkness of the grave. None of these devils will be of any help to her then. "But your time will come!"

The sounds died down, indicating the end of the ceremony, and the grave digger took a few steps toward him but was stopped by the man standing on his right. "Let me deal with this. I know these people." He felt revulsion again, but as he realized that it was all over, his sense of loneliness overcame all else. He cast one last look at the grave, feeling at peace with its orderly appearance. Through the bars of the window he could see the creepers growing on the wall of the tomb. His mother, God rest her soul, was fond of the good life, but now all she had left was the grave.

The people moved slowly to offer him their condolences. First the women, who despite their weeping and wailing and mourning dress could not hide the licentious look in their eyes; then the men, drug peddlers, ruffians, hustlers, pimps, all muttering incoherent words of condolence. He looked at them all coldly, knowing full well that the feeling was reciprocated.

On his way home a refreshing breeze fanned him, carrying with it the fragrance of spring. His house on Nabi Danial Street was the scene of a happy, comfortable period in his life. However, the only signs of comfort remaining were the large hall and an abandoned water pipe under his mother's empty bed.

He sat on the balcony overlooking the intersection of Nabi Danial and Saad Zaghlul streets, smoking a cigarette. His attention was drawn to a flat across the street; foreigners lived there, and preparations were being made for a party. He could see a man and a woman embracing, rather inappropriate for that early time of the day.

He decided that as of today he would know life as it really was. He was lonely, without friends, work, or family, and he was left with nothing but a dreamlike hope. He must as of this moment fend for himself; that was previously his mother's domain, and he had been free to enjoy life to the fullest. Only yesterday thoughts of death could not have been further from his mind. It was yesterday, too, at about the same time, that the carriage had arrived bringing his mother home. He led her into the house, the house she had prepared for her son. She was weak and haggard, looking thirty years older than her fifty-odd years. That's how he remembered Basima Omran, as she was when she came home the previous day after having spent five years in jail.

"Your mother is through, Saber."

Carrying her effortlessly in his arms, he said, "Nonsense, you are in the prime of your youth."

She lay down on the bed fully clothed, leaned over to look in the mirror, and repeated, "Your mother is through, Saber. Who would believe that this is Basima Omran's face?"

How true. A round, handsome face, and the pink coloring of a ripening apple. Her laughter that had reverberated through every drawing room in Alexandria now failed to cause the slightest ripple on her large, fat body.

"May God curse sickness and disease."

Wiping her face, despite the cool weather, she said, "It's not sickness, but jail. I fell ill in jail. Your mother wasn't made for jails. They said it was my liver, my blood pressure, then my heart, curse them. Can I ever again be what I was?"

"And even better, with rest, and medicine."

"And money?"

He winced and said nothing.

"How much have you got left?"

"Very little."

"I was wise to register the house at Ras el-Tin in your name; otherwise they would have taken that, too."

"But I sold it when I ran out of money. I told you at the time."

She groaned and placed her hand on her forehead. "Oh, my head, I wish you hadn't sold the house. You had a lot of money; I wanted you to lead the good life, to live like the aristocracy. I wanted to leave you a fortune, but . . ."

"Everything was lost in one stroke."

"Yes, may God forgive them, a mean revenge from a mean man, a man who enjoyed my wealth, then dropped me for a worthless slut. Suddenly he remembered the call of duty, law, and honor and discarded me, the bastard. I spat on him in court."

She asked for a cigarette; he lit one for her, saying, "It's better that you don't smoke now. Did you smoke in there?"

"Cigarettes, hashish, opium, but I always worried about you." She drew on the cigarette breathlessly, wiped her damp face and neck, and said, "What about your future, my boy?"

"How should I know? There's nothing for me to do but become a ruffian, a hustler or a pimp."

"You?"

"I know, you taught me a better life, but I'm afraid that won't do me any good."

"You weren't made for that kind of life."

"What else can I do in this world?" Then with sudden rage he exclaimed, "How my enemies gloated when you were away."

"Saber. Avoid anger. It's anger that sent me to jail; it would have been easier to appease that scoundrel who betrayed me."

"Everywhere I find people I'd like to crush."

"Let them say what they want, but don't use your fists."

Clenching his hands, he growled, "If it weren't for these fists I'd have been humiliated everywhere I went; no one dared mention a word about you when you were in jail."

She blew out the smoke angrily and said, "Your mother is far more honorable than their mothers. I mean it. They don't know, but if it weren't for their mothers my business would have floundered!"

Saber smiled, in spite of the oppressive atmosphere. His mother continued: "They're very clever at fooling people with their appearance, cars, clothes, expensive cigarettes. Well-spoken, smelling good, but I know them as they really are. I know them in the bedroom, naked except for their defects. I have endless stories about them, those dirty, sly bastards. Before the trial, many of them contacted me and urged me with great persistence not to mention their names at the trial, and in return they promised me freedom. Such people have no right to speak ill of your mother, for she is far more honorable than their mothers, wives, and daughters. Believe me, if it weren't for them I would be out of business."

The smile returned to his lips.

"Where have those laughing, carefree days gone?" She sighed. "I loved you with all my heart; everything I had was at your disposal. I let you live here in this lovely house far from my world. If I ever wronged you it was unknowingly. Your looks and elegance are unequaled, but you must avoid losing your temper or worry about what's happened to me." Her sadness was contagious.

He said softly, "Everything will be just as it was."

"As it was . . . I'm finished. The Basima of days long ago will never return; my health would not permit it, and neither would the police."

He looked at the floor. "Very little of the price of the house is left."

"What is there to do? You must maintain the standard of living I have accustomed you to."

"I've never known you to lose hope before."

"Only this once."

"Then I must either work or kill."

She put out her cigarette and closed her eyes as if trying to concentrate on a single idea.

"There must be a way out," continued Saber.

"Yes, I've given the matter much thought in jail."

For the first time his confidence in his mother was shaken.

"Yes," she continued, "I've thought about it a lot, and I am now convinced that I have no right to keep you here, since it is no longer good for you."

He looked at her, a questioning glance in his dark eyes.

Then with a tone of defeat she whispered, "You don't understand. The government took you away from me at the same time that they confiscated my wealth. I don't have the right to own you either. I knew that the day they sentenced me." She was silent for a while, utter despair on her face. "Saber, this means that you must leave me," she said.

"Where to?" he asked resentfully.

"To your father," she replied in a barely audible voice.

He raised his eyebrows in bewilderment and cried, "My father . . ."

She nodded.

"But he's dead. You told me he died before I was born."

"I told you so. But it wasn't true."

"My father, alive . . . Incredible . . . My father . . . alive."

She looked at him with sudden disdain as he continued: "My father alive . . . Why did you hide this from me?"

"Yes, the hour of reckoning has come." She sighed.

"No, no. But I've got a right to know."

"What father could have done for you all that I've done, your happiness . . . ?"

"I don't deny this at all . . ."

"Then don't reproach me and start searching for him."

"Searching?"

"Yes. I'm talking about a man whom I married thirty years ago, and now I don't know anything about him."

In a calmer vein but still bewildered, he asked, "Mother, what does all this mean?"

"It means that I'm trying to show you the only way out of your dilemma."

"But he might be dead."

"Or alive."

"Must I waste my life, then, looking for someone I'm not even sure exists?"

"You'll never be sure unless you find out. Anyway, it's better than staying as you are with no work and no hope."

"It's a very strange and unenviable situation!"

"Your only alternative is to become a hustler, a crook, a pimp, or a murderer. So you must do what must be done."

"How can I find him?"

She sighed, and an even greater sadness fell upon her. "His name is on your birth certificate, Sayed Sayed el-Reheimy." Her eyes grew misty as she continued: "He fell in love with me thirty years ago. That was in Cairo."

"Cairo . . . Then he's not even in Alexandria."

"I know that your real problem will be to find him."

"Why didn't he try to find me?"

"He doesn't know about you."

A look of resentment and indignation crept into his eyes. "Wait," she said, "don't look at me like that. Listen to the rest of it. He is a man of means in every sense of the word. At the time he was a student, but even then he had considerable means and prestige."

He looked at her with increasing interest but somewhat distantly.

"He loved me. I was a beautiful, lost girl. He kept me secretly, in a golden cage."

"He married you?"

"Yes. I still have the marriage certificate."

"He divorced you?"

She sighed, "I ran away."

"You ran away?"

"I ran away after some years. I was pregnant. I ran away with a man from the gutter."

"Unbelievable," he muttered, shaking his head.

"Now you are going to blame me for your problem."

"I'm not blaming you for anything. But didn't he look for you?"

"I don't know. I ran away to Alexandria and never

heard any more about him. Many times I expected to see him in one of my establishments, but I never set eyes on him again."

He laughed coldly and said, "And thirty years later you send me to look for him."

"Despair drives us to do even stranger things. You'll have the marriage certificate to help you. Also the wedding photograph. You'll see the striking resemblance."

"Strange that you kept the certificate and photograph."

"I was thinking of the picture. I was a poor girl living with a hustler, and when I became successful my intentions of avenging you were realized."

"And yet you never got rid of the rest of your memories."

She wiped her face and neck impatiently and said, "I intended to many times but changed my mind, as though I had a premonition of what would happen."

He paced back and forth, then stopped in front of her bed. "What if after all my efforts he denies me?"

"Who can deny you after seeing the photograph?"

"Cairo is a big city, and I've never been there before."

"Who says he's in Cairo? He might be in Alexandria, Assiut, or Damanhour. I have no idea. Where is he today? What is he doing? Is he married or single? God only knows."

He waved his arm angrily. "And how am I supposed to find him?"

"I know it won't be easy. But it's also not impossible. You know some police officers and lawyers. No prominent personality is unknown in Cairo."

"I'm afraid that my money might run out before I find him."

"That is why you must start at once."

He thought for a moment, then asked, "Is he worth all that effort?"

"Without the least doubt. You will find the life you want with him. You won't suffer the indignities of work or be forced to lead a life of crime."

"And if I find him poor? Weren't you extremely rich?"

"I assure you that money is only one of his assets. It's true that I was rich, but I never provided you an honorable life, and all you did was go about using your fists to defend your mother's and your own honor."

I must be dreaming, he thought. "Do you really believe that I'll find him?"

"Something tells me that he is alive, and that if you don't despair, you'll find him."

He shook his head, torn between bewilderment and hopelessness. "Should I really start searching for him? If my enemies know of this, won't they treat me as an insane freak?"

"And what will they say if they find you pimping? You have no alternative but to look for him." She closed her eyes, muttering about how exhausted she was, so he begged her to sleep, saying that they would resume their talk tomorrow. He took off her shoes and covered her, but she tossed off the cover with a nervous gesture and fell into a deep sleep punctuated by light snoring.

He awoke at nine o'clock next morning after a restless, sleepless night. He went to her room to wake her, and found his mother dead. Had she passed away in her sleep, or did she cry out in the night? An unheeded cry. No matter. Here she was, dead, in the same clothes as those in which she had left prison the day before. He looked closely at the wedding photograph. The only evidence of the existence of a father thirty years ago. How true. He was the image of his father. A handsome, virile-looking man, his tarboosh slightly tilted to the right, enhancing an already impressive figure.

The guests had started to arrive at the neighbors', the sound of music blending with the chants of the Qur'an in the dead woman's bedroom.

Where is reality, and where is dream? Your mother, whose last words are still echoing in your ears, now lies dead. Your dead father is seeking resurrection. And you, penniless, persecuted, tarnished with crime and sin, looking for a miracle that will lead you to a life of honor, freedom, and peace of mind.

Two

Better to let the matter remain secret for the moment. Should he despair of the search, he could seek aid from his acquaintances. He'd start with Alexandria, although it was unlikely that someone like his father would be in Alexandria without his mother's knowing about it.

The telephone directory for a start. The letter S, Sayed el-Reheimy. Aha . . . if only luck were on his side. Sayed Sayed el-Reheimy, owner of el-Manshiya bookshop. Very unlikely for a person of his father's social condition. In any case, el-Manshiya was an area worked by his mother for more than a quarter of a century. Still, this might be a useful clue.

The bookshop owner was a man over fifty, bearing no resemblance to the photograph. Covering his mother's face, he showed him the picture.

"No, I don't know this man," said the bookshop owner.

Saber explained that the photograph was taken thirty years before.

"I don't remember seeing him."

"Is he perhaps a relative?"

"We are Alexandrians, and all my relatives live here. Some of my relatives on my mother's side live in the countryside. Why are you looking for this man?"

He hesitated a moment, then said quickly, "He's an old friend of my deceased father. Do any of the Reheimys live elsewhere?"

The man looked at him suspiciously and said, "El-Reheimy is my grandfather, and there are only my sister and me."

There was no other course but to be patient. He had only two hundred pounds, and these were dwindling away with every passing hour. When they were gone, so went the hope of an honorable life. His eyes ached from scrutinizing every passerby. He consulted a lawyer of his acquaintance, who suggested that his father might have an unlisted number. "Ask the local Sheikh el-Hara,"* he suggested.

"My father is an important man," retorted Saber indignantly.

"Strange things can happen in thirty years. I was going to suggest that you ask about him in the various jails."

"Jails!"

"Why not? A jail is like a mosque, open to all. Sometimes people go to jail for noble reasons." With a short laugh, the lawyer continued: "Let's start with the registry offices, then the jails and the property registrars. If there is no trace there, we have no alternative but to ask the local sheikhs."

Saber rejected the idea of an advertisement in the paper.

---

*Literally "The Elder of the Alley." He is a person who has lived for a long time in a particular quarter of the city and who is relied upon by the authorities to assist in maintaining a register of births, deaths, and addresses in the quarter.

This would give his enemies an opportunity to make fun of him. The advertisement would have to wait until he left the city. He made the rounds of the local sheikhs, from one end of Alexandria to the other.

"What does he do?"

"I don't know anything about him except that he is a well-known personality and of ample means. This is a photograph of him taken thirty years ago."

"Why are you looking for him?"

"He's an old friend of my father's and I've been asked to look for him."

"Are you sure he's still alive?"

"I'm not sure of anything."

"How did you know he's in Alexandria?"

"Only a hunch, nothing more."

Then the final answer would resound like the clanging of a cell door, "Sorry, we don't know him." He did not cease his scrutiny of every passerby, in a continuous whirlpool of searching, without success. The raindrops forced him to retreat from the seashore and move on to Miramar. He looked up to the late afternoon sky with the first shades of darkness gently edging away the remaining daylight. A voice cried out in welcome, "Come."

He shook hands and sat down.

"I wasn't able to pay you my condolences, but I waited until you came to Le Canard. Everyone is asking about you." The rain had stopped. He stood up, making some excuse about an appointment. She got up and said softly, "Are you in financial straits?"

So they've begun talking!

Temptingly she continued: "Someone like you should never be in want of money."

He shook hands coldly and left. Someone like you should never be in want of money. The call of the madam. That's just what your enemies want. I'd rather be dead. What's left in Alexandria?

The palm reader; but nothing new.

The sheikh, all-knowing perhaps. He visited him in his ground-floor room, shuttered and musty. The sheikh, sitting cross-legged on the floor lost in thought, said, "Seek and ye shall find." The sound of waves seemed to augur a promising start. "A search as tedious as the winter nights," the sheikh added. Every day is like a year, and at what expense! "You shall obtain what you seek."

With a startled voice: "What is it that I'm seeking?"

"He is waiting for you impatiently."

"Does he know about me?"

"He's waiting for you."

Maybe his mother didn't tell him everything.

"Then, he is alive!"

"Thanks be to God."

"Where do I find him? That's what I really want to know."

"Patience."

"I can't be patient indefinitely."

"You've just begun."

"In Alexandria?"

The sheikh closed his eyes. "Patience, patience," he murmured.

"You've told me nothing," retorted Saber angrily.

"I've told you everything," replied the sheikh.

He walked out cursing and was greeted by the introductory rumbles of a thunderstorm. He decided to sell his furniture and leave for Cairo. He had already sold the costly objects in order to maintain his expensive tastes and extravagant living. He hated having the secondhand dealers and buyers come to his flat, so he paid a visit to "Madame" Nabawiya, a close friend of his mother's, and the only one in that circle he did not dislike.

"I'll be glad to buy your furniture, but why are you leaving?" she asked, offering him a puff from her narghile.

"I'll make a new life for myself in Cairo, away from all this."

"May God have mercy on her soul. She loved you and ruined you for any other kind of life."

He understood what she meant and said, "I'm no longer fit for this kind of life."

"What will you do in Cairo?"

"I have a friend who promised he'd help me."

"Believe me, our work is suited only to the proud."

He spat in a large incense bowl. That was his response.

Alexandria faded in the distance as the train sped south toward Cairo. A quarter of a century of memories faded away in the autumn twilight, enveloped in dark clouds heralding November with its cold winds blowing through half-deserted streets. He bade a silent farewell to the city, wondering what the future held in store for him. His sole companions for the journey were his thoughts, thoughts about his father. The questions he had asked, the evasive answer from his mother. He had always assumed that he was the product of a moment of pleasure in any one of the numerous brothels. A bastard.

The sudden din of the Cairo station cut through his thoughts. His immediate impulse was to board the next train for Alexandria. But he thought better of it, left his luggage at the station, and walked out into the late afternoon sun. He was struck by all the appurtenances of a big city, the cars, buses, pedestrians, street vendors, noise, wide streets, noise, narrow streets, noise. Contradiction and contrasts everywhere. Even the weather, the hot rays of a sun struggling to the last before setting, and a pleasant cool breeze waiting to take over after the struggle was inevitably finished.

He eventually found himself in an arcaded street across from the Cairo Hotel, an establishment that looked like it was within his means. And as though to emphasize this fact, a beggar was sitting cross-legged near the doorway chanting a religious song. The street was crowded with shops on both sides, and piles of merchandise were strewn all over the sidewalks.

The hotel was an old building with sand-colored walls rising four floors above him. An arched doorway led into a long corridor with a stairway at the end. In the middle of the corridor stood the reception desk presided over by a seated old man, and beside him stood a woman. What a woman! He felt an immediate awakening of long-dormant desires and memories lost in the fog of time. The sound and smell of the sea and moments of insane passion, inflamed by the darkness of night. An intimate relationship sprang up between him and the hotel; it was as though they were destined to meet.

He crossed the street and entered with a burning curiosity. The beautiful dark girl, her almond eyes flashing with temptation and seduction. A clinging, pale-colored dress, long fingernails suggesting an exciting animal desire.

She reminded him of her. Ten, maybe more years ago, the name long forgotten but the moment recaptured in its entirety. The girl of long past was of no consequence, but here she was now, bringing back the past, calling out, just as his father was doing. A call from the dead that brought him from the sea to this exciting, teeming city. She gave him a fleeting glance full of meaning, then quickly turned her face toward the hotel lounge on her right. Saber walked up to the desk, where the old man was bent over a large register, a magnifying glass in his trembling hand. The old man did not notice him, so he stole a glance at the woman and assured himself of the promise he had first detected. She glanced back at him with a touch of scorn and nudged the old man, upon which Saber immediately greeted him. "Good evening, sir."

The old man raised his head to display a deeply lined face with a prominent hooked nose. The look in his pale eyes indicated a total lack of interest in the whys and wherefores of this world.

"I'm looking for a room," Saber said.

"Twenty piastres a night."

"And if I stay for two weeks?"

"Twenty piastres is worth nothing nowadays."

"I might stay for a month or more."

The old man gave up the bargaining and murmured, "As you wish."

Saber gave his name and place of origin, and when asked about his occupation simply said, "I have private means." He gave the old man his identity card, stealing glances at the woman while the man was busy writing down the details. Their eyes met, but he failed to read the meanings he had first seen. Nevertheless, he convinced himself that she was that girl of his past. Once more the smell of the sea stung his nostrils as well as the scent of the carnations that had adorned her hair. All of a sudden he was optimistic about the success of his mission and did not doubt for a moment that this woman was ready and willing. She appeared to be disinterested, but an enchantress lay beneath that cool façade.

The old man returned the identity card, saying, "You are from Alexandria?"

He nodded and smiled, and said slyly, looking to the girl, "I bet you like Alexandria?"

The old man smiled, but the girl, contrary to his expectations, did not appear even to have heard, so he quickly asked, "Did you ever know Sayed Sayed el-Reheimy?"

"It's not improbable that I did."

Saber became keenly interested, forgetting the girl. "Where and when?"

"I can't remember, I'm not sure."

"But he is an important man."

"I've known many, but now I don't remember one."

His optimism increased. He glanced at the girl and saw a look of doubt and mockery in her eyes, as though she were asking why a man of private means should stay in this hotel. It didn't bother him. The truth would appear when she discovered the reason for his being there. And she would find out sooner or later.

Did she remember him? He felt the long fingernails dig into his flesh after the long chase along the Corniche in Alexandria. The chase that ended in the dark with the sea breeze blowing over their naked bodies. But where was her father then? And when did he move to Cairo to run this hotel?

The woman called out, "Mohamed el-Sawi."

An old man stood up from his seat near the door and answered her call. He was very dark, short, and lightly built. He wore a gray-striped galabiya and a white skull-cap.

She pointed to Saber and said, "Room thirteen."

Saber smiled at the number. He excused himself and went back to the station to get his luggage. When he returned, he followed Mohamed el-Sawi to his room on the third floor. A middle-aged porter, moving far too quickly for his profession, carried his bags. The porter had small, closely set eyes and a very small head that gave him an air of naivete.

"What's your name?" asked Saber.

"Aly Seriakous."

The way he said it told Saber that he was a man who could be bought.

"Is the old man at the desk the owner of the hotel?"

"Yes, Mr. Khalil Abul Naga."

He was about to ask about the woman when he warned himself that naivete can be a two-edged sword.

When he was alone he looked over his surroundings. The immediate impression was that of age. High ceiling and a four-poster bed. His father must have enjoyed such surroundings when he made love to his mother. He looked out the window onto a square at the northern end of the street. Children were splashing about in the fountain in the center of the square. He switched on the light and sat on the old divan, closing his eyes. Sexual fantasies, intermingled with dreams of finding his father, swept over him.

He could hear the call of those almond eyes. She might now be thinking of him and asking herself about the reason for his presence. There was no doubt that she was the girl. He could hear her voice above the din of the festival, telling him sharply not to come near her in this manner.

You had replied haughtily that no girl had ever spoken to you like that before. She retorted that she did and would repeat it. She left with a vulgar-looking woman, the breeze caressing her hair. Where was Mr. Khalil then? Your eyes met today more than once, and the looks were full of meaning. But no hint of memories past. No hint of long talks by the sea near the overturned fishing boats, conversations that disguised passion and powerful desires. A stolen kiss followed by a friendly tussle. Then you cried out, "One day I'll pull out those long fingernails!"

As to the long chase which ended in the dark, that was a total victory, a victory that was followed by disappearance and a long silence. Then sorrow that lasted for a long time until your mother moved from one quarter to the other, and ended in the elegant flat in the Nabi Danial district. Who knows? This hotel might have some connection with that dark night and the girl with carnations in her hair. This woman arouses a tempest of passion in your veins. And you need moments of warmth and passion to ease your search and alleviate the pangs of loneliness. And then, when the miracle occurs, you will cry out, "I'm Saber, Saber Sayed Sayed el-Reheimy! Here is my birth certificate and here is the marriage certificate, and look carefully at this photograph."

Then you will open your arms and all evil thoughts and doubts will vanish forever.

You have become a lady in every sense of the word. Where is that girl covered with salty spray? Where is that pure virgin smell?

Three

He rose early, after only three hours' sleep, feeling surprisingly refreshed.

Opening the window, he saw a world he had never seen before. The familiar Alexandria scene, the buildings and usual morning sights were replaced by those of an alien world. Even the air he breathed was different. The strange surroundings conjured up an image of his father, the object of his search. Aly Seriakous brought in his breakfast, which he wolfed down hungrily. When the servant returned to take the tray Saber asked him, "Who was the girl sitting next to Mr. Khalil yesterday?"

"His wife."

This was unexpected. With what sounded like shocked indignation he asked, "From Alexandria?"

"I have no idea."

"When did Mr. Khalil buy the hotel?"

"I don't know. I've only been working here for five years."

"Was he married then?"

"Yes."

There was no doubt about it. She was the girl from his past. The old man bought her from that vulgar woman and made her a lady. But he must concentrate on his search, before the money runs out. He left his room and went downstairs, and found Mr. Khalil talking to Mohamed el-Sawi, the doorman. Some of the hotel residents were in the lounge, reading newspapers or drinking coffee, and some were just chatting together. He walked up to Mr. Khalil, greeted him, and asked for the telephone directory.

Sayed . . . Sayed . . . Sayed . . . Sayed . . . Aha. Sayed Sayed el-Reheimy. There it is . . . His heart beat faster. A doctor and professor at the Faculty of Medicine. Now that's something! He could not contain his joy, and cried out, "It seems that the Almighty is on my side."

The old man looked up with his weak, distant look. "It looks as though I shall succeed in what I came for," Saber continued.

"Success is a wonderful thing," murmured the old man.

Just as you succeeded in possessing that beautiful girl!

The old man was still looking at him, with mounting curiosity. "I'm looking for a man. Someone who means the world to me," Saber explained.

"No one comes to this hotel to stay. They always have some specific mission or particular purpose that takes them a day, a week, or a month to fulfill, then they leave," said the old man.

"That's normal," replied Saber.

"That's why even though they share the same roof and have their meals together, they never get to know each other."

"I imagine that your work must be interesting," said Saber, trying to maintain the conversation.

"Absolutely not!"

What about the vicissitudes of fate! The girl, for example! He heard footsteps behind him, and she appeared wearing a black skirt and red blouse and, around her head, a white polka-dotted scarf. His heart almost stopped beating. The look in her eyes showed the promise of virgin land! The smell of sea breeze hit his nostrils once more. The doorman stood and picked up a battered gray suitcase. The old man raised his head from the hotel register.

"Are you leaving now?"

"Yes, I'll see you later. Goodbye." She left the hotel followed by Mohamed el-Sawi. You are truly a mystery, Khalil! That face of yours, expressionless like a death mask. Saber got up with apparent calmness, excused himself, and walked out of the hotel. His eyes scanned the street. There they are! Walking toward the square. He hurried after them, quickly catching up. The doorman turned around, questioningly. With an apologetic smile Saber asked, "Excuse me, Mr. Mohamed. Can you tell me the way to Azhar Square?"

The woman looked at him with surprise. The doorman started to point out the directions. He pretended to listen, frequently stealing glances. The promising, provocative look was in her eyes. He was about to ask her about the carnations in her hair, the salty sea breeze, and the naked darkness. The doorman had stopped talking. He thanked him and left them. Where was she going with her watchdog? Was he perhaps overly presumptuous? He had always been forward. But perhaps this time it might ruin everything.

Arriving at the address, he found the doctor's assistant, who told him that the doctor usually came around noontime. He sat down and waited. Was this the place where his father worked? Fear, despair, hope, anxiety all came crowding in. What would he do if his father denied him? He would fight for his rights to the bitter end! In his excitement he suddenly realized that he didn't know what the doctor specialized in. He walked out of the waiting room and approached the assistant.

"Please, what branch of medicine does the doctor specialize in?"

"He is a cardiologist."

"I just wanted to make sure. You see, I'm from Alexandria." He realized how foolish he must have sounded, but he didn't care. "Do you have any idea as to the doctor's age?" he asked.

"I have no idea," replied the assistant with surprise.

"But you can guess, roughly?"

"He is a professor at the Faculty of Medicine."

"Is he married?"

"Yes, and he has a son, who is a medical student."

Now, that is an obstacle! The family will certainly have something to say about the new member coming from the brothels. Nevertheless, he was determined.

The patients started arriving and the waiting room filled up. His turn came. Anxious and full of doubt, he walked into the consulting room. The face bore no resemblance to the photograph. He sat opposite the doctor and started answering his questions.

"My name is Saber Sayed Sayed el-Reheimy."

"Then you must be my son," said the doctor with a loud laugh.

"Actually, I'm not here for your professional advice."

The doctor looked at him questioningly.

"I am looking for Sayed Sayed el-Reheimy."

"You are looking for me?"

"I don't know. But please take a look at this photograph."

The doctor looked at it carefully and shook his head.

"This is not your photograph?"

"Definitely not," he answered with a laugh. "Who is that beautiful woman?"

"Perhaps one of your relatives? It was taken thirty years ago."

"No, no."

"You are from the Reheimy family?"

"My father is Sayed el-Reheimy. He worked at the post office."

"Are there any other branches of your family?"

"No. My family is a very small one."

He stood up, despair lining his face. "I am sorry to have troubled you. But maybe you've heard of someone with that name?"

"I don't know anyone of that name. What exactly are you looking for?"

"I'm looking for Sayed Sayed el-Reheimy, the man in this photograph, taken thirty years ago."

"He might be anywhere. In any case, I'm not an authority on missing persons," said the doctor in a tone that indicated the end of the interview.

He walked into the first bar he found and ordered a brandy. He had to start all over again. The telephone directory was nothing more than a cruel mockery. The optimism that had swept over him when he saw Khalil's wife was now fading fast. He remembered his fruitless search in Alexandria, the registry offices, the local sheikhs. But here in Cairo he knew no one. Perhaps it was best to place an advertisement in the paper. He looked at the old barman and asked, "Do you know a Sayed Sayed el-Reheimy?"

"Yes, he is a doctor in a building not far from here."

"No. Not that one. He is an important person. A man of considerable means."

The barman, a foreigner, repeated the name a couple of times, and then said, "I don't recall any of my customers with such a name."

"Have you ever tried looking for someone without knowing where to start?"

"A lost son since the war?"

Saber shook his head.

"But the war is long over. And everyone's fate is now known."

"Rather lost, than dead." Saber asked the barman about the *Sphinx,* a newspaper, and was told that it was in Tahrir Square.

The paper was located in a large white building. A fountain gurgled in the quadrangle. It reminded him of a villa belonging to a rich Greek in Alexandria, one of his mother's friends. He walked through the main door and was surprised by a woman beckoning to him. But he soon realized that she was calling a messenger boy who was standing behind him. The boy gave her a parcel and went through another door, leaving him standing in front of her. Slim and elegant. A dark face and deep blue eyes that attracted him. She radiated warmth and confidence. He greeted her and asked for the advertising department. She answered in a pleasant, warm voice, "Come with me, I'm going there myself."

He followed her with mixed feelings of admiration, desire, and respect. They entered the advertising office and she pointed to a man sitting at one of the desks. A plaque bore his name, Ihsan el-Tantawi.

"I'm looking for a Sayed el-Reheimy."

"The cardiologist?"

He shook his head, expecting him to recite a long list of persons bearing that name. But he didn't.

"I don't know anyone except Reheimy the cardiologist, but don't you know anything about him? What he does, or where he lives?"

"Not at all. Only that he is a man of means. But I found only the doctor in the telephone directory."

"He might have an unlisted number, or perhaps he lives in the suburbs. In any case, an advertisement is the best means of finding him."

"Please make it a small advertisement. Let it run daily for one week. Ask them to contact me at the Cairo Hotel by telephone or mail."

"We must mention your name in the advertisement."

He thought for a moment. "Saber Sayed."

The man started filing the advertisement. Saber noticed that the girl had been following their conversation. No doubt the advertisement had aroused her curiosity. Her colleagues in the office called her Elham.

"Do you wish to state the purpose of the advertisement?" asked Tantawi.

"No." After a brief moment he added, "I imagined that he would have a large number of acquaintances, but it seems that no one knows him."

"Yours is a strange case indeed," said Tantawi. "How can you be sure that whoever contacts you is not an impostor?"

"I've got evidence."

Curiosity got the better of Elham. "This is really mysterious. Just like a movie."

Saber smiled, delighted that she was taking an interest. "I wish it could be solved as easily as in the movies."

"At least you know that he is a man of means. How did you know that?"

Saber was silent. Tantawi interjected sharply, "This sounds like an interrogation."

What a charming girl. Perhaps she would take to him. She is a pleasant breeze compared with the roaring flame at the hotel. "Miss Elham, I'm a stranger in your city."

"A stranger."

"Yes, I've just arrived from Alexandria, and I must find this man. Now that I've seen you, I feel optimistic."

She smiled, a warm, confident smile. He remembered the wine he used to drink in the Taverna with the soft strains of a violin in the background.

Four

He left the newspaper at the same time the employees departed. Thinking that perhaps he might get another glimpse of Elham, he stood for a while at the bus stop. The advertisement would take over his search for the moment. A cool breeze was blowing gently; he saw her chatting casually with a group of young people in front of the building. She took her leave from her friends and crossed into a side street and into a small cafeteria called Votre Coin. He followed her without hesitating, and seeing her sitting alone at a table, he walked in and made for the counter. He stopped at her table.

"What a pleasant coincidence! May I join you?"

"Please do," she said without undue enthusiasm. The waiter had just brought her sandwiches and an orange juice. He ordered the same.

"I hope that I'm not a nuisance. But this is usually the way with strangers."

"I welcome strangers."

"Thank you. What I meant is that strangers are always

overly keen to strike up friendships. It sometimes puts people off."

"No. Not at all. You've done nothing to put me off."

"Perhaps you are going to the cinema?" he asked, taking a bite of his sandwich.

"No. We go back to work in a couple of hours. I live at the end of Giza, and you know what public transportation is like. I prefer to take my lunch here."

"Do you spend your entire lunch hour here?"

"Sometimes I go for a walk along the Nile."

They ate in silence, Saber stealing a glance whenever she wasn't looking. Her blue eyes contrasted startlingly with her dark attractive features, altogether a very pretty sight.

"What do you think of the advertisement?" he asked. "Do you think it will achieve its purpose?"

"It always does," she replied.

He was trying to arouse her curiosity, but she failed to rise to the bait. "The result is very important to me."

"Don't you really know anything about the man you're looking for?"

"I've got a photograph and some hazy information." Then, after a moment's thought: "My father has sent me to look for him. He knew him many years ago." He saw a questioning look in her eyes. "An old acquaintance," he added, smiling. "They had dealings together many years ago."

"Financial?"

"That as well."

You are trying to achieve the impossible. This girl is the type that can arouse passions. "I've never felt like this before," he said, changing the subject. She raised her eyebrows with a cynical look. "I mean, being a stranger, living on a hope, and of course, your charming presence," he explained quickly.

"I've heard that before."

"At work?"

"That's one example."

"Are you satisfied with your work?"

"Huh?"

"Would you give it up and keep house?"

"I consider this my career, not just a temporary stopgap."

His ideas of the opposite sex were firmly entrenched. They were beautiful, savage beings looking for love and passion, without principles or scruples. His mother and her circle of friends reinforced this idea. However, he did not undress her in his mind, as he usually did with any member of the opposite sex. There was something more to this girl. A certain mystery, a certain magic. Some secret he had never come across before. He would not be able to enjoy her as he had others, savagely, passionately, with an animal lust. She was unique. Something quite new to him.

"But look at the care you take over your fingernails, for example."

Indignation showed on her face, and she said sharply, "What about the care you take over your hair!"

"Please excuse me," he said hastily. "I was merely expressing my admiration." And somewhat apologetically, he added, "When I return to Alexandria I shall take back the sweetest memories of our meeting."

"Why didn't you advertise in Alexandria?"

"Well, advertising is only part of my search." He was about to settle both their bills, but she objected strongly. "If you had offered, I wouldn't have objected," he said, laughing.

He noticed that she was looking at his reflection in the mirror on the left-hand wall. A feeling of satisfaction swept over him. Perhaps he had made the same impression on her as he had made on other women. They stood up, shook hands, and separated. He fought the strong desire to follow her. When he returned to the hotel, he notified Mr. Khalil Abul Naga and Mohamed el-Sawi that he was expecting a phone call from a Sayed Sayed el-Reheimy.

"Then you are searching for your father?" said the old man, Khalil. "How did you lose him?"

"The same way that he lost me. And here I am looking for him."

"What a strange story," said the old man.

"There's nothing strange about it," he said, annoyed at the questions. "Please call me if there is a phone call."

A young man in search of his father, that's what they'll say about him. He picked up a newspaper and sat in the lounge. The telephone rang. Sayed Reheimy, hairdresser from Bulaq, Reheimy the schoolteacher, the tram driver, the grocer. Where is Sayed Sayed el-Reheimy? Why doesn't he contact him like the others? If he's dead, where is his next of kin? His funds were being rapidly depleted. The other hotel guests sat around smoking, drinking coffee, chatting. No one noticed him. Thank God. They didn't read the advertisements. Your money will run out. Where is your father? You are nothing but a pimp and a hustler. Life was beautiful when your mother was alive. Money, pleasure, more money, more pleasure. Fighting for your mother's name, in vain perhaps. But nevertheless fighting. Money, pleasure, and bloody battles.

"Cotton . . . Everything now depends on cotton," said one of the guests as he looked up from the paper at his companion.

"But this impending war? Won't it guarantee our cotton?" asked his companion.

"It won't be like previous wars."

"That's true. Nothing will remain."

"And where is God? The Creator and Protector of all this?" That's true. Where was God? He knew of the name. But that was about all. He lived in a world without religion. The telephone vigil continued. Thoughts of Elham and Khalil's wife flashed through his mind. The breeze and the flame. We need both. If my father doesn't put in an appearance, it's back to fear, hunger, and a tainted past filled with crime and sin.

The telephone rang. It wasn't for him. But as he looked toward the phone booth, he saw her. His heart stopped beating and his breathing became heavy. So she's back. That look again. A conspiracy of desire and mockery. Reheimy and Elham were soon forgotten. He left the lounge and went up to his room on the third floor. Footsteps were approaching. He opened the door. "Welcome back."

She nodded, smiling.

"We really missed you."

She laughed quietly and hurried up to the fourth floor.

"Alexandria," he said suddenly, summoning up his courage.

She stopped. "Alexandria?"

"Yes."

"I don't understand."

"If you've forgotten, I can't."

"You're mad."

That sapped his newfound courage. "But aren't . . . ?"

"Don't try these old tricks on me," she interrupted and continued up the stairs.

"Well, anyway, please accept my unbounded admiration!"

She disappeared up the stairs. He leaned on the banister to get his breath and allow the fires of desire to die down. The night of the chase reappeared vividly in his imagination. Aly Seriakous, the porter, was coming down the stairs.

"I think I hear someone calling you," Saber told him slyly. "Maybe it was Madame."

"Madame?"

"Mr. Khalil's wife."

"No. I don't think so. It might be the guest in room fifteen. I've just seen Madame enter her flat."

"Ah. Maybe. Does Madame live in the flat?"

"Mr. Khalil's flat. On the roof."

"Where was she these past few days?"

"At her mother's. She goes there every month."

He saw Khalil coming down the stairs. Hatred and resentment suddenly filled him. Beauty and the beast! He couldn't bear the idea of staying one minute longer in the hotel. The sun and fresh wind lifted his feelings of depression, anger, and envy. How he wished he had more time to go sightseeing. The advertisement would not be published after tomorrow.

"Anything new?" asked Elham as he walked into her office at the paper.

"Telephone calls and meetings, all to no avail."

"Patience."

He watched her fingers skip over the keys of the typewriter. A sudden feeling of sadness came over him in spite of the happiness at seeing her.

Ihsan Tantawi was busy writing an obituary. He remembered the last night in his mother's life. All his happiness and future were now hanging on a fine thread lost in an enveloping fog. Tantawi finished writing and looked up. "A renewal?" he asked, smiling.

"I've seen many people, but not him," said Saber with despair in his voice.

"Such an advertisement requires patience," said Tantawi encouragingly.

"But he is supposed to be very well-known."

"You only know his name. All the rest is hearsay. I've lived in many districts over the past thirty years, and I've never heard of him."

"But I trust the person who sent me to look for him."

"Then there must be a secret which only time will reveal."

"I've got a photograph of him. It was taken thirty years ago."

"We can put it in the advertisement; it will help."

He showed him the photograph.

"He certainly looks impressive," murmured Tantawi.

Saber waited for Tantawi to comment on the resemblance. He didn't, and proceeded to discuss the costs of the new advertisement, to which Saber reluctantly agreed. His money was dwindling, and dwindling fast. He walked into the cafeteria and sat at Elham's table, waiting for her. She walked in, saw him, hesitated for a moment, then sat at his table. He ordered lunch for two.

"I've seen the photograph," she said.

"Really?"

"The resemblance is striking."

"You mean the man?"

She nodded, looking at him searchingly.

"He's my brother," he lied.

"Your brother! Why didn't you say so before?"

He smiled, but did not answer.

"Who is the beautiful woman in the photograph?"

"His late wife."

"Oh. And, your brother . . . I mean how . . . ?"

"He disappeared before I was born. It was the usual

chain of events. A quarrel, then disappearance. And now thirty years later, my father sent me to look for him."

"What a strange story. But what makes you think he is a well-known personality?"

"My father told me. Maybe it's mere supposition. But what strikes me as strange is that Mr. Tantawi didn't notice the resemblance. Did he mention anything after I left?"

"No. But Tantawi's head is full of figures and statistics."

The waiter brought their lunch. They started eating. He stopped and said apologetically, "I'm sorry to be intruding on you like this, but I'm a lonely stranger in a big city."

She smiled at him. "How do you spend your spare time?"

"Waiting."

"How boring. But searching doesn't entail waiting."

"Waiting is unavoidable."

"What do you do while waiting?"

"Nothing."

"Impossible!"

"Now you realize how badly I need a friend," he said with a pleading look in his eyes. The sympathetic look on her face encouraged him. "You are the friend I need." She took a sip of her orange juice. "Well, what do you say?" he asked.

"You might be disappointed."

"Don't worry about that. In these matters, only the heart can tell."

"We might meet when you come in to renew the advertisement."

Laughing, he said, "In that case, you want me to keep renewing the advertisement indefinitely."

"If you are so keen on finding him."

"I am. But if the advertisement doesn't find him, I must."

She raised her glass; he raised his. "Cheers."

"I think I'd better tread carefully with you," she said with a smile.

They drank, exchanging glances and smiles. He wouldn't have chased her that night long ago had she been the other girl, the seaside girl with the salty taste and carnations in her hair. She was very dear to him. He was in love with her.

You ask who the beautiful girl is in the photograph. You didn't see her on her last night on earth. Her body wrapped in the white shroud, wasted and worn out. Suddenly he looked up and said, "I'm truly grateful!"

She recognized the trap but did not object. A happy silence reigned. The seeds were sown. The search is long and arduous and requires an occasional rest in the shade.

Five

Sore eyes from looking, searching, scrutinizing the teeming Cairo streets. The autumn clouds sailing from Alexandria are dispersed long before arriving in Cairo. But the memories of his hometown linger on. The hotel lounge has now become a torture chamber since her return. How often you've watched her sitting next to the old man, her husband. Her eyes sparkling with promise and desire. How many times did you attempt, but in vain.

Elham was lost in a dark corner of his mind, enveloped in his all-consuming fire of desire for this woman. The lounge atmosphere, cigarettes, coffee, small talk, would occasionally draw him away from his madly passionate thoughts. Maybe these people are also searching for a hope. Lost in thought, he was abruptly aroused by the doorman, Mohamed el-Sawi. "Mr. Saber . . . telephone."

At last! Was it?

"Hello?"

"Are you the person mentioned in the advertisement?"

Breathlessly, he answered, "Yes, who's calling? Sayed Sayed el-Reheimy?"

"Yes."

"Is it your photograph?"

"Yes."

He was finding it increasingly difficult to breathe. "Where can I meet you?" he almost whispered.

"Why are you looking for me?"

"Let's wait until we meet."

"Just give me an idea."

"I can't over the telephone. There's no harm in waiting till we meet."

"Can you at least tell me who you are?"

"My name is in the advertisement."

"What do you do?"

"Nothing; I've got private means."

"Why do you want me?"

"I'll tell you when we meet, anytime, at your convenience."

A brief silence at the other end. "Come now. Villa fourteen, Telbana Street in Shubra."

No one in the hotel had heard of the street. "Go to Shubra and inquire," suggested Mohamed el-Sawi.

He went to Shubra. No Telbana Street. It didn't exist. It never had. Perhaps he had heard wrong. Perhaps he was being fooled. The woman, sitting next to her husband, added to his dark mood, driving him almost to a bloodthirsty passion.

Someone had rung several times in his absence. Hope surged again.

"Were you successful?" asked Mr. Khalil.

"Almost," he replied, trying to sound cheerful. He walked to the lounge, glancing quickly at the woman. The lights had just been switched on, adding a gloomy touch to the atmosphere, which lent itself to his mood. The telephone rang.

"Hello?"

"Saber? I waited all day," the voice said accusingly.

"I didn't find the street!"

"Did you really look for it?"

"All day! Telbana, number fourteen."

"What an ass you are." A wicked laugh, then the line went dead. The bastard! Back where I started, without hope.

He left the hotel and walked into a nearby restaurant, ordered a brandy and a fish dinner. A useless day. Might as well end it on a full stomach. He had several drinks, ignoring the cost. Just like the old days. Days of wine and roses, literally, you might say. But this city has nothing but heartache and despair to offer. Every passing hour brings nearer a frightening end. What comes after waiting and searching in the dark?

He would be the laughingstock of Alexandria. His fists, the only language he used, would now be turned against him. What did he have to look forward to? A life of crime, and not hope, and inevitably punishment. The woman crept back into his thoughts; the raging fire, and Elham, the gentle breeze. But of what use was all this, before he found his father? He left the restaurant and walked through the arcaded street. Passion was the only emotion driving him after his day's failure. A mad passion, just like the night of the chase. He remembered his mother. Smoking her narghile and ruling the desires of men. Beware how you spend, my son. Poverty is the real enemy. Love many, but never be dominated by one. Love, money, nightclubs, pleasure, women. But where is Sayed Sayed el-Reheimy?

Reheimy! . . . A cry in the wilderness. The brandy stimulated his imagination. That woman dominated his thoughts momentarily. He conjured up images of wild seduction. He returned to the hotel. It was past midnight, and everyone had retired. He lit a cigarette in his ancient room. More thoughts of the woman. Then sleep. He was awakened by a sound. Opening his eyes in the dark, he heard a gentle tapping on his door. He sat up unbelievingly. Could it be! The tapping again. He got out of bed and slowly opened the door. It was barely open when a figure rushed in, closing it again quickly.

"You."

She looked around her as though trying to recognize the surroundings. "Where am I . . . ? I'm sorry, I seem . . ." She gathered her dressing gown around her, covering her almost visible breasts. She was smiling. He pulled her toward him savagely, with all the fury and frustration that had been building up in him. I have been waiting a hundred years . . .

He pulled her toward the bed and turned the lights off. "I don't even know your name."

"Karima."*

"Very . . ." he murmured.

The only sounds were those of two creatures locked in passion, longing, and lust. Love in the dark, as he'd always known it. The dream was being realized in a whirlpool of passion, occasionally, but only imperceptibly, cooled by disbelief. The smell of the sea breeze once again. Memories rushing in, but being pushed into the background by passion and lust. The roar of the sea accompanying their violent lovemaking. Deep breathing, sighs, then calm reigns.

"Light me a cigarette, please."

*Karima means "generous."

"I didn't think you smoked."

"Only occasionally."

The match lit up her naked body, but she quickly blew it out. The smell of phosphorus blended with that of love.

"Why have you fought me all these days?"

"I never fight. I do nothing."

"I expressed my feelings about you from the very first."

She laughed softly and said, "When I saw you ten days ago I said to myself, this is it."

Triumphantly he cried out, "Alexandria?"

"No, no. I don't mean that. I said, this is the man I've been waiting for."

"What about Alexandria?"

"What about it?"

"Really? Come off it!"

"Why should I lie to you?"

"Strange that there could be two of you. Identical."

"Let's not waste time."

"How did you manage to come to my room?"

"He took his sleeping pills. All his troubles and worries converge on him in the evening."

"You have disappointed me. I told myself if you were the girl from Alexandria, then it was a good omen for my search."

"You mean your father?"

"Yes."

"What's your real story?"

"I always thought he was dead. Then I was told otherwise. That's all there is to my story."

"Maybe you're looking for money?"

"That doesn't matter now. Promise me you'll come here every night."

"Whenever I can."

He kissed her in a passionate embrace, which inevitably led to more lovemaking.

"Whenever I feel like it," she said breathlessly when they had spent themselves.

He lay on her breast, pleasantly exhausted. "Don't deny Alexandria."

"You are obsessed by an image. Take care that your search is not just a mere fantasy."

"I wish it were. Then I could rest," he said sadly.

"You really do have worries. More than I thought."

"Yes. But now my main concern is to stay here as long as possible."

"What's to stop you?"

He thought for a while, then said, "If my money runs out before I find my father, I'll have to go back to Alexandria."

"And when would you return?"

"I must look for a job."

She caressed his hand. "No," she said gently but firmly. He suddenly become aware of the trend the conversation was taking. She asked, "Why don't you look for a job here?"

"Impossible!"

"You're very mysterious. But let me tell you that money is not a problem!"

His heart missed a beat. "You must be a millionairess."

"The hotel, the money, they're all in my name."

"And your husband? Is he merely an employee?"

"No. As long as he's alive, he runs the show."

"But that doesn't concern me!" He felt himself blushing at the sly innuendo.

"Well, let's hope you find your father. That is a much better solution."

"Yes, that's very important. But from now on my main

concern will be to wait for you." He tried to embrace her, but she slipped out of bed.

"Dawn is breaking. I've got to go."

He returned to his bed. The rumpled sheets and the memory of her embrace were evidence that it had all happened.

He felt that now he could do without his father. The telephone rang.

"Hello?"

A serious voice said, "Is this Saber Sayed of the advertisement?"

"Yes, yes."

"I am Sayed Sayed el-Reheimy. What do you want?"

"I must meet you."

"I am waiting for you at the Votre Coin café near the newspaper."

"I'll be there in a few minutes."

Looking around the café, he saw a man sitting at the table usually occupied by Elham. Without a doubt, it was he. He hadn't changed in thirty years. Some white hairs and a few lines on his face. Nothing more. He moved toward him, and a new fear gripped him.

The man felt him approach and stood up. "Mr. Saber?"

"Yes. And you are the man in the photograph!"

The man sat down. "You are a very young man; I have a feeling that I've seen you somewhere before. Where? I wonder."

"I'm from Alexandria and am staying at the Cairo Hotel. All day I walk the streets. I've come here several times, at this very table."

"Maybe I saw you on one of the streets. I, too, go to Alexandria occasionally. I also come here from time to time."

"When did you see the advertisement?"

"The very first day."

"Really! Well, why didn't you contact me?"

"Your advertisement indicated that you had failed to find me by other means. But I'm well-known, and it's not difficult to find me. I decided to contact you when I noticed your persistent advertising."

"But that's very strange. No one I met had ever heard of you."

"Never mind about that now. Tell me what it is you want."

"I want you! But don't you notice anything?" Saber looked intently into the man's face, hoping to find a glimmer of recognition.

There was no sign of it on the man's face. "Look at my face," he said, almost shouting.

"What's wrong with it?" asked the man.

Suddenly a soft voice called out, "Saber!"

He turned to find Elham. He got up to introduce her to his father, when suddenly, to his surprise, the man rose and said, "Elham. How are you?"

To his utter amazement the girl kissed the man's forehead. "You know him!"

The man looked astonished. "When did you meet my daughter?"

"Your daughter! Oh my God!"

Before anyone could stop her, Elham rushed out of the café. Reheimy sat down and in his calm voice said, "Now tell me what it is you want."

Shaking, Saber sat down. Automatically, he took out the photograph, his birth certificate, and the marriage certificate. The man looked at each document calmly, placed them in a neat pile on the table, and just as calmly tore them to pieces. Saber jumped up and grabbed the man by his jacket, screaming, "You are denying my existence!"

"Get away from me! Don't ever let me see your face again! You're a good-for-nothing, just like your mother. I've got nothing to do with you!" He pushed him violently; Saber staggered back, fell, and banged his head on the lunch counter.

He woke up in a cold sweat, breathing heavily. He was in his hotel room, naked under the bedclothes. The sun was seeping through the shuttered window. The search; was it a dreamlike hope? A fantasy, as Karima suggested? He would have many more dreams like this one.

Six

Every night the dreams haunt him. He wakes up tired and depressed, a silence continuously surrounding him. A deepening, grave-like silence. Similar to a wave before it rolls and breaks. What then? Another wave follows. His father appears in every dream. But the search is no longer the main aim of his life. Rather, it is the snatched moments of love. Love in the dark, savage, passionate with an animal desire. Darkness brings back the memories of his early youth when he was almost fatally ill.

He had panicked when he met death face-to-face. It was this panic that became his driving force, that drove him to a life of violence; swimming, maybe drowning, in a sea of sin, lust, and pleasure, continuously having to use his fists to defend his mother's fictitious honor.

He went to the newspaper office and was greeted by Elham's calm smile. How refreshing she looks. A rock in his stormy sea.

"Any news?" she asked.

"I've come to renew the advertisement even though I doubt it will be of much use."

"Have you thought of any other method?"

He smiled. Little did she know that the search was now of secondary importance in his life.

"We've got a surprise for you," said Tantawi.

He sat down, his curiosity aroused.

"A woman inquired about you."

"A woman?"

"She asked about the advertisement."

"Who was she?"

"She didn't say anything; she just asked about the advertisement."

"Maybe she knows of him. Reheimy, I mean," Saber said hopefully.

"Maybe, and maybe . . ."

"What's the other maybe?"

"She might know you."

"Or maybe someone's playing a trick. It's happened before," he said bitterly. Could she be his wife? His widow? Maybe it was Karima, just curious. That woman was a volatile mixture of passions and emotions, cunning and destruction.

Saber and Elham sat at their usual table in the neighboring café. He remembered his strange dream.

"You don't seem as enthusiastic as before," she remarked.

If you only knew the real reason! "It's better this way," he said, "I must not raise my hopes too high."

"Yes," she agreed, "let time be your ally in this search."

"Please let me buy you lunch, at least once."

"You are the guest, not I."

They ate in silence. He noticed a thousand questions

going through her mind, mirrored in her eyes. He thought of the previous night. How strange to be two people at the same time, divided between two women, one a raging fire, the other a gentle spring breeze.

"Are you taking a holiday to carry out your search?"

She's probing now. He felt slightly uncomfortable. "I'm not employed in the real sense of the word. I have private means."

"Land?"

"My father owns some property." He could see that she wasn't convinced. "I run his properties for him. Believe me, that's harder than holding down any job." The second lie! How he hated lying to her.

"Well, as long as you've got something to do. Idleness is man's worst enemy."

"That's very true. These past two weeks have proved it. But what do you know about idleness?"

"I can imagine it. Anyway, I've read about it."

"You have to try it to really understand it," he said bitterly.

"That's true."

"It's difficult for someone your age to have experienced enough, at least the way I have."

"If you think I'm still a child, you'd better think again!"

How delightful she is. I think I love her. He mustered more courage and said, "You know everything about me. Now tell me something about yourself."

"What do I know about you?"

"You know my name, what I do, why I'm here. And also how fond I am of you."

She smiled. "Don't mix fact with fiction!"

That is the only fact, he told himself. A dark cloud hid

the sun momentarily and plunged the café in a deep gloom. "Well, I know your name and job," he said.

"What more do you want to know?"

"When did you start working?"

"Three years ago, when I graduated. I'm still studying, though. Higher studies, you know."

Thank God, she doesn't ask about my qualifications. She's too tactful for that.

"You, er, live in Giza?"

"I live with my mother. Our family is in Qalyoub. My uncle lives in Heliopolis. We also have someone missing from the family."

"Who?" he asked, surprised.

"My father," she said, trying to hide a smile.

How incredible. He remembered his dream. Lost fathers are plentiful, it seems. Maybe they're looking for the same one. "How did you lose your father?"

"Not like your brother. Don't you think I'm giving away too much?"

He looked at her reproachfully and yet curiously.

"Actually, my parents separated when I was just a baby," she continued.

"He abandoned you?"

She laughed loudly, making him aware of his mounting curiosity. "I mean, he disappeared?" he added hastily.

"He's a well-known lawyer in Assiut. Maybe you've heard of him. Amr Zayed."

He immediately relaxed.

"I thought you were going to say Sayed Sayed el-Reheimy!"

"Would you have liked to be my uncle?" she asked, laughing.

"No," he retorted firmly.

She blushed. "My mother," she continued, "insisted on keeping me. That suited my father, as he was intent on remarrying. He paid her alimony, and we moved to my grandfather's house in Cairo. He died, and we now live alone, my mother and I."

He listened carefully, but nevertheless with some skepticism. He always doubted women and especially mothers. Elham obviously had never heard of his kind of life. Whores, pimps, bastards, and many other choice varieties. Could he give her such details as she had done? Clouds of despair and gloom hung over him. Elham was still talking. "One day my uncle said that I should meet my father. My mother was furious. He doesn't deserve it, she argued, he never once asked about you. But my uncle insisted, saying that I was growing day by day, and I would definitely need a father."

He murmured unthinkingly, "Freedom, honor, and peace of mind."

She shrugged her shoulders and said, "My mother insisted on my not seeing him. I agreed with her point of view, that my job was more important than a father, at least more permanent. She was frightened lest he should decide to take me away from her."

Oh, just listen to her talk, that delightful child. What job or career could possibly replace freedom, honor, and peace of mind?

"I continued my studies and applied for this job, and now I'm pursuing my higher studies at night school."

"Don't you ever think of your father?" he asked.

"No. To me, he does not exist. That was his choice."

"Because you don't need him?"

"No. I don't need my mother either, but I love her and can't imagine my world without her."

You are obviously not on the brink of despair, my girl. You don't thirst for freedom, honor, and peace of mind. You are not threatened by a tainted past that could become your future overnight.

"I'm happy in my job even though I haven't got private means like you." She hit him where it hurt, unintentionally of course. How he wished he could tell her all. But he did not dare. Loneliness enveloped him when she left him to go back to the office. Despite her charm and gentleness, she aroused the animal instincts in him. He imagined her shock and horror at seduction and his ensuing shame and defeat. But to him seduction was a natural instinct, one could even say a hallowed tradition. That was his defense mechanism. To destroy every possible virtue. Elham was a shining beacon in his life but also a threat to his ego. She shook the world he was accustomed to. He could only forget his torture in Karima's fire. The beacon lighting the other half of his newfound dual life.

He walked out into the nippy November evening and strolled back to the hotel. The newly familiar sight greeted him: Khalil bent over his desk and Mohamed el-Sawi by the door.

He sat in the lounge for about an hour, smoking and scanning the papers.

He got up, went to the telephone, and dialed. "Elham, will you meet me tomorrow in the café?"

"With pleasure. Is anything wrong?"

"No, no, not at all. I want to see you whenever I can."

Seven

The nights he spends in passion with Karima. The sound of breathing echoes the rhythm and savagery of the jungle. He forgets himself then. Transcends this earth and universe, far above all fears and worries. Karima offers the pleasures and pains of a heavy meal, in contrast to the loneliness left by Elham every time they part.

Karima's nocturnal visits were uninterrupted since that first night when her gentle knock awakened him from his drunken sleep. Her influence dominating him, leaving no way for escape from these moments of passion. He pretending to be the dominant partner but fooling neither himself nor her. Never had a woman dominated him like this before. And yet he always doubted everything she said.

"I can't live without you," she whispered one night as she lay in his arms. How familiar were those words! He'd heard them in all the nightclubs and whorehouses that had been his life in Alexandria. He fought against the tide of her passion and influence. In vain. She was everything to him. Love, the hope that sent him searching for his lost father. On other evenings, she would just lie silent and still, submitting quietly and without much passion or concern. Then he would cry out in his mind for Elham, the fresh breeze to cool him in his hell with Karima. Yet it was a hell he could not live without.

How simple it had been that night on the beach by the fishing boats. You are still stubbornly attached to a memory that has long disappeared without a trace, like the waves. Karima represents not only love but also a magic potion that alleviates the agonies of his fruitless search and the whirlpool of anxieties stirred by Elham.

"You're not yourself," he said one night.

"Do you sometimes find me different?" she asked with the naivete of a child. The cunning devil. Had she forgotten her passionate confessions of love for him? He remembered his mother on one occasion. A man had come to "visit" her, and she had thrown him out furiously; then, when he left, she had broken down, hysterically weeping. Such was the way of women.

Casually he said, "I thought you were not feeling well."

"I'm fine," she said simply. And he detected a challenge in her voice.

"I'm glad."

She caressed his cheek, saying softly, "Don't you see that you mean everything to me?"

Meaningless words. "You are everything to me as well, and more," he said slyly, "and that explains my sadness at my impending departure."

"You are talking of leaving?"

"Not talking about it doesn't mean it won't happen."

"We'll postpone it as long as possible. Unfortunately, the money instinct is strongly ingrained in men."

"There's no other solution."

"He can help when necessary."

"Is he careful about financial matters?"

"Very. He doesn't care about money so much as how it's spent."

"Is he jealous?"

"Beyond belief. We've come to an arrangement about this matter. I must keep to my bargain or I lose everything. But you, what about you? Have you nothing to do but wait for a phone call?"

"A phone call could solve everything."

"My father never meant much to me."

"Well, mine means everything."

"How did you lose him?"

"It's ancient history. I'll tell you about it one day."

"Why doesn't he contact you?"

That's the question. The cause of his torture. So many possibilities. What will happen to you if you don't find him? Disaster, calamity, a life without hope, him, or work.

"How did you manage before?" she asked, interrupting his thoughts.

"I owned thousands, once; now only tens remain."

"What work did you do?"

"No work."

"Why don't you look for work?"

"Any work I do must come through my father. It's worthless otherwise."

"I don't understand."

"Believe me."

"Go into business."

"No capital or experience."

"A job?"

"No qualifications." Then, after a pause, he said bitterly, "I'm not fit for any job."

"Only love," she whispered, running her fingers through his hair.

He smiled. "I wonder what the future holds in store for us."

"Matters are complicated, and I can't depend on my husband."

"But he's so old!"

"That's very true. I think that death has passed him by without taking too much notice of him."

"Anyway, he'll live longer than my money will last."

"And he might smell a rat, and we'd never meet again."

He pulled her closer to him. "We'll run away when all hope has gone," he whispered fiercely.

"I'm ready. But what'll we do then?"

"Hmm . . . Even our love is worthless without my father."

"Be practical and stop dreaming."

"Does that mean that we must wait?"

"How can we bear waiting? And after we wait, then what?"

"Death." He sounded ominous.

"I sometimes think that he'll bury me. He's as healthy as anything. And me, I've got trouble with my liver and kidneys."

"How ironic." He laughed bitterly.

"He's a crafty old devil. At the first suspicion, I'll stop seeing you."

"I'll go mad," he almost screamed.

"So will I. But what can we do?"

"Waiting is useless, escaping futile, the telephone call, a dream; what's to be done?"

"Yes. What's to be done?"

"I think escape is the only way out."

"Never," she said breathlessly.

"Then waiting."

"Not that either," she said, almost urging him to utter some hidden thought.

"Then what?"

"Oh. Well," she said resignedly, "if we are unable to do anything, we'd better stop seeing each other."

He put his hand firmly on her mouth. "I'd rather die," he said.

"Death," she sighed. Then, as though speaking to herself, she repeated, "Yes, death."

He felt his heart beating faster, and his heavy breathing was deafening in the ensuing silence. "Why are you silent?"

"I'm tired," she answered. "Enough questions."

"But we're back where we started."

"Let it be."

"But there must be a solution," he almost pleaded.

"What?"

"I'm asking you."

"And I'm asking you."

"I was expecting a suggestion from you, a word, anything."

"No. I've no suggestions. It's a dream. Just like your telephone call. If I could inherit the money and the hotel, we'd live together forever."

He sighed. She continued: "The trouble is that we dream whenever we fail to find a way out, an escape. Dreams are our only escape."

"But the dream may be realized."

"How?"

"All by itself."

"You don't believe that, do you?"

"No!"

"And now dawn is breaking, and we've said all that can be said," she muttered.

He watched her shadow dressing in the dark. One last passionate embrace, and she left. Alone in the dark once again. Darkness like death and the grave. Your mother's grave. Alone with just your thoughts. Alone, cold, dark. In court, when sentence was passed, she cried out, "I know the monster who is behind this. I'll kill him." But her term in jail killed her, slowly but surely.

Oh, if only I could tell everything to Elham. How much easier things would be. She told me everything. I told her nothing but lies. Oh, Father, who do you insist on remaining lost?

Your mother thought she killed me. But it is I who killed her.

Then you are a criminal, a murderer; but I'll find you. The seduction of Elham. The bloody struggle. Her screams, I'll kill you! Her torn dress revealing a naked, ravished body.

The muezzin calling the dawn prayer. Another sleepless night? But no, there was the dream, his mother, his father, and the seduction of Elham.

He got up at seven, opened the window, and heard the beggar down in the square chanting his nonsensical rhymes. Oh! One with the beautiful face, Christians and Jews have embraced your faith. He saw Khalil being helped down the stairs by the porter, Aly Seriakous.

He sat in the lounge watching the old man. His trembling hand, adding up the money in his ledger. The money. Oh, if only you'd drop dead, old man. What possible joy can life offer you now? Karima's beauty wasted on your sterile love. The only pleasure you get is watching her undress and having her rub your back so as to get you to sleep. Either you die or my father appears. He remembered his days of violence. That evening in one of the dingy cabarets. He almost killed a police officer in a fight.

"Don't ever get involved in a fight again," his mother had said. "I can't bear the thought of losing you. If anyone gives you trouble, just tell me. I have means of sending him to the grave." That's true; she had once dispatched one of her competitors. One of her men had taken care of her and then escaped to Libya. Everyone said Basima Omran had killed her. But there was no evidence. As for you, Khalil, death won't really make much difference to you!

Eight

"I don't think continuing with the advertisement is much use," said Saber to Tantawi the next morning. Tantawi agreed. "He must have seen the ad by now," continued Saber.

"Yes, that's almost certain," said Tantawi.

Elham joined the conversation. "Then he is refusing to make an appearance."

"Maybe he is out of the country," said Saber. "In any case, there's no sense running the advertisement any longer."

Elham's enthusiasm was mounting. "It really all depends on him now. Time is the only thing we can rely on. He'll return when he wants to. We read of many similar cases."

Little does she know that he needs his father far more than his father needs him. He needs him not only for his future but out of fear of his own dark, tainted past. A life of crime. What will happen when his money runs out anytime now? There's no one he can turn to. The only thing driving him on is his fear of a return to the past. To stop his search will mean a plunge back into a life of crime.

These dark thoughts led him to say resignedly, "Well, let's renew the advertisement."

He waited for her in the café. Their daily meeting became a sacred ritual, one to be looked forward to with eager anticipation. Then the nights of lovemaking with Karima, forgetting the calm, tender moments with Elham, only to remember them again at daybreak. A pendulum-like life, swinging between animal lust and tender love, neither one overshadowing the other.

He feels attracted to and repelled by both. Each has a strong hold over him, arousing a feeling of protest within him. And yet he can't give either up. The choice can never be made. Elham representing clear, cloudless skies, Karima thunder and rain, but also like the Alexandria skies. Beloved Alexandria. The nights he spent at home in Alexandria, drinking beneath a cloudy sky, warming himself with creatures of lust and desire. Why does she deny that she hails from his past? She who is reminiscent of those wild nights made spicy by the salty air, wild like the stormy sea. She who is so much like him, hot-blooded, passionate, angry. Elham, so much the opposite, remote on a hill, out of reach.

She remarked on his silence, so he said heavily, "When this search is over, one way or the other, there'll no longer be any reason for me to stay."

She cast her eyes to the floor and said, "Have you decided when you're leaving?"

"I can't bear the thought of life away from Cairo."

"A lovely thought. I hope you realize it," she said earnestly, looking straight at him.

"I think of nothing else."

"But what about your family and your work?"

"There is always a way. Sometimes I think . . ." He was silent for a moment, then continued: "Sometimes I think that I didn't come here to look for Sayed Sayed el-Reheimy at all, but rather to find you. We sometimes go chasing something, and during the chase we come across the thing we are really looking for."

A look of tenderness and warmth crept into her eyes, and she said seriously, "In that case, I'm heavily indebted to Sayed Sayed el-Reheimy."

The dam burst. "Elham, I love you. My love has been growing ever since I met you. You mean everything to me, the very reason for my existence. I've never felt like this before. Every word I'm saying I mean from the very bottom of my heart."

Her lips moved silently.

"Isn't it so with you?" he asked, urging her out of her silence.

"Yes, and more," she said quietly.

He touched her hand and stroked it gently. Every fiber in him was singing; then he remembered Karima and their forthcoming meeting in a few hours. Clouds suddenly darkened his mood. He had loved more than one woman before, but now when he was with Karima, Elham pulled him, and vice versa. If only he could make them one person, one soul, one body!

"Have you ever been in love before?" he asked, trying to blot out his thoughts.

"No, never. Childhood romances maybe. I was once in love with a film star who is long since dead. No, Saber, I have never loved before. I was engaged once, but we broke up when he asked me to leave my job. My colleagues at work, they make their passes, that's inevitable. I'll tell you all about that later, if you promise that you won't leave; well, at least not forget Cairo."

"If I go to the ends of the earth, I'll never forget Cairo."

"That's good to hear. Now tell me what you know about love."

"I never knew it could be like this."

"I know a little about life, and I feel that when I look into your eyes I see a person of great goodness."

He quickly hid his surprise. "What do you mean?"

"I don't know. Please don't ask me to explain. You, you, it's something in the look in your eyes. It's reassuring, confident."

Oh. These beautiful, blue, unseeing eyes. Me, a good person? What about the old days? Where have the wild nights gone? Have they vanished without a trace? Oh, Father, please come and save me from my predicament.

"I don't want to praise myself, but my love for you, Elham, proves to me that I'm a better person than I thought I was," he said, half believing himself.

"You're better than that. Look at the relentless way you are looking for your brother. Did you ever know him?"

"No."

"And yet you are searching for him as though you knew him all your life. This alone proves to me what a noble person you are."

Damn! All my lying. Elham's words are as empty as a silence.

"I've only been asked to look for him, just like any other task."

"No. Even if you find him, that won't be to your advantage, at least materially; don't deny your good qualities."

Karima, like him, had been rubbed in the dirt for a long time. They had that in common. They could communicate, even at a distance. At the climax of their lovemaking she would whisper, "When will the obstacle to our love vanish?" That would fill him with fear, a fear compounded in the dark love nest, a darkness that could easily lead to crime.

Karima wouldn't imagine that he could kill just to avenge another woman. Yet he had done so before. He had blood on his hands; it was not a new experience for him.

The old man's clinging to life had no meaning except to drive him to an inevitable end. Elham, you have fallen in love with a criminal. I'll go mad if I continue lying to you.

The thought of murder fills your mind. You've done it before. Confess . . . Confess that you are worthless and poor, and that Reheimy is your father, not your brother. Confess that without him you are not worth a fistful of dust. Confess your past. She'll scream with fright and pain. The light in her eyes will go out. Then she'll discover the truth. If your mother had brought you up properly, you would have been a successful pimp by now. But no . . . she protected you in her golden cage, and now you suffer eternal torture. She resurrected your father and thus took away from you the comforts of despair and hopelessness.

"My mother thinks you should start a business in Cairo. She knows a lot about you," said Elham, interrupting his thoughts.

Mother! He feared mothers. Like his mother, she might find out the truth. She wouldn't be fooled by the look in his eyes.

"What kind of business?"

"That depends on what you can do."

Drinking, dancing, fighting, and lovemaking.

"Real estate management is the only thing I know."

"I don't know anything about your schooling."

He remembered that transient phase in his life. His brief sojourns in Arabic and foreign schools.

"My father didn't give me the chance to finish my education. He needed me to help him, especially when he fell ill."

"Think of some business. I've got some friends who can help you."

"All right. But I must first consult my father."

They got up to leave. "I wish I could kiss you, Elham, but it's impossible here."

His senses all screamed out: Leave Elham. She's like your father, full of promise but only a dream. Karima is just an extension of your mother. She represents pleasure and crime. Go back to Alexandria. Pimp for your enemies. Kill. Take Karima; take her money. Draw Reheimy out of the darkness. Marry Elham. Cairo winters are cruel. Streets are crowded, a marketplace of humanity. There you are lost in a fruitless search. You can have any woman you choose, offering a life of pleasure and no worries. But instead you choose Reheimy. Maybe he's just a charlatan who convinced your mother he was somebody.

You must have seen your father a thousand times every day while scanning the countless faces in the Cairo streets. He rejects you, or perhaps fears you. Maybe he's dead? Winter speeds up the darkness. It springs upon you suddenly and closes over you like the waves, drawing you in.

The porter of the hotel had told him of a soothsayer; perhaps he might help. He had gone to him, only to find that he had been arrested as a humbug. Since when was that a crime? The hotel became his prison. The lounge was filled with people, smoke, and noise. The faces changed, but the conversation always remained the same. He heard a man ask, "But doesn't that mean the end of the world?"

"To hell with it," said another.

Laughter and smoke filled the room. A man asked him, "Are you for the East or the West?"

"Neither," he replied disinterestedly. Then he remembered his plight and said, "I am for war . . ."

Nine

Karima didn't come that night. He lay on his bed in an alcoholic stupor imagining the absent lovemaking, trying to quench his lust. It was past midnight and still no Karima. She had never missed a night in his arms before. He kept a constant vigil all night, gradually losing all hope of her turning up. The dawn prayer announced the end of his hopeless wait. He slept for a few hours and woke up at ten.

As Saber breakfasted in the lounge, he watched the old man chat with the doorman. When will he wake up and find the old man not at his desk? How was he going to ask Karima about her absence last night? A heated argument broke out between two of the residents. He watched the vigorous gesticulations and the empty threats. Intensely annoyed, he got up and walked out of the hotel.

At lunch Elham looked serious. He felt much better than he had earlier. He always did when he saw her. "Our meeting every day is the only meaningful thing in my life," he told her with happiness clearly ringing in his voice.

"I don't cease to think about us," she said, looking at him with love and tenderness in her eyes.

He felt a tightness in his chest at her innocent attempts to capture him. He felt annoyed at the nightly defeats Elham suffered at the hands of her powerful enemy. "I'm glad to hear that. Me, too, I think of nothing else."

"Tell me, then," she said coyly.

"I think of work, and marriage."

"So you're finally convinced by my suggestion?"

"Yes, but first I must finish my mission here, one way or the other; then I'll leave and make arrangements with my father." He despised himself for his lies. How he wished he could confess all, come what may. The dilemma was something totally novel to him, a constant torment. "Let's go to the cinema," he said almost desperately.

They held hands in the dark. Always in the dark. But he felt at peace and kissed her hand; the gentle, intoxicating whiff of her perfume stirred his passions. He remembered the torture that lay in store for him at night. Karima. Desperately he tried to obliterate the thoughts.

"How cruel," whispered Elham, referring to the scene from the film.

He wasn't following, so he quickly said, "One moment away from you is far more cruel."

He watched the scene unfolding on the screen. A man was abusing a girl. The dialogue to him was disjointed and meaningless. Just like watching people's lives out of context, detached, disinterested. We laugh when tears are called for and cry when we are supposed to laugh. Your search for your father, for example, must appear amusing to people reading the advertisement. Will Karima come tonight? Is it going to be another night of agony and torture? He watched Elham's face; she was following the film intently. He tried slipping his hand out of hers, but she clung tightly to it.

They walked to the bus stop; she got on, and he stood for a moment watching the bus disappear around the corner. He walked to the grocer next to the hotel, ordered a sardine and pastrami sandwich, and washed it down with half a bottle of brandy. The vigil in his room began shortly after midnight. Oh, the humiliation he suffered. Never before had he felt like this. A hungry fear, fear of futile search, fear of fear itself. The night passed slowly and no Karima.

There she was the following afternoon. Sitting next to her husband. Just as he had seen her the first time. She avoided his long, hungry look as he sat in the lounge. She didn't know the madness of his passion, or she wouldn't provoke him so. She got up and went upstairs. As their eyes met for a moment, there was a clear warning in her glance. What does her look mean? The old man hadn't changed in his behavior toward her. He was too old to hide his emotions. Saber thought of following her, but as though she had read his thoughts, she raced up the stairs.

His money was running out. The search had become nothing more than a meaningless farce. The nights followed in the same monotonous pattern. A meal and heavy drinking. Hope by midnight. Waiting in the dark, night after night.

"Someone called you today," said the doorman one evening as Saber returned, drunk as usual. The telephone. Its ring lacked the excitement and anticipation it had had previously. But still a miracle could always occur.

"A woman's voice," continued the doorman, noticing Saber's indifference.

"Concerning the advertisement?"

"No. She just asked if you were here."

Elham. He had not seen her for a couple of days. His mood was such . . . He lay in the dark. A knock on the door. He jumped up like a maniac, opened the door, and dragged her violently inside.

"You!" he almost screamed out. He pulled her savagely toward the bed, unable to contain his passion. "You, damn you, you devil!"

"You're tearing my skin," she cried.

"You tore my nerves."

"What about me! Don't you know how I felt?"

He tried to tear off her gown, but she struggled.

"No, no don't. It's dangerous. I've got to tell you something, then I must leave."

"The devil himself can't save you now," he snarled.

"Shut up! You're drunk. One false move, and you'll spoil everything."

He sat her down on the bed. "What happened?"

"When I returned to my flat the last time I was here, he was awake. I made the usual excuses for being out of the room. But I think Aly Seriakous, the porter, saw me. I'm not sure, but I'm very scared."

"You're imagining things."

"Perhaps. And perhaps not. We can't risk it. We'll lose everything. Love, hope, our future. One word from him will condemn us to eternal poverty and misery. Don't you ever forget that." She sighed heavily, then continued: "That's why I stopped coming to you. I obviously couldn't explain to you before. I imagined your torture through mine. But my husband has given me all his wealth only on the condition that I'm absolutely faithful to him. He told me I'm his hands, eyes, daughter, wife; in fact, everything. I must be true to him during his few remaining days."

"Then what are we going to do?"

"I must stop coming here."

"But this is madness!" he growled.

"This is the only sane thing to do."

"How long must I wait? Till when?"

"I don't know," she sighed.

"My money will run out, and I'll have to leave."

"I can give you some to keep you here as long as possible."

"That won't change the inevitable."

"I know. But what can we do? I'm suffering just as you are."

"My plight is worse. I'm threatened with torture and poverty."

"I'm suffering for both of us. Why can't you realize this?"

"When will the old man die?" he muttered to himself.

"Do you think I know? I'm not a clairvoyant."

"Then what are you?" he snapped.

"An unhappy woman. Unhappier than you can imagine."

"Maybe death will answer our call, and he'll die suddenly."

"Maybe."

"He's an old man; he can't live forever."

"He might die tonight or in twenty years' time. His elder sister died two years ago," she said with a sigh. Dawn, the cock crowing, the muezzin calling the faithful to prayer. "There's nothing we can do. I must go."

"I won't see you unless he dies?"

"There's nothing we can do."

"There is," he said forcefully. The silence was deafening. He continued: "We've so far spoken in riddles, in the dark. We are going to speak frankly now. I must kill him!"

Her body trembled and so did her voice. "You don't really believe what you're saying. I'm not cruel or savage.

My only fault is that I love you beyond measure. We must wait."

"So that he lives as long as his sister?" he retorted with contempt.

"Or whenever the Almighty decides."

He had already decided. His blood was boiling and he felt hot despite his nakedness and the cool winter night. He paced the room furiously. "What happens after the crime?" he asked in a matter-of-fact tone of voice. She was silent. The darkness was oppressive. "Don't waste time," he snapped. "What happens after the crime?"

She gasped slightly as though choking over words, then very softly she said, "We wait a while. We can meet secretly, then I'll be yours. Me and the money."

He clenched his fists. "We have no choice. Desperation has driven us to this."

"Yes, unfortunately that's true."

"How must we set about it?" he asked.

She replied, quicker than he expected, "Study the neighboring building carefully."

So. She's got everything planned. But never mind. It's all because of her love for me.

"The apartment opposite the hotel is used as a second-hand clothing store. It's always empty at night. And it's easily accessible. The roof of the building and our roof adjoin," she continued in a hushed voice. "You can cross over to our side easily. You must wait for him in the flat."

"He comes up at about half past eight, nine?" asked Saber.

"Yes. Choose a date when I go to visit my mother. I go regularly once a month."

"Incredible that I've been here almost a month already," he said.

"You can then cross back to the other roof and leave the building without anyone noticing you."

His voice trembled slightly as he said, "We often hear of such crimes, after they are discovered."

Coldly, she replied, "But we never hear of those that are not discovered."

She was just like his mother. Utterly ruthless. "Is there anything else we haven't covered?" he asked.

"Yes. You must steal something as a motive for the crime."

"What shall I steal?"

"Leave that to me. But be sure to leave no traces."

"I'd better be careful, hadn't I?" he muttered.

"Our lives are now bound together. Should anything happen to you, it will also be my fate. We have no other choice."

He shook his head as if he couldn't believe the entire conversation. "Madness . . . madness . . . do you think all this will really happen?"

"Study the building carefully. Make sure no one sees you. There are a few days left before I go to my mother. You've got the guts it takes. Now let's go over it once again, step by step."

He was not listening, lost in deep, dark thoughts.

Ten

He breakfasted on eggs, cheese, fruit, and a glass of milk. He watched the other guests in the lounge. Look carefully at them; in a short while a vast chasm will separate you from them.

When night falls you are going to sign a blood pact as your gateway to crime. There goes old man Khalil, facing the cold morning, his hand trembling unceasingly, not thinking of death. Your life will end at ten this evening. You don't know that, but I do. Take the advice of one who has lost hope; don't bother about trivial matters any longer. I share with God the realm of the unknown. The telephone rang. Saber laughed audibly. Was that his father ringing at the eleventh hour?

Mohamed el-Sawi answered, "No, no, you've got the wrong number."

No, no. And no to you, Sayed el-Reheimy! You've denied your son, and now your son denies you. Your son will seek freedom, honor, and peace of mind somewhere else. Don't yawn, Khalil. Soon you'll sleep forever. Why do you persist in following an inevitable destiny? Explain to me what it all means; I, your killer, will enjoy your fortune, my mother sunk to the lowest depths, my father mercilessly silent, my hopes dependent on destruction. Explain all this. What is it all about? A week has passed, and I think of nothing but the crime. How different were my dreams as the train left Alexandria. These other men, the guests, have none of them committed a crime? All this talk of money, war, luck, will it never cease? They predict the future and yet are so ignorant about what is going to happen right here under their very noses.

Saber left the hotel at ten, nodding to Khalil on his way out. *I left the hotel at ten and didn't return till one in the morning*, he kept repeating to himself. He looked at the entrance of the neighboring building. Like a teeming marketplace. People going in and out. The roof was empty, and no other overlooked it. It would get dark after five.

He thought of visiting Elham, but the idea was crowded out by his immediate thoughts. He couldn't bear to talk to her while he was contemplating blood. What was he going to tell her before he left her forever?

He passed the newspaper building, and an overwhelming sadness descended upon him. He remembered their meetings, her concern over his problem, his inability to match her love. He killed time by walking aimlessly, had lunch at the grocery in Clot Bey Street, and washed it down with a couple of brandies.

"Terrible weather," said the grocer.

"I'm a criminal descended from criminals," he cried out as he left the shop. The grocer laughed; brandy does strange things to people!

He suddenly decided that he must see Elham. She was not at the café; the waiter told him that she had left immediately after lunch. His sudden desire to see her waned. He waited until five o'clock and then walked back to the arcaded street, standing in the darkness opposite the entrance to the building adjoining the hotel. The beggar was singing loudly, as usual. He noticed the doorman of the building busy in conversation with a street vendor. He took this opportunity to cross the street and enter the building. It was crowded with people. Many eyes fell upon him, but none saw him. He looked at every face carefully, to check whether any of the hotel guests were in this building for one reason or another.

He finally reached the roof. It was light enough to see that the roof was deserted. He looked around and saw that no other building overlooked it. His eyes rested on the hotel roof. Karima was there gathering the washing from the line. The sudden sight of her shook him. She must have been waiting for him. Maybe she had even watched him cross the street and enter the building.

She beckoned to him to approach. He did; seeing her renewed his determination to carry out his task.

"Did anyone see you?" she asked, turning her back to him.

"No one."

"Aly Seriakous is downstairs. I'll wait at the top of the stairs until you cross over."

She left with the washing and disappeared around the corner. He waited a moment, looked around him, then jumped onto the hotel roof. He proceeded cautiously until he arrived at the door of the apartment.

"The door is open. Come in," she whispered.

He took a deep breath and entered, finding himself in a darkened hall. She joined him, closing the door behind her, and switched the light on. Her eyes were sparkling but her face was deathly pale. Gone were her seductive looks. They hugged, nervously and without passion, looking at each other with some bewilderment, like two frightened, lost children.

"Any slipup and we're lost," he said.

"Get hold of yourself," she said. "No one suspects a thing. Everything will turn out the way we planned it."

She took him through the flat. The hall led into a large bedroom with an adjoining door to a smaller dining room. He glanced at the furniture in the bedroom. The large bed, the sofa, the Turkish divan, all seemed to stare at him with disinterested eyes. He was about to tell her his feelings, then thought better of it.

"What an ugly room," he said instead.

She seemed to recover from the tension of the moment. "Yes. You must hide here in the bedroom. The moment you hear the front door, get under the bed."

"Is it a wooden floor?"

"Yes, it's carpeted all over."

"He'll close the front door?"

"Yes. Sawi takes him up. Especially when I'm away. He locks the door himself and leaves the key either in the lock or on the table, here. You unlock it and leave."

"I might meet someone on the roof."

"No. Seriakous, the porter, retires after my husband comes up. His room is on the third floor."

"They'll ask how the . . ."

"The windows will be closed, so either he forgot to lock the door after Sawi left or else someone knocked and he opened the door," she said quickly.

"Is it possible that he'd open the door to someone without asking who it was?"

"Maybe he heard a familiar voice."

"Then suspicion will fall on those he knows in the hotel."

Coldly and impatiently, she answered, "They won't pin it on an innocent person. The important thing is that you get away." She pointed to her handbag. "I've taken the money and some jewelry. I opened the cupboard with a knife and threw some clothes on the floor. Did you get gloves?"

"Yes."

"Very good; here is the iron bar." She pointed to the table in the middle of the room. "Don't touch it without your gloves on, and be careful not to drop anything under the bed." Her face seemed even paler contrasted with her glittering eyes. "I must go," she said. They embraced.

"Stay for a while," he pleaded, clinging to her.

"No, I must go."

"Have you forgotten anything?"

"Pluck up your courage and act calmly, and . . ."

"What?"

She gave him a strange, distant look. "Nothing," she whispered. "Get under the bed."

They embraced a third time. She broke away quickly and left him, calling loudly for Aly Seriakous. Quickly, he hid under the bed. Karima returned with the servant and told him to close the windows. She waited until he had done so, then switched off the lights and left the room.

Saber got out from under the bed. It was pitch-dark. He put on his gloves and groped toward the table and found the bar. He gripped it firmly and crossed the room and sat down on the edge of the bed. Nothing else existed at the moment. Just the feel of the bed, the smell of her perfume, and the crescendo of silence. No escape now. One death-dealing blow. One blow is better than all this endless waiting and futile searching. Karima's love, like a thin cloud and yet more dangerous than the task he was about to perform. The beggar was still chanting away. Did he ever stop? It was a lost call. Just like the advertisement, and his mother's wealth, and those days of long ago. When would he see Karima again? Embrace passionately and safely?

He heard the servant Seriakous humming softly on the roof. Then silence and darkness. After what seemed an eternity, he heard the key turn in the lock. He quickly crawled under the bed. Footsteps approached, the door opened, and the room flooded with light. He could scarcely breathe, and he thought that his heartbeats could be heard a mile away. Six feet appeared to him. The old man was saying, "You can go now, Aly, but don't forget the plumber."

Two feet disappeared. Khalil sat on the edge of the bed, his feet a mere two inches from Saber's face. "I'll meet him tomorrow. But I won't stand for any nonsense," Khalil said.

"Yes, I agree," said Sawi, the doorman.

"He's a cunning devil. He came close to death four times, and he still hasn't learned his lesson."

"You are a generous man, master." After a short silence, Sawi asked, "May I leave you now, Mr. Khalil?"

"No. Stay a while. My back is aching, and I have a terrible headache."

How long will he stay? Will he spend the night with the old man? Saber shuddered at the thought. Khalil was busy saying his prayers. How appropriate. When he had finished, he said, "Help me with my robe and shoes, Sawi." Rustling and movement then, "Get me my sleeping tablets from the drawer."

Where is that drawer?! If it was in the cupboard, the fake theft would be discovered. He held his breath in anticipation. He breathed again when he heard the old man drink water, swallowing the tablet. Then he felt Khalil lie on the bed and pull the covers around him.

"Sawi, I can't get up. Lock the door and open it at the usual time tomorrow morning. Good night."

Darkness, then the dim light of a small lamp. You will find your master a corpse tomorrow morning. How did the killer enter? How will he escape afterward? The window, the one overlooking the roof. How will they reconstruct the crime? He was going to explode with tension and fear. All these thoughts, all this planning. You must carry it out. You must. Your heartbeats are deafening. You can't think. Will he fall asleep before I explode? Snoring. Just like his mother on her last night. The death shroud, the weeping skies in Alexandria. Forget that now. He crawled out from under the bed. He stood up, gripping the bar firmly in his gloved hand.

Khalil was hidden under the bedclothes. Only his head showed slightly under the pillow. He felt better at not seeing his face. He approached with renewed courage. He raised the bar. Suddenly the old man turned restlessly. Saber stood rooted in his place, arm raised, bar above his head. The old man opened his eyes. Their eyes met. No sign of recognition in Khalil's eyes. Saber realized his plight and brought his arm crashing down. He was taken aback by the fantastic force of the blow and the sickening sound of the impact. The old man uttered one soft cry, then a whimper, then silence. The body shuddered once violently, then was still. Saber didn't bother to make sure he was dead. He rushed to the window, opened it, looked out, and jumped quickly onto the roof, closing the window behind him.

Was the iron bar soaked with blood? Was the roof

deserted? What time was it? He crossed the roof. Why didn't he wash the bar in the bathroom? Should he throw it from the roof of the building? That would be idiotic. He heard voices on the stairs. He looked over the banister. The third floor was dark, but the light shone on the second floor. He wiped the bar with his left glove, then slowly went down the stairs. He came to the second floor. The light was shining from an open apartment. Three men came out and followed him down the stairs. He slowed down until they passed him. He came to the ground floor and left the building with the three men as though he were one of them. He noticed the doorman of the building sitting in his small room by the entrance. Outside he took a deep breath. Did anyone recognize him? Were his clothes bloody? He saw a taxi on the other side of the street. But he dared not cross. Someone might see him from the hotel. He turned away from the building and crossed the street, and then doubled back toward the taxi. The beggar was through for the day. He was getting up and moving toward him. He waited a few paces away from the taxi.

The beggar passed him. For the first time he got a good look at him. How repulsive. A thin, sallow face, a crooked nose, and red, bloodshot eyes. A dirty bedraggled beard and a head covered by a black patchy skullcap. What did this man have to sing about? And yet he sang all day. The beggar passed him with the expected stench that went with his appearance. He rushed toward the taxi and asked the driver to take him to the Nile, at the place where some boats were moored. Had anyone seen him leave the building? Did anyone notice the glove and the bar? Why was the taxi moving so slowly? The driver was annoying him with meaningless chatter.

"Isn't that right?"

"Huh . . ."

"I mean, instead of this madness, I tell myself, patience is a virtue." Why doesn't this idiot shut up? What is he saying anyhow? The banks of the Nile were plunged in darkness. No one would see the glove, the bar, the blood. Rowing at such an hour must surely be strange. But not strange when compared with other things.

Now you can get rid of the glove and the bar. Wash your hands carefully in the muddy Nile waters. He suddenly felt exhausted. He let the boat drift with the current. Nothing on shore was worthwhile. How pleasant it was just to drift with the tide. The eyes and their look, the cry; these could never be forgotten. The beggar's eyes, did they issue forth tears or blood? Nothing mattered now, not even the search for his supposed father. But where are you drifting?

Suddenly a piercing blast woke him from his trance. A river steamer passed within inches of him. His boat rocked violently in its wake. He took the oars and rowed back to the mooring place. The sky was pitch-black. Not a star in sight. He suddenly shivered and for the first time that evening felt the winter cold. He walked along the island briskly to keep warm.

It happened while he was crossing the Kasr el-Nil bridge. A large sedan was waiting at the traffic light. A man sat at the wheel. Dignified and obviously well-to-do. That face. Was it possible? The light turned, and the car moved.

Sayed el-Reheimy! The cry rent the cold night air. He chased after the car, running like a maniac. But the car sped on and disappeared from sight. He stopped running, gasping for breath. It was him. Reheimy. After thirty years. He didn't even get the car's number. What was the use now? How could he trust his eyes if he didn't even feel the cold?

His senses had deserted him. Reheimy meant nothing to him now. His only hope lay in Karima.

She must be awake now, thinking. A strong bond held them, and yet how he wished to see Elham and confess. The clock in the square showed midnight. He decided to return to the hotel. What a hateful prospect. He shuddered as he passed the building next to the hotel. He remembered the repulsive beggar and wondered where to seek refuge.

Sawi, the doorman, was sitting in Khalil's chair. He was still awake. Saber dared not enter. But to go out again might raise suspicions.

"You look exhausted," Sawi said.

"It's very cold outside," he said cautiously.

"She rang again," the doorman said, with a knowing smile.

"Who?"

"You know best."

Elham! Cowardly! Just like Reheimy.

"Your city offers nothing but problems," he said bitterly.

"Life is nothing but problems. Any news?"

He realized Sawi was asking about his search. "I'll look for him tomorrow. At the cemetery."

He nodded and went up the stairs to his room. Room number thirteen!

Eleven

He left his bed at six in the morning without having had a moment's sleep. All night haunted by dreams, dreams, and more dreams. A quarrel between him and Karima in front of the old man, who didn't seem to notice him. But if he had dreamed, then he must have fallen asleep. It's very cold. But you can take it. After all, you're a hardened criminal. He switched on the light and was shocked to see his right glove still on! He stared at it in horror. He must have gotten rid of the bar and the left glove and forgotten this one. He had gone to the riverbank, strolled around the island, chased after the car, crossed streets, waved to the doorman, and all the time he had his right glove on!

He felt a cold, creeping terror. What happened to all your careful planning? What traces have you left behind? You must check everything, the bedsheets, the blanket, the floor, your shoes, socks, jacket, shirt, handkerchief. He felt physically sick with fear and doubt. The investigating eyes will not miss a thing. He must get rid of the glove. He wrapped it in his towel, grabbed his soap, and went to the bathroom, his small scissors in his pajama pocket. He cut the glove into small pieces and flushed them down the toilet He then washed his face and left the bathroom to return to his room, only to meet Aly Seriakous in the corridor.

"Good morning, Mr. Saber, you're up early this morning."

Damn . . . What are you doing here? . . . The guest in room thirteen was up earlier than usual, that's the only thing I noticed, Officer. That's exactly what the wretch will say. Damn! Damn! This was a bad omen. Did he wipe the floor after having disposed of the glove? Curses! He's going to the bathroom. He thought he had seen what looked like bloodstains on the sink. He stood rooted to the spot, his eyes glued to the bathroom door. The porter came out of the bathroom.

"Can I do anything for you, sir?"

He ignored him and went straight for the bathroom to look for bloodstains.

"I forgot my soap," he said apologetically, trying to appear calm as he left the bathroom again. The man smiled.

"You had it in your left hand."

Catastrophe! Laughing nervously: "That's the hazard of waking early. I couldn't sleep, there was a terrible racket outside." He entered his room still laughing nervously. What a bad start. But no need to exaggerate the dangers. He inspected his clothes carefully while dressing. Looking up at the ceiling, he imagined Khalil lying on his bed. He shuddered. Murders happen every day, he reassured himself. It would be madness to leave now for Alexandria. Have I forgotten anything? Evidence could be found in the strangest places. He thought of taking his jacket to be dry-cleaned. But how would he wrap it? This would certainly draw attention to him. Probably by this afternoon he would be answering questions. The dangers of his situation weighed heavily upon him. He must leave the hotel before they discover the crime. That was more important than the jacket. He took a last look around the room. Will it betray him? Mohamed el-Sawi was performing his morning prayers as Saber walked into the lounge. There were a few people around as he sat down to his breakfast. The porter, Aly Seriakous, walked up to him.

"You forgot this, Mr. Saber."

His wallet! It must have fallen out of his jacket as he was looking through it. He opened it.

"Thank you very much, Aly," he said, giving him ten piastres.

"I found it on the floor by your bed."

How many mistakes were still undiscovered? he wondered. This blind force driving you will soon bare you before the whole world. You will stand naked, just as you were born. Just as your mother delivered you into this world. Your mother, the real killer! Khalil had snored, just as she had done on her last night. He noticed one of the residents smiling at him, as though he were reading his thoughts. The lounge became unbearable. He walked out of the hotel and was greeted by the singing of the beggar. How repulsive he looks. Maybe he's happy just singing away all day and every day. Sawi, the doorman, going up to the apartment on the roof. Knocking on the bedroom door.

"Mr. Khalil! Wake up! Wake up! Mr. Khalil, it's almost eight o'clock. Mr. Khalil! Mr. Khalil!" He pushes the door open and looks carefully in. "Mr. Khalil," quietly. Then: "Oh my God! Mr. Khalil! Master! Master! Help! Help! Aly! Aly! Help! Mr. Khalil has been murdered! Police! Police! Help!"

My mother disappeared, never to be found by my

father. My father disappeared, never to be found by me. Maybe I can also disappear. Just vanish without a trace. Then sometime, somewhere, Karima will be in my arms, the promises of a comfortable, happy, secure life finally fulfilled.

He walked, not seeing anyone, not hearing anyone. Just walked, occasionally sitting down at a café for a brief rest. But for him there could be no rest. He passed by the High Court building. Dark clouds were passing overhead. Clouds, reminiscent of Alexandria.

He must see Elham. Toward the late afternoon he headed for the café, their usual meeting place. It looked strange to him today. Everything was strange today. He felt a sudden mad urge to confess everything. The truth! For once!

She looked at him reproachfully. "Why should I greet you if you've been avoiding me?" she said, looking at him with her deep blue eyes, pretending to be cross. She sat down, staring at him uncomprehendingly. "And you're not even talking," she continued.

"I'm sorry, Elham. I was very busy and completely exhausted."

"Not even a call on the telephone?"

"Not even. Let's not discuss this now. Let me just look at you."

They were silent. Just sitting there looking at each other. The beggar's chant ringing in his ears. Why did he insist on meeting her? Maybe their meeting was a temporary shelter from the storm that was about to break. She's smiling even though she shook my bloodied hand! He felt tears creeping into his eyes. The farewell tears.

"You look exhausted."

"I've seen him," he said quietly, almost in a whisper.

Her eyes widened. "Your brother?"

"Sayed. Sayed el-Reheimy."

"Then your mission is over?" she cried, overjoyed.

He recounted the story wearily.

"There is a possibility that it's him," she said hopefully.

"And also that it isn't," he retorted.

"When will all this be over?" she asked pleadingly.

"I consider it finished."

"You really look tired."

"I've been meeting a lot of people during the past few days."

"About your brother?"

"Yes."

They drank their juice in silence. A smile crossed her lips and she asked, "Didn't you have any time to think of me?"

"All the time."

"What did you think?"

When are you going to confess? When, when? Save yourself all these lies.

"Say something," she said, still coyly. "Last time, we spoke of a new job here in Cairo."

Confess. Confess. That's all you're thinking of. Otherwise, you'll explode.

"Yes, yes," he said hastily, "I haven't forgotten."

"In spite of your worries?"

"I've been thinking of the various aspects of the new job."

He could not resist any longer. "Elham. I love you. I love you with all my heart. I've been lying to you all this time."

"What do you mean?" she asked, bewildered.

"My love for you is what drove me to lie."

"I don't understand." Confusion covered her face.

"I told you I was searching for my brother. Well, the truth is that I'm searching for my father."

"Your father?"

"Yes, yes. My father."

"How did he disappear? Perhaps like my father?"

"No. I always believed that he was dead. But my mother, just before dying, told me that he was alive and said that I must find him."

"Well, that doesn't change anything," she said, looking him straight in the eye.

"But I'm broke," he cried. "I don't own a thing. My mother was rich, and I always led a comfortable life. But when she died all she left me was her marriage certificate and the photograph as evidence. Other than that, I'm not worth a thing."

Bewilderment and shock filled her eyes. What if he told her the whole truth about his mother?

"You look worried," he said quickly.

"No, no. Just surprised," she replied haltingly.

"I'm not worthy of you, Elham. I'll never forgive myself for deceiving you."

"I understand everything. I understand why you lied."

"What I can't bear is that I made you love someone not worthy of you."

"Your love for me, is that a lie?"

"Never. Never. I love you with all my heart."

She sighed. "It's your love for me that forced you to tell the truth, isn't it?"

"Yes, yes. That's true."

"Then you've done nothing wrong by hiding the truth."

"But I must leave you."

"Why?" she cried out, swallowing hard.

"I'm penniless; I have no one; I can't do anything."

"Money is not everything. As for having no family, what do we need family for? And besides, there are many things you can try your hand at."

"I doubt that. I've no education, no experience, I never had a job before. You see, there is no hope unless I find my father."

"And will your father be a substitute for everything else?"

"My mother told me that he was a man of considerable means."

She paused briefly, then: "But the advertisement . . . the name . . . the telephone directory . . . I mean . . ."

"Yes, you're right. I no longer believe that he is a man of position or even that he is in Cairo. But he might be in any one of the other governorates. Not necessarily Cairo."

"You say you saw him yesterday?"

"I thought so. But I've lost faith in everything now."

"How long are you going to wait?"

"That's a good question. I can no longer afford searching, or waiting."

"And so?"

"I don't know. All the avenues seem to come to a dead end. I must return home and look for any job, or else . . . or else kill myself."

"And you say that you love me," she choked, biting her lips.

"Yes, Elham. I do. With every fiber in my being."

"And you talk of leaving and suicide?"

"Everything is lost now. I feel like someone slowly being strangled to death."

"But you love me. And I love you too."

Pain and hopelessness were all over his face. "But, Elham, I'm far beneath you."

"You must be patient, Saber," she pleaded. "I will stand by you."

"Oh, what's the use? I was dreaming when I thought I'd

find my father. That's why I allowed you to enter my life. That's why I fell in love with you."

"Work. That's what will solve our problem."

"But I've already told you, there's nothing I know how to do."

"Give me a chance to think. You'll see, everything will turn out the way we want it to."

And what about the murder? How can things turn out for the better? It's all over now. How is it that the confession has not brought on the holocaust?

"Things won't turn out the way we want them to, Elham," he said quietly.

"Give me a couple of days," she said determinedly. "Don't make any decisions. I know what we want."

Tell her about your mother. Tell her what you did yesterday. Confess that you married another woman, a marriage that was sealed and consummated in blood. Tell her that you want to scream, scream, scream.

Twelve

Here they are. The police and the calamity. Just as you had imagined all day long. The crime has been discovered, and only the criminal remains to be found.

There's no alternative but to go forward. Control yourself. Forget the look, the last look on Khalil's face. Forget also the last cry uttered by a dying man, a murdered man. The return to the hotel was a terrifying experience. Just like confessing. Your careful planning, useless. You should have left the hotel long before the crime. Enough of this dithering. The beggar, still singing despite everything. He made his way through the crowd of onlookers. A policeman stopped him.

"What happened? I'm a resident here." He saw Sawi, his face tear-stained and pale. "What happened, Sawi?"

Sawi burst into tears. "Mr. Khalil has been murdered!"

"Murdered!"

"He was found murdered in his bed. God's curses on the killer."

The lobby was crowded with policemen and detectives. In Khalil's chair sat the senior officer, and on his right, in Karima's chair, was another man. The senior officer was busy looking through some papers. One of the guests was sitting opposite the officer. The officer reminded him very much of his father. He felt suddenly weak at the thought but then noticed that the officer was a much younger man. How silly, he thought; everyone seems to look like my father. Should he wait or go straight to his room? He was just about to go upstairs when the man sitting in Karima's chair said, "Please wait in the lounge."

He walked into the lounge and sat with a group of hotel guests. "What happened?" he asked.

"Mr. Khalil was found murdered."

"How?"

"Who knows? The police have asked us all to stay here for the investigation. They've searched everywhere."

He heard subdued, choking sobs. There in the opposite corner of the lounge sat Karima. She was sitting between an old woman and an elderly-looking man. How could he have not noticed her when he entered? What should he do? After some hesitation he went over to her. "My profoundest sympathies, madame. You must be strong."

She didn't look up, but continued to sob. He went back to his corner, shaking his head as though in shock at the crime. Was it a mistake, what he just did? Could this old woman be the mother of the Alexandria sweetheart? What are the police thinking? Did they inquire about the resident in room thirteen? Was he already the subject of investigation? Do they understand criminals, as he understands loose women? He hated them all. Hated them to the point of killing!

"What now?" he asked the group.

"You've only been here a few minutes. We've been here since morning."

"Have they questioned the other guests?"

"Yes, and they let them go. Our turn has not come yet. They also questioned the wife, her mother, and her uncle."

"But I believe she wasn't here."

That was rash! The guest continued: "That makes no difference. This place is full of surprises. They found a large amount of hashish in room six, and they arrested the man living there. Also, in room three they discovered a professional thief."

"Ah. Maybe."

"Yes, that's quite possible. It all depends on the motive."

"No doubt it was theft."

Again rash. You'd better be careful. Did they find any evidence? he wondered. He wanted to be with Karima, if only for a moment. Don't look in her direction. She must have some important information for him. It's not as you imagine. Damn that beggar and his incessant chant. I visit my mother at this time every month.

Money and jewelry are missing. Aly Seriakous closed the windows in front of me. I locked up myself. No. I don't think he has enemies.

Why does this man remind him of his father? A guest interrupted his thoughts. "We are innocent, and yet we're nervous and on edge. What must the guilty feel?"

Said another, "What's worse, that one false slip or a wrong expression can start endless troubles."

"But never was an innocent hanged."

"Hah!"

But the guilty may escape. Your mother and the man who escaped to Libya. You were mad to return to the hotel. There must have been some other way. Your need for your father becomes more urgent with the growing danger.

The guests were called one by one. His turn came. He sat before the investigator, hating him immensely. He must defeat him at all costs. The man looked at Saber's identity card.

"You've been here for over a month, as the hotel register shows."

No, he doesn't resemble his father. "I got up as usual, got dressed, and came down to have my breakfast."

"Not exactly as usual. You woke up early."

"I don't wake up at a set hour."

"The porter said that on this particular morning you were up earlier than usual."

"Probably he didn't see me on other occasions."

"Did you hear anything unusual at night?"

"No. I slept soundly the moment I got back to my room."

"Did you notice anything unusual when you woke up?"

"No."

"When did you see the porter, Aly Seriakous?"

"On my way out of the bathroom."

"Did he seem somewhat different to you?"

"No. He looked just as he does every day."

"And you? Tell me, is there anything about yourself that you haven't told me?"

"No."

"Didn't you forget your wallet?"

"Yes, yes. I did. Aly Seriakous brought it to the lounge."

"What impression did you have then? I mean after getting the wallet?"

"Naturally, I was pleased."

"What else?"

"That's all."

"Weren't you surprised at his honesty?"

"Maybe. I don't remember. It probably didn't occur to me."

"But it's natural that it should occur to you."

"Perhaps I was slightly surprised."

"Slightly?"

"I mean, I wasn't astounded or anything like that."

"How honest do you think he is?"

"I never noticed anything about him that would suggest dishonesty."

"Where did you go from the time you left until your return?"

"Walking about, here and there."

"No job, of course. That's clearly stated on your identity card. But also no friends?"

"I have no one here in Cairo."

"Yesterday. When did you leave the hotel?"

"Around ten in the morning."

"When did you return?"

"At midnight."

"You didn't return at any time during the day?"

"No."

"Is that your usual habit?"

How did you change your regular pattern yesterday? Why?

"I've done it maybe once or twice."

"Nobody here recalls that."

"But I do!" he said indignantly.

"Once or twice, you say?"

"Probably twice."

"And how do you spend your day, then?"

"Walking around. I'm a stranger here, and everywhere I go is new to me."

"What did you find upon your return?"

"I saw the doorman, Mohamed el-Sawi, here, and the porter, Seriakous, in front of the door of my room."

"What was he doing?"

"He asked me if I needed anything."

"Did you meet any of the other residents?"

"No."

"What did you do yesterday from ten in the morning until midnight?"

"I walked until lunchtime."

"Where did you have your lunch?"

"I had a sandwich at the grocer's on Clot Bey Street."

"Strange for someone of your means."

His hatred for this officer grew intensely. "I came across this grocer when I first arrived. You might say I became attached to him."

"Then what did you do?"

"I walked along the Nile."

"In this weather?"

"I'm from Alexandria, remember," he said, laughing, trying to conceal his fear and anger.

"Then what?"

The café? No. He must not drag Elham into all this. In Alexandria I saw the film showing at the Metro Cinema here. "I went to the Metro Cinema," he said quickly.

"When?"

"At six o'clock."

"Which film was showing?"

"*On Top of the Clouds.*"

"And after nine, what did you do?"

"I walked around as usual. I also took the Heliopolis bus to the end of the line. Just to kill time." Kill! What a choice of words.

"Where did you have dinner?"

Be careful! "At the cinema. I had a sandwich and some chocolate."

"Did you meet anyone?"

"No."

"You know no one here?"

"No one." He paused a while, then added: "I contacted the advertising manager of the *Sphinx* newspaper. Purely business, you know." Was that a mistake? Could it implicate Elham?

"Why did you come from Alexandria to Cairo?"

"A visit. Tourist, you might say."

"But this hotel is not appropriate for a tourist of your means."

"It's very economical."

"Do you really possess private means?"

"Yes, of course."

"Tourism, is that the real purpose of your visit?"

The circle is closing. Lies will get you nowhere now. You never expected these questions when you planned all this. "I do have another purpose, apart from tourism."

"Tell me."

"It's family business."

"Tell me something about the property you own."

"Just money."

"No land or buildings?"

"Just money, cash."

"And your address in Alexandria. Is it what is stated on your identity card?"

Questions. Investigations. His home, the nightclubs.

Basima Omran. You will invite suspicion, you cannot escape it.

"Yes, that's where I live."

"Which bank do you use?"

"Bank?"

"Yes. Where is your money deposited?"

"I don't use banks."

"Where do you keep your money?"

"In . . . in my pocket."

"Your pocket? Aren't you afraid you might lose it?"

"There's very little left," he said quietly, with bitterness.

"But your identity card points out that you are wealthy."

"I was."

"What are you planning to do?"

Don't hesitate. I'll challenge him with the truth, or in spite of it.

"I was searching for my father. That's my future."

"You're looking for your father?"

"Yes. He left us when I was just a baby. I told you I had family problems; they're of no importance, not worth mentioning. Now that I've gone through my money, I've no recourse but to look for him."

"Have you any idea where he might be?"

"No. The advertisement in the newspaper is my last hope."

"Maybe that's the real reason why you are here in Cairo."

"Perhaps."

"How long will your money last?"

"A month at most."

"May I?"

With mounting but restrained anger, Saber handed him his wallet. The officer looked through it and then gave it back. "What are you going to do when the money runs out?"

"I was planning on finding a job."

"What are your qualifications?"

"None."

"What kind of a job?"

"Any kind of commercial enterprise."

"Do you think that'll be easy?"

"I've got friends in Alexandria; they will help me."

"Do you owe the hotel money?"

"No. I paid this week in advance."

"How did you find this hotel?"

"Purely by chance. I was looking for a cheap place to stay."

"Did you know anyone in this hotel before coming?"

"No."

"But since then? You know many people here, no doubt?"

"Mohamed el-Sawi, Aly Seriakous."

"Mr. Khalil, I mean. The deceased, Khalil Abul Naga?"

"Naturally."

"What did you think of him?"

"A very old, very kind man."

"And yet someone saw fit to kill him."

"That's very sad."

"Did you know where he lived?"

"In a flat on the roof, I think."

"You're not sure?"

"No."

"How do you know?"

"Aly Seriakous told me."

"Or did you ask him?"

"Perhaps."

"I wonder why."

"I don't really remember. I usually chatted with the porter whenever I saw him."

"Did you ask him any other questions?"

His heart beat violently. "Perhaps. I cannot recall any specific questions. It was ordinary conversation, you know."

He felt the trap closing. The officer asked, "How long are you staying in Cairo?"

"Until I find my father or a job, or until my funds dry up."

The officer lit a cigarette and took a deep puff, then asked, "Have you anything else to add?"

"No."

"We might require you later; please don't leave without informing us."

"Yes, of course."

What an idiotic, incomplete scheme it was. Escape now would be madness. You'll be watched every minute of the day. You'd better think back over every question and try to find out where you stand.

Thirteen

Your position is precarious, obscure, just like death. Most probably they are already investigating you, watching you closely, your every move. You won't realize it. Just like Khalil before the fatal blow. Weigh your every move. You cannot afford a false one. The hotel is quieter now. The smell of death drove many of the guests away. But others will come. The lounge is cold, cold as the grave. Nothing new in today's paper. Talk about cotton, currency, and war. The wind howling outside as though chorusing the perpetual chant of the beggar.

He heard footsteps, looked up, and saw Sawi greeting Karima. He felt his stomach turn with emotion. Karima sat down with her old mother and Sawi. Did she come to take over the hotel? Will their eyes meet? He felt much better seeing her. When will we meet? Somehow she'll contact you. She's even more beautiful and sensuous in her mourning dress.

You're in desperate need of her passionate condolences, consoling you in your plight. She was talking quietly to

Sawi. He heard him say, "I don't know when they'll allow us to enter the flat."

Where is she staying? It would be insane to follow her. How could you have possibly overlooked asking her mother's address? She must contact you by phone. She must remember how badly you're in need of money.

"Telephone, Mr. Saber."

Damn the telephone. What now? Has Reheimy perfected the art of mocking me? He walked to the telephone and, passing her, offered his hand. "I repeat, Madame, my sincerest condolences."

She shook his hand without looking up. He kept his eyes on her while speaking on the phone.

"It's Elham, Saber."

Why isn't it Reheimy? Why did I come to Cairo? Why this hotel in particular?

"How are you, Elham?"

"Are you all right?" She sounded anxious.

"Yes, thank you."

"Why didn't you come yesterday?"

"I'm sorry. I was rather tired."

"Well, I won't reproach you now. You're coming today?"

"No, not today. As soon as I get rid of my cold."

"Well, I won't trouble you. You know where to find me." She seemed hurt.

"Goodbye."

"Goodbye." He didn't put the receiver down but pretended to continue with the conversation, looking straight at Karima.

"You must contact me in any way. By telephone perhaps."

She turned her eyes; she must have gotten the message.

"I want to know several things," he continued. "I am

sure that you are aware of my situation; we must talk, and don't forget that my money is running out."

She gave him a warning glance. "I'm fully aware of your problems," he added quietly, "but I'm sure you'll find a way." He walked back to his seat in the lounge, feeling slightly relieved although still very worried. Karima got up, followed by her mother. He felt that he was seeing her for the last time. The crime was meaningless without her. He waited, hoping for that phone call. No call. A terrible silence was left in her wake. The lounge was empty except for him. He noticed Sawi looking at him, so he nodded to him, smiling.

The man asked, "Why are you here all alone?"

"It's my cold. I've taken a couple of aspirins. I'll go out if I feel better." He moved to the chair that had been occupied by Karima and sat down. "The telephone has driven me to utter despair."

"Well, I'm sure there must be a good reason for his not calling."

Saber looked at Sawi and said with some sympathy, "You've been going through very hard times."

The old man's face contorted with pain and sorrow. "May you never go through what I'm going through."

"It must have been a terrible sight. I've never seen a dead body before. Even my mother, I closed my eyes."

"Yes, but murder, that's something else."

"Yes, that's true. Murder, blood, savagery."

"Unbelievable savagery. No punishment is sufficient."

"I've often asked myself, what would drive a person to murder?"

"Yes, I wonder."

"And the murderer. What kind of person can he be?"

"I saw a murderer once, an errand boy. I had always thought he was so kind and gentle."

"Incredible."

"Yes, but what can we do?"

"How true. What can we do? We'll soon hear that he's been arrested."

The old man looked sadly at him. "He already has been arrested."

"Who?"

"The killer."

"The killer! But we didn't hear anything about it."

The old man nodded.

"Who is it?" asked Saber almost in a whisper.

"Aly Seriakous."

"That . . . that idiot."

"Just like the errand boy."

"Is that why I didn't see him around yesterday evening or today?"

"May God have mercy on us all."

"Has the wife been informed?"

"Naturally."

"Man is truly an enigma."

"They found the money on him."

"It could have been his money."

"He confessed to the theft."

"And to the murder?"

"I don't know."

"But you just said that they've arrested the murderer."

"That's what Karima said."

"Does that mean that theft was the motive?"

"I think so."

"He could have stolen without killing."

"Probably Mr. Khalil woke up and saw him, so he had to kill him."

"He was kind to the point of idiocy almost."

"As you said, man is an enigma."

"He's more than that," said Saber.

"Did you know that the poor beggar we hear singing every day was once the tough guy around here?"

"That decrepit old man?"

"He lost everything, money, health, his sight. He had no other recourse but to beg."

"But Aly Seriakous showed great honesty when he returned my wallet, which I had misplaced."

"He's smarter than we think."

Do such things happen so easily? Or is it purely our imagining based on emptiness? Nothing, nothing at all.

"Wouldn't it have been easier for him to escape?"

"Escape would be tantamount to confession."

"How could he have hidden the stolen articles in his room?"

"Maybe they found them at his home."

"Taking them there would have been foolish."

The old man sighed. "Such is the will of the Almighty."

"When I saw him the morning of the crime—before it was discovered, that is—he appeared calm and pleasant as usual." Saber's heart was pounding.

"Some people kill and attend their victim's funeral!"

Be careful. Don't let your hidden fears surface. The telephone might throw some light on matters.

The old man continued, still in a sad, tired voice: "I was the first to be questioned by the police."

"You?"

"Yes, of course. I was the last to see him alive last night and the first to enter his apartment this morning."

"But who could think . . . ?"

"I was bombarded with questions. I had closed the door myself. The windows were shut, but I found a window ajar."

"Maybe he forgot to close it."

"No. She insisted that all the windows were closed."

"Did Seriakous break in?"

"No, that's impossible. The noise would have woken everybody up, certainly Mr. Khalil."

"Maybe he knocked on the door and Mr. Khalil opened it."

"But why open the window? And also it was established that he was killed in his sleep."

Saber stared in silence. Then he said somewhat hopefully, "Maybe he hid in the bedroom?"

"No. He left the apartment before me. I locked up myself."

"Well, maybe . . ." The sentence died abruptly. It was stifled by a sudden fear. He was about to say that maybe Seriakous pretended that he was closing the windows. He is not supposed to know that Scriakous closed the windows. That was a close shave! It left him ice cold with fear.

"Maybe what?" the man asked.

"Maybe he used another key to open the door."

"Possibly. But why open the window?"

"It is most probable that they were left open. Forgotten."

"God knows."

"It must have been hard on you," Saber said sympathetically.

"I don't understand how they let me go. But they know their job."

"There's no more talk of the murder in the papers. All news stopped suddenly."

The old man was close to tears. "May God rest your soul, Mr. Khalil. I knew him for sixty years."

"How old was he?"

"Over eighty."

"When did he marry?"

"Ten years ago."

"It's a strange marriage, don't you think?"

"He married when he was young. He had a child; then suddenly, tragically, he lost his family. He remained single for a long time until she came along. He loved her as a father would his daughter, above anything else."

"That sounds reasonable, considering."

"He was a good man, kind and generous. He helped me raise and educate my children."

"How did he get married?"

"He used to travel frequently to Alexandria."

"Alexandria! Is she from Alexandria?"

"No. He used to stay with a friend of his who lived in Tanta. She was married at that time."

"Married?"

"Yes, to her cousin, a good-for-nothing. He met her at this friend's."

I am talking too much. "How did they get married?" Saber's curiosity made him reckless in his questions.

"She got a divorce, and they were married."

"She married a man over seventy?"

"Why not? He gave her honor and security."

"And peace of mind," Saber interjected heavily. He remembered his mother's last words. "But a good-for-nothing, as you describe her ex-husband, wouldn't divorce such a beautiful woman. Why did he divorce her?"

"Everything has its price." The old man immediately regretted this remark.

Saber noticed and said quickly, "Anyway, those things are past."

"I've said more than I should. Ever since I saw him lying in his blood, I'm not myself. May God forgive me."

A pimp's whore. A purchased slave. A coolheaded criminal, a vessel of unbelievable pleasures, your torturer to the end. Groundless intuition, nothing else, led you to this bloody hotel and flung you into crime, murder, blood. Just like the intuition that made you chase the car like a maniac.

Fourteen

Coffee and more coffee to alleviate the rigors of a sleepless night. He watched the telephone through a cloud of cigarette smoke. When will Karima ring? A heavy downpour lasted for a few minutes, leaving the streets soaked and muddy. Karima, silent as the dead, not realizing his agony. Heavy drinking, sleepless nights, nightmares. All this will leave traces on you, easily observed by watchful eyes. As for Karima, she doesn't care. One of the residents approached his table and asked if he might share it with him. The lounge was very crowded. He must be the last of the residents who were here when it happened. Obviously he is seeking some juicy gossip.

"They've arrested the killer," the man said.

"Yes, I know," said Saber, hiding his fear and annoyance behind a smile.

"Aly Seriakous?"

"Yes."

"Theft was the motive, I believe," said the man, settling comfortably into his chair. "I was wrong."

"What did you think?"

"Well, to be quite frank, I always suspect women."

Saber looked at him sharply; he continued: "A beautiful young woman who stands to inherit a good-sized fortune."

"I thought of the same thing," said Saber, feeling his nerves almost twanging with fear. Did the investigator think the same? But Karima is silent, like death. The telephone does not ring. The rain, cold, and mud haven't silenced the beggar's singing. Mohamed el-Sawi called him, pointing to the telephone. He got up and moved toward it with heavy, tortured steps.

"Hello?"

"Saber?"

Never did he think that he would hear her voice while in such a state of despair. "Elham. How are you?"

"Am I disturbing you?"

"No. No. You'll see for yourself I've been sick. I'll wait for you today."

He must get her out of his life, no matter how painful it is. He must get her out of the mud he is floundering in. They met. There she was, ignorant of everything, smiling reproachfully. How could he love so deeply and sincerely?

"Don't you feel guilty?" she asked, smiling. He couldn't answer. She took off her gloves and sat down.

"That cold must really have affected you."

"It was a nasty bout with the flu."

"And no one to take care of you?"

"No one at all."

"Did you see a doctor?"

"No. I just let it run its course."

"Good. You must drink a lot of juice. It's good for you."

They ate in silence, her eyes never leaving him.

"I thought many times of coming to visit you."

"Thank God you didn't," he almost snapped.

She shrugged her shoulders, but didn't pursue the matter further. Then, full of enthusiasm, she said, "I haven't wasted a minute."

Oh! The pain you cause, Elham! Why don't you go away? "You're an angel," he said quietly.

"Don't you believe me?" she chirped, her eyes dancing with joy. "Well, you're about to start . . . *we* are about to start a new life. What do you say to that?"

He tried desperately to overcome his gloom. "I say that you are an angel, and me, I'm a crippled beast."

"The capital you need," she continued, undaunted, "is now available."

"Capital?"

"Yes. All that I've saved for the future. Also some of the jewelry I never wear. It's not a fortune, but it's quite sufficient. I asked people in the know, and believe me, we'll start out on solid ground."

Are such miracles possible? In your wildest dreams you never thought this could happen. Money without crime, and love to top it all. Resurrect the old man and awaken from your nightmare! He sighed woefully. "Elham, the more you do for me, the more I'm convinced that I'm not worthy of you."

"Stop trying to be a poet. There's no time."

Her happiness is burning like a bright flame. To extinguish it will be your second crime. But she is reaching out for something that does not exist. You never dreamed that there was such a simple solution to your problems. Well, there you have love, freedom, honor, peace of mind. And where do you stand? So much, so late.

"Why are you so pensive? I expected you to jump with joy."

The time has come! "I told you many times that I was not worthy of you; why didn't you believe me?"

"I expected you to jump with joy."

"It's too late," he almost wailed.

"Oh my God, you don't love me."

"Elham. Things are much more complicated. I loved you at first sight. But who am I?"

"Don't tell me about your father, your poverty, or your worthiness."

Oh, the hell I'm going through. There's no other way but to tell the truth.

"You are still suffering from the flu. You're sitting with me, but where is Saber? The Saber I knew when we first met?"

"Don't ever ask that question again."

"If you're ill . . ."

"No. It's not illness."

"Then what, what? What is the matter? Why did you say it's too late?" She was very close to tears.

"Did I say that?"

"Just a few seconds ago."

"I mean only one thing. I'm not worthy of you."

"Don't be idiotic. I love you," she said angrily.

"That's my crime. Unfortunately we thought only of love."

"And why is that a crime?"

"Because I should have told you the truth about myself."

"You did. And I accepted it."

"I spoke of my father, but . . ." Then bitterly he continued: "But not about my mother."

She looked at him defiantly. "I love you, you. Your past has got nothing to do with it."

"You must listen."

"For God's sake, let her rest in peace."

"All of Alexandria knows what I'm going to tell you."

Then with vehemence mixed with bitterness and sorrow, he burst out: "She ended her days in jail!"

She started, disbelievingly, as if she were looking at a madman.

"Now do you understand?" Swallowing hard, he continued: "The government confiscated all her property, and that is the reason for my poverty. She left me with a hope that has destroyed me." The shock was brutal. But she'll recover. "I have no right to love someone like you. Only the loose women I've known all my life. But what could I do? I was helpless in my love for you."

She was silent. Struck dumb. That's good. No questions. Otherwise, you would have had to tell the whole story.

"My pure love for you is my only compensation. All my life I've spent in sin. It's the only thing I can do. Sin."

The biggest hurdle is now behind you. You almost feel happy. Oh, if only night wouldn't fall. Probably the investigator knows all these things by now. He got up and left without a word.

The telephone rang the following afternoon. "Elham!"

A low quivering voice said, "Saber. I just want to say that all you said yesterday, well, it doesn't change anything."

Fifteen

Elham. You're nothing but a constant torturing pain. As for Karima, you are linked in a bloody tie that will be broken only with death. Your need for her is like a maddening hunger that keeps you in a constant hell. You'll find a way of contacting her. You must!

The best thing we can do then will be to sell the hotel and live in some other town. You will lead a passionate, spontaneous, carefree life, not like Elham, whose voice calls for a change in your life and causes you endless pain. But when will Karima contact him? What happens after the money runs out? He would accept any job, even Seriakous', just to wait for Karima. I wonder, are they going to hang him? Poor Seriakous! You've killed a man with your own hands; no harm in killing another, but using different hands. When, when will this nightmare be over?

Before leaving the hotel, Elham telephoned him. "Are you going to renew the advertisement?" She sounded subdued.

"No," he replied wearily.

"I asked someone to find out if he's got an unlisted number," she said softly.

"And of course he didn't find anything."

"No, unfortunately."

"Don't worry about it," he sighed.

"We've got correspondents in other towns. They're inquiring as to his whereabouts."

"I don't know how to thank you, Elham."

"Aren't you thinking of coming to pay us a visit?" she asked shyly.

"No," he replied firmly. "I'm thinking of your welfare."

"I wonder how you are taking all this."

"I told you, it doesn't matter to me."

"It does to me," she whispered.

They lost contact after this. The pain was unbearable. What's the use of beauty in a world soiled with blood? Her eyes can only see what is beautiful. They are blind to ugliness.

Sawi saw him on his way out and smiled. Saber smiled back nervously. The man offered him a seat. He sat hiding his impatience and tension.

"Are you in a hurry?" asked the old doorman.

"No, not at all. I've got nothing to do."

"Then stay a while. To tell you the truth, I feel very lonely after the death of Mr. Khalil. I've no one to talk to."

"What about your sons?"

"They're not in Cairo."

There were only two guests in the lounge. The traffic noises drowned out the beggar's chant.

"Anything new turn up?" asked Saber.

"I've got a friend on the force. He seems to know, although he brags a bit."

"What does he say?"

"Aly Seriakous. They've found no one else."

"Perhaps he confessed?"

"I don't know."

"He was tempted by petty thievery."

"He denied the theft."

"But he had already confessed to it," Saber said, as though defending himself.

"Yes, but later he denied it."

"But they found the money at his home."

"He said the wife gave it to him."

"Mr. Khalil's wife?"

"Yes."

"But why?"

"Charity, maybe."

"But did she give charity to the other servants?"

"No. All the others were questioned. He's the only one."

"That's very strange," said Saber, swallowing hard.

"What is stranger still is that he then confessed again to the theft."

"And what about the so-called charity?"

"He said that she normally gave him tips for jobs that she wanted done. He saw where she kept the money, and this tempted him."

"He went to steal, and he killed."

"That's it, I think."

"What does the investigator think?"

"Who knows? But they seem convinced that he's the murderer."

"He has probably confessed," Saber said hopefully.

"Probably."

"No doubt the lady used to tip him."

"Perhaps."

"But why did he deny it and then confess?"

"Who knows?"

"There must be another facet to the problem."

"Ah. Who can be sure?"

For the first time he inspected the old man's face. Green, faded eyes. The closer he looked, the more he felt that he was seeing a new face, forgetting the old one. "Do you think that there is another facet?" asked Saber.

"How can I know?" replied Sawi, showing no interest in the matter.

Yes! That's how men will feel approaching the gates of hell! "You know much more than you're willing to tell," said Saber cunningly.

"I'm afraid that the opposite is more correct."

"Did they ask the wife any more questions?"

"The officer called her more than once."

"Did Seriakous' statement have anything to do with that?"

"Yes."

"Do you have confidence in your friend? The one who gave you this news?"

"But she said so herself."

"The wife?"

"Yes. She was here yesterday evening."

She chose a time when he would be out! That cunning, wicked devil! Of what consequence can the investigation be compared with his predicament? Beware; the old man might read more than just curiosity into your questions. But how can I avoid these burning questions?

"Did she speak about her gift to Seriakous?"

"Yes, it was only charity, of course."

"That's reasonable."

"Why?"

"Aly Seriakous doesn't strike me as a man . . ."

"Are you aware of these things?" asked Sawi.

"Not every man is capable."

"But I've lived far longer than you," said the old man.

"Are you doubting her character?"

"I didn't say that."

"Then you are confident she's honest?"

The old man closed his eyes sadly. "I don't doubt her, I know."

Observe how matters are being revealed. Your investigation is proving more successful than the real investigation!

"Then she is dishonest?"

"Unfortunately . . . Yes . . ."

"Did you know this before your friend's death?"

"Yes, but I cared for his peace of mind more than the truth."

"Did you give your opinion in the investigation?"

"Of course."

"You mentioned the relationship between her and Aly Seriakous?"

"Aly Seriakous . . . I'm not thinking of him."

Was this the trap? And had he fallen for it? "We were talking about him."

"Yes, but then we talked about her."

"As the other party."

"No. There is another man."

Can her fires consume more than one man? Of course they can! It is known as hell!

"Another man?"

"Her previous husband."

"The man who sold her," said Saber breathlessly.

"It was merely a business deal."

"But how do you know all this?"

"I saw him several times at her mother's house when I was there."

Hell's gates were opened wide. "And you didn't mention it to anyone?"

"It would have killed my master to know."

"He was killed in spite of it."

"Yes, and that's the tragedy."

"Why did he allow those visits?"

"His age destroyed his ability to doubt."

"You also mentioned this during the investigation?"

"I did."

"Did they question the other man?"

"He was not in Cairo on the night of the murder."

"That doesn't preclude that he planned it."

"Yes, that's true. But they let him go."

"Why?"

"They have their reasons, I suppose."

"They must have used the servant with incredible cunning."

"Or some other idiot like him."

Saber swallowed hard. "Maybe these are all groundless doubts."

"Perhaps," said Sawi, noncommittally.

"But you said that you're sure."

"Maybe I used the wrong expression."

"Well, we're back where we started."

The old man shook his head gravely. "My heart tells me that my doubts are well founded."

"But there might not be any connection between her adultery and the crime."

"That's possible. Otherwise they wouldn't have let them go."

"In any case, Seriakous has served them well," said Saber spitefully.

"If he's the murderer."

"Do you doubt that?"

"Everything is possible."

"Sometimes I think that you don't believe it."

"And why not? You remember what I told you about that errand boy?"

"Maybe he's the killer."

The old man sighed. "I think that the killer will strike again. Perhaps not right away. But he'll strike again."

You'll not sleep a wink until you question her yourself. What a devil of a woman. But she'd be a fool if she thinks she can trick you. She knows that you can kill. But how to find her?

"Her previous husband," said the old man, "didn't plan the murder. Otherwise they wouldn't have let him off so quickly. But the other crime . . ."

"He's her cousin," Saber interrupted, "and it's not strange that he should visit her."

"Actually, I had my doubts long ago. Her mother used to live very near here, and her husband would take her there whenever she wanted. Then suddenly the mother moved to number twenty Sahil Street, in Zeitoun, miles away. Why? I could find no logical reason except that the wife could use it as an excuse to spend some days at her mother's. Mr. Khalil objected at first, but then gave in."

How easy it all was! Number twenty Sahil Street, Zeitoun. No effort at all.

Saber was now lost in a raging tempest of madness. The smell of blood was strong in his nostrils.

Sixteen

He knew he was being watched; otherwise he would have gone immediately to Zeitoun. Patience and a plan were both required. Sawi was sitting in the old man's, the dead man's, chair. For a moment Saber thought it was Khalil, then for the first time the truth of his actions hit him with a ferocious impact: he had taken a life.

I wonder if Khalil is thinking of me now? If he can, what thoughts must be passing through his mind?

He greeted Sawi, who returned the greeting quickly and looked back into the register, as though he had forgotten yesterday's conversation.

He took his breakfast in the lounge, halfheartedly, without any appetite. Karima. No one is going to make a fool of me. Karima will not escape me. She can try what she will, but the hangman's rope is in my hands. Nothing seemed changed in the lounge, the same chatter about war and money, and outside, the beggar chanting. Elham was on the phone.

"Can I see you today just for a few minutes?"

"I can't."

"Give me a good reason why not."

"I can't."

"Even if it has to do with your father?"

"My father?"

"Yes."

"What do you mean?"

"Let's meet today."

"I can't." Even his father could not save him from the whirlpool of his fury.

"But it's about your father. The object of your search."

"So what?"

"Shall I come?"

"No," he said impatiently. What news could she have? Anyway, what difference is it to him now? Zeitoun, that's the objective. His father. That was probably a trick to get him to see her. He drank heavily. Cheap wine. Walking around trying to think of a plan to fool the watchful eyes.

I'll go up to my room. But I shall not sleep. The detective will. At dawn, he crept slowly downstairs. A servant was sleeping in the lobby in front of the door, the locked door. He dared not wake the man up. He might be the detective. Slowly, he went back up the stairs. Suddenly an idea occurred to him. He raced up the stairs, all the way to the roof. A shiver ran through him as he passed the closed apartment. He crossed the roof to the wall of the adjoining building, and without hesitating for a second, jumped over to the building. Breathing heavily, he went down the stairs to the entrance. The doorman's room was closed. The front door was closed. Damn! Nothing but obstacles. He tried the key that was in the lock. It didn't work. Why? He tried the door handle. It worked. The door wasn't locked. Why? He opened the door slowly, quietly. Suddenly a man blocked the now open doorway. "Who's there?" a voice cried.

Without hesitation, he drove his fist violently into the man's face and kicked him in the stomach as he doubled up. The man fell, silent, motionless. He rushed out into the cold empty dawn. Crossing the street quickly and racing toward the square. Without warning, he collided with something.

"Oh! Help! Please, please, I'm blind."

"I'm sorry, it's very dark," he said as he hurried on. He shuddered. That cursed beggar. Ubiquitous.

The taxi drove toward Zeitoun. The detective is going to have a long wait. He got out of the cab at the beginning of Sahil Street. He walked toward the small bungalow. Daybreak was slowly filtering through the dark.

He knocked on the front door, not caring what lay ahead. Karima! There she was, just as she appeared on her first nocturnal visit. He pushed past her.

"Are you mad?"

They faced each other under a bare, glaring lamp.

"You must be insane."

"Maybe." He looked at her with his bloodshot eyes.

"Don't you realize the consequences of your action?"

"It's better than waiting without hope," he hissed.

"You must wait. Don't you see that my situation is far more critical than yours?"

"And how long must I wait? Till death? Why didn't you phone?"

"Sawi would have recognized my voice."

"Anyone could have spoken instead of you."

"They asked me so many questions. I panicked."

"You panicked? You who plot murders in bed while making love?"

"Don't raise your voice. My mother's asleep."

"Isn't she your accomplice?"

"You're mad. You look so strange."

"I must see your bedroom."

"It's just like any other room."

"Don't be funny, I must see who shares it with you."

"Have you gone out of your mind?"

"Your cousin. Your previous husband. Isn't he here?" he shouted.

"Who said so? No one is here. You've brought disaster upon us now by coming here."

"I don't care. I must see for myself."

He pushed her roughly out of his way and opened the first door he saw. An old woman was fast asleep. Another door, another bedroom. Hers, most probably. He searched every room. No trace. "You've driven me crazy," he cried, returning to the hall. "You must avoid him during the investigation."

"Saber, I think someone is behind all this. Some cunning devil," she said, trying to calm him down.

"Weren't you married to your cousin?"

"I was."

"And didn't he sell you to the man you plotted to murder?"

"They'll arrest us, you fool. Today."

"Answer me."

"You're an idiot. I risked my life because I love you."

"He came to sleep with you in this . . . whorehouse!"

"Can't you see the truth? Have you forgotten what was between us?"

"Every woman is an accomplished actress in bed."

"Please, please believe me. These are all lies!" She was almost hysterical.

"Do you think I'm afraid of hanging? I'll never leave you to another man."

"There is no other man. Believe me. If you don't, they'll get us before sunrise."

"Whore! Liar! You destroyed my life with a lie."

"Believe me, I beg you. I love you. All I've done is for your sake!"

"You destroyed me to enjoy the fruits of my crime with your lover."

"You are my lover! Believe me before it's too late. This man stepped out of my life years ago!"

"You divided things like only the devil can. I get the murder and you, the money."

"Oh, what's the use? We're finished. Once more, won't you believe me?"

"No."

"Then what do you want?"

"To kill you."

"And hang?" she screamed.

"I don't give a damn anymore!"

Several footsteps, followed by thunderous banging on the door. Karima screamed loudly, "The police! It's too late!"

He pounced on her savagely, blindly, his hands closing around her neck. Screams, the door banging, more screams, the door crashing open.

Seventeen

And where now, Saber? In jail, alone. No one visits you. You have no one. Elham is now a distant dream, a vision. She must have gotten over her love. She must be cursing it!

The newspapers carry the full story, Karima, Mr. Khalil, Mohamed Ragab, her first husband. Your photograph. The wedding photograph, even Elham, and of course, Basima Omran. The papers leave no stone unturned.

But in jail you are liberated from the vicissitudes of life, just as in the womb. Saber, arrested while murdering his mistress. Saber, there's a story behind him. Basima Omran, queen of the Alexandria nightlife. She offered him in his poverty and despair an unknown father, a lost hope. The search for Sayed Sayed el-Reheimy. Love. Murder. Saber's amorous adventures and conquests. Saber, the symbol of cruelty and corruption. They admired his love for Elham. How noble that was in the midst of a sordid story.

His mother afforded him a brief life of luxury; when that inevitably collapsed, he had to find a father or kill. The investigator suspected you from the first. You were constantly watched. Sawi spoke to you of Karima's infidelity. That cunning old devil! What an idiot I've been!

Her first husband, Mohamed Ragab, denied any connection with the victim. It was the lover who fell in the trap. Was Ragab lying, or was he simply telling the truth? The papers don't give any details of the part that resulted in your destruction. Will you find out the truth after death?

Mohamed el-Sawi, the doorman, spun his web of lies which ensnared you in the trap. The address you got out of him so effortlessly. The doorman of the building who almost caught you on your way to her. The detective recognized your voice as you apologized to the beggar when you bowled him over. Curse that beggar!

The papers splash your scandalous life just as they do your mother's. A magazine made a study of your case. Learned men gave their opinions. Incompatible marriage between the old man and Karima. The prime cause of the murder. Poverty is the cause. Karima's first husband sold her because of poverty. Karima is the martyr of the class war. Saber's upbringing in a den of sin. Saber's Oedipus complex. In Karima he saw a mother substitute, and Khalil was a symbol of power, which he had to destroy.

He avenged the confiscation of his mother's wealth. It's a matter of a lost religious faith. If Saber had spent only a fraction of his efforts searching for God rather than searching for his father, none of this would have happened.

Saber shrugged his shoulders as he read all these comments. No one knows whether Karima was lying or telling the truth, or whether Reheimy existed or not, he told himself.

A lawyer called one day to see Saber. He thought he'd seen him somewhere before. But where and when, he could not remember. He felt comfortable in the lawyer's presence. He was an elderly, distinguished-looking man.

"Are you the lawyer chosen by the court to defend me?"

"No." Then, in a quiet voice, the lawyer said, "I am Mohamed el-Tantawi."

Saber did not recognize the name. "Who gave you my case?"

"Consider me your friend."

"But I have no money."

The man smiled. "I'm Ihsan Tantawi's elder brother. You know, the advertising manager of the *Sphinx*."

"Oh! I see. I thought I had seen your face before." Then sadly he asked, "Are you going to defend me?"

"Yes. If you'll allow me."

Suddenly Saber cried out, "Elham!"

The lawyer smiled but did not say anything.

"What about your fee?"

"Just the necessary expenses."

Was it possible? Her love paying for his funeral!

"I'm afraid you'll be wasting your time, sir."

"The word 'hopeless' does not exist in our dictionary."

"But I killed two people, premeditated murder, confessed."

"And so . . ."

"And Elham. Why?"

"You don't have relatives, but that doesn't mean you don't have a friend."

"Even after I confessed?"

"She accepts that."

He wiped at his tears. "The second tear in my life."

"There's nothing wrong with tears. Let's get down to business."

"I confessed everything."

"There are circumstances."

"What circumstances could possibly help me?"

"Your upbringing, love, jealousy, your feelings for Elham!"

"That'll only give the newspapers more fodder."

"We shall not give up."

"It's all like a strange dream. I came from Alexandria to look for my father, and then strange things happened which led me to forget my original purpose and finally drove me to jail." He sighed and continued: "And now I have forgotten everything else and only remember my original intentions. Well, there's not much use thinking about this now."

"I might use it in the defense. I will say that this was the first crime. A crime that took place before you were born."

"But now I remember something. Elham called me one day saying she had news about my father."

"What did she say?"

"I didn't see her. I was busy seeking revenge!"

"Well, I assure you, she knows nothing about him."

Saber shook his head, bewildered and in despair. "The crime coverage in the papers, that is the best possible advertisement. Maybe it will bring some results."

"I'm sure that any concern shown by your father now will make no difference whatsoever."

"Maybe if he turns up some miracle will happen."

"How?"

"If he really is important and influential."

"He cannot change the law."

"Listen, sir, my mother wielded influence once, and she was able to change the law right under the noses of the lawmakers!"

"Well, please explain to me how your father could possibly help you."

Saber hesitated, then: "Escape maybe."

"Your imagination is running away with you! Stop thinking about these possibilities; it'll only bring on heartache."

"Well, in any case, sir, I thank you, and I'll be at your disposal in any way you wish. As for my wild hopes, well, sir, as you said, 'hopeless' is not a word in my dictionary!"

The judge pronounced sentence. Hanging. Saber followed the trial closely and expected his sentence. Nevertheless, he was stunned.

"We still have a chance to appeal," said the lawyer.

"How is Elham?" asked Saber dejectedly.

"Not so well. The story in the papers, it seems, brought her father back from Assiut, and he insisted on taking her back with him, for a change of air."

"So he crept out of his hole!" Saber cried out. "But my father . . ."

The lawyer smiled. "That reminds me. Would you believe that I have some news of your father?"

"No!"

"Yes." The lawyer continued: "Did you ever hear of a newspaper commentator who used to sign his column 'The Old Pressman'? Of course not; that was long before your time. He stopped writing twenty years ago. Well, he's my neighbor in Heliopolis. He was also my teacher at the Faculty of Law. We were talking about your case, and I mentioned your father. He then cut me short and said, 'Do you mean Sayed Sayed el-Reheimy? Well, I know him. The rich, handsome Reheimy. He was about twenty-five years old. That must have been over thirty years ago."

"But didn't your friend see the photograph in the paper?"

"He hasn't picked up a paper in twenty years. And besides, he's blind!"

"But the name, the description, the age."

"Yes, that's true."

"Where is he now?"

"I'm afraid he doesn't know."

"Did he tell you about my father's first marriage?"

The lawyer smiled. "He told me that his only pleasure was love."

"But my mother deserted him. Surely that's something he wouldn't forget."

"In the life of a man like Reheimy, women change daily. You can't distinguish between the deserter and the deserted."

"My mother never spoke to me about this aspect of his life."

"Maybe she didn't know about it."

"But you cannot hide marriage."

"My friend, Aly Borhan, I mean 'The Old Pressman,' said that he married, very frequently, all sorts of women, old, young, rich, poor, widowed, married, divorced, even maidservants and prostitutes."

"Amazing!"

"True."

"But didn't this pose problems?"

"Nothing stood in his way."

Saber could not believe his ears. "What work did he do?"

"He was a millionaire. Love was his sole profession. Every time he was trapped, he just moved away somewhere else."

"But my mother's marriage certificate, I've still got it."

"You'll probably find countless others."

"Was he never sued in court?"

"Who knows? He is divorced, that's quite sufficient."

"And what about the law?" said Saber sarcastically.

"He was never caught. Mr. Borhan said that once he

had trouble with a virgin girl from a wealthy family. He left the country at the appropriate time."

"When did he return?"

"He didn't. The world became his playground. He could afford to pursue his hobby anywhere."

"How did your friend know all this?"

"They used to correspond occasionally."

"Does he have any idea where he might be now?"

"No. He never gave his address. And he never stayed too long in one place."

"He must be well-known abroad."

"Every millionaire is well-known. But he probably used different names. It's more prudent in his line of work!"

"When did your friend receive the last letter from him?"

"You know, my friend is over ninety now. He doesn't remember things too clearly. All he remembers is that he received letters from every corner of the globe."

"But he surely knows everything about his family."

"He has none in Egypt. His father was an immigrant from India. My friend knew his father, and through him, his only son, Sayed. The father died forty years ago, leaving his fortune to his sole heir. He made his fortune in spirits. He has no heirs in Egypt except those that may have resulted from his amorous adventures."

"Like me."

"Yes, like you, if he is really your father."

"I don't doubt it, now that you've told me of his habits."

The lawyer smiled and said nothing.

"Yes, his habits are my habits. But while he pursues them around the world, here I am in jail awaiting the hangman."

"But he didn't kill."

"Your old blind friend doesn't know everything," said Saber bitterly.

"In any case, he is a millionaire."

"What's more important is that the law cannot touch him."

"But you know that you are poor and subject to the law."

"And I also know who my father was."

"And to what avail?"

"Yes, unfortunately. My mother knew him better than your old friend. She made her fortune through him and was able to defy the law; she was unfortunate."

"But he never knew misfortune."

"It was impossible that I should have accepted work as a pimp after I discovered my true origin."

"Unfortunately, you did not live up to your origin."

"I looked for him."

"And forgot about him. You said so yourself."

"Because of a woman. He would understand that."

"But he is not your judge."

"But he is the one who deserted me."

"He might have thought that you were as capable as he, and didn't have any need of him."

"Had my mother not deserted him, maybe."

"But she did desert him."

"It's not my fault."

"That's true."

"That was the real reason for the crime."

"No. That's too far-fetched."

"But it's a better reason than a chance meeting with someone like Karima."

"The law is the law."

Saber sighed deeply. "Maybe it would have been better if I denied that he's my father."

"That was my opinion. But I saw how eager you were to know anything about him."

"And what did I learn? Nothing useful."

The lawyer nodded.

"Everything is lost now; freedom, honor, peace of mind, Elham, Karima. Only the hangman's rope remains," he said with a deep sigh.

"We can still appeal," said the lawyer. "There's something else Mr. Borhan told me."

"What?"

"One day, to his surprise, Reheimy came knocking on his door!"

"What! When?"

"Last October."

"October!"

"Yes."

"I was searching in Alexandria at the time."

"He spent six days in Alexandria."

"This is utter madness! I asked everywhere about him. I didn't advertise in Alexandria; I was afraid that my enemies might make fun of me."

"Surely finding him was more important than worrying about mockery."

"Yes, yes! Oh, yes!" he wailed.

"Don't upset yourself. Maybe he didn't read the papers."

"Oh! Don't try to soften my despair."

"I'm sorry I told you all this." The lawyer watched Saber's agonized face, then, trying to comfort him, said, "He was on his way to India. He gave my friend a book on how to stay young for a hundred years. Also a case of the finest whiskey."

"Probably it was him in the car that night. Did he sign the book?"

"I think so."

"Can I see it?"

"I'll bring it."

"May I keep it for a while?"

"I don't think my friend would object."

"Thank you. What else did your friend say?"

"Mr. Borhan said that Reheimy was still as young and virile as he was thirty years back. He told him how he moved around the world and that he could not consider himself among the living unless he had made love in the four corners of the globe."

"Did he mention any of his offspring?"

"He might have. But he speaks only of love. They spent the evening drinking heavily, Reheimy telling his countless stories. He even sang a love song he had heard in the Congo."

"Drinking and singing and not a question about his sons?"

"Maybe fatherhood changes when it is practiced to excess."

"But sons remain sons, regardless of their number."

"Often strange contradictions occur when a strong father believes his sons will follow his example."

"What an excuse," said Saber scornfully.

"We forgive perverts deviations we wouldn't forgive others, so we would surely forgive someone like this incredible person."

"Oh! My head! It's spinning. I can't believe all this."

"I'm sorry I told you."

"Maybe he's still in Egypt."

"No. He sent a postcard from abroad."

"Maybe he'll visit me before I hang."

"Nothing is impossible."

"You know, I used to visit Elham and your brother Ihsan every week and little did I know then that I would one day be close to you, you the neighbor of Borhan, the friend of Reheimy."

"Sometimes life is like that."

"What a unique opportunity that could have been."

"There is still hope."

"How . . . what hope?"

"We might get you a life sentence instead of death."

"What hope!"

"You'll still have another opportunity to appeal."

"And if the appeal is quashed?"

The lawyer did not answer. He clenched and unclenched his fists nervously. Saber continued: "If the appeal is quashed, and I still have some time, please do me a favor and try to contact the man."

"My son, the law is the law. My duty lies in studying your case, not going on a wild-goose chase."

"But all you've heard of him, doesn't that convince you how strange he is?"

"I am a lawyer. I know that it is only the law that will decide your fate."

"There might be a chance. I might be foolish, but during the little time I've got, please do what I ask of you."

"I have no means of finding him."

"You are a man of experience. Your neighbor seems . . ."

"Contacting him is not impossible, but it requires a lot

of time, one thing we haven't got. We must contact all our embassies abroad. He might have moved in the meantime."

The memory that is fading, dying away. So far and yet almost there, almost. The cloud formations in the sky, blown about carelessly in the wind. Pain tearing away at you behind prison bars. The blind questions leading to the oppressing answer. "It seems there's no use relying on anyone."

The lawyer smiled understandingly. "There is only use in what is reasonable."

Saber shrugged his shoulders and sighed. "Oh! Let anything happen now."

Translated from the Arabic by Mohamed Islam.
Edited by Magdi Wahba.